JUNK MAIL

JUNK MAIL

Will Self

Black Cat
New York
a paperback original imprint of Grove/Atlantic, Inc.

Published simultaneously in Canada
Printed in the United States of America

Some of this material has been previously published in two collections of Will Self's journalism published in the United Kingdom under the titles *Junk Mail* and *Feeding Frenzy*.

FIRST EDITION

Library of Congress Cataloging-in-Publication Data
Self, Will.
Junk mail / Will Self.
p. cm.
A collection of the author's nonfiction.
ISBN-10: 0-8021-7023-4
ISBN-13: 978-0-8021-7023-1
I. Title
PR6069.E3654J86 2006
824'.914—dc22   2006041219

Black Cat
a paperback original imprint of Grove/Atlantic, Inc.
841 Broadway
New York, NY 10003

Distributed by Publishers Group West

www.groveatlantic.com

06 07 08 09 10   10 9 8 7 6 5 4 3 2 1

In memory of my father, Peter Self,
1919–1999, who kept on at me

Contents

CONTENTS

Introduction

I want to make a few remarks to preface this collection of my journalism and occasional writings from the last fifteen years for the American reader. Because of the centralization of the print media in London, there is a long-established British tradition of writers being jacks-of-all-trades. We write books, prospectuses, screenplays, articles, reviews, political commentary, feuilletons—whatever will pay the rent. We are denizens of a Grub Street that stretches through time: a grimy boulevard littered with torn-up contracts and spiked copy. The notion that the authorship of literary fiction somehow places us beyond the daily weal of labourers in the word-mines is inimical to us. One of the few compliments I've ever cherished about my work is that a British newspaper editor once said of me: 'He can write about anything, at any time, to any length.'

I had no formal training in journalism, but when I had published my first book in 1991, I decided to capitalize on its favourable reception by writing for newspapers and magazines. I didn't want to go the route of teaching creative writing, or doing the kind of literary jobbing that sustains many authors unable to make a living from their books. I was getting quite enough literature writing the damn stuff. I also felt that at twenty-nine it was too early for me to retreat to my cork-lined room and spend the rest of my life processing what little experience I had into fiction. I needed more of the world and journalism was as good a way as any of obtaining it.

INTRODUCTION

Of course, I soon discovered one of the sad facts about Grub Street: the glibber and more facile the pieces I wrote, the better they were paid. Weighty, elegant discourses on matters cultural and philosophical attracted derisory fees, while upbeat pap on ephemera commanded hefty word rates. Unsurprisingly I also became very quickly addicted to the daily and weekly fix of the by-line. This is an addiction which has stayed with me well past the point where I, quite reasonably, could have relied on the income from my books. Still, I can't be too severe with myself about this: I always earned enough to support my family, and my immersion in the contemporary world prevented me leaping to my death from an ivory tower, yet another literary victim who took himself too seriously.

This collection includes pieces from the two compendious volumes of nonfiction I've published in Britain, together with a long essay on modern masculinity I wrote to accompany a book of photographs. There are also interviews I conducted with well-known men and women, and a number of miscellaneous pieces—diversions if you will—which fit into no easy category.

I'd like to think it's a biopsy of our times, a tissue sample of diseased cultural and political organs. Doubtless some of the material may feel a little dated by now: near-recency is not valued by any era. Certainly, from my perspective, the preoccupation with illegal narcotics strikes me as a little *de trop*. Or rather, having stopped taking drugs myself for some years, I now feel that the insights of the problematic drug user on the whole vexed question of intoxicants are at best partisan, and at worst ridiculous. Nevertheless, for those not similarly afflicted there may be something of value in my drugs writing; at least I was there, if stoned. And I stand by the introduction to Burroughs's *Junky* which I wrote in 2002 as perhaps my final statement on the subject in general, as well as his oeuvre.

I still get asked to comment and write on drugs a great deal, and this is understandable. Mostly I decline, explaining being relieved of the obsession to drink and use drugs by this analogy: 'Imagine that for twenty-odd years of your life you could only think about chives. You woke up every morning with chives on your mind, and all day you sought out chives wherever you could find them. You read books on chives, you saw movies about chives, you listened to chive music and chived about the house playing air-onion. If you finally managed to rid yourself of this vegetative hysteria, surely the last thing you'd want to do is ever contemplate the damn things again?' After this they usually leave me alone.

For the American reader, a number of the cultural referents in these pieces may be a little out of focus—but not, I think, altogether obscure. The important thing to remember is the extent to which the cheesy grin of Prime Minister 'Call me Tony' Blair shone out over the dingy heart of Olde England, throughout the second half of the 1990s, and into the new millennium. From across the pond, Blair may acquire some of the lineaments of statesmanship, but to those of us who have been up close and personal, he's always been a makeweight of the first order, whose principled stands have been utterly supine. During the 1997 election which brought him to power I stuck a poster in my window which read: 'A Vote for Labour Isn't Necessarily a Vote for that Sanctimonious Git Blair.' How wrong I was.

The other British phenomenon Americans tend to be a little hazy about is the monarchy. Believe me, there's nothing in the least bit charming or historic about this institution. At a constitutional level, far from being a guarantor of the people's rights, it's a barrier to British political maturity. At an economic level it's a loss-leader for the tourist trade, and at the psychic level of the personalities involved, well, words fail me. That a posh girl with an eating disorder could be the only one to come close to buckling the foundations of the Windsor's cardboard castle is proof positive—if any were needed—of what a sorry charade it all is.

INTRODUCTION

And then there's London. There may be some pieces in this collection that I've fashioned off the back of travel, but these were only excursions: the dark gravity of this two-millennia-old metropolis drags me back again and again. I was born at Charing Cross, in the epicentre of the city, and even now I only live a half hour's walk away from my personal omphalos. I don't think it was just the drugs, because there seems to be a general consensus now that between 1994 and 2000 the World Spirit of Cool did, once more, animate the British capital. Certainly, it seemed an exciting time to be here, with the burgeoning art scene (they threw the best parties), the massive improvements in cuisine and a decent soundtrack courtesy of Blur, Oasis, Massive Attack et al. I hope at least some of my writing from this period manages to convey the sense of surfing on a wave of contemporaneity, rather than floundering in the tidal wrack of a bygone age.

Lastly, there's an element of paradox in this introduction, because since 9/11, I myself have become an American writer. Of course, I was always a US citizen—my mother was American, I was registered at birth—but only since the inception of the Orwellian 'Homeland Security' has it become necessary for me to obtain an American passport. The explanation for this lies, in part, in this volume: with criminal convictions for narcotics it became impossible for me to obtain a visa on my British passport. The curious thing is, that since I've become more properly American, I feel much less so. Samuel Johnson said that patriotism was the last refuge of the scoundrel. Sadly, in this increasingly ugly and partisan world, this particular scoundrel still finds no refuge in it at all.

London, 2006

New Crack City

A journalist friend of mine asks me to take her out on the street and show her some crack dealing in action. I can't understand why she needs my help. You only have to stand outside the main entrance to King's Cross for five minutes to start spotting the street people who are involved with drugs. King's Cross has always had a name for prostitution, and where there are brasses there's always smack; and nowadays if you're anywhere in London where there's smack, then there will be crack as well. The two go together like *foie gras* and toast.

Still, I suppose I can understand why my journalist friend needs me. The London street drug scene is as subject to the caste principle as any other part of English society; druggies identify one another by eye contact and little else. As Raymond Chandler once remarked: 'It's difficult to tell a well-controlled doper apart from a vegetarian bookkeeper.' All up and down the promenade outside King's Cross, druggies are making eye contact with one another. There are Italians—they're principally interested in smack—and a contingent of young black men hanging out with white prostitutes. These men are pimps as well as being crack dealers.

We watch the scene: dealers carry rocks of crack or tiny packets of smack wrapped up in silver foil and cling-film inside their cheeks. When a punter scores, he discreetly tucks the money into the dealer's hand, the dealer drops the rock or the smack out of his mouth and into the punter's palm. The whole transaction takes only a few seconds. 'Why aren't the police doing anything?' moans my journalist friend. 'It's all so blatant.'

And it is. But what can the police do? Snarl up the whole of King's Cross in the middle of the rush hour while they try and nab a few street dealers? Supposing they do manage to collar them: the dealers will have swallowed their stash. Fear is a fantastic lubricant.

We've seen the street action, and my journalist friend wants to check out a crack den: do I know of one? Well, yes, as a matter of fact, I have some friends in the East End who are well-established crack and smack dealers, but they're not the sort of people who accept house calls, especially from journalists. What a shame I can't take my voyeuristic friend, but I can take you . . .

The day's action is just beginning up at Bob's place. It's about seven in the evening. Someone has been to see the Cypriot and they're washing up a quarter ounce of powdered cocaine in the kitchen of Bob's flat.

Bob's flat is situated at the very end of the outside walkway on the top floor of a thirties council block in Hackney. It's a good position for a drug dealer. The police have to come up four flights and get through a locked, bolted and chained door and a barred gate set in the flat's internal passageway before they can gain access. The windows are also barred.

Not that this deters them. To give the constabulary their due, they have turned Bob's place over several times recently, but they never find anything. Bob keeps his stash up his anus. The police know this but they can't be bothered to pull him in and fence with his brief while they wait for it to come out. Bob would have a good brief as well. Bob's family are well established in this area; this has been their manor for years. Three generations of the family have been hard men around here, respected men. Before they got into drugs they were into another kind of blag altogether: armed robbery.

Bob once told me how they made the switch: 'Chance, really. We were doing a number on this Nigerian bloke. We knew he had something but we didn't know what. It was six kilos of brown. I got the fucker down on the floor with my shooter in his ear and said: "You're fucking lucky we're not the old bill!"'

Bob is a talkative soul: bright, articulate and possessed of a gallows humour that counts for wit in this society. But Bob is mighty keen on that rock. Sometimes he'll be up for several days on end rocking it. Not that the crack is his core business—that's still smack.

As William Burroughs so pithily observed, smack is the only commodity that you don't have to sell to people; instead, you sell people to it. And the people who *it* buys come in all shapes and sizes. At Bob's, most of them get dealt with through the bars of the safety gate in the long, dark corridor that runs the length of the flat. The clientele are a really mixed bunch; all the way from shot-to-pieces street junkies, indistinguishable from alcoholics apart from the abscesses on their hands, to the smart end of the carriage trade: a young man, incongruously dressed in a velvet-collared crombie, is buying a rock and a bag of brown when we arrive. He has an accent that would sit more comfortably in St James's than in a Hackney council estate.

Bob doesn't have a pit bull or a Rottweiler; he doesn't need one. The other dealers around here all know who his family are and they respect them. But what about the Yardies? They don't respect man or beast. The word on the scene is that they carry automatic weapons and aren't afraid to use them. They have no respect for the conventions of the London criminal world. I asked Bob about it. 'Yardies?' he snorted. 'They're just another bunch of coons.'

In truth, there are always a lot of black people around at Bob's place. They're heavily involved in the crack scene. Most of them are second- and even third-generation English. They talk like Bob and his family, and a lot of them have done bird together. Bob's current dealing partner, Bruno, is black, and Bob himself has been scoring half ounces of smack through a Yardie.

I'll take you down the dark corridor to the kitchen where Bruno is washing up. Bob's place is always pretty cluttered, so mind the stuff lying around in the hall. Like a lot of professional dealers, Bob is eclectic in his activities. There are always consumer durables lying around the flat that have either been swapped for drugs, or are stolen goods waiting for a buyer. Bob loves gadgets, and he'll often detain an antsy punter and force him to watch while Bob takes the latest laptop computing device through its paces.

Bruno is holding a whisky miniature over the steam that's spouting from an electric kettle. The little bottle has a solution of acetone, water and powdered cocaine in it. As we watch, Bruno takes a long metal rod and dips it down the neck of the bottle. A large crystal forms around the rod almost immediately. This is crack cocaine. The fresh rocks have to dry out on a bit of kitchen towel for a while, but then they're ready to smoke.

There are no Coke cans with holes in them round at Bob's. This is a piping household. The pipes are small glass things that look like they belong in the laboratory. The bowl is formed by pressing a piece of gauze down the barrel of a thin Pyrex stem; fragments of crack are sprinkled on top of a bed of ash; the outside of the stem is heated with a blowtorch until the crack begins to deliquesce and melt, then the thick white smoke is drawn off, through the glass body of the pipe and out through a long, flat stem. Smoking a crack pipe properly is an art form.

If you came at the right time, Bob might ask you to join him—if he likes you, that is. And you could while away the evening doing pipe after pipe, with the odd chase of smack in between to stop yourself having a heart attack, or a stroke or the screaming ad dabs. If you stay, you'll have some amicable conversations with people—one of the Yardies might drop by. The English blacks are also dismissive of them. Bruno says: 'Yardies? They're just down from the trees, man.' It is almost universally agreed that the Yardies overplayed their hand in London. They were easy to spot, too flamboyant for our pinched, *petit bourgeois* drug culture. The Met has managed to have the bulk of them deported, but their influence as a catalyst to the drug scene has gone on working.

But now Bob is expecting his dad, whose flat this is and who is due out on a spot of home leave. It's not that he doesn't want his dad to know that he's dealing out of the flat; far from it. In fact, Bob's dad will expect a commission. It's rather that he won't want to see a lot of low-life punters hanging around the place. So we say our goodbyes:

'Stay safe, man.'

'Yeah, mind yer backs.'

Security is always variable at Bob's; sometimes, when he's especially lucid, it's fantastic. He drills punters to carefully wrap crack and smack and stash the little waterproof bundles, either up their anuses or in their mouths. As Bob says: 'The filth pull a lot of punters as they're leaving here, and they sweat you, so make sure you stash that gear 'cos I don't want to do ten because some dozy prannet had it in his hand.' But at other times, you'll find six or seven addicts scratching outside the door of the flat, waiting for the Man. And there are young black kids running up and down the walkways of the flats, taunting the addicts, especially the white ones.

Even out in the street, Bob's influence is still felt. A tall, young black dude in a BMW CSi notices us coming out of Bob's block and calls us over. 'Have we come from Bob's? And do we want to go somewhere else where we can go on rocking?' Well, of course we do! We have our public to satisfy.

Basie drives us back up towards the Cross. It's dark now. He keeps up a running monologue for our benefit; it's sheer braggadocio: 'Yeah, I've bin back to Africa, man. I hung so much paper in Morocco they probably thought I was decorating the place.' He isn't altogether bullshitting. I know from Bob that Basie is both successful at 'hanging paper' (passing false cheques) and at Bob's traditional blag: sprinting into financial institutions with the old sawn-off. I've seen Basie round at Bob's before. Sometimes he'll have a couple of quite classy tarts with him who look vaguely Mayfairy: all caramel tan streaky blonde hair and bright pink lips. If it wasn't for the hungry look and the strained eyes, one might almost take them for PR account handlers.

Up at the Cross, we turn into a backstreet and park the wedge. There's a crack house here that conforms a little more to our public's expectation. It's a squat with smashed windows and no electricity. Once Basie has got us inside, we are confronted with a throng of black faces. Everyone here is either buying, selling or smoking crack. Candles form islands of yellow light around which ivoried faces contort with drawing on the little glass pipes.

The atmosphere here is a lot heavier. Sure, Bob's place isn't exactly a picnic, but at least at his flat there is the sense that there actually *are* rules to be transgressed. Of course, it's bullshit to say there is honour among thieves, but there is a hierarchy of modified trust: 'I think you're a pukkah bloke, and I'll trust you and look out for you until it's slightly more in my favour to do otherwise.' It's an ethic of enlightened self-interest that isn't that dissimilar to any other rapacious free market where young men vie with one another to possess and trade in commodities. And, after all, isn't that what Mrs T wanted us to do? Tool around London in our Peugeot 205s and Golf GTIs, cellular phones at the ready, hanging out to cut the competitive mustard.

But, at the crack house in King's Cross, we have no cachet, and we have the feeling here of being very isolated: a wrong move, a word out of place, and these people might get very nasty. The people here are much more 'streety' and they have very little to lose.

We've seen what we wanted to see, we've come full circle; you don't want to stay in the crack zone, do you? No, I didn't think so. Turn the page, get on with the next article, go home.

Evening Standard, September 1991

On *Junky*

I have it on the desk beside me as I write—the first edition of *Junky* by William S. Burroughs. The world has changed a great deal in the fifty-odd years since it was originally published, and some of those changes are evident in the differences between the first edition of this memorable work and the one you are currently holding in your hands.

Entitled *Junkie: Confessions of an Unredeemed Drug Addict* and authored pseudonymously by 'William Lee' (Burroughs's mother's maiden name—he didn't look too far for a nom de plume), the Ace Original retailed for thirty-five cents, and as a 'Double Book' was bound back-to-back with *Narcotic Agent* by Maurice Helbrant. The two-books-in-one format was not uncommon in 1950s America, but besides the obvious similarity in subject matter, A. A. Wyn, Burroughs's publisher, felt that he had to balance such an unapologetic account of drug addiction with an abridgement of these memoirs of a Federal Bureau of Narcotics' agent, which originally appeared in 1941.

Since, in the hysterical, anti-drug culture of post-war America, potential censure could easily induce self-censorship, it's remarkable that *Junky* found a publisher at all. Despite its subhead, Wyn did think the book had a redemptive capability, as the protagonist made efforts to free himself of his addiction, but he also insisted that Burroughs preface the work with an autobiographical sketch that would explain to the reader how it was that someone such as himself—a Harvard graduate from a Social Register family—came to be a drug addict. The same cautious instinct led Wyn to interpolate bracketed disclaimers after most of Burroughs's (often factually correct but radically unorthodox, and sometimes outright wacky) statements about the nature of intoxication and chemical dependency. Thus, when Burroughs stated: 'Perhaps if a junkie could keep himself in a constant state of kicking, he would live to a phenomenal age.' The bracket reads '(Ed. Note: This is contradicted by recognized medical authority.)'

Burroughs's preface (now restyled as a 'prologue') still stands first in the current edition, but relegated to the rear of the text is the glossary of junk lingo and jive talk with which he sought to initiate his square readership to the hip world. And for Burroughs the term 'hip' referred resolutely to the heroin subculture. The bracketed editorial notes have been excised.

Both *Junkie* and *Narcotic Agent* have covers of beautiful garishness, featuring 1950s damsels in distress. The blonde lovely on the cover of Helbrant's book is being handcuffed (presumably by the eponymous 'Agent', although his face and figure are hidden in the shadows), while clad only in her slip. The presence of ashtray, hypodermic and spoon on the table in front of her goes a long way to explain her expression of serene indifference. However, on the cover of *Junkie* we are given a more actively dramatic portrayal: a craggy-browed man is grabbing a blonde lovely from behind, one of his arms is around her neck, while the other grasps her hand, within which is paper package. The table beside them has been knocked in the fray, propelling a spoon, a hypodermic and even a gas ring, into inner space.

This cover illustration is, in fact, just that: an illustration of a scene described by Burroughs in the book. 'When my wife saw I was getting the habit again, she did something she had never done before. I was cooking up a shot two days after I'd connected with Old Ike. My wife grabbed the spoon and threw the junk on the floor. I slapped her twice across the face and she threw herself on the bed, sobbing . . . ' That this uncredited—and now forgotten—hack artist should have chosen one of the small handful of episodes featuring the protagonist's wife to use for the cover illustration, represents one of those nastily serendipitous ironies that Burroughs himself almost always chose to view as evidence of the magical universe.

From double book to stand alone; from Ace Original to Penguin Modern Classic; from unredeemed confession to cult novel; from a cheap shocker to a refined taste—the history of this text in a strange way acts as an allegory of the way the heroin subculture Burroughs depicted has mutated, spread and engrafted itself with the corpus of the wider society, in the process irretrievably altering that upon which it parasitises. Just as—if you turn to his glossary—you will see how many arcane drug terms have metastasised into the vigorous language.

Burroughs observed a discrete—if international—urban phenomenon, confined to the physical as well as the psychic margins of society: 'Junk is often found adjacent to ambiguous or transitional districts: East Fourteenth near Third in New York; Poydras and St. Charles in New Orleans; San Juan Létran in Mexico City. Stores selling artificial limbs, wig-makers, dental mechanics, loft manufacturers of perfumes, pomades, novelties, essential oils. A point where dubious business enterprise touches Skid Row.'

Today junk is everywhere, on housing estates and in penthouses; sniffed, smoked and shot up by models and model makers alike. Heroin chic has been and gone as a stylistic affectation—and will doubtless return again. Countless books and films have been predicated on the use and abuse of the drug. The heroin addict has become a stock figure in soap operas. Conservative estimates of the numbers of heroin addicts in Britain indicate a thousandfold increase in the past half century.

Burroughs wrote *Junky* on the very cusp of a transformation in Western culture. His junkies were creatures of the Depression, many of whose addiction predated even the Harrison Act of 1922, which outlawed the legal sale of heroin and cocaine in the USA. In *Junky* the protagonist speaks scathingly of the new generation: 'The young hipsters seem lacking in energy and spontaneous enjoyment of life. The mention of pot or junk will galvanize them like a shot of coke. They jump around and say, "Too much! Man, let's pick up! Let's get loaded." But after a shot, they slump into a chair like a resigned baby waiting for life to bring the bottle again.'

Is it too much to hypothesise that as it was to the demimonde, so has it been for the wider world? That as addicts have increased in number and become more tightly integrated into society, so has the addictive character of the collective consciousness become more horribly evident. The mass obsessions with polymorphous sexuality, and the awesome death of affect implied by the worship of celebrity, are matched by a compulsive consumerism, characterised by the built-in obsolescence not only of products, but also the 'lifestyles' and the 'mind sets' within which they are placed. And, of course, there is the 'War on Drugs' itself, which has lopped off arm after arm after arm, only for six more, then twelve more, then thirty-six more to grow from their stumps, all of them being shot up into.

Certainly, Burroughs himself viewed the post-war era as a Götterdämmerung and a convulsive reevaluation of all values. With his anomic inclinations and his Mandarin intellect, Burroughs was in a paradoxical position vis a vis the coming cultural revolution of the 1960s. An open homosexual and a drug addict, his quintessentially Midwestern libertarianism led him to eschew any command economy of ethics, while his personal inclinations meant he had to travel with distastefully socialist and liberal fellows. For Burroughs, the reevaluation

11

was both discount and markup, and perhaps it was this that made him such a great avatar of the emergent counterculture.

Janus-faced, and like some terminally cadaverous butler, Burroughs ushers in the new society of kicks for insight as well as kick's sake. In the final paragraph of *Junky* he writes: 'Kick is seeing things from a special angle. Kick is momentary freedom from the claims of the ageing, cautious, nagging, frightened flesh.' He might have added that kicking is what you do to God's ribs once he's down on the ground and begging for mercy.

By all of which you can take it as stated that in a very important sense I view Burroughs's *Junky* not to be a book about heroin addiction at all, anymore than I perceive Camus's *The Fall* (1956) to be about the legal profession, or Sartre's *Nausea* (1938) to be concerned with the problems of historical research. All three are works in which an alienated protagonist grapples with a world perceived as irretrievably external and irredeemably meaningless. All three are trajected at the reader in the form of insistent monologues. As Burroughs writes of the hoodlum 'Jack' in *Junky:* 'He had a knack of throwing his voice directly into your consciousness. No external noise drowned him out.' The same could be said of 'William Lee' himself, or Clemance or Roquentin.

But before grappling with the existential lode of *Junky,* let's return to that cover illustration with its portrayal of 'William Lee' as Rock Hudson and his common law wife, Joan Vollmer, as Kim Novak. When I say Burroughs himself must have regarded the illustration—if he thought of it at all—as evidence of the magical universe he conceived of as underpinning and interpenetrating our own, it is because the first draft of the book was completed in the months immediately preceding his killing of Vollmer on September 6th 1951 in Mexico City. Burroughs himself wrote in his 1985 foreword to *Queer* (which was completed in the year after Vollmer's death, but remained unpublished until thirty-four years later),

'I am forced to the appalling conclusion that I would never have become a writer but for Joan's death, and to a realization of the extent to which this event has motivated and formulated my writing.'

Much has been written and even more conjectured about the killing. Burroughs himself described it as 'the accidental shooting death'; and although he jumped bail, he was only convicted—*in absentia* by the Mexican court—of homicide. However, to my mind this rings false with the way he characterised his life—and his writing—thereafter: 'I live with the constant threat of possession and the constant need to escape from possession, from Control.' Burroughs saw the agent of possession implicated in the killing as external to himself, 'a definite entity'. He went further, hypothesising that such an entity might devise the modern, psychological conception of possession as a function of the subject's own psyche: 'since nothing is more dangerous to a possessor than being seen as a separate invading creature by the host it has invaded.'

Personally, I think Burroughs's definition of 'possession' was tantamount to an admission of intent. Certainly, the hypothesis of murderous impulsiveness squares better with the impromptu 'William Tell act' (whereby he called upon Vollmer to place a glass upon her head which he would then shoot off), than his own bewilderment in the face of an act of such cruel stupidity and fatal rashness. (He knew the gun to shoot low, and what would've happened to the glass shards even if he had succeeded? There were others in the room.)

I belabour these events for two reasons. First, because I think an understanding of the milieu within which Burroughs and Vollmer operated, and the nature of their life together is essential in disentangling the *post hoc* mythologising of the writer and his life, from the very grim reality of active drug addiction that constitutes the action of *Junky*. When Burroughs was off heroin at all he was a bad, blackout drunk (for evidence of this you need look no further than his own confirmation in *Junky*). However much he cared for Vollmer, their life together was clearly at an impasse (their sexuality was incompatible—she was even beginning to object to his drug use); and what could be more natural—if only momentarily—than to conceive of ridding himself of an obvious blockage?

Second, although the bulk of *Junky* was in place before the killing, Burroughs continued to revise the text at least as late as July 1952, including current events such as the arrival from New York of his old heroin dealing partner Bill Garver (whose name is changed to 'Bill Gains' in the text). Indeed, such is the contemporary character of what Burroughs was writing about, that at one point in the book (and this remains uncorrected in the present edition), he actually lapses into the present tense: 'Our Lady of Chalma seems to be the patron saint of junkies and cheap thieves because all Lupita's customers make the pilgrimage once a year. The Black Bastard rents a cubicle in the church and pushes papers of junk outrageously cut with milk sugar.'

The meat of the text of *Junky* is as close as Burroughs could get to a factual account of his own experience of heroin. In a letter to Allen Ginsberg (who had worried that the book constituted a justification of Burroughs's addiction), he inveighed: 'As a matter of fact the book is the only accurate account I ever read of the real horror of junk. But I don't mean it as justification or deterrent or anything but an accurate account of what I experienced while I was on the junk. You might say it was a travel book more than anything else. It starts where I first make contact with junk, and it ends where no more contact is possible.' To analyse the exactness of the correspondence between the text of *Junky* and what is known of the author's life between 1944 and 1952 (the time span of the book), one has only to read through his collected letters for this period[1], or Ted Morgan's excellent biography[2].

All of which is by way of saying: *Junky* is not a novel at all, it is a memoir; 'William Lee' and William Burroughs are one and the same person. I realise that in the light of what I've said above—positioning *Junky* as an existentialist text on a par with the work of Sartre and Camus—this must seem bizarre, but I think it's simply another aspect of the author's own Janus face makes fact serve for fiction. Burroughs's own conception of himself was essentially fictional, and it's not superfluous to observe that before he began to write with any fixity he had already become a character in other writer's works, most notably Jack Kerouac's *On the Road*. He also signed his letters to Ginsberg, Kerouac et al. with his nom de plume, as well as using his correspondence as a form of work in progress, peppering his Epistles to the Beats with his trademark riffs and routines. By the time Burroughs was living in Tangier in the late 1950s, his sense of being little more than a cipher, or a fictional construct, had become so plangent that he practised the art of insubstantiality with true zeal, revelling in the moniker 'El Hombre Invisible'.

For Burroughs, with his increasingly fluid view of reality, the confabulation of fact and fiction was inevitable, the separation of life and work impossible. Doubtless, he himself would seek to underpin—if not justify—this with an appeal to metaphysics, but from the vantage of a half century later, with Burroughs dead, and the counter-culture he helped spawn reduced to little more than attitudinising, T-shirt slogans and global chains of coffee shops, it seems about time to accept that his drug addiction was psychologically anterior to all of this, rather than some optional add-on. It's time to take Burroughs at his most truthful and gimlet-eyed, when he writes in *Junky:* 'Junk is not a kick. It is a way of life.' Burroughs was the perfect incarnation of late twentieth-century Western angst precisely because he was an addict. Self-deluding, vain, narcissistic, self-obsessed and yet curiously perceptive about the sickness of the world if not his own malaise, Burroughs both offered up (and was compelled to provide) his psyche as a form of petri dish, within which were cultured the obsessive and compulsive viruses of modernity.

Burroughs never managed to recover from his addiction at all, and died in 1997 physically dependent on the synthetic opiate methadone. I find this a delicious irony: the great hero of freedom from social restrain, himself in bondage to a drug originally synthesised by Nazi chemists, and dubbed 'Dolophine' in honour of the Fuhrer; the fearless libertarian expiring in the arms of an ersatz Morpheus, actively promoted by the Federal Government as a 'cure' for heroin addiction. In the prologue to *Junky* and the introduction to *Naked Lunch,* Burroughs writes of his own addiction as if it were a thing of the past, but this was never the case. In a thin-as-a-rake's progress that saw him move from America to Mexico, to Morocco, to France, to Britain, back to New York and eventually to small-town Kansas, Burroughs was in flight either from the consequences of his chemical dependency, or seeking to avoid the drugs he craved.

But really the die was cast long before, in the dingy apartments of wartime New York, and the ramshackle habitations of his exile, where Burroughs saw 'life measured out in eyedroppers of morphine solution'. By the time he and Vollmer were ensconced in Mexico City, the pronounced deterioration of their long-term addictions (hers to amphetamine), had already taken its heavy toll. Contemporary accounts describe the once pretty Vollmer as 'a large, shapeless woman, with a doughy face and the kind of eyes that used to be placed in antique dolls, made of blue glass and quite vacant . . .' while Burroughs was 'cadaverous-looking—thin lips, bad teeth, yellow fingers and eyes like death.'[3]

Burroughs was incapable of confronting the real physical degradation implied by their *folie a deux,* and, as with Vollmer herself, the text of *Junky* avoids the subject altogether, or glosses it—as above—with flat untruths and slurred shibboleths about heroin's life preserving properties. The writer's wife isn't mentioned at all until page 61, and then only in the context of an aside when 'William Lee' is being inducted into the

Federal Hospital at Lexington for a 'cure': 'Patient seems secure and states his reason for seeking cure is necessity of providing for his family.' Thereafter, she is allocated a walk-on
part when 'Lee' is busted in New Orleans, before evaporat-
ing once more, until, in Mexico City 'she did something she
had never done before . . . '

In a postscript to a letter to Allen Ginsberg (who was acting as Burroughs's literary agent) written seven months after
Vollmer's death, Burroughs said 'About death of Joan. I do
not see how this could be worked in. I wish you would talk
them out of that idea. I will take care of her disappearance. I
did not go into my domestic life in *Junk* because it was, in the
words of Sam Johnson, "Nothing to the purpose."' In the text
Lee and his wife are said to be 'separated', but while being
perhaps a little de trop '(taking) care of her disappearance' was
more to the purpose.

As for the text itself, it reads today as fresh and unvarnished
as it ever has. Burroughs's deadpan reportage owes as much to
the hard-boiled style of the detective thriller writer Dashiell
Hammett, as it does to his more elevated philosophical inclinations. At the time of writing Burroughs was still much in thrall
to the proto-Wittgensteinian ideas of Count Korzybski, whose
lecture series he had attended at the University of Chicago in
1939. Korzybski propounded a theory of 'General Semantics',
which held that it is the gulf between language and reality which
fosters so many philosophical conundrums of the either/or form.
In eschewing rhetorical flourish or adjectival excess, Burroughs
sought to remain silent about what could not be said, just like
the drug subculture he was so enchanted by: 'She shoved the
package of weed at me. "Take this and get out," she said.
"You're both mother fuckers." She was half asleep. Her voice
was matter-of-fact as if referring to actual incest.'

But while Burroughs aims at a plain-speaking style, he cannot avoid his propensity for the mot juste, anymore than he
can escape his destiny as a natural raconteur. His later, more

free-form works—such as *Naked Lunch*—were often worked up out of his own conversational routines, and so it is that *Junky* maintains its high level of entertainment by juxtaposing acute descriptions with acutely remembered conversations. Only Burroughs could characterise the movement of a posse of young thugs as being 'as stylized as a ballet'; describe a lie as 'worn smooth' by repetition; or write of an addict's aggression thus: 'Waves of hostility and suspicion flowed out from his large brown eyes like some sort of television broadcast. The effect was almost like a physical impact.' Burroughs's humour is as dry as a tinder, so that while he refuses his authorial persona the comfortable clothing of a physical description, we are nonetheless given a frighteningly clear picture of who he is in every snide put-down—'Affability, however, did not come natural to him'—and snappy one liner: '. . . a terrific bore once he has spotted you as "a man of intelligence."' And his apothegms are apt, if revolting, as if La Rochefoucauld were an arrested adolescent: 'When people start talking about their bowel movements they are as inexorable as the processes of which they speak.'

Burroughs also employs his own special version of the pathetic fallacy—for him everyone has the face he deserves: 'He had the embalmed look of all bondsmen, as though paraffin had been injected under the skin.' Moreover, the capacity of someone's face to imprint itself upon the observer is a function of their status in reality: 'If you walked fast down a crowded street, and passed Dupré, his face would be forced on your memory—like in the card trick where the operator fans the cards rapidly, saying, "Take a card, any card," as he forces a certain card into your hand.' And again: 'Some people you can spot as far as you can see; others you can't be sure of until you are close enough to touch them. Junkies are mostly in sharp focus.' Except—please note—when they are withdrawing from the drug: 'His face was blurred, unrecognizable, at the same time shrunken and tumescent.'

These parings of description are sufficient to give the lie entirely to the idea that there is any profound break between the apparent 'objectivity' of *Junky* and the stylistic excesses of *Naked Lunch*. All of Burroughs's dystopian world picture is here, in this text, in embryo. The milieu of heroin addiction, as described by Burroughs, is one fraught with magical thinking. And indeed, this does correspond to the mentality of most addicts, who, because of their psychological and physical dependence on a commodity viewed by the rest of society as an unmitigated evil, find themselves habitual participants in a form of black mass.

Burroughs's preoccupation with the viral quality of addiction, as if it is an external organism transmitted from heroin user to heroin user, is concomitant with his sublimation of its very real character as an aspect of the individual psychopathology. But he widens the ambit of this metaphor to include a portrayal of a dystopian community in the section of *Junky* dealing with the Rio Grande Valley, where he and Kells Elvins ('Evans' in the text), unsuccessfully farmed citrus fruit in 1946. 'Death hangs over the Valley like an invisible smog. The place exerts a curious magnetism on the moribund. The dying cell gravitates to the Valley . . . ' Burroughs's coinage of 'the cellular equation of junk', with all that it implies, is his synecdoche for all of the ills of the post-atomic age, and it will reappear in this guise throughout many of his later works.

Present too in *Junky* is the unsettling notion of quasi-human organisms, that both prefigure and mutate from humanity itself. Burroughs's 'mugwump' makes its appearance: 'He has a large straight nose. His lips are thin and purple-blue like the lips of a penis. The skin is tight and smooth over his face. He is basically obscene beyond any possible vile act or practice . . . Perhaps he stores something in his body—a substance to prolong life—of which he is periodically milked by his masters. He is as specialized as an insect, for the performance of some inconceivably vile function.' Burroughs and Elvins travelled to Mexico in 1946 to take the Bogomoletz serum, an alleged anti-ageing agent, and together with this, there are veiled references in *Junky* to Wilhelm Reich's theory of the 'cancer biopathy': the idea that cancer—and by extension social ills as well—is a function of sexual repression.

Burroughs's raptor propensity for looting the wilder cliff-top eyries of intellectual speculation and mixing their eggs with his own embryonic ideas, is what makes *Junky* such a nourishing omelette. When Burroughs says of a stool pigeon (or informer): 'You could see him bustling into Black and Tan headquarters during the Irish Trouble, in a dirty gray toga turning in Christians, giving information to the Gestapo, the GPU, sitting in a café talking to a narcotics agent. Always the same thin, ratty face, shabby out-of-date clothes, whiny, penetrating voice.' He is with this single image evoking the circular historians Spengler and Vico, quite as much as he is describing a real individual. Just as when he writes—of a homosexual—'I could see him moving in the light of camp-fires, the ambiguous gestures fading out into the dark. Sodomy is as old as the human species.' Burroughs prefigures his later experiments that 'cut up' and 'fold in' texts, in an effort to annihilate all dualisms and abolish the linear time of conventional narrative.

And in the drunken phantasmagoria that follow his cessation of heroin in Mexico City, Burroughs scrys out the place of dead roads, where all his fictional vehicles will terminate decades hence. 'A series of faces, hieroglyphs, distorted and leading to the final place where the human road ends, where the human form can no longer contain the crustacean horror that has grown inside it.'

These signposts to future fictional topographies may be what makes *Junky* such a key text for the committed Burroughsian, but what will impress the first-time reader is the author's take on the nature of intoxication itself. From Burroughs's first description of a shot of morphine as: 'a spreading wave of relaxation slackening the muscles away from the bones so that you seem to float without outlines, like lying in warm salt water.' To his neat encapsulations of using cocaine, marijuana and even peyote, he remains simultaneously deep and sharp about the realities of drug experience. In this vital respect *Junky* is the 'true account' of which he speaks. From the vantage point of my own—not inconsiderable—experience of intoxication, I can say that *Junky* is unrivalled as a book about taking drugs.

What it isn't, for the reasons outlined above, is any kind of true analysis of the nature of addiction itself. Burroughs's own view—'You become a narcotics addict because you do not have strong motivations in any other direction. Junk wins by default'—is a deceptively thin, Pandora's portfolio of an idea that entirely begs the question: for what kind of person could drug addiction represent a 'strong motivation'? Surely only one for whom alienation, and a lack of either moral or spiritual direction, was inbuilt.

Indeed, this is the great sadness of *Junky* (and Burroughs himself) as I conceive it. You can reread this entire text, assuming the hypothesis of addiction as a latent pathology, present in the individual prior to his having any direct experience of chemical dependency, and everything that Burroughs says about habitual heroin use begins to make perfect sense. But taking him at his own, self-justifying estimation (predicated on a renunciation of drugs that never, ever came), Burroughs's *Junky* becomes the very archetype of the romanticisation of excess that has so typified our era: 'I loosened the tie, and the dropper emptied into my vein. Coke hit my head, a pleasant dizziness and tension, while the morphine spread through my body in relaxing waves. "Was that alright?" asked Ike, smiling. "If God made anything better, he kept it for himself," I said.'

In conclusion, to return to *Junky* as a key existentialist text, it is Burroughs's own denial of the nature of his addiction that makes this book capable of being read as a fiendish parable of modern alienation. For, in describing addiction as 'a way of life', Burroughs makes of the hypodermic a microscope, through which he can examine the soul of man under late twentieth-century capitalism[4]. His descriptions of the 'junk territories' his alter-ego inhabits are, in fact, depictions of urban alienation itself. And just as in these areas junk is 'a ghost in daylight on a crowded street', so his junkie characters—who are invariably described as 'invisible', 'dematerialized' and 'boneless'—are, like the pseudonymous 'William Lee' himself, the sentient residue left behind when the soul has been cooked up and injected into space.

Saint Germain, Paris, September 6, 2001

NOTES

1 *The Letters of William S. Burroughs 1945 to 1950*, edited by Oliver Harris.

2 *Literary Outlaw: The Life and Times of William S. Burroughs.*

3 Marianne Elvins, reported by Ted Morgan in *Literary Outlaw* Ted Morgan.

4 'Junk is the ideal product . . . the ultimate merchandise. No sales talk necessary. The client will crawl through a sewer and beg to buy . . . The junk merchant does not sell his product to the consumer, he sells the consumer to his product. He does not improve and simplify his merchandise. He degrades and simplifies the client. He pays his staff in junk.' *Naked Lunch* (1959).

A Conversation
with J. G. Ballard

J. G. BALLARD: Americans are so different from us, there is no question about that. There is a strangeness about America, it is not the pop-art aspect of the place, which of course most British visitors are struck by, and the huge advance that the American standard of living represents over ours, but their strange way of thinking. There is something very odd about the place.

WILL SELF: I wonder if I am missing out on something by not finding it as bizarre as perhaps I should. The other thing is that it is so polyglot now, and increasingly polyglot.

J. G. B.: I don't think it is bizarre, but their minds move in ways that one can't fathom all that easily. In a different way, the Japanese mind is a very difficult one to read. Whenever I go to the US, I love it, it is a marvellous place, so exhilarating and visually exciting. It is intensely in the present, which is wonderful. We barely touch the present here because of the dead weight of the past, but there the present envelops everything. It is like moving from a small TV screen to a huge cinema screen, you are conscious of a million little details that one can't find in the small-screen world. I am always aware there, after a while, of a missing dimension. I don't know what that missing dimension is—I have thought about it for years—but there is a missing dimension.

W. S.: I am a writer who is very attached to the idea of place. I am concerned with the notion of topography, of visceral shape underlying the imaginative skin of the book.

23

J. G. B.: Yes, that comes through in your style.

W. S.: And once you are settled in that topography, uprooting yourself would be like pulling the tablecloth from under your imagination: you are not sure that everything would be left standing in the same place. Or whether you would wish it. Was there a certain point in your career where you knew that . . . I mean know that for all sorts of practical reasons you were settled here, but was there a point in your emotional relation to your work where you thought, 'Yes, I am stuck here'?

J. G. B.: I am stuck here, and I realized that I was stuck here quite a few years ago, but I think that imaginatively I have always assumed I would be leaving England and settling somewhere abroad, somewhere in the Mediterranean. I have not actually drawn a lot of my fiction from the English landscape so it is rather different in my case. You have to remember I didn't come here until I was sixteen, and the brain is hard-wired by the time you are sixteen. You are constantly aware of what may seem trivial things: the density of light, the angle of light, the temperature, the cloud cover, a thousand and one social constructs, the shape of rooms and the way people furnish them, the way they furnish themselves. All these things, which a true native takes totally for granted and is unaware of, still seem . . . there is still an underlying strangeness for me about the English landscape and there is even about this little town of Shepperton where I have lived for thirty-four years. If you settle in a country after a certain age, after your early teens, then it will always seem slightly strange. In my case this has probably been a good thing, it has urged me to look beyond Little England for the source of what interested me as a writer.

W. S.: When you first arrived, and docked at Liverpool, you looked at the cars in the streets and they seemed like little prams to you, the sense of scale was wrong, you were used to an opulent and Americanized environment.

J. G. B.: Absolutely. There is nothing particularly unique in that. I think that any sixteen-year-old crossing the globe and going to a radically different environment, radically different culture, is going to be conscious of those differences forever. But I think that in my case it has worked well because I have always been interested, keenly interested, in the next five minutes, where we are and what happens next. It has helped to have that distance. A lot of English fiction is too rooted. The writers are too comfortable, one feels. They are like people returning again and again to the same restaurant, they are comfortable with the flavours on offer, and the dishes on offer.

W. S.: You have fostered contradictions both in your self-presentation as a writer and in what you have allowed . . . well, you don't allow people to interpret you as they wish. On the one hand, I feel that you like to reject, as I do, the English image of the writer as a superior craftsman who wears a tweed jacket with leather arm patches and who stands up after a day's work and says 'There's another good coffee table I have sanded down today.' But on the other hand, you seem to embody the Magrittian idea of a very bourgeois lifestyle and a wild imagination. So there is a sort of contradiction there, isn't there?

J. G. B.: Magrittian? Bourgeois? I don't live a bourgeois lifestyle, none of my fellow residents in Shepperton considers this ménage bourgeois in the least. I live like a kind of student.

W. S.: I mean in terms of this *RE-Search* volume, which I read many years ago and am now looking over again: 'I live a solitary life. I get up in the morning. I type.' That sort of angle rather than 'I am wired up to sophisticated recording equipment, tripping on LSD in an upper bedroom.'

J. G. B.: Right. People are amazed by the low-tech state in which I live. I don't even own a hi-fi system. I don't have a PC. I write my stuff in longhand, which amazes Americans.

My eye is fairly sharp, even at my age I am still interested in change.

w. s.: You wrote that essay on William Burroughs in the late fifties, at a time when he was languishing and out of favour. Well, I suppose Girodias was just publishing *Naked Lunch* at that time. I was interested in your remarks upon Burroughs. Again, you said that you found it difficult to establish a rapport with him when you actually met him, though judging from the dates when you interviewed him, he was in the midst of a serious smack period.

j. g. b.: Have you met him yourself?

w. s.: No, I have never met him.

j. g. b.: I admire him enormously. I think he is the most important, innovative American writer, and possibly world writer, since the Second World War. But the man himself . . . the thing to remember about him is that he is a Midwesterner. He comes from an upper-class, provincial American family and he is not cosmopolitan, he doesn't have the natural cosmopolitanism of, say, a New York writer. He is very much a product of his Midwestern background, he has that built-in contempt for doctors, small-town politicos and policemen that a Bournemouth colonel might have, to use a counterpart from here. It is very difficult to penetrate that almost aristocratic mind-set of his.

w. s.: He has gone home to Kansas, he has gone home to die.

j. g. b.: Absolutely. We have met a number of times over the last thirty years and we always chat in a friendly way. Obviously I steer the conversation towards those things that I know interest him. But I have never been able to relax with him, partly because he is a homosexual . . . that is an important element, I think, because he comes from a generation which had to be careful. You could go to jail. This is true of Angus Wilson too, though he was a very different type, but you sense with older homosexuals that they have developed a system of private codes

26

whereby they recognize one another and ease themselves into each other's company and friendship without endangering themselves in any way. Strangers can be dangerous. There is something of that in Burroughs, complicated of course because he had been a lifelong drug user, at a time when that too was extremely dangerous. It is difficult for an outsider like me who is not a drug user, not a homosexual, to penetrate.

... I remember going to see Burroughs when he was living in St James's, Piccadilly, way back in the late sixties. We had dinner together and he was distracted—he had this boyfriend who had 'hate' and 'love' tattooed on his knuckles and he was nervous about where this young man was going. The boyfriend cooked us a roast chicken, then slipped out, and I think Burroughs was unsettled by this. He had an obsession with handguns and how you kill somebody, where you stab them in the chest—all weird stuff out of popular magazines. Then he started talking about the CIA. He had to be careful when walking up and down the sreet, this little street in St James's, he said, 'because they are keeping a watch on me from a laundry van'. He wasn't that old then, about fifty, and I thought, 'This guy is paranoid.'

w. s.: The impression I got—not so much from reading the Morgan biography, although that joined all the dots, more from the letters to Allen Ginsberg—was that there was a point at which Burroughs decided to live in the world of the imagination and take excursions into the world of observable fact, rather than the other way around. He went fully underground into his imaginative world.

j. g. b.: And that is probably why he is the great writer he is. That is the only way you can tackle life in the twentieth century and write a fiction about it.

w. s.: But you don't seem to have done that, yet you have produced an enormous amount of prescient work.

j. g. b.: Yes. Well, people are always saying that I have been strongly influenced by Burroughs, but it is not really true. I am much more influenced by the surrealists. They are the biggest influence on my stuff.

w. s.: You are certainly keen on the contemporary period. There is no air of disdain in your work, of 'I don't want to know what is going on now at all.'

j. g. b.: Oh, no, I am very interested in what is going on now. What I am not interested in is what happened twenty years ago. What happened twenty years ago, or thirty years ago, or even half an hour ago tends to be the subject-matter of most English fiction; it is profoundly retrospective. I wasn't interested in the English past—and the reason why, which I discovered when I first came here, was that the English past had led to the English present. One wanted to press the plunger and blow the whole thing up.

w. s.: Given your melioristic, if not optimistic, attitude towards the current period, I wonder if you find it difficult to look at how things have regressed in the last twenty years. There has been a move back towards a preoccupation with class, there has been more economic inequality, there has been a resurrection of Little England.

j. g. b.: I agree and I find it deplorable. I thought the sixties—which you didn't experience at first hand—were a wonderfully exhilarating and releasing period. All those energies, particularly of working-class youth, burst out; class divisions, which had absolutely strangled and imprisoned the English, seemed to evaporate. Those divisions genuinely seemed to vanish or become as unimportant as they are in America, where there is a class system but one that doesn't serve a political function of controlling the population. Here the class system has always served a political function as an instrument or expression of political control. Everybody is segregated—*hoi polloi* at one end of the lifeboat and toffs sitting around the captain as he holds the tiller—and this prevents anyone from rocking the boat and sending us all to the bottom. In America the class system is not an instrument of political control. When the class system began to . . . well, it didn't disintegrate but it seemed irrelevant in the sixties, I thought, 'How wonderful, this country is about to join the twentieth century.' And then in 1971— I think Heath had just got back into power—I heard someone use the phrase 'working class' and I thought, 'Oh, God, here we go again.'

w. s.: Would that be your opinion of what happened when André Breton tried to link the original surrealist movement to Marxism?

J. G. B.: Yes, that was an absolute blunder. I don't think Breton ever really understood or responded deeply to the painters who are now seen as the main exponents of surrealism, because he came from the literary side of surrealism, which was much more dominant in the early days. He saw it as a literary movement, and it was much easier to link a literary movement to Marxism than it was to yoke together this strange collection of painters— Magritte, Dali in particular. The whole point of surrealist painting is that it is answerable to nobody. It is unprogrammable because it all comes from the unconscious.

w. s.: If one were to derive a message from all this, it would be that arationality and the unfettered pursuit of what the imagination is prepared to throw up is fine as long as it is not coupled to some programmatic political aim.

J. G. B.: Absolutely. It is dangerous to follow anything to its logical end. The history of this century is the history of a few obsessives, some of the most dangerous men who have ever existed on this planet, being allowed to follow their obsessions to wherever they wanted to take them, as we saw in Nazi Germany, or Pol Pot's Cambodia or Mao's China.

w. s.: In *Rushing to Paradise,* the fact that Dr Barbara has been convicted for euthanasia in the past seems to be a reprise of the Ballard preoccupation with the way the progress of technology is once again queering human destiny, whether or not it is mastered. And yet there are images in the book— the defunct camera towers and what they symbolize, for example—that suggest to me that we have arrived in a post-Ballard world which is not dominated by technology. That we have now reached a strange plateau where for a time human ideals and aspirations are mattering again. Am I wrong to see that in the book?

J. G. B.: No, I think that is fair enough. Saint-Esprit, the disused nuclear island in the novel, is loosely based on Mururoa, which is still a French nuclear test island. In fact the *Rainbow Warrior,* when it was sunk in Auckland harbour, was about to sail to Mururoa—the Greenpeace protesters later landed on Mururoa, not from the *Rainbow Warrior* but from other craft, and were thrown back into the surf by French soldiers. So I was referring to true-life attempts by animal rightists to defend the turtles. But beyond that, the point is that both the boy, who is myself, and Dr Barbara are, in their very different ways, obsessed with death. My depiction of the young boy, Neil, obviously draws on my own childhood experiences in Shanghai during the Second World War and my own personal obsession with nuclear weapons; these weapons represent a glamorous apocalypse, providing those great mushroom clouds over Eniwetok and Bikini Atoll. The idea that the human spirit might be somehow transfigured by an apocalyptic nuclear war, even at the cost of hundreds of millions of deaths, that this is a necessary step for mankind—this obsessed me for many years, and it comes through in a lot of my fiction; it informs the mind and imagination of my teenage hero. I provide him with a father who died as a result of cancer that he developed after observing a British nuclear test in Australia many years before. Dr Rafferty is not interested in the nuclear aspect of the island, she has her own agenda. She is obsessed with death but she sees it as some kind of minor detour that we will have to take at some point in our lives. Death for her is a door to safety.

w. s.: To what extent do you view yourself as an orthodox Freudian?

A CONVERSATION WITH J. G. BALLARD

J. G. B.: It depends on the perspective one takes. As a therapeutic process, psychoanalysis is a complete flop, it doesn't work. But Freud has enormous authority. He has the authority of a great imaginative writer. If you think of him as a novelist ... Thomas Szasz, the anti-psychiatrist, refers to psychoanalysis as an ideology, and I think that is almost right. If you regard all the aspects of Freud's view of the psyche as symbolic structures, as metaphors, then they have enormous power. I don't think that there is such a thing as a death-wish wired into our brains, along with all the instinctive apparatus—the need to reproduce ourselves, the need for physical freedom, the need for food, water, light—I don't believe that there is a death instinct. It might have evolved as nature's way of . . . there may be an advantage to the gene pool as a whole if there are genes that predispose the sick and the dying to wander off to some elephant's graveyard to keep out of healthy people's way. Now, that could have evolved as a death instinct, a way in which the community cleansed itself of potentially dangerous toxins. But that hasn't happened. Nobody who is close to death wants to do anything but live. Very few people actually look forward to dying. Very few people will their own deaths. On the other hand, death has an enormous romantic appeal, there is no doubt about that. There would probably be more entries in a dictionary of quotations under death than under any other subject. Death has an enormous appeal for the romantic imagination. Obviously it stands for more than just physical dissolution of the body and the brain. It represents something else.

w. s.: Does it point up the notion of soul?

J. G. B.: Could be. Perhaps by visualizing our own death we are cocking a snook at the Creator, we are challenging the unseen powers of the universe with our own small but nonetheless real ability to destroy a portion of that universe.

w. s.: Just to pull you back to Freud, does not the characterization of him as one of the great twentieth-century novelists

31

explain why the nineteenth-century novel is as dead as you have always said it is, particularly in your introduction to the French edition of *Crash*?

J. G. B.: I went wrong in two ways in that introduction. First, in the final paragraph, which I have always regretted, I claimed that in *Crash* there is a moral indictment of the sinister marriage between sex and technology. Of course it isn't anything of the sort. *Crash* is not a cautionary tale. *Crash* is what it appears to be. It is a psychopathic hymn. But it is a psychopathic hymn which has a point. The other way in which I went wrong was in all my talk about science fiction. Of course *Crash* is not science fiction.

W. S.: You developed this concept of inner space, didn't you?

J. G. B.: I still had hopes in those days—the sixties had just ended, science fiction had at last begun to escape from its ghetto. A whole new raft of science fiction writers had come along who had read their Kafka, their James Joyce; they were aware of the larger world of the twentieth-century experimental novel, they were interested in surrealism—and they could see that science fiction needed to rejoin the mainstream, even if, as I claimed then and now, it wasn't the mainstream. There were hopes then, what with films like *Dr Strangelove* and *Alphaville,* and the imagery of the modern techno-media landscape starting to appear in dozens of films, and on TV too in series like *The Avengers,* which now looks quaintly folkloric. But in those days it seemed so chic and hard and gleaming, like a brand-new showroom radiator grille. There was a hope that science fiction could take a great leap forward and transform itself into a more sophisticated kind of fiction altogether. It didn't happen, sadly. By the mid-seventies the whole shebang had slammed into reverse, and science fiction entered its most commercial phase ever.

W. S.: I was thinking of the decoupling of the literary enterprise from the relationship of individual characters to social change. In that piece you say that the nineteenth-century novelist could move in and out of the individual psyche to show its relationship to society. Coming back to Freud, he is the great deconstructive novelist because he made it impossible for other writers to undertake that project.

J. G. B.: The notion of the novelist as moral arbiter has gone for good. The idea that the novelist can sit like a magistrate above his characters, who are figures in the dark, or a collection of witnesses, or the accused in a shabby scandal—the notion of the novel as a moral structure in which the novelist can acquit some of his characters and sentence others, let others off with a stern warning—this Leavisite notion of the novel as a moral criticism of life doesn't belong in the present world. This was the world of the past. A world of static human values. We now live in a huge goulash of competing appetites and dreams and aspirations and activities. The novelist can't take a moral standpoint any more, he can't sit in judgement on his characters, he can't set in motion a series of divining machines which engage his characters and draw them out, and test them. The writer can rely only on his own obsessions.

W. S.: I was interested in your categorization of *Rushing to Paradise* as satire.

J. G. B.: I have written a lot of satire or skits, particularly in my short fiction. And in *The Atrocity Exhibition* with the pseudo-scientific papers at the end: 'Why I Want to Fuck Ronald Reagan' or 'Plan for the Assassination of Jacqueline Kennedy'. These are not satires exactly, although they contain satiric elements. I am satirizing the world of laboratory-obsessed researchers who are crashing pigs into concrete blocks, or showing pornographic imagery to disturbed housewives. Many of the things I invented subsequently happened. In *Rushing to Paradise,* the frame in which the satiric elements are set works against the satire. The author seems to endorse what is being satirized. The obvious example is that I appear to lend my moral support to Dr Barbara and her activities. Maybe she is right. It may be horrible to think of a world run by Dr Barbara Rafferty and her ilk. This is what I hope the reader will feel when he or she comes to the end of the book.

w. s.: You are making a very precise point that the technologies of bio-engineering and contraception enable women to adopt all the necessary roles that men can adopt, so given a few cups of well-preserved semen, the need for men simply isn't there any more.

j. g. b.: And this is true, isn't it?

w. s.: It is.

j. g. b.: There have been news reports from China over the last week or so of a marked imbalance between the sexes. There are several million more men than there are women. When, in the next twenty or thirty years, parents are able to choose the gender of their children I assume most people will choose a boy first. But bearing in mind that a lot of women who have one child never have another for all sorts of gynaecological, social and personal reasons, that will lead inevitably to an imbalance between the sexes. Now if you have high unemployment and a huge army of young men who can't find wives, or even mates, or sexual partners, then that is a recipe for civil unrest on a vast scale.

w. s.: Given your personal experience, as someone who was denied the opportunity to exercise and define your male sexuality through manifest aggression, are you saying that that is all there is to masculinity? And further, that a lot of the traditional divisions between the public life and the private, intimate world were predicated upon men being allowed to go out and kick the shit out of each other somewhere else?

j. g. b.: That is true. Of course men, on account of their greater physical strength, were the dominant figures in most social activities: commerce, industry, agriculture, transportation. These activities no longer require man's great physical strength. A woman can just as easily fly a 747 across the Atlantic. A very small part of industry requires brute muscle. A woman computer programmer can control a machine tool that

34

cuts out a car door. A large number of traditional masculine strengths, in both senses of the term, are no longer needed. The male sex is a rust bowl.

w. s.: And is in danger of becoming a genetic sport.

J. G. B.: Yes. There is another element in *Rushing to Paradise* that is equally important, and that is Dr Barbara's attitude towards sex. She represents the way that women have begun—thanks to the feminist movement in large part—to resexualize themselves. They have begun to resexualize their imaginations. I imagine that Dr Barbara would endorse the pro-pornography feminist lobbyists who believe that women have as much right to make, read and enjoy pornography, to express their own sexual imaginations, as men do. Dr Barbara has resexualized herself. Sex for her is as intense as it is for anyone else. She has not allowed herself to be stereotyped in a way that the traditional middle-class professional women would probably have been. She is a sexual predator.

w. s.: Do you think there is anything definitively masculine that is worth preserving aside from aggression?

J. G. B.: Well, of course.

w. s.: Well, what?

J. G. B.: This is a novel that presents an extreme hypothesis, it is not intended to be . . . no more than I am suggesting in *Crash* that we should go out and crash our cars.

w. s.: I know, but you speak to my condition. I feel genuinely pessimistic because if you look at the men's movement, the attempt to resexualize and recondition male sexuality, men are considered either effete or aggressive with nothing in between.

J. G. B.: Men are going to have to cope with the huge task of deciding who they are. And they are going to have intense competition from the world of women.

w. s.: But you're not pessimistic?

J. G. B.: Me? No, I'm not. One can't speak collectively of human beings and discount sex roles. I am a great believer in the power of the human imagination to transcend almost anything, and the future is so unpredictable.

w. s.: Unlike some other writers, such as William Gibson, you don't seem to be enthralled by the technology. You forecast the possibility of major revolutions in social organization and collective thought, as a function of technological change.

j. g. b.: I do think that we are limited by our own central nervous systems. It is very difficult to say whether real evolution on the human brain is going to take place. It is possible that it will only take place at one remove, in those outer electronic shells . . . the externalizations of the central nervous system represented by computer systems.

j. g. b.: People used to come to this little suburban house expecting a miasma of drug addiction and perversion of every conceivable kind. Instead they found this easy-going man playing with his golden retriever and bringing up a family of happy young children. I used to find this a mystery myself. I would sit down at my desk and start writing about mutilation and perversion. Going back to Burroughs, his imagination and mine—I recognize the similarities instantly whenever I read Burroughs. People say I have been heavily influenced by him, but I don't think I have at all. My fiction is highly structured, I know where I am going, I always plot my novels and short stories very carefully, I always write an extended synopsis. Burroughs doesn't do this at all. I don't think he starts a book with any sense of structure whatsoever. *Naked Lunch* in particular. I have a scientific imagination, my fiction is not generated by my emotions but by a natural inquisitiveness.

w. s.: A forensic imagination.

j. g. b.: Yes. I am in the position of someone performing an autopsy.

w. s.: With your view of Freud as the great novelist of the twentieth century, you can write things like *Crash* and then experience a car accident without viewing your psyche as the toy of terrifying forces over which you have no control. Burroughs is the true Freudian. He believes in fate and thanatos and just about everything.

J. G. B.: I think that is true. As I said, I haven't looked at *Crash* since I read the proofs, but when I think of it, or when other people talk about it, I don't feel any emotional tie to the book. Which I do feel in the case of the straightforwardly autobiographical *Empire of the Sun*. When people say 'What was your camp like?' or describe scenes in the book, I feel a flood of emotional feelings of all sorts. Because I was directly involved. In a sense, *Empire of the Sun* is true. It represents a still-living body of experience that part of my mind is immersed in. That is not true of *Crash*. Had *Crash* been inspired by a real car crash, had I been lying drowsily, pumped full of morphine, and gazing at the nurses around me, feeling a strange, erotic merging of images of technological violence, the enticements of the flesh—had *Crash* emerged from that, it would be a completely different book from the one I wrote.

J. G. B.: The imagination is not a moral structure. The imagination is totally free of any moral constraints or overtones. It is up to society as a whole to say whether the novels of de Sade should be available or not. Society has social needs that the individual imagination doesn't have. There is no reason why a mass murderer shouldn't write a beautiful poem.

W. S.: Don't you think that evil is incorrigibly banal? I am reading Shirer's *The Rise and Fall of the Third Reich* at the moment and even in translation—I shudder to think what it is like in the German—Hitler's table talk is crushingly banal.

J. G. B.: Is that really true? I have read Hitler's table talk, *Mein Kampf* and speeches and so on. A totally evil man, of course . . . but there is something compelling about his diction.

W. S.: It is the compulsion of obviousness.

J. G. B.: He was a product of the self-improvement manual, the public library . . .

W. S.: Dale Carnegie Man.

J. G. B.: He was the product of the first popular newspapers, the first product of the era of mass literacy.

W. S.: The Great Autodidact.

J. G. B.: His strange mix of Wagner, Darwin, Nietzsche, culled from newspapers and improvement manuals, culled from popular encyclopaedia accounts of Darwinism and Nietzsche, biology and race. There were an awful lot of race theories around in the last decades of the nineteenth century. He assembled these together in the way an autodidact does. It was rather like a science fiction fantasy. But what he added was this tremendously compelling spin to it all. You can almost believe that what he writes and claims is true. There is an insane logic that you almost have to acknowledge. Almost, but you have got to be careful.

W. S.: What is fascinating about reading *The Rise and Fall of the Third Reich* is how damn modern it all was. It was right up to date.

J. G. B.: Absolutely, and that was a large part of its appeal. If you think of Hitler's contemporaries—Herbert Hoover and Balfour, men in frock-coats and wing collars who rode around in the world of hansom cabs. Whereas the Nazi order was the world of neon . . .

W. S.: New drugs.

J. G. B.: . . . New drugs, fast aeroplanes, fast cars, uniforms worn for their theatrical effect, the whole society conceived as a dramatic and imaginative statement. This was absolutely new, it had never been done before except in the heyday of ancient Rome or ancient Egypt or Babylonia. They brought technology into it all. You have technology at the service of madness.

W. S.: Technology is the key. What are your feelings on the role of technology today, when things seem so undefined? I am not asking you to play the Seer of Shepperton . . .

J. G. B.: The nightmare marriage of sex and technology that I wrote about in *Crash* may not have taken place. Still, I would maintain that the thesis advanced by *Crash* may be just beginning, if not literally at least imaginatively: with video arcade games, a culture of violence in the cinema, the first hints of virtual reality systems, a culture of sensation for its own sake. We are walking through the shallows of a great, deep sea of possibility; at any moment we are going to feel the seabed drop away beneath our feet. I think we are in a lull before a momentous change that you will see but I won't.

W. S.: I'd rather not see it, personally.

J. G. B.: I think it will come.

W. S.: Not that I wish to be a reactionary but I don't share your melioristic temperament. I am a pessimist by nature. Surely it is the climb-down of the Soviet Union that has given us this sense of a false lull? But you are horrified, as I am, by the prospect of a future of boredom, a Switzerland of the soul.

J. G. B.: Not just a planetary suburbia, a future of utter boredom, lit by totally unpredictable acts of violence. The forces of social cohesion will ensure we get the drab city of the plain again. These unpredictable acts of sudden violence may take all sorts of forms, not necessarily physical violence. There could be weird consumer trends or bizarre vacation schemes, financial scams. All sorts of strange diseases may well flare up, and they will be welcomed by the bored inhabitants of the super-Switzerland of the future. More like a Düsseldorf suburb actually. They will be welcomed in the way that people like reading about serial killers, or rent videos about psychopaths, because these deviant acts provide some sort of compass bearing. I think what we are seeing now in the post-Soviet Union breakdown is the consumer culture finally settling globally into place. In Russia there is the equivalent of a land rush, they are all charging forward trying to get their piece of the consumer society—of course it is a total cock-up. Sooner or later eastern Europe and the Soviet Union will embrace suburbanization, and the global consumer economy will finally have wrapped itself around the planet, leaving tragic sections of the Third World out in the cold forever. Then we will get this Kafka-esque prospect—you can already see it in place. How dull it all is.

August, 1994

Martin Amis: The Misinformation

It's a dun, early afternoon in the basement of Julie's, a restaurant off Holland Park Avenue in West London. The décor is late Klingon, as are the waitresses, who sashay around in long, velour coat robes underneath big hair. The muzak plays, frog-tongues of receipt are being extruded from the cash register with an angry whirr. And I'm witnessing an oxymoron made flesh: Martin Amis lost for words. He's discussing the beast bumping under the bed of his life—a hideous chimera made up of teeth, women and a £500,000 advance for his new novel, *The Information*.

'It's just that it got out of hand is all I have to say about it . . . It just . . . It was a spiral . . . as these things are . . . I sort of . . . I am slightly thrown by it . . . I don't think I . . .' He breaks off to order an espresso from a Klingon who's wafting by and continues: 'The ironies inherent in it are very very striking, and every day something new about it strikes me. It feels like I really am caught up in some *post-modern* joke. You know it's very disturbing to feel *disliked* and that gravity exerted by that mass of dislike is not pleasant . . . um . . . But one of the things Salman lost for a while as a result of his situation was the right to sober literary consideration. And I feel a kind of danger that I might lose it for this book. I'm hoping the book will *bite* through that shit and stand on its own two feet. But it's an awful thing to be treated phenomenally rather than in a literary way.'

Amis sighs. 'It's really a story about the English character and not about me. What *got into* people? Basically. It brought out a tabloid streak in people who shouldn't have a tabloid streak.

'It goes back to my unique situation, in that I do think I'm pretty thick-skinned because *I've seen it,* it's been around the house, I've *seen* my dad lampooned when he broke up with his wife, it goes with the territory. So, I think that's what qualified me to write the novel and it qualifies me to say that all this stuff, it ain't *my* trouble, it's England's trouble, it's A. S. Byatt's trouble.'

He pauses. There's a hollowness in the room—we're the only customers—the atmosphere is both nervous and enervated, if that's possible: 'It doesn't weigh on me . . .' His slight shoulders sag. 'Actually, sometimes it does put the wind up me a bit. It's just that it's all out of control and that I'm exposed . . . That's what happened early on in the deal and that's where everything went wrong. It *should* have been kept confidential. *Why* wasn't it kept confidential? The whole thing. How did it get out that *I*—supposedly *I*—was demanding this money? That's where it all went sour, right there, and then it was just a sort of *maelstrom.*'

Yeah, it goes with the territory. Or as one of the lowlife characters in *The Information* puts it: 'Terry-terry . . . That what it all come down to. Every man want to be cock of the walk. All the Indians want to be chief. That what it all come down to: terry-terry.' And today I'm lunching with the chief in the far corner of his particular terry-terry: Amiscountry.

If you cross beneath the Westway from Shepherd's Bush and then turn right, you enter a very particular region. From here to Westbourne Park in the east, to the Harrow Road in the north, and to Holland Park Avenue in the south, stretches Amiscountry.

One of Martin Amis's great literary heroes, Vladimir Nabokov, believed that in order to understand the fictional topography of a novel, you needed to have an exact appreciation of the physical spaces within which the action takes place. He would commence his lectures on literature at Cornell by rendering diagrams of the two crucial 'ways' at Combray, or the floor plan of Mansfield Park.

The implied comparisons with Proust and Austen are not as outlandish as you might think. Like Proust, Amis is a novelist of psychological interiority projected on to the world: skies, streets, cities are for him the tangible simulacra of states of mind. And like Austen, Amis is a miniaturist, dissecting the verbal tics and nuances of the middle class with a well-stropped razor. His characters may venture further afield—in *The Information* trips are undertaken to Soho, to Islington, the sticks, there is even a whirlwind tour of the USA—but their true nature remains defined within this ragged rectangle.

Amiscountry is a variegated place. It stretches all the way from 'Calchalk Street' in the north, home of Richard Tull, the failed-novelist, book-reviewing protagonist of *The Information,* to Holland Park Avenue in the south, where the egregiously glib Gwyn Barry, purveyor of literary 'trex' and Tull's enemy-cum-friend, lives in palatial splendour. Still further north the modernist silhouette of Trellet Tower, home to Keith Talent, the darts-playing yob of Amis's *London Fields,* looms up.

The elegant terraces and squares that flank Ladbroke Grove may have been built to form aristocratic estates, but they now comprise elements in one of England's most prized literary estates. There is little greenery in the area, just the occasional little patch of grass, usually shit-bedizened, where someone or other stands tethered to their dog. In *The Information* Richard Tull takes his children on regular sorties to 'Dogshit Park'.

I decided to walk over to see Martin Amis from Shepherd's Bush, in the hope of clearing my head. You want to have a clear head if you're going to lock antlers with Amis. To say he is not a man to suffer fools gladly is a gross understatement.

He often pounces on misusages of English in conversation, and will demand the authentication of examples used in arguments—or even discussions.

Furthermore, Amis has achieved that most useful of occult abilities over the years: the ability to swap height. I don't know if he sojourned with sadhus at the headwaters of the Ganges in order to acquire this skill, but the fact remains that when I am with Amis (approximately 5' 5") I, Self (6' 5"), feel small. I've known Amis as an acquaintance-cum-family-friend for about six years and often wondered why it is that when we meet, instead of him, as you might expect, adopting some perspective at the far end of a room or a seated position which might to some extent blur the distinction, he comes right up to me and stands with the crown of his head aligned with my collar-bone: using sympathetic magic to steal my eminence.

Martin Amis is coming out of the main door of the house his work flat is situated in when I arrive at about midday. He's wearing a greenish suit in some lightweight fabric and an open-necked shirt. He's midway through his dental work and his face is all caved in at the cheeks and his nose appears to be pushed to one side. He looks a bit like my mother did after she died—when they had taken her dental plate out. I do a sort of double take, because Amis really doesn't look good . . . not at all *clever,* as he might say himself. He kind of shrugs, twists his deflated face in a moue, as if to say: Yeah, this is about the size of it, this is what *happens* when they remove all your *teeth*.

He goes off to post a letter and I head upstairs. The flat is messier than I remember. Ashtrays and glasses on unwiped surfaces, the former full, the latter half-empty. A shirt lies like a collapsed balloon on the divan. Most of the curtains are drawn. There isn't much light for the windows to admit any-way: it's a monochrome London day. I notice a few things: an invitation to the memorial service of Lucy Partington, Amis's second cousin who was murdered by the serial killer

Frederick West in 1973, and to whom (along with his sons, Louis and Jacob) he has dedicated the new novel. On the fax machine rests a note to one of his publishers concerning some business. It's on A5 headed notepaper, typed and neatly signed.

The main room of the flat is unostentatious in the extreme: television and video module, sound system, wall of books, a few award citations from British and American press bodies. In *The Information* Richard Tull meditates on the 'shapelessness' of writers' lives. By which he means that writers—unlike, perhaps, visual artists, or musicians—are uninterested in the trappings of style, either personal or interior. And it is this that comes to my mind as I sit on the World of Leather-ish divan and await Amis's return.

At forty-five, Amis has for some years been at the peak of his profession. Whether it is a shibboleth or not, he is almost ceaselessly referred to as 'the leading writer of his generation'; 'the most talented contemporary English writer'; 'the writer who has had most influence . . .' and so on, and so on, each blurbacious formulation further gilding the lily of his achievement.

And in what does that achievement consist? To date he has written eight novels including *The Information,* a collection of short stories and three collections of journalism and occasional writings.

While the early quartet of novels, *The Rachel Papers, Dead Babies, Success* and *Other People,* can be viewed as of a piece, cruel but essentially local satirical dissections of the English class system, with Amis's fifth novel, *Money,* he seemed to go global—or at any rate transatlantic—producing a furious absurdist burlesque on the excesses of eighties materialism. Many people consider this novel to be his finest work. It was followed five years later by *London Fields,* a great doorstop of a book which reprised all of his preoccupations with the nature of the fictive art, the millennial condition of Western cities, the implosion of public space and the threat of a global pandemic.

The eighties also saw Amis focusing his attentions abroad and away from Amiscountry. In 1987 he published *Einstein's Monsters,* a collection of short stories that gave form to the writer's preoccupation with the imminence of nuclear holocaust.

In his journalism from this period, collected in two volumes, *The Moronic Inferno* (1986) and *Visiting Mrs Nabokov* (1993), Amis's acerbic *tour d'horizon* took in personalities (mostly fellow writers) as well as politics in the form of disquisitions on the Republican Party and the 'Megadeth Intellectuals' of Washington.

This strain in his writing and public pronouncements, towards the political, has always been characterized by a kind of bilious liberalism. Amis, one often feels reading his political pieces, is more than anything annoyed at being forced to venture beyond the confines of Amiscountry and tick these people off. In *The Information* Richard Tull muses: 'It often seemed to him, moving in the circles he moved in and reading what he read, that everyone in England was Labour, except the government.' And to me Amis says: 'There is nothing else to be, is there? The other stuff is *repulsive.*' Although he agrees the new Labour Party 'image' turns its leader into 'Bambi, a wuss'.

Interest in Jewish culture and in particular the enduring influence of the American-Jewish novel on his own work must have been part of what led him to a contemplation of the meaning and resonance of the Jewish Holocaust. But in particular it was a reading of the book *The Nazi Doctors,* by Robert Jay Lifton, that was the inspiration for the novel *Time's Arrow.* In this relatively short book, Amis married all of his technical skills as a writer to a subject-matter that not only was beyond the confines of Amiscountry but even antedated its establishment.

In the *Spectator,* James Buchan reviewed the book, saying: 'I find it creepy to see Primo Levi rearranged for literary fun and profit.' Amis considered it a hideous slur, and one that he felt incumbent to reply to (the first time he has ever broken the rule of not replying to public criticism, and he hopes the last). For a while it looked as if the controversy might catch fire, and that with the preternatural sensitivity of the Jewish community (particularly in the USA) to the idea of gentiles writing about the Holocaust, Amis might become a victim of what he himself terms 'literalism', that category mistake whereby a writer's work is treated 'in a phenomenal rather than a literary fashion'.

In the event this didn't transpire, and for good reasons. *Time's Arrow,* far from being a sensationalist or meretricious account of the Holocaust, is a wrenching, heartfelt plea against those who yoke themselves to the march of history or the destiny of nations. It is a book firmly of the Enlightenment, in the strongest sense.

Recently Amis has proved one of the staunchest public defenders of Salman Rushdie. At a *Sunday Times* literary dinner a couple of years ago, where Amis was the guest of honour, I found myself sitting next to a woman who turned to me and said: 'Bloody Martin Amis, he's a misogynist and a pain in the arse, what do you think?' I demurred, saying that he was a friend. We sat in silence throughout the meal. When Amis rose to speak he delivered a fearless and cleverly structured defence of Rushdie, which included a comprehensive attack on the media and political powers that were ignoring the writer's plight, including News International itself. As nice an example of biting the feeding hand as I can think of. When Amis sat down, to huge applause, the woman turned to me again and said she was humbled.

But now Amis has himself fallen victim to another kind of 'literalism'. Since the breakup of his marriage to Antonia Phillips eighteen months ago, there is a sense that the carrion-eaters circling the Amis encampment have begun to close in. A rash of tabloid-style articles covered the breakup, speculating on Amis's motivations and conduct. Photographs of Amis and his new girlfriend, Isabel Fonseca, appeared in the press, the latter usually insultingly termed 'a literary groupie'. Some hacks said that Amis was falling victim to the crime of hubris, and that having for so long critically dissected the morals of others, it was now his turn to be exposed for his peccadilloes.

It had been long known that Amis's new novel would be concerned with the notion of literary envy and achievement, and when an extract appeared in *Granta* last year, commentators and gossips were quick to pick up on the characterizations of Gwyn Barry, the successful but facile novelist, and Richard Tull, his failing friend, and cast round for real-life counterparts. Initially the word was (and I heard this at every gathering at which there were more than two 'litewawy' types present) that *The Information* contained a systematic character assassination of Amis's estranged wife, and that following the *Granta* extract there had been representations to him from friends and colleagues (in particular his agent Pat Kavanagh) to tone it down.

But however implausible this might seem—it is of course logical that those who can't imagine are also incapable of understanding the imagination—there was worse to come. Sooner or later we will know what went on in the meeting between Pat Kavanagh and representatives of Cape (Amis's then hardback publishers) and Penguin (Amis's then paperback publishers). Amis himself may be being slightly disingenuous when he implies that it wasn't he who was pushing for a £500,000 advance. Andrew Wylie, who has subsequently taken over Amis's global agenting, was already at that time in *de facto* control of Amis's American agenting, and the whisper in a writer's ear along the lines of: 'You're not being paid what you're worth', is the so-called Jackal's usual calling card when he goes out to poach a client.

Suffice to say, parties at the meeting were given the impression by Kavanagh that it was Amis who was pushing for the figure, and this in itself—the implication being that the

relationship between agent and author was under stress—
would have been sufficient to engender the leak.

From then on it was open season. The heady mixture of
money and sex was mixed into a cake of pure literalism and
pure 'trex'. People began to say that *The Information* was in
fact about the rivalry between Amis and Julian Barnes (husband to Kavanagh and close friend of Amis), and that it was
this that had precipitated the split between Amis and Kavanagh
and resulted in him bringing in Andrew Wylie to secure the
half-million advance.

The truth is there is a rich *mélange* of personal tensions here,
some of them no doubt relating to the breakup of Amis's
marriage, and to the presence of a new woman in his life. But
wherever the onus of blame for the breakup in the agent-
author relationship lies, it is the media reaction that has now
overtaken all parties concerned and fractured friendships that
had endured over many years.

This media reaction has been extreme, even by Amis's standards. When we had last 'formally' talked together (for an 'in
conversation' piece for an American literary review) he had
told me about a seminar in Boston on his work that he had
attended. At the end he asked the academic convening the
event why it was that given the respect his work was being
shown in the USA he was still the repository of such odium
in his native country. The academic told him succinctly: 'It
isn't your work that they hate—it's *you*.'

In a way this 'hatred' for Amis is a paper tiger. For as many
people who 'hate' him in the publishing world, you can find
an equal number who have nothing but good things to say
about him personally. But somewhere between the light source
itself and what is projected on to the screen of public aware-
ness a kind of distortion takes place in the image of the writer.

There's no question that Amis is being treated phenomenally. Not content with regarding his new novel as a phenomenon, the media have even zeroed in on a phenomenon

that has been a source of pain and acute anxiety for him for many years. His teeth. He says: 'Not to be too self-pitying, but when you're *reeling around* outside some dentist's office in New York, coughing up blood like some terrible old *sap* who keeps getting into fights and always ends up yeurgh!—I thought, I knew this was going to happen but I didn't know I going to get *shat* on for it. But that's because the voracious idiot of publicity, when it hears something like $20,000 in dental work, thinks I'm after a Liberace effect, that what I want is a *dazzling smile*. All I want to do is to be able to *eat*. But everything is taken negatively, so that is what happened.

'It's actually liberated me in lots of ways. I used to leave the room when people talked about teeth for the last fifteen years. If I'd known this was going to be in the paper . . .' And here his normally basso voice drops into a ravine of irony: '. . . I think I'd have *killed* myself a year ago. But within days of finishing the novel it was crunch in the dentist's chair.'

One of my central quibbles with *London Fields* was with Amis's characterization of Keith Talent, the darts-player and all-round yob. For me there was always a suggestion that lying behind Talent's awfulness was a doubly inverted form of snobbery, along the lines of: 'I'm not afraid to show what it is the middle class really think and fear about the working class, namely that they are a bunch of loutish, vicious thugs.'

In *The Information* the Talent role is taken by Steve Cousins, a criminal entrepreneur and *farouche-savant* who reads Canetti in his van while staking people out. Cousins's argot, and that of his accomplice, Thirteen, a black street kid, seems far more convincing than that of their counterparts in earlier novels. Had Amis, I wondered, been doing more than the usual research in this direction?

'No, it's made up really. I read up a bit, that wonderful book by Roger Graef, *Living Dangerously: Young Offenders in Their Own Words,* and what makes it great is that it is in their own words. Things like "They chief me out, they fucking chief me out" . . . but the thing about argot is that you have to generalize it, otherwise it's going to date.'

There is a whole aspect of *The Information* that is concerned with the idiocies of political correctness—Amis gets some of his best jokes from this Möbius strip of an ideology. But the smashing of these commandments is also connected to the brooding theme of physical violence in the book: Richard Tull plots to beat up Gwyn Barry, but there is also aggro in store for him: 'It's the dramatization of literary envy. There was a bit I was going to add this morning when I handed in the proofs saying violence is always a category mistake.'

But it's a category mistake that Amis must fear as well. It's the fear of not having *The Information* judged on its own merits, and it's the fear of the *ad hominem* and frankly odious criticism that must feel like being beaten up. And when you've made the protagonist of your novel a book reviewer, and *then* heaped all sorts of misfortune on him, and *then* introduced a gallimaufry of other litewawy types (some recognizably drawn from life) and shot them down with marvelously acidic darts, well, your anxiety levels would *have* to be fairly healthy.

Richard Tull is himself a fairly vicious reviewer: 'One doesn't soften up,' says Amis. 'I was like that myself. It *is* cruel. You know, everyone who writes a serious book puts a lot of pain into it, and ragging is to me like ragging is to *no one* else on this planet, in that I entered the house of someone who was making a living by his pen, and that has always been in my domestic landscape, and there is no other case of a writing son—*so I see it clearly*. Maybe not clearly in other ways, maybe too close to see some things about it.'

Amis realizes that it is a strange kind of *pas de deux* that he and the media are involved in: 'The relationship that I have with the media is different from before and it is not just to do with more shit and more attention. I am in the dance with them now.'

Talk turned—as it will—to impotence. Impotence is big in *The Information*. One of the finest comic riffs in the novel concerns Richard Tull's inability to make love to his beautiful wife, Gina: 'In the last month alone he had been impotent with her on the stairs, on the sofa in the sitting-room and on the kitchen table. Once, after a party outside Oxford, he had been impotent with her right there on the back seat of the Maestro.'

Tull's career as a high-speed book reviewer leads him to muse on impotence through the fictional ages, concluding with the memorable line: 'And as for Casaubon in *Middlemarch,* as for Casaubon and poor Dorothea: it must have been like trying to get a raw oyster into a parking meter.'

But why should impotence be such an obsession? Impotence and fellatio. In *The Information* there is even a riff that begins 'Whither fellatio?' And the principal McGuffin in the plot hinges on who has been sucking off whom. Amis obviously thinks that fellatio is the high-water mark of sexiness, the most profound form of ingress. I tackled him on it, but all his references to 'swallowers' and 'non-swallowers' are drawn from literature, rather than life: Amis keeps his penis close to his chest.

But the issue of fellatio relates to one of the wider charges against the writer, that of misogynism. This has stuck over the years to the extent that when a clique of women publishers in London were looking for someone to receive 'The Hooker Prize' (their spoof version of the Booker Prize, awarded for services to literary male chauvinism), Amis was the first candidate.

In *The Information* the female characters—the wives of the two writers—are better drawn than previous Amis females, but one still feels it's a depiction from the outside, that Amis can't really—in the metaphorical sense—get inside his women.

Of the character Richard Tull he says: 'He is averagely fucked up along the usual male lines. He is not a woman-hater at all, but he is a bit fucked up, he is English and he is middle class.' I think that this is the key, if there is one, to under-standing Amis's approach to women: it isn't that he hates them, it's that—as with class—there is a certain disarming quality to his admission of ignorance.

A certain disarming quality, but one that doesn't disarm altogether. It's partly to do with Amis's strengths as a writer in projecting a 'universal' voice, that one finds oneself disagreeing—as a man—with his pronouncements. No, Mart, not all of us wish for a notional 'brother' to substitute for us when we're having flop-on difficulties; no, Mart, not all of us are preoccupied with fellatio; no, Mart, not all men view their condition as one of being on a rickety stage in front of a lot of other men . . . and so on.

In *The Information* the penultimate nail in the coffin of Richard Tull's hatred of Gwyn Barry comes when the glib and successful writer wins something called a 'Profundity Requital', a vast, yearly sinecure with no strings attached. It doesn't take much imagination to see this concept as a reification of all of the author's concerns with the notion of posterity. I ventured heresy: had he ever considered jacking in the whole game of writing fiction?

'I worked through a big crisis when I was finishing this book. But it was just writer's midway-through-last-version pain, a kind I am used to.'

'The constipation grind . . .'

'. . . Yeah. And you recognize it and are ready for it, but like the mother of seven children, even the seventh time it happens you say, Jesus I didn't think it would be this bad. So it *flashed* across my mind to abandon the novel. And if I had known what was going to happen to it even before it came out I don't know what I would have done.'

The strongest elements in *The Information* are the satirical skits on the literary world itself. From the *Little Magazine* where Richard Tull grinds out critical essays to the depiction of Rory

Plantagenet, the odious purveyor of literary tittle-tattle, Amis has the suffocatingly self-regarding book world to a T. But while journalists may go hunting for real-life counterparts to Richard Tull and Gwyn Barry it was always self-evident to me that the real-life model for both characters was Amis himself.

'Thank you. That is exactly what I was saying to one of the journalists who was trying to tee Julian up. I said, listen, that is one hundred per cent gossip . . . If you want the scoop on this book it is that both Gwyn and Richard are *me*. One is the over-rewarded side and the other is the whimper of neglect side.'

Lunch is over. We wander down to Holland Park Avenue, the border of his fiefdom. Amis is going to pick his kids up from school. After that he is off to the New World to pick up his new teeth.

'I can go anywhere I like,' he had said to me, with reference to the 'literalism' that has placed Salman Rushdie in internal exile. And while this may be practically true, psychically the world for Martin Amis has become an unpleasant place. The following day, a woman I was speaking to said to me, 'I saw Martin Amis yesterday—my son goes to the same school as his boys. I tried to get a look at his teeth . . .' Now that's all you need as a writer. You may be used to people trying to get inside your head, but your mouth, that's what I call true literalism.

Esquire, April 1995

Where Did I Go Wrong?

A Father's Story, Lionel Dahmer's analysis of his hopelessly flawed relationship with his son Jeffrey, is particularly unpleasant for a parent to read. It might be possible to dismiss the book as just another example of the breast beating occasioned when someone lights on a new-found jargon to explain his life mistakes ('denial' is made much of in this book), were it not for the palpable pain and despair that gusts from the text.

Of course, nothing is easier than to impose a retrospective interpretation of events. What makes Lionel Dahmer's narrative so compelling is that he is trying in this ascription to peer not just into the soul of his son but into his own.

A Father's Story is fairly straightforward, running chronologically from the son's birth and childhood in the Middle West through to his arrest in July 1991 at the age of thirty-one, conviction seven months later (for killing and dismembering fifteen boys and young men to gratify his sexual desires with their bodies) and his incarceration for life.

Throughout, the sense of someone constitutionally ill-equipped for introspection of any kind groping toward a realization is gripping. Lionel Dahmer comes across as he presumably intends to—as an emotionally and spiritually absent parent. A chemist who describes his emotional make-up as 'a broad, flat plain', he buried himself in the laboratory where 'the ironclad laws of science governed', rather than face up to the 'chaotic' world of human relationships and to the impact that his disintegrating marriage to a seriously depressed woman was having on his younger son.

The details of Jeffrey L. Dahmer's life—from his increasing lack of affect to his growing obsession with bones, his teenage alcoholism and his arrest for child molestation—are brought into grotesque salience. And as Lionel Dahmer writes of his chronically moody, asocial son, one wants to grab hold of the author and shake him out of his withdrawn state.

Clearly Lionel Dahmer is not a professional writer, and the text bears the evidences of strong editing. Whether or not this makes its execution and publication a wholly meretricious act is quite difficult to judge. Undoubtedly Lionel Dahmer believes he is acting in good faith, but then according to him, he has always done that.

The tone of *A Father's Story* stands in interesting contrast to that of Brian Masters's fine *Killing for Company,* which I first read in 1985, when it was published in Britain (it came out in the United States a year later and was minimally distributed). Mr Masters's unconventional biography of the British mass murderer Dennis Nilsen is long and graphic, yet in reading it one doesn't feel macabre or like a voyeur. Lionel Dahmer's memoir of his homicidal son, Jeffrey, is a lot shorter and a lot less graphic, yet the sense of spying on the mechanics of evil can be almost overpowering.

I was fascinated by Dennis Nilsen, for he lived and killed in the same area of North London where I grew up and still live. He was an interviewer for a state employment bureau in Kentish Town—his task was to assess people's suitability for employment—and one of the people he interviewed was me.

It is now almost aphoristic to say of evil that it is banal, chillingly ordinary. But the fact remains that the Dennis Nilsen I met seemed to me, as he did to his colleagues and acquaintances, to have had no charge, no resonance, no aura about him whatsoever. His chain of fifteen murders between 1978 and 1983, when he was arrested at age thirty-seven, their attendant necrophilia and dismemberments, and his hoarding of the body parts, had yet to be discovered.

Like Jeffrey Dahmer, Dennis Nilsen had a largely loveless and isolated childhood (he came from a poor background in the Buchan, a culturally distinct enclave of Aberdeenshire in Scotland). In attempting to scour this upbringing for evidence, Brian Masters seizes on one episode that in the time-honoured tradition of psychoanalytic biography he sees as key to what Nilsen became: as a five-year-old, he was without preamble thrust into the parlour to pay his respects to the bloated corpse of his grandfather, a fisherman who had drowned. Masters identifies this as the point at which eros, agape and thanatos became hopelessly commingled in Nilsen's mind.

Whether or not this is a good explanation, it suits the dramatic cadences of this perceptive book, which Random House brought out in the United States late last year with a preface linking Nilsen's and Dahmer's pathologies. Masters, the author of books on less unsettling figures like the British novelists Marie Corelli and E. F. Benson, has a style remarkable for its clarity, and that is a good thing, because he had unusual access to the killer's own writings after his arrest; Nilsen is now serving a life sentence. Not since Dr Karl Berg wrote *The Sadist,* his book on the German serial killer Peter Kurten, in the 1920s has such a garrulous and intelligent embodiment of evil come forward to tell us of his inner life.

For if listening to the Celtic mystic pop music of Clannad while drinking Bacardi and Coke, preparatory to sawing up the corpse of a young drifter you have garrotted, performed various sex acts with and then kept sitting in an armchair for several days isn't evil, then I don't know what is.

Masters himself isn't sure about this question. At some points he seems to suggest that the moral-religious perspective on evil and the forensic-psychological definition of mental disorder converge. At others he implies that Nilsen worried him enough to bring him to question his acceptance of the Freudian view of the need to acknowledge rather than repress violent impulses.

Masters is among those who make the point that serial murderers like Nilsen and Dahmer are becoming more common. Some would argue—indeed, Lionel Dahmer comes close to doing so—that this is a function of the violence and anomie of modern mass society. This may be true, but I would be inclined to see both the killers and the society that obsessively contemplates them as involved in a colossal fabrication of collective memory and moral perception.

Lionel Dahmer writes about a recurrent dream in which he is aware of having committed a violent murder but with no knowledge of why, and then identifies it as a wellspring of homicidal intent that he shares with his son. I have such a recurrent dream, and I would wager that many reading this do as well. 'I see and hear my son,' he writes at another point, 'and I think, "Am I like that?"' I can think of no better place to begin the much-needed examination of the dark side of our natures than with a careful reading of these two remarkable books.

New York Times Book Review, April 1994

Thomas Szasz:
Shrinking from Psychiatry

Ross Perot was talking to CBS News. 'Raisin' taxes,' he drawled, 'is like givin' a cocaine addict maw co-caine.' I knew I was in the right place. Outside, the sirens wailed in the New York night, while on the flickering screen the presidential hopeful defined the collective American psyche in terms of obsession and compulsion.

When I walked out of my midtown Manhattan hotel the following morning, the discarded crack vials crunched like gravel under the soles of my shoes. I was on my way to interview Dr Thomas Szasz, the maverick 'anti-psychiatric' thinker who advocates the legalization of all drugs and puts forward the radical view that both drug addiction and mental illness are not diseases at all.

By noon I was sitting with Dr Szasz in his immaculately neat office at the New York University Medical Center in Syracuse. I started off by asking him what he felt about R. D. Laing, who had put forward theories similar to Dr Szasz's, and then, paradoxically, had himself suffered a mental breakdown.

'There are no second acts in academic notoriety,' said Dr Szasz. Paraphrasing Gore Vidal is very much Dr Szasz's style. 'Laing agreed with me that there is no mental illness but claimed to have a cure for schizophrenia. Perhaps that's something like the Greek idea of hubris. I think that in many ways what happened to Laing . . . obviously there is a problem with self-honesty.'

A small, neat man, who still has a pronounced Hungarian accent after fifty years living in the United States, Dr Szasz could never be accused of courting popularity for its own sake. On the contrary, his radical views on mental illness and drug addiction have been presented with great consistency and courage in the twenty-or-more books he has published since the 1950s. And Dr Szasz has stuck to his guns despite public vilification and professional skulduggery.

In his latest book, *Our Right to Drugs: The Case for a Free Market,* Dr Szasz returns to themes he first explored in his ground-breaking work *Ceremonial Chemistry,* published in 1974. Put succinctly, Dr Szasz holds that we have substituted scientism for morality and allowed a category error to permeate our thinking about mental illnesses and other 'diseases' such as drug addiction, alcoholism, anorexia and obesity. Szasz sees their current 'pathological' status as the inevitable result of a society that is unprepared to accept the hard work involved in personal responsibility. During our conversation he quoted Burke approvingly: 'Men are qualified for civil liberty in exact proportion to their disposition to put moral chains on their own appetites . . .'

'You can see when we allow doctors to take over the area of communal life that is concerned with how we communicate and how we morally judge, we open a Pandora's box. I'm not suggesting that there is a conscious conspiracy, it's rather a collective urge, a sort of Puritan desire to be smacked with one of Mummy State's hands, while being stroked with the other.'

But Dr Szasz is not just a conventional libertarian philosopher, and his case for the complete legalization of all drugs rests as much on his sophisticated analysis of the language of medicine, and his careful reading of social mores, as it does on appeals to individual liberty.

'The whole area is full of absurdities,' he told me. 'On the one hand, if you can drink and drive, you can be jailed. But on the other hand, you can take a prescribed drug like Halcion, murder someone, and get acquitted. You can carry a loaded gun, but not a loaded syringe. It's almost as if we want to be punished in this way, deprived of our rights and turned into adult children. Or take the smoking debate. People forget the issue of private property. If I own a restaurant and wish to have people smoke in it—it's my own affair. No one has to come there.'

Dr Szasz's arguments rest, he says, 'on firmly held, rather traditional values. I am not conventionally religious, but I do think that personal responsibility is enormously important.' Had he ever taken drugs himself? 'Oh, no, never. Partly because they don't really interest me, but more importantly because of their legal status. I just couldn't afford to give any ammunition to my critics.'

In 1962 he published *The Myth of Mental Illness* in which he argued the symptoms of mental illness are not those of a disease but merely examples of behaviour that is generally disapproved of. Following this there were attempts by members of the American Psychiatric Association to have Dr Szasz removed from his post. 'They made mistakes,' he said, 'and I was lucky. They actually wrote a letter to the university saying that I was "unfit to hold the chair in psychiatry" because of the book. Imagine that! They tried to act as if the First Amendment didn't exist! Such foolishness. That's why censorship is a much better concept for the understanding of drug prohibition than any "disease model".'

Certainly, by arguing that state-run drug programmes are nothing but 'legalized drug peddling' and that the war on drugs is not only a waste of time, but also positively pernicious, Dr Szasz was bound to earn himself enemies. 'But it is ridiculous,' he says. 'Putting drug addicts in treatment centres is somewhat like confining people with tuberculosis together and then getting them to cough over one another.'

But what about the actual suffering involved in mental illness and drug addiction: surely Dr Szasz couldn't gainsay that?

What would he have felt like if one of his two daughters had been a drug addict or a schizophrenic? Wouldn't it have made him alter his views?

'Well, you know a lot of people ask me that question. I have been fortunate. But, you know, what is the impulse to ask these questions? Surely it's an attempt to make me look bad . . . It's really compassion-mongering, trying to adopt the high moral ground of someone else's suffering. It's analogous to the way people raise money for charity: "Give us your money for people starving in the Third World," they say. But of course they live well using other people's money to indulge their own altruism.

'Of course I cannot imagine forcing my daughters to be hospitalized. To the extent that I style myself an "anti-psychiatrist" it is only the involuntary type of psychiatry that I mean.'

So what about psychotherapy, where the individual actively seeks help? 'Well, I don't call what I do "psychotherapy", I just call it talking to people. If I can help them, then that's good, but I hope I never fall into the mistake of believing that I can help people because of my professional status.'

According to Szaszian philosophy, self-help groups such as Alcoholics Anonymous would appear to be the most pernicious and misguided of 'therapies'. But at least they have the honesty to give their theories an overtly religious character.

Did he agree? 'I suppose so. If people think that they can be helped by these things, that's their own affair. Just as it's their own affair if they want to belong to a religion or take a certain drug. But as far as I am concerned they are all equally stupid. It's just a case of *chacun à son goût.*'

But there is an increasing amount of research that seems to show that drug addiction and alcoholism may be genetically inherited. Wouldn't this seem to fly in the face of his theories? 'No, not really. I mean I'm not competent to judge this evidence, but even if a person does have a disposition to react unfavourably to a drug, all his susceptibility does is to enlarge his responsibility to avoid it.

'Really all of this preoccupation with medical care of one kind and another, as a political and a social issue, is a displacement. Instead of giving the people bread and circuses, politicians give them wars against diseases and drugs, and all kinds of therapies. If you look at it carefully you will see that involuntary mental hospitalization at taxpayers' expense is really a kind of poor relief.'

Dr Szasz is no faddist or crank, nor a 1960s maverick who has had his day. Indeed he said that he had been hardly aware of the counter-cultural antics of the Learys and Hoffmans. Rather, the key to Dr Szasz comes from his cry early on in our discussion when I touched upon the tension in America between the collectivism of public health laws and the individualism of capitalism. 'But it's all in de Tocqueville,' exclaimed Dr Szasz. 'He understood this and wrote about it 150 years ago!'

And that is why I predict that Dr Szasz's work and thought, prompted by the publication of his new book, will once again come to the fore: he takes the long view.

The Times, June 1992

Self's London

From where I lie, I can't see much of the world, save for a pro-jecting wall of my own house still fringed by green wisteria, the grey slate line of the next row of houses, and beyond this, the pill-box hat of one of the council blocks on the Wandsworth Road. Of course, if I sat up, I could get a bearing on at least a small part of iconic London—I could see the very tips of two of Battersea Power Station's stacks nestling same-sized amongst closer chimneys. And from this angle I'd also be able to see the gardens of this terrace, below and to my right; long strips of urban verdancy, most with their own dinky hut, sawn lawn and dwarf terrace: *urbs in rure in urbe in rure.*

Levi-Strauss said that all world cities are constructed on an east-to-west schema, with the poor in the east and the rich in the west. Some ascribe this to the prevalent winds; the poor, as it were, being swept into the gutter. I think Claude saw it as a deeper structural phenomenon than this; humanity dis-playing some of the instinctive, orienting behaviour of the social insects. But I've never experienced London in Levi-Strauss terms. I inhabit a city within which, no matter where I look, or in which direction I turn, I still find myself hid-eously oriented. I suffer from a kind of claustro-agoraphobia, if such a thing is possible. I fear going outside in London because it is so cramped and confining.

When you grow up in a great city (and by great I mean a city that is not readily geographically encompassed, even by an adult with mature visuo-spatial abilities), your sense of it is at first straightforwardly crazy—like a film with appalling continuity. (Characters turn the corner of St James's and find themselves standing, grinning foolishly, on the Aldwych.) 'Daddy,' asks my eight-year-old as we drive past Clissold Park, 'is that Battersea Park?' Poor dog, nodding his way into comprehension, as the jump-cut scenes of the city are projected at him through the windscreen.

Then comes the integration, the coalescence of the two hundred billion neurones that will comprise the city-brain. The *faux* villages of London—the tiny zones around friends' houses, or known haunts—spread over a grey waste of overpopulation, strung out along ribbon developments of short-term memory. And then, in adult life, there is the long, long shading in of the rest, the even adumbration which constitutes regular experience. Even ten years ago, and certainly fifteen, I could patrol central London and still avoid my past self when I saw him coming in the opposite direction. I could take alternative routes to avoid the districts of failed love affairs, I knew short cuts that would circumvent the neighbourhood of an abandoned friendship, I had only to swerve to miss the precincts of a snubbing acquaintance. But now the city is filled in with narratives, which have been extruded like psychic mastic into its fissures. There is no road I haven't fought on, no cul-de-sac I haven't ended it all in and no alley I haven't done it down. To traverse central London today, even in a car, even on autopilot, is still to run over a hundred memoirs.

The irregular, cracked flags of the driveway outside my childhood home in N2 have remained exactly the same for four decades. I know this, because I've been home. Not often, but a few times since the house was sold in the late seventies. Most recently, after a gap of a decade or so, I took my own children there and was amazed at the continuities of the topiary and the bricolage, set against the transitoriness of my own feelings. Of course, my last bitter memories of this house and its environs are of an insufferably stuffy, ultimate *ur*-suburb; Kate Greenaway on Largactil; the sort of place that could grow a J. G. Ballard out of the mildest and least imaginative of psyches. But that's because I was seventeen when I left here. Now, with my own kids chucking each other into the hedges and running on the wide, grass-bordered pavements, all I can see is how green it is; all I can hear is how quiet it is, the soundlessness of the suburbs.

It was on this driveway that we trundled our toys, small-scale precursors of the commuters we would become. It was here that we constructed rooms on the outside, cosy dens containing little stories; here we picked up the trails of our first narratives, worming in the crannies and clefts alongside virulent moss. In my childhood home, how many days would I spend, stowed in the hold of the upstairs back bedroom, imagining the oceanic city all around. There—or here, it makes no difference. In either place and time I have the same sense of residing in a permanent mid-morning, of avoiding the workaday world, of being marooned by the audience drain from Radio 4. Beached, here or there, on a grainy mattress, while outside the city hums and beeps and bumps and grinds and pulses and pullulates with a crazed sense of its own capacity to ceaselessly mutate, its fanatical ability to construct stories out of its rooms and its streets, its vestibules and its courtyards, its cars and its discarded fag packets. Any object the eye pursues becomes a story, another track scored in time. Any person is a potential Medusa, Gorgon-headed with writhing, serpentine tales.

Which is why I lie here in the spare room, safely barricaded by other people's stories, the tales of other cities. This refuge is almost completely lined with books, most of which have little to do with London. The wall opposite the sunny window is tiled with the spines of some 1,600 battered paperbacks. They are umber, grey, brown and blue, they are as pleasingly textured and involving to the eye as the robes of the couple in Klimt's *The Kiss,* a reproduction of which hangs on the wall opposite me. Their battered backs are a mnemonic of my own history. Despite the gearing of my own book collection into that of my wife, this impression has been enhanced, rather than diminished. It must be because we are both the same kind of trampish bibliophagists. Unlike other, more fastidious types, our collecting instinct is akin to the spirit in which homeless people acquire shopping trolleys, then use them to mass everything the verge, the bin and the gutter have to offer, creating small mobile monuments to obsolescence.

Thus we have all the books no one else wanted—as well as most of the ones we did. That's why we have Tony Buzan's *Memory: How to Improve It,* as well as *Extracts From Gramsci's Prison Notebooks;* that's why there are all of my dead mother's Viragos, and the family Penguins, Pelicans and Puffins, paperback generics which have come together in chunks, after generation upon generation of packing them into cardboard boxes, resulting in the evolution of a crude librarianism. But only very crude. J. K. Galbraith still abuts C. S. Lewis abutting Arthur C. Clarke, who in turn leans on *Zen Comics* and a collection of *Helpful Hints* compiled by some upper-class supernumerary. Good cladding—and an entirely suitable housing within which to stay firmly at home. In fact, it *is* my childhood home—or more like anywhere else could ever be like it again. And looking to the wall outside, its particular pocks, chips and coarseness of mortar, I am oppressed by the notion that the bricks may be texts as well, the spines of buried tablets, covered in cuneiform script, which bear, etched into the very mucilaginous matter of the city, the histories of all who live here now, lived here then, or could ever live here.

I can't believe this is exclusively a writer's problem. Consciousness is, after all, simply another story, another string of metaphors, another gag. I think all of us Londoners are like the young schizophrenic man who knocked on the door of my Shepherd's Bush house on a dull winter evening in 1989:

'Could you lend me £13.27,' he said, his voice jagged with the fateful snicker-snack of psychosis, 'and drive me to Leytonstone?'

'All right,' I replied, keen as ever to experience a random act of senseless generosity. As we were scooting under the Euston Road underpass, and his delusional babble was mounting in volume and intensity, I decided that I'd better check out his destination. I pulled over. 'Show me,' I said to him, opening the *A–Z* to the relevant page, 'exactly where it is you want to go in Leytonstone.'

He looked at me warily. 'Come on, man,' he said, 'you know as well as I do that the *A–Z* is a plan of a city—it hasn't been built yet.'

The *A–Z*, the colouring book of London. Some of us live in this plan more than we do in the physical reality of London. Some of us even live more in the diagram of the tube than we do in the physical reality of London. After all, the tube imparts a sense of the city that is not unlike the child's unintegrated vision described above: you disappear down a hole in the Mile End Road and then pop out of another one in Chalk Farm. Some people's whole lives must be like that, with no coherent sense of the city's geography; they must find it impossible to circumvent old lovers, evade defunct friendships.

Of course, I've been orienting myself for a lifetime, which is why it's so hideous, but it wasn't until the mid-eighties that I had my first epiphany, the first coming-together of all these disordered ideas and impressions and imaginings of London. I was standing in Hill Street, Mayfair, on a warm, early summer morning, when the realisation came that I had never been to the mouth of the river that ran through the city of my birth. You couldn't have had more solid confirmation of the fact that London's geography remained, for me, exclusively emotional. What would you think of a peasant who had farmed all his life on the banks of a river if he told you he had never been to where that river meets the sea, some thirty miles away? You'd think he was a very ignorant, very insular, very landlocked peasant. There are millions of peasants like that in London; in imagining themselves to be at the very navel of the world, Londoners have forgotten the rest of their anatomy.

I got in the car and drove east. I had an idea, a visual image even, of Southend, the town on the northern bank of the estuary, though it was someone else's image, smuggled into my memory by photograph or film. But the south bank was unknown, and so potentially the more exciting, although in common with the other peasants, I was certain there was nothing there, only mudflats and defunct industries.

The Isle of Grain, the southernmost extremity of the Thames, was the provider of a parallax, a point of reference that allowed me to sense the overall shape of the city and its peculiar cosmology. Once you've spotted one parallax, you begin to apprehend more and more. Central London may seem curiously flat, but if you drive up the Bayswater Road towards Marble Arch and focus on the very tips of those same iconic, twin chimneys which you can see poking up from behind the green swell of Hyde Park to your right, you'll be able to realise the overall shape of the city moving beneath you. Or walk east across Wormwood Scrubs, under the machine eyes of the prison security cameras, but keep your eyes firmly fixed on the Trellick Tower, the block that dominates Notting Hill: you'll have the same sensation. I've now taken so many bearings that I am paralysed, ensnared by my own earlier sightings, lost in a tangled undergrowth of points of view. It took several more years and several more acts of geographic foolhardiness (the worst of which was undoubtedly making a film about the M25) before I could acknowledge the full extent of my own sense of confinement.

I adopted two stratagems to deal with the problem of being a small metropolis boy. The first was to take purposeless walks across the city; the second was to write fictions. The

walks, in order to be purposeless, had to unite two parts of
London that could not in any way be construed as bearing a
functional relationship to each other; they were lines drawn
on the *A–Z:* Perivale to Acton; Wood Green to Wandsworth;
Hammersmith to Hackney.

This sense of confinement was enhanced by the fact that I
was commuting at the time from Shepherd's Bush in the west
to Southwark in the southeast. It was the first—and last—
proper office job. It came with a company car, a Ford Sierra
so new that there was wrapping paper on the accelerator and
the interior smelled the way I remember new bicycle brakes
smelling when I was a child. The temporal margins within
which I had to operate were astonishingly narrow: five minutes too late leaving in the morning could mean another twenty
on the journey time. Twenty minutes of giving children
asthma, smoking cigarettes, merging with the collective ulcer.
Twenty more minutes pinned like some automotive butterfly on the card of the Westway flyover, or the Gray's Inn
Road or Blackfriars Bridge. When there were tube strikes—
and there were a lot around then—the journey could last
three hours.

I was overwhelmed by a sense of the totality of the traffic
in the city, and of its complete interconnection. I began to
imagine it might be possible to analyse it on a purely physical
level, and from this to derive a complete knowledge of traffic
flows throughout an entire built-up area. It would be like
having an awesomely powered Trafficator computer—but
inside your head.

I started work on a story that expressed this idea of a metaphoric meta-jam; this world of driverless cars, of ultimate claustrophobia. Soon I was getting up at six-thirty in the morning,
rushing through London by car in order to sit down and write
about it. I began to work on other stories in parallel—and I
began to see their ontogeny, and to see that they were all about
London. By this I don't mean simply that they were all set in

London, I mean that the city was the main—and possibly the only—protagonist.

Although it seemed as if the city had sucked me in, it was a consummation I had no will to resist. For in order to avoid the massive and destructive sense of irony that I felt whenever I came to the act of writing fiction, I *had* to write about something I knew very well indeed. I was forced on my subject—and it was forced on me. We were locked up together, tapping the monotonous, plastic piano.

Needless to say, my stratagems didn't work. London wasn't going away. Now I was a writer, I thought I needn't actually live in the place. It might be nice to live in the country, to write about London from a position of rural reclusion, or even not write about London at all. What a fool. The country was crowded, noisy and polluted. My infant son's asthma got worse. At night the sky was bruised with the massive explosion of halogen, forty miles away to the south. In the day I fancied I could hear the distant rumble of the Great Wen's traffic, mocking my bucolic idyll. I began writing a novel, most of which was set in London. It was disturbing and involving, and I didn't want to get into it. We took a holiday in Morocco and as a piece of *jeu d'esprit* I wrote a novella, a light thing about a woman who grows a penis and uses it to rape her husband. Naturally this takes place in Muswell Hill, another theoretically anonymous north London suburb. I scrawled away, with the shouts of Berbers hawking in the Djemaa el Fna ringing in my ears, describing a pedestrian narrative around familiar precincts.

Eventually I forced myself back to the novel. The London it was set in was a bewildering place containing many different levels of reality: my protagonist really could turn the corner of St James's and find himself mysteriously in the Aldwych. The city, once again, had usurped the tale, stolen the narrative. In the novel it was 'a mighty ergot fungus, erupting from the very crust of the earth; a growing, mutating thing, capable

71

WILL SELF

of taking on the most fantastic profusion of shapes. The people
who live in this hallucinogenic development partake of its
tryptamines, and so it bends itself to the secret dreams of its
beholders.' This was, in fact, my own dark view. It was now
not simply a matter of being in a confined, well-known place,
it was like being in a confined space with a brooding, potentially violent presence.

My marriage broke up. I moved to the far north of Scotland. I wrote a collection of short stories, most of which were
set in the M40 corridor. London was an enormous absence in
these stories, but it was there, beyond the horizon, like a giant
lodestone, attracting the cars down the motorway and then
aligning them like iron fillings around the M25.

I moved to Suffolk. It was a tired, eroded landscape which
I walked ceaselessly, attempting to map it, but my subject
matter, when I did manage to write at all, was exile. My pro-
tagonists were all writers who had left the city. I reached a
point where my life and my writing life horribly intersected.
I started to know people in the locale, there were invitations
to gatherings of stultifying chit-chat. I was obliged to 'look
in' at the craft shop. After four years, it was over in two days.
A van was hired, a house was rented. I went home.

Initially I found myself to be pleasingly disorientated, occasionally even lost. My internal *A–Z* had faded with desue-
tude. But soon it was back, and worse than ever. The city
was punishing me for my defection. Before I left, my
fictionalised London might have been banjaxed and strange,
but it exhibited no more anachronism than the real thing.
Now this sinisterly altered. I began to perceive the city as
not simply filled with my own lifelines and storylines, but
choked with those of everyone else as well. I began to write
stories set in a London where the opium den that Dorian
Gray frequented in Limehouse was still mysteriously open,
despite being shadowed by the Legoland of Canary Wharf

72

Tower. This was a predictably more claustrophobic city than the one that had preceded it. It swarmed with humankind: humans running, humans walking, humans scratching, belching, farting, like a pack of apes. I decided to write a novel set in a London entirely populated by chimpanzees. My protagonist found the city to be about two-thirds to scale with the London he knew. That, and the way in which the chimps would ceaselessly and publicly copulate, served to make him feel overpoweringly claustrophobic.

I remarried and we bought this house in Vauxhall, closer to the centre of town than I've ever lived before. The great paperback miscegenation took place. My claustrophobia was now so complete that in some strange way it wasn't really claustrophobia any longer, more a case of my own partaking of too many London tryptamines: a bit of a bad trip. In the past I would welcome that sensation, familiar to all city dwellers, of suddenly noticing a building that I'd never paid any attention to before, even though it had been in my purview many thousands of times. Now I'm afflicted by a more ominous but related sensation, which involves suddenly noticing a new building and not being able to remember what it's replaced. This is unpleasant. This is like conceptualist burglars breaking into your house during the night and millimetrically realigning all the furniture.

There's only one way to arrest this entropy of the city—keep writing about it. I've learned to accept London as my muse. Initially, there I was, sitting on the tube, when she came in: filthy, raddled, smelly, old and drunk. Like everyone else I wanted to get up and move to the next carriage, especially when she elected to sit down right next to me. But now we're inseparable, going round and around the Circle Line, arm in arm, perhaps for eternity.

The measure of my acceptance is that I'm now prepared to fictionalise an area as soon as I move into it—like a dog marking its territory. I've set a short story in Vauxhall already, and to celebrate the hideousness of my orientation the climax takes place in the hot-air balloon that has recently been tethered here. Tourists pay a tenner to rise up four hundred feet over London. On a clear day you can see almost the entire city spread out beneath you. When I did my research ascent, I was struck anew by the immensity of the urban hinterland to the south; it needs a big book, a really long novel. The Great South London Novel has a ring to it—I think.

In conclusion: when I was a child my unhappily married parents would drive us, almost every weekend, to Brighton, where we would stay with my grandparents. My parents would argue all the way there and all the way back; the trip was synonymous with misery for me. In time I came to associate any leaving of London with this wrenching sadness. I began to conceive of the city itself as a kind of loving parent, vast but womb-like and surmounted by an overarching dome. By accepting the city as a source of fictional inspiration I've made this dome a reality—for me. My only wish now is that everyone else should experience the same peculiar sense of interiority, of being in London, that I have. So, my only objection to the Millennium Dome is that it should have been far, far bigger—and I could have told them what to put in it.

Granta 65, Spring 1999

At the Mevlevi Festival

Having purchased a Mobylette moped while travelling in central Anatolia—despite the considerable derision of John, my companion—I looked forward to driving it into central London. But after puttering happily over Waterloo Bridge and beginning the descent into the Kingsway underpass, I encountered a hold-up. The gates were closed at the entrance to the tunnel and the traffic was backed up for fifty metres. So I propped the Mobylette on its stand, clambered up on to the roadway and began looking for someone to blame for this impasse. I only saw a few obviously innocent passers-by, but on returning to where my moped had been parked I found it gone! 'What the hell's going on!' I bellowed, as quick as any Londoner to embrace road rage. How could it have been stolen when it was blocked in fore and aft? Had a weightlifting thief managed to manhandle it out of the underpass?

I leapt back on to the roadway above and moved purposively towards the passers-by I'd seen before. Obviously they weren't innocent after all—they were massively culpable. I'd give them what for . . . ! But then, just as I was closing in on the knot of putative motorised-bicycle thieves, something bizarre happened. No, bizarre is a grotesque understatement— something marvelously, triumphantly, unimpeachably transcendent, something the like of which I never thought I could experience. I realised—in one delirious surge of giggling, intoxicated, sympathetic glory—that I had become . . .

ENLIGHTENED; that I had shucked off my tedious old ego as easily as if it were a raincoat, and left it lying in the road; that I felt no anger towards the people who might have stolen my moped, because it didn't matter AT ALL. Nothing mattered, except this sense of hilarious, total identification with all things sentient, with the godly hydra-head that is all creatures. If I looked into the eyes of the urban foot sloggers all around me, I was instantly at one with all their dreams and hopes and longings, but not in a painful, burdensome way—this was a dynamic, beautiful and extremely funny form of sympathy.

Giggling like a small boy, I strolled away from the underpass. Obviously, I couldn't really be enlightened—that would be absurd. It took years, I knew, of disciplined meditation and prayer, under the firm tutelage of a spiritual master—whether Sufi sheikh, eastern guru, or Christian divine—to achieve such a state. No, I must be suffering from one of those delusory states that come upon mystical initiates. What I needed was a sharp blow on the head from the person who knew the condition of my soul better than any other: my wife.

Without being aware of getting there I found myself standing at home, in the entrance hall of my house. The front door swung open and in came Deborah. She looked at me strangely and said, 'What's got into you?' I knew what she was thinking, that I was drunk, or in a still more unsavoury state. I could conceal the truth no longer. 'It's very funny,' I tittered, 'but I've become enlightened!' She stared deep into what had once been my eyes, and in a matter-of-fact way said, 'Oh, so you have . . .' And the 'have' lengthened and deepened, oscillating up and down the scale, until it became an amplified ululation . . . until it became the muezzin, howling out over the public address system of the mosque adjoining the Mevlana Müzesi across the road. I was jerked awake. It was a late-December dawn in Konya, central Turkey, and so far was I from really being enlightened that my first thoughts on coming to consciousness were of how narrow and hard my bed was, and just how overheated Room 217 of the Hotel Balikcilar remained, despite the window having been wide open all night.

I retell this peculiar dream at such length purely because it really did happen, complete with its distinct levels of lucidity. After all, it's one thing to dream that you've been enlightened, quite another to be aware within the dream itself that this may be false. It's one thing to go looking for a vicarious religious experience—but it's altogether stranger to have one thrust upon you unbidden. I suppose I'm as cynical about spiritual tourism as I am about any travel that makes you a voyeur, extracting trivial pleasures from the profundities of other cultures. When Westerners are young we tend to do this in a material dimension, taking our cheap holidays in other peoples' misery. But when we grow old enough and rich enough we might think we're behaving more laudably by taking expensive ones in other peoples' piety.

On the face of it I was as bad as any other in this respect. My friend John had suggested the trip to the Mevlevi Festival, where the dervishes famously whirl. Until then I knew no more of this Sufi sect than that raw fact: they whirl. In English parlance, to act like a 'whirling dervish' is to behave with an uncontrolled frenzy. As for the Sufis and Sufism in general, I had no more acquaintance with these than a back-of-the-cereal-packet fact file. I knew they represented the mystic, heterodox wing of Islam; and once or twice in Morocco, I'd ended up chatting late at night, in pidgin French, to young men who were members of Sufi brotherhoods. But was it the smallness of the hour, the inadequacy of my French, or the potency of their hashish, that led me to mystical appreciation of their wisdom, when they uttered such sentiments as 'God is breath'?

My vision of modern Turkey was similarly warped and occluded. Edward Said has propounded the thesis that the West's view of the Orient has always been a distorted projection of its own negative cultural capabilities, and certainly I had absorbed plenty on Turkey's downside. This vast oblong of territory between the Black Sea and the Mediterranean, the Middle East and the Aegean, styled itself as a democratic, modernising bulwark against Islamic fundamentalism. But was Turkey not also the implacable pursuer of territorial claims in Cyprus and Kurdistan, which meant that the former had remained for three decades with its sovereignty in escrow, and the latter was an unmentionable word, a non-designation? Shortly before I arrived in December 2000, the case of Abdullah Ocalan, the Kurdish rebel leader captured by the Turks and sentenced to death, was referred to the European Court of Human Rights. The Turkish government had agreed to abide by the Court's decision, and in a sense this was the very pivot around which Turkish membership in the European Community—for so long a matter of debate—revolved.

Then there was a $10 billion emergency loan from the IMF to bail out the Turkish economy and the ongoing hunger strikes by Marxist rebels in Turkish prisons (which culminated, the week after I left, in an armed assault by the security forces leaving fifteen prisoners dead—they'd set themselves on fire). With the cosmically vexed question of the Armenian holocaust of 1915–17—a fact the assertion of which remains a criminal offence in Turkey to this day—it was difficult not to think of the nation as, if not the proverbially 'sick man' of Europe, at any rate a fervid-to-overheated kind of a place, physically proximate, but linguistically and culturally isolated. And, of course, there were also those dervishes.

On the BA flight out from Heathrow to Istanbul I began my crash programme of instruction in Sufism and the cult of the Mevlana or 'teacher'. Known as 'Rumi' (literally 'from Roman Anatolia'), but called 'Jelaluddin Balkhi' by the Persians and Afghans, the poet was born in Balkh, Afghanistan, in 1207. Sometime between 1215 and 1220 he and his family fled the threat of invading Mongols and emigrated to Konya in Turkey. Rumi's father, Bahaeddin Veled, was a theologian and mystic, and after his death Rumi took over the role of sheikh in the dervish community in Konya. The word 'dervish' derives from the Persian *darvish* meaning 'poor man' (this expresses the poverty of man in relation to the richness of God rather than literal poverty), but up until 1244 when he encountered the wandering dervish Shams of Tabriz, Rumi's life was that of a relatively orthodox religious scholar. Shams changed all of that with a single question about the primacy of Muhammad's teaching, and the two then embarked on a *sohbet,* or mystical conversation, which was only interrupted by Shams's disappearance to Damascus when he sensed the jealousy of Rumi's disciples. On Shams's return the *sohbet* was resumed, only to be finally interrupted when the mendicant was murdered, possibly by Rumi's own son.

It's difficult to express the intensity of the friendship between the two men in any conventional framework—this was a total melding of minds. It's said that when Rumi and Shams were in convocation they had no need of sleep or food for weeks on end. It was his relationship with Shams that made Rumi into a mystical poet, and after his disappearance Rumi reached the conclusion that he had wholly absorbed Shams's identity; indeed, that Shams was now writing through him. He called his huge collection of odes and quatrains 'The Works of Shams of Tabriz': and during the last years of his life he composed and dictated the vast, six-volume masterpiece called simply *Mathnawi,* or *Spiritual Couplets.*

Just as it's impossible to place one definition of Sufism itself, which is in reality a vast, multi-stranded skein of Islamic practice, commentary, interpretation and belief, so Rumi's poetry, some sixty-five thousand verses in Persian, defies any reduction to this, or that. Rumi has been compared to Shakespeare in the range of his impact and his cultural centrality to his own, emerging world. Like Shakespeare's writing, his poetry can seem, even on slight acquaintance, to be a vast palimpsest, a working-up out of diverse sources—mythic, folkloric, lyrical, ecstatic—of an entire metaphoric realm. Some of Rumi's verses are couplets with all the paradoxical confusion of Zen Buddhist koans—'I am the kebab, God is the spit'—while others have the pithy air of tough, homespun advice, and still others the feel of love poetry, only in Rumi's case the beloved is God himself.

Suffice to say, even in four hours I'd read enough to feel enthusiastic about my trip to Konya for the *sema* or Mevlevi Festival. Each year, in the week preceding the anniversary of Rumi's death—17 December 1273—the whirling ceremony is held twice daily. My guidebook was disparaging about the modern version, saying that it was inauthentic: it took place in a basketball court, the tickets were 'pricey', and the whirlers themselves were not even professing Mevlevis. It painted a picture of Konya as a conservative, unlovely, close-faced metropolis of half a million, beset by the sub-zero temperatures of the Anatolian plateau, and where hotels and restaurants doubled up their prices for the pilgrims, while the shops were full of kitschy whirling-dervish memorabilia.

How wrong the guide was. Authentic is not a synonym for 'picturesque', and our experience of off-season Turkey felt profoundly real. From the moment I rendezvoused with John—who for the purposes of my narrative occupies a Shams of Tabriz–type role—at Pandeli's, a famous restaurant in the Egyptian Bazaar of Istanbul, we were plunged into a conversation which, if not evidence of a profound mystical union, was at any rate tantamount to a philosophic discourse, while entering a milieu shorn of tourists and occupied by Turks who consistently displayed towards us a manner of weary acceptance, verging on the bullying intimacy of an older brother: 'Don't cross the road there!' they shouted to us as we barrelled across the cobbles. 'There is a tram coming.'

AT THE MEVLEVI FESTIVAL

We ate lamb at Pandeli's and talked of religion and science ('I am the kebab, God is the spit'); we ate lamb in Konya. When we got to Cappadocia we ate lamb there too. There was traditional, limp salad, and occasionally some chickpeas. We didn't object—we were visiting slap-bang in the middle of Ramadan, and while it wasn't impossible to get things to eat and drink during daylight hours, there was a persistent atmosphere of strained tolerance when we asked for food. In Konya no one smoked in the street, and when dusk fell the restaurants and cafés were filled, then evacuated, by the populace within the space of an hour, as if the city itself were some voracious bivalve.

John, who'd visited Istanbul before, gave me three hours of edited highlights. At the Aya Sofya—'the Church of the Divine Wisdom'—which was for a millennium the largest enclosed space in the world, I marvelled at the louring interior of the giant dome, complete with its stalagmite of scaffolding, so dense and complex that in the gloom it appeared like charcoal shading. We admired the porphyry columns, the ecstatic mosaics, the ramp-like staircases Byzantine noblewomen had ridden their horses up. Then on to Yerebatan Saray, 'the Underground Palace', a fourth-century cistern—again on such an enormous scale, with its four-storey columns sunk in a pellucid pool, that whole legions could have tenanted it. And finally to the Blue Mosque, where we made our obeisance under the calligraphic literalism of another vast dome.

Outside it was dusk. In the precincts of the mosque people were beginning to throng. You could feel the tension of the fast on the verge of being broken. Around a small fair, urchins were running, shouting and playing. Young women sat at the outside tables of cafés, smoking hookahs and chatting. Men strolled arm in arm. We sat and drank several of the ubiquitous glasses of strong tea that fuel Turkey, and continued the philosophic debate that had been driving us forward all afternoon. John, an avid reader of those modern Tao-of-physics-style books, inclines to a sense of awe at the intellectual comprehensibility of creation; while I, already slightly tipsy with culture shock, and the sips I had taken of Rumi's poetry (which frequently employs drunkenness as a metaphor for abandonment to God), was already cruising for a mystical experience.

At the airport, a mere twenty minutes' cab ride from the mosque (a further disorientation in this ancient city of confusion), we had two more hours of circular debate before we boarded our flight for Konya. By the time the Turkish Airlines flight was aloft, we were so dizzy with speculation that neither of us nervous flyers remembered to be anxious. Edward Said's thesis was entirely forgotten as John flipped through *Sky Life,* the Turkish Airlines equivalent of the magazine you're now holding, and after an hour tunnelling through the sky we landed in the darkness of central Anatolia.

The next morning, in Konya, the sunlight had a milky quality that suggested it was only the sub-zero temperature that was keeping the dust of the steppes at bay. The city is situated in the middle of a region styled 'the bread-basket of Turkey'; but in midwinter, in the bustle of headscarfed women pilgrims, lottery-ticket sellers and shoeshine operatives, with the omnipresent hoot of traffic, we felt suffused with urbanity. Our hotel, the Balikcilar, boasted peculiar murals in the dining room depicting the famous troglodyte dwellings of Cappadocia. The lobby too was encrusted with knobbly stonework. The night had not been a comfortable one. There was the heat of the rooms, the narrowness of the beds, and in next door to John the mounting hysteria of a woman having a full-scale nervous breakdown. While we were consulting in the corridor as to what to do, a huge Nordic character had emerged from a room further along, and after gaining admission succeeded in either comforting or eliminating her. On the television I watched the *sema* on the local station, eighteen dervishes fluidly revolving on the floor of a basketball court, their white skirts flaring out. Even in black and white their smooth synchrony seemed the antithesis of religious frenzy.

We had one of those days that only happen in remote places where you don't speak the language, hardly anyone speaks yours and you're otherwise ill prepared. We visited the Mevlana shrine itself and saw the tombs of Rumi, his father and his acolytes, all caparisoned with iridescent drapery. Chandeliers hung on long wires from the high ceilings. The tombs were canted at an angle, their curiously phallic, turbaned tops like the pommels of saddles. They looked like suspended-animation chambers carrying their occupants to some distant planet. The literalism of Islam was on every available surface, and as we were carried forward in the press of pilgrims—the headscarfed, keening women holding their hands open beseechingly in front of their faces—eerie, ululating singing played from hidden speakers. We examined some hairs from the Prophet's beard in the adjoining chamber, together with brilliantly illuminated manuscripts of the poet's works. And everywhere, despite the press of worshippers, there was the same air of grudging yet total tolerance of our presence, and the handful of other Westerners in attendance.

Outside the shrine we met Arum, a young man intent on improving his English. And improve it he needed to. We spent two hours in his company, trekking on foot down the dusty boulevards to the Atatürk Sports Stadium, to this office, to that office, to an ethnographic museum, to a third office, hunting for where we thought they might have our reserved tickets for that evening's *sema*, while revelling in the full weight of each other's incomprehension. About the only point of true communication was summed up by the words 'Britney Spears', and that's a very low denominator indeed. Eventually, in a side-street, we found a crowded office where an envelope was discovered bearing John's name, phonetically transcribed. We were given free posters depicting a whirling dervish and the legend that this was the 727th Mevlevi Festival.

That evening, as we sat on part of an island of leatherette sofas in the lobby of the Balikcilar, I felt a strange, liquid undulating beneath me. For a full twenty seconds I thought it was the motions of the distinctly heavyweight people in the seat behind, but then I noticed the staff had left off serving tea and were bolting for the door. It was over within a minute, and we were all outside, standing across the road on a traffic island oddly decorated with a bed of cabbages. It wasn't until the following evening, when we were having a telly supper three hundred kilometres away in Cappadocia, that we learned via *BBC World Report* that the earthquake had toppled a minaret in Konya, killing six.

The tremor was a fitting preamble to our visit to the *sema* itself, introducing a further note of disorientation to our experience of the Orient. Back at the Atatürk Sports Stadium there were headscarves in abundance. At an urn in the dusty lobby a man performed a tea ceremonial of high-speed riskiness, whipping four glasses at a time under the stream of boiling water, as if attempting to manicure his outstretched hands with third-degree burns. Inside the auditorium about two thousand people were settling themselves on plastic chairs. Photographers and camera crews were roving around the edge of the court. There was even a camera positioned on the gantry holding the basketball net. Banners inscribed with the verses of Rumi were hung up around the walls, together with many others bearing the single word 'ARCELIK'. Later, by a deductive process involving scrutinising advertising hoardings, I worked out that this was the name of a Turkish washing-machine manufacturer. Washing machines? Whiter-than-white robes? Whirling dervishes? Could this be some form of commercial sponsorship? On the one hand, it would seem a desecration of the religious character of the *sema;* on the other—it made perfect sense.

AT THE MEVLEVI FESTIVAL

For, as the lights went down, and the musicians in their long robes filed in to take up their positions, it occurred to me that while the whirling-dervish order remained to some extent clandestine, this officially sanctioned exhibition was the public, popular face of contemporary Sufism in Turkey. Atatürk banned the Sufi sects (which had enormous political influence under the Ottoman Empire) outright in the 1920s, and although the ban never really took, there is still a sense in which such practices are frowned on. Not that you would have realised it from the speech of an official from the Ministry of Culture at the lectern, who, in between the musical and the dancing parts of the programme, told us that the Mevlana had anticipated the theory of relativity, genetic engineering and the moon landing; as well as exhorting us not to use mobile phones or take flash photographs during the *sema*.

For an hour and a half we listened to hypnotic *ayin*. These complex compositions are played by a small orchestra including the *ney* (an end-blown reed flute), the kettledrum, the *rebab* (a pear-shaped fiddle played with a bow) and the *kanun* (a large zither), among other instruments. Vocal pieces preceded and followed the *ayin: ilahi,* hymns comprising words from Rumi; and *zikr,* trance-like repetitions of some of the ninety-nine names of God by a soloist with an electrifying ability to shift his tone.

When the dervishes entered—from beneath the opposition's basket—they looked imposing, in their floor-length black cloaks, which symbolise the tomb itself, and their high, conical, camel-hair hats, which symbolise the tombstone. Filing down the tramlines of the court they took their places in several colloquies of cushions and proceeded to enact in dumb show various aspects of the dervish lifestyle, such as discoursing over religious texts and welcoming a new initiate, who poignantly—if a little fetishistically—was called upon by the *seyh* (the current head of the sect—or the man *playing* the current head of the sect) to kiss his hat.

85

Eventually the *seyh* marshalled them together again, and they dropped their black robes to denote that they had escaped the tomb and all other worldly ties—a piece of symbolism perhaps a tad undercut by the fact that the white skirts they wear underneath are intended to resemble the funeral shroud. But no matter how morbid these accoutrements, or how hammy the performance of the *seyh* (who paced about looking distinctly self-important and performing his obeisance with all the gravity of a small-town mayor), when the dervishes began to whirl all was explained, all was clarified, and all the background camera flashes and rumblings of the audience faded into the darkness of the auditorium.

The dervishes whirl steadily and metrically. Their motion is intended to represent the heavenly bodies, and there is something other-worldly about these men as they revolve, their skirts flaring out, canted at an angle. They hold one arm extended up, receiving grace from God, and one down, distributing it to humanity. Their feet, moving one about the other in a tight three-step, seem wholly disconnected from their static torsos. They are released by the *seyh,* one after the other, and float up one side of the court, then down the other, then into the middle, until the whole area is carpeted with their white blooms, yet at no point—despite the fact that their eyes are half closed—is there any possibility of collision. While they whirl, the musicians sing of the desire for mystic union.

The whirling was over in an hour or so, and after it had finished we rushed for the cab rank in the darkness as if we'd been at any other kind of gig—Britney Spears perhaps. The next day we hired a car (expensive, but not catastrophically so) and drove two hundred kilometres over empty roads, through a landscape of blue hills that seemed in their very contours to be remembering the tramp of the myriad civilisations that have passed through them.

In Cappadocia we saw the wind-eroded rock valley of Göreme, and the fairy chimneys of Ürgüp. We climbed into the tiny churches hewn out of the volcanic tuff, and at night, in a deserted hammam a masseur lathered us and cracked our vertebrae. We returned to Konya the following afternoon and attended the *sema* again. For some reason the faces of the dervishes appeared to be those of old friends: the young one with the swan's neck; the middle-aged guy with the notably black beard; the small old one with the face of a British comedian. However, whether it was the daylight streaming into the hall, or our familiarity with the ritual, this second helping felt like one too many. It was the first that stayed with me.

As I walked back to the hotel, exhausted by four of the most incident-filled days I can remember ever having, a cavalcade of sinister black Mercedes with tinted windows screeched to a halt outside the Mevlana Müzesi. Behind them came uniformed police who sealed off this busy section of road. From the darkened cars a politician, complete with his entourage, emerged in double-quick time—the apparatchiks all in sharp suits, the security men fanning out about them, ostentatiously patting their armpits to check their firearms were still concealed. The largest and most threatening of the minders walked straight towards where I was standing, by the outdoor fountain of the mosque. For a few seconds I thought he was going to accost me, but then he veered off, went over to one of the taps, took off his jacket—exposing his shoulder holster—and draped it over the stone balustrade, then sat down and removed his shoes and socks so that he might wash his feet.

Modern Turkey—ancient Turkey. Who would've thought so much could be absorbed in so little time? But then, that night, there came the dream.

High Life, May 2001

The Red Centre

In the desert the dawn of the third millennium breaks in a pale, thin smile, which lengthens and lengthens until the skullcap of the night peels away from the circumference of the horizon. The features of the landscape swim out of the haze and yet again the world reveals its primordial character, devoid of the diminishing presence of man. The gigantic bulk of Uluru, the largest single lithic outcropping in the world emerges from the darkness, first charcoal grey, then purple, then a throbbing, dark red. The Rock is isolated in this waste of scrub and scree, the only other eminences are similarly vast formations rearing up from the crepuscular terrain. Einstein said that 'God does not play dice', but looking upon these stupendous chunks of the world littering the desert floor, it's difficult to resist the thought that this is the aftermath of some divine game of chance, and these are the abandoned counters.

Certainly the locals are in little doubt about the spiritual significance of Uluru; just as they equally revere the thirty-six rock domes of Kata Tjuta (the Olgas), which rise a thousand metres out of the earth forty kilometres to the west. But the Aboriginal world view, which regards the consciousness of humans as the reverie of the earth's very ecology, fits these monuments into a quite different kind of cosmology. Some are the petrified bodies of mighty animals; beings who once moved over the surface of the earth during a protean period called—in English—'the Dreamtime'. Others—like Uluru itself—are monuments to great conflicts between the Dreamtime spirits. But for the aboriginal individual this is a living past, a permanent now the great antiquity of which—Aboriginal myth refers with consistency and accuracy to geological events which occurred tens of thousands of years ago—testifies to its importance.

Here, according to the Pitjantjatjara people, was once a flat expanse of land dominated by Uluru waterhole and Mutitjilda Spring. This latter place was—and is—the abode of Wanambi, the Rainbow Snake. The Rainbow Snake is possibly the most ancient, but certainly the most widely known of the Dreamtime spirits. To the original Australians, this amalgam of creature and natural phenomenon, is the very chord which connects spirit and matter. When contemplating the mythology of Uluru it's better to think of the *Bhagavad Gita* or the *Iliad* than any monotheistic tale. For, the environs of where the Rock now looms, were once the scene of a battle to rival any staged between Arjuna and Karna, under the gaze of Vishnu.

Most of the major indentations which form the 'wumbuluru' or shade side of the Rock (the southwest face) are petrified reminders of the conflict between the Kunia (or carpet-snake people) and the Mala (or Hare-wallaby people). The point at which the dawning rays of the third millennium first strike is exactly where, in the wake of more trials and tribulations than there is space-time here to recall, the Kunia finally gathered together and sang themselves to death.

Yet as the desert floor begins to resonate beneath your feet, as if it were flexing itself in preparation for the pulverising heat of the day, you can see that you are not alone in the lee of this majestic massif. Far from alone, silhouetted against the rapidly blanching sky, inching their way up the gargantuan buttress, are an ant-like file of human figures. And as the busy, unruly sun mounts the empyrean, all around you on the desert floor are revealed the members of a mighty motorcade: coaches from the four corners of the continent; ditto camper vans; ditto cars;

ditto motorcycles. There are even a few cyclists and walkers in amongst this throng, Mad Maxes who've pounded the eighteen kilometres of tarmac out from Yulara, the tourist resort beyond the border of the National Park.

It isn't, you now realise, the eerie rustling of a Dreamtime spirit which you can hear above the moan of the wind coming from the desert. It's the click, whirr and whine of a thousand cameras—digital, camcorder, automatic—registering the first daylight of a new age. And that murmuring all around, it isn't—you acknowledge to your companion—the voices of the Pungalunga Men, on their way towards the west, where they'll transmogrify into the thirty-six rock domes of Kata Tjuta. Oh no. These are the voices of twenty-five thousand very real Japanese salary men and their wives. These are the voices of thousands of others who have come to inaugurate their new era by snapping and snooping around the timeless grandeur of some other people's immemorial past.

Do I think there's anything wrong with visiting Uluru (or Ayer's Rock as it's known in the West)? No, not particularly. Would I climb the Rock itself? You've got to be joking—it's the psychic equivalent of pissing on the Wailing Wall or spreading a picnic out on the Ka'ba. Would I go there on the eve of the millennium—as so many are planning to do"? Not if you paid me a vast amount of money and fully insured me (in a weird, cosmic fashion) against eruptions of the Rainbow Snake, mass hysteria or any other unsettling phenomenon which may occur.

Not that there's much chance of my going—or you for that matter. Unless, that is, you've taken the precaution of finalising your itinerary an aeon ago. Not only is the Yulara Resort long since fully booked, but the flights into Australia itself have been full up for months now. Of course, you could get there—and stay there—if you really really wanted to be at Uluru for the millennium experience, but you have to ask yourself what kind of people are likely to descend on an incredibly remote place, en masse, in order to simultaneously revere and profane the sacred beliefs of the people who own it? Tie-dye nutters is who; the patchouli and bangle mob; types who think the Rainbow Snake is a clothes shop in London's Knightsbridge. Yes them, the tofu heads and the Tantrically incorrect.

Actually, to say that the Pitjantjatjara 'own' Uluru is a reversal of the real state of affairs. It is rather the land that owns the people; and this land is the omphalos, the very navel of the body that is their world. To trample upon it has to be a mistake, especially in the midst of the odd psychic maelstrom generated by partying—because it is—like it's 1999. It's not that I'm superstitious, it's simply that I have slight acquaintance with the very periphery of the Aboriginals' world picture, to know better than to advance further—unless having respectfully requested to.

These Pitjantjatjara, like many desert peoples are ascetics, fanatics and magicians. Think of the same environment that nurtured successive waves of Sufi brotherhoods out of the fastnesses of the Sahara and then imagine its impact on a people who've been profoundly culturally isolated since the Upper Palaeolithic period. These are people whose initiation rites include infibulation and subcision (a slit along the length of the boy's urethra); whose minor punishments are spearings and beatings; and who regard all deaths as caused by some agency, human or otherwise. I well remember one friend of mine, who negotiated with mining companies on behalf of an Aboriginal mob, saying of his employers: 'When they say "jump", I ask how high.'

And I too have had my fair share of odd experiences in the red centre, experiences which while falling short of sundering the laws of nature, certainly impressed upon me that they can be significantly warped. The first time I ever ventured there, I was thudding north to Alice Springs on a corrugated dirt road (at that time, in the early eighties, there was no sealed road across the continent), when the two Aboriginal men who had been sleeping (sleeping!) all the way from Port Augustus on the south coast, despite the fiendish jolting of the un-airconditioned bus, awoke simultaneously, and walked to the front. They didn't say a word but the driver pulled over. The Aboriginals got down and without so much as a backward glance disappeared into the Tanami Desert.

I subsequently learned that the majority of Aboriginal people—including the blind—have perfect orientation in this way. I suppose in an ordinary country the familiarity of its inhabitants with the land can be taken for granted. But here, in a continent the size of the USA, with a Westernised popu-lation of a mere fifteen million, living in densely populated cities on the coasts, the ability of a few scattered individuals to find their way unerringly around this oceanic interior, seems little short of miraculous—particularly given that I myself, with all the comfort, ease and power afforded by technology tee-tering on the edge of the twenty-first century, was unable to make it the five hundred kilometres from Alice Springs to Uluru without getting lost. How, it is reasonable to ask, can anyone get lost in perfectly clear weather conditions, on a near flat, straight route, which involves only one righthand turn-ing the whole way? The answer is: you miss the turning.

In fairness to me, I was intoxicated by the sheer scale of land-scape and its brooding beauty. I was also pushing our rental Ford Falcon along and savouring the sensation of the big car beneath me slicing its way through the turbid, hot air. I was also engag-ing in a slightly manic conversation with my wife, Deborah, our seventeen-month-old son Ivan, and a recently acquired hitchhiker: Colin the Canadian. Nevertheless, to zip past the turning for the Lasseter Highway was one thing, but to con-tinue for another hundred kilometres south, and still not realise our mistake, even when we'd gone well over the South Aus-tralian border, smacks of lunacy.

A literal lunacy I suppose, because this, the oddest of the Earth's inhabited continents, always seems—to me—like another world which has been inadequately terraformed. And it's always ultra wide-screen in the red centre; this is a vista which requires a one-hundred-and-forty degree lens. And it's always very harsh in the red centre, whether the harshness be heat, or cold, or rain or wind. Oh, and there was also the red bird incident—enough to unsettle anybody.

It was just after we'd acquired Colin, and Ivan was getting a little fractious so Deborah began reading to him from a book called *Brown Bear*. This happy little fable involves the reader chanting: 'Brown Bear Brown Bear What Do You See . . . ?' and then turning the page to reveal to the child the next animal in the sequence. She was on the verge of completing the couplet thus: '. . . I See a Red Bird Looking at Me.' When out of the red centre and smack into our wide-screen windscreen flew a suicidal red bird. The impact was so loud I was certain the windscreen had shattered—but it was the bird. A grisly smear of feathers, blood and a single claw was the evidence. 'Phew!' Deborah exclaimed, 'That was close, the next animal in the book is a blue horse.'

I realise now that we were suffering from spatial shock, the result of having been standing in Sydney Airport only a few short hours before. Colin was more acclimatised by virtue of being young, Canadian and having travelled overland to Alice on the Ghan, the railway line which, at the turn of the century, was forged through the desert from the south, by Afghani labourers using camel power. We were spaced out; Colin was spaced in. He didn't even bat an eyelid when, having discovered that he was an amiable computer nerd, I teased him that I had a satellite phone which he could link up to my laptop, so that he might spend the rest of the dull drive to Uluru surfing the net!

However, I think the majesty of our surroundings began to impinge upon him at last, when he realised how far off course we were. There were two hours of daylight remaining and we still had three-hundred-and-fifty kilometres to go.

Given that the wildlife—indigenous and otherwise—are subject to strolling towards the beams of oncoming headlights, this is not a situation you want to find yourself in in the red centre, unless your car is equipped with protective steel bumpers, or 'roo bars' as they're know locally.

We kept on through the gloaming at a healthier 80 kph. From nearly seventy kilometres away we could see the massive flat-topped bulk of Mount Cotter towering over the plain to the southeast. Apart from the gentle furrowing of the ranges to the north, it was the only thing we saw until, at last, the lights of the Yulara Resort showed in the stygian darkness. We dropped Colin at the campsite and went in search of a room at the inn.

The resort may have been designed so as to blend in with its desert surroundings, but despite its low, moulded bulk, its predominant colourings of sand and ochre and its crenellation of rigid, sail-shaped awnings, it completely fails. It may not be as gauche as its counterpart in Nevada, but the Desert Sands Hotel is still a fanfare of cacophonous materialism in the ancient calm of the interior. There are four different hotels within the complex, and I'd been quite keen on trying out the most luxurious. While it may gibe with the environment to the extent, frankly, of surrealism, it's well worth experiencing the contrast between Australia's—usually—tremendous infrastructure, and its uninhabited hinterland. However, the marble floors and acres of plate glass, the trilling receptionists behind their reef-like desk, and most of all, the huge display of Aboriginal 'artefacts'—all conspired to make me feel like a member of the rat pack. And I'm not talking about a cool gang of sixties film stars here.

We settled for the second best hotel, and spent a humid night enfolded in its modernity. Deborah and Ivan slept, whilst I read an account of the discovery of the last Aboriginal people to be brought out of the Western Desert. In 1986 an elderly Walpiri couple was brought out of the Tanami, having lived there for thirty years in fear of tribal retribution for having married across totemic groups. Right until the bitter end of their free existence, these people were living entirely off the land and employing tools and equipment unchanged for many many millennia. I wondered what they would have made of the Desert Sands, with its minibars and swimming pools, and its rapid turnover of well-paid maids and porters, and its still more rapid turnover of the world's more prosaic travellers.

It was still dark when we awoke and dragged the somnolent baby along with us to the campsite where we looped in the adorably clean-cut Colin. As we drove towards the Rock, the dawn came up as rapidly as if some titan were yanking upon a solar dimmer switch. Each time I looked towards our destination its colour, its size, its position—all had altered. It was sublime, the way this mammoth, granite entity hopped about the land. Less sublime was the apparatus of the national park—cattle grids, admission charges, signs galore—and still less sublime were the rank upon rank of coaches and cars and tourists, all the panoply of humanity I evoked at the outset of this piece.

We were at Uluru on a weekday morning in the off season and there must have been five-thousand-odd gawpers around the base of the Rock; how many more will there be come dawn on the first of January 2000? I shudder to think. Of course, there's no question that the creation of the national park has helped to preserve the Rock, and Kata Tjuta to the west. In the dark old days there were, I'm reliably informed, corrugated iron 'hotels' which backed directly on to the Rock itself. I wonder what the Rainbow Snake made of that! But it's debatable whether any of the developments around Uluru will ultimately help to preserve the sacred sites, or simply hasten their erosion by a myriad of sightseers' feet.

No, we didn't climb the Rock. We had Ivan to think of, and respect for the site was neatly conjoined with indolence. Anyway, we could despatch Colin, like a denim–trousered mountain goat, to do the hike for us. I think that had I been his age I would have gone with him. Not simply because of being more limber, but because when I was younger I felt the need to confront other peoples' belief systems—now I simply admire them from afar. Colin asked me whether I wanted him to take my camera with him up to the summit, and I thought this the most amazing idea of tourism-by-proxy. Instead we repaired to the Desert Sands for a breakfast of cow's milk and reconstituted wheat granules.

To prove the point that the Aboriginal omphalos has become an Antipodean sink, down which packaged tourists disappear anticlockwise, later that morning we drove out to Kata Tjuta. Despite the fact that these bizarre rock formations are larger—and if anything more spectacular—than Uluru, there were no coaches, no synchronised snappers, no brouhaha. Puffing a generous Havana (in my experience the best possible flyspray for all concerned) I carried Ivan up into the awesome fissure which cut through the core of this kilometre-high granite plug. And at the top of the track there was a wooden platform, from which you could stare back down the way we'd come: out from the shady, verdancy and into the harsh irradiation of the noonday sun.

That evening we found ourselves a hundred kilometres to the north at the King's Canyon Resort. King's Canyon is a medium-sized gulch leading into the Petermann Hills. There are cliffs and rock paintings there, an edenic water pool and honey catchers in the tangled roundabout. At the Resort itself there are the necessary mod cons—swimming pools, showers, airconditioning—but none of the ersatz pizzazz of Yulara. And of course all around was the red centre. Plenty of it.

While Deborah slumbered I took Ivan for a roast dinner in the restaurant. One of the rather more endearing features of British colonialism in the Antipodes is this obstinate adherence to the culinary mores of a remote northwest corner of Europe. Great tranches of roast meat, potatoes and boiled greens are served up in forty-degree heat; food which was intended to have the internal effect of swallowing an immersion heater. Nevertheless Ivan and I wolfed it down while pink travellers noshed all around. Afterwards we drove at a snail's pace around the adjacent camping ground. Under the massy stars of the southern hemisphere every conceivable type of temporary, mobile accommodation had been assembled into a compact little village. There were transparent tents with built-in barbeque areas, tiny igloo tents, enormous Winnebagos, and khaki army twenty-pounders. The quiet murmur of conversation floated through our open windows as we rolled by and on out of the tiny settlement. As we sat out in the bush, listening to the night sounds, I meditated on how much better it would be to see-in the millennium at King's Canyon with all these solid, calm families about. The Mad Maxes will be down at Uluru, screaming at the sun and invoking the Rainbow Snake, while the Sane Maxes will stop at King's Canyon, drinking from thermoses and eating the occasional sandwich.

It was the briefest of Centralian sojourns, the following day we headed back to Alice Springs. There, in the dried-out river-bed of the Todd River were seated groups of Aboriginals. Some quietly erect, some drunkenly comatose, some out for the count. They were the first significant numbers of the Traditionally Owned we'd seen since leaving Alice two days earlier. There had been none in evidence at Uluru and just the one propping up the bar at King's Canyon. However, the bar at King's Canyon was also being run by a most distinctive looking individual: burnished copper skin, shaven head, smooth features with a sharp, triangular nose—and big, very big. He was a Maori, naturally. It's estimated that there are anything up to three quarters of a million Maoris in Australia—a huge minority of the total world population. They do well there, working as barmen and bouncers. They're industrious and they stick together. It's said ruefully by white Australians: The Maoris are the indigenous people we wish we had—and the Aboriginals are the ones we've got.

Certainly this guy was running a beautifully efficient bar, and with his Hawaiian shirt and pressed chinos he looked right at home amongst his clientele, but out there in the red centre, set beside the awesome Uluru, he'd look just as out of place as all the rest of us.

High Life, June 1999

A Little Cottage Industry

'You're loss adjusters for the Northern Ireland Office?'
    'That's right.'
    'So you come in fairly quickly?'
    'Yeah, we come in very fast, as soon as we can get here.'
    'I'm here doing a feature for the *Observer,* so I'm interested in the whole process.'
    'Well, we got the call at around 2.30 p.m. and came straight down here, but we have to wait until the army and police have cleared the area before we can actually get in.'
    'So the Northern Ireland Office pays out compensation to private individuals . . . ?'
    '. . . Even commercial property as well they pay out on.'
    'And do you think the reason you come in so fast is a psychological one, to show that the NIO cares in that way?'
    'Yeah, it's a little bit of both. It's psychological to show, number one, that they care, but it's also that they want to see the damage as quickly as possible, so they have an idea first-hand exactly what it is; they want to create reserves for this incident, to see how much money they need to put aside for it. Plus, there's also the factor that they want to make sure that nothing happens over the weekend that is added to the damage in any way sort of thing, you know, they don't want ornaments getting knocked over or anything else. So, the idea is they want us here fast to see it straightaway.'
    'So you'll hang in now until they let you in?'

WILL SELF

'We'll hang in until they let us in.'

'And where are you based?'

'In Belfast.'

'You've driven all the way down? This only happened at ten past one . . .'

'Yeah, well we were instructed at about half past two, and we literally left the office about ten minutes after that.'

'And what you're involved in is basically a kind of negative quantity surveying?'

'Err . . . I suppose it is really. I started off as a quantity surveyor and we do come from either an insurance or a quantity surveying discipline. Most people have their own loss assessors acting for them, who will present a claim to us, ahh . . . and then we will agree the amount of damage with them. Most people on . . . on domestic property have their own insurance cover, so they'll involve the insurance company as well. But the company will then get their recovery from the Northern Ireland Office . . .'

'. . . I see . . .'

'. . . We will ultimately put forward a figure and if the insurance company pays out they will be covered by the NIO.'

'But people must have to pay out a pretty brutal premium to be fully covered in this area?'

'Well, yeah, that's right, it would be hefty from that point of view. Although some people—to be honest with you—don't claim, especially more than one claim. They don't want to have their insurers sit back and think . . . one company here has actually said to some of the people: one more claim and you're off cover for everything. Forget about it, we won't give storm cover, fire cover . . . So the people have just literally stopped claiming from the insurance company, and just rely upon the NIO, just work it that way.'

'There's a lot of stuff written in the press about how that's bad politically, because it's building up a sort of negative economy, where there's a lot of money slushing around.'

'Oh yeah, oh yeah, that's very true. It does become a little cottage industry at times.'

'Oh well . . .'

'We don't even know what extent of damage there is, they say there's some properties down there pretty extensively damaged, but . . .'

'The impression I got was that the house had been pretty much blown out.'

'I've dealt with claims down there not that long ago.'

'In this patch here?'

'Yeah, actually there was a bomb in the square here not that long ago. Very minor damage down here, as you can imagine, just some plaster cracks or whatever but . . .'

'But the RUC station here was taken out . . . ?'

'Yeah, that was the 25th of April . . . it was Saturday the 19th of March, the whatever . . . 10th of January. I think this is our eighteenth incident down here in the last, sort of, three or four years. They're getting fairly regular. But from our point of view it's quarter past four now on a Friday, and we normally finish at five . . .'

'Thanks for talking.'

'OK. All the best.'

He left me and walked off down to where the security forces had stretched white lengths of tape across the road. A big, gingerish man wearing a sharp, dark double-breasted suit, an aggressively op-art tie—all bold geometric patterns—and accompanied by a colleague attired so similarly that the two of them looked like some strange paramilitary insurance unit.

The NIO loss adjusters were the most concrete thing I had managed to latch on to in Crossmaglen, South Armagh. How suitable, I thought to myself; that an English ironist should light on these figures of consummately jokey normalcy, whilst Lynx helicopters buzz the rooftops. In its own peculiar way this summed up the sensation I had had of entering a hall of mirrors ever since I arrived in Northern Ireland. It was the business of the place to supply the stuff of narrative, of anecdote, of story; and it was the business of the English voyeur to provide the necessary irony, the distancing, that could render the situation simultaneously comprehensible and yet redundant.

I went to Northern Ireland with no firm convictions about anything other than my own inability to make a reasonable comment. In Belfast three nights before the Crossmaglen incident, the novelist Robert McLiam Wilson had bellowed at me across a dinner table: 'But don't you see, we need people to come from outside and comment on what's going on here. It's no good you saying you're not qualified. You have to have the courage to be sincerely insincere—if that's what you feel.'

But I didn't even feel sincerely insincere—I felt worse than that, I felt ashamed. Robert Wilson, like the two other novelists I spent time with in Northern Ireland, Glenn Patterson and Carlo Gébler, extolled the virtues of the long piece on the Province that Rian Malan wrote for the *Guardian* last year. But, of course, Malan could bring a valid outsider's view to the Troubles. He's a South African and when he says that the Troubles are as nothing compared to the suffering of his own country, it carries clout.

In Britain we've become accustomed to only accepting such validity: the high moral ground of someone else's suffering. But if there's to be any movement at all in the intractable nastiness of politics in Northern Ireland, then we must cease adopting such perspectives, confront our insincerity and our shame. I feel ashamed about the Troubles because for many years I supported the Republican cause, if not the 'armed struggle', for reasons that were so simple-minded that they now make me blush.

The events that 'politicized' me in relation to Northern Ireland were the hunger strikes of the early 1980s. I became a signatory of a human rights declaration that was meant to do for Northern Ireland what Charter 77 had done for the Czechs, but which in reality was probably little more than a front for the Republicans. I remember marching on a wet day in 1981, from Trafalgar Square to Quex Avenue in Kilburn, together with the oddest mixture of trendy lefties and working-class Irish people. Constantly harassed by the police, the demonstration was eventually broken up altogether, while H-Block Committee activists shouted through megaphones.

The reasoning was thus: if Thatcher is bad, then, QED, it follows that the hunger strikers must have some good in them. Furthermore, any minority group that forces the British state apparatus into such galvanisms of military activity must be acting as a proxy, drawing down on to them the repressive measures that the British government might well like to deploy against the left wing on the mainland.

But more than that, there was the fact that an espousal of the Republican cause was absolutely guaranteed to reduce all sorts of people to apoplexy. It was the acid test of British patriotism. If you wanted to *épater* them to the hilt, you merely had to challenge the right to exist of the United Kingdom. I've never had a Damascene conversion from this point of view. Rather it has ebbed away, just as the political certainties of most youth seem to ebb away, to be replaced by the fuzzy, 'I'm not fit to comment' lack-of-attitudinizing so redolent of incipient middle age. But contributing to this falling away of my 'convictions' was the growing acknowledgement that, not only did I not know much about Northern Ireland, for much of the time Northern Ireland hasn't existed for me.

The Australian writer Peter Carey wrote a story called 'The Cartographers'. In it, the portions of a vast country that are not regularly mapped start to disappear. Gradually this attrition of the very landform begins to effect things closer to home. Buildings in the centre of the capital city that people have taken for granted for too long and never properly regarded begin to disappear as well. Eventually, people who are not loved begin to evaporate too. The story ends with the narrator's father

103

screaming at him, as through the old man's back we begin to ascertain the pattern of the wallpaper.

Northern Ireland is, for me, the country described in Carey's 'The Cartographers'. A country where 'politics' has ceased to function as the arena within which to manage the concerns of the people. When that happens the very physical geography of a place begins to deteriorate. The disappearing parts of Northern Ireland are the no-go areas on either side of the sectarian divide. The most extreme examples of disappearance are the gaps in cityscapes where buildings have been bombed, and the gaps in people's lives when those they loved have been killed.

In Northern Ireland people were keen on telling me what politics were, I think because the word 'politics' no longer serves to describe what is happening. 'Politics isn't politics here,' Robert Wilson told me, 'it's geography.' 'Elections aren't fought on political issues here,' pronounced Richard McAuley, the Sinn Fein press officer, 'they're fought on constitutional ones.' There was another shibboleth that I heard time and again, until it was polished smooth by repetition: 'There aren't any current affairs in Northern Ireland, only history.'

'I'm doing some research for my new novel,' a snort of laughter from Robert Wilson—he's about to coin an epithet. 'I'm studying Irish history seriously for the first time. Studying it so that I can lie more effectively!' He was pinpointing another get-out for those of us on the other side of the Irish Sea. We sit here, and bewildered by the 'complexities', relapse into the idea that both sides of the divide are guarding historical arcana, privileged knowledge we cannot hope to understand. It salves our conscience, renders the conflict in some way tribal, puts it beyond the purlieus of reason.

My time in Belfast was a busman's holiday. I surveyed the conflict not through the eyes of a reporter, or a journalist, but through those of fiction writers. How did they respond to the challenge to their imaginations that their country represented? How was it possible to write true fictions in a place where fictional truths were being produced with such frantic abandon?

I felt embarrassed about pushing Robert Wilson, Glenn Patterson and Carlo Gébler to mull over these issues for hour upon hour, but needn't have. It gradually dawned on me, as we talked and talked and talked, that this was another of the little cottage industries that has been created by the Troubles. Whether it was the loss adjusters in Crossmaglen or the prize-winning novelists in Belfast, all had become narrative artisans. People had to fabricate their stories with a will, because the story the society was telling itself was so warped.

In Crossmaglen I stood and watched as cliché after cliché framed itself, hackneyed images from a million news reports. Squaddies talking to children leaning on a fence, an elderly woman ambling up the road while a prone rifleman draws a bead on her shopping, another squaddie in a sniping position under one of the ubiquitous 'Sniper at Work' mock road signs. The images were worn thin—I talked to the news reporters instead: 'Well, you see, that was one of the things, whenever you were working on the *Irish News*, or the *Newsletter*, whenever there was an incident you sometimes had to phone up and find out if they were Protestant or Catholic victims before you decided to go. If you were working for the *Newsletter* and it was a Catholic victim you might not bother going. And when I was working on the *Irish News* I remember the shootings up in Castlerock, those four workmen, you remember? We spent a good half-hour, wasting time, finding out if they were Catholic or Protestant before we went. Eventually I was sent only to find out they were Catholic. Crazy really.'

But the young radio reporter had another anecdote as well, concerning himself. His story, so to speak, and that was that he was from a mixed family, but had been brought up a Protestant in a highly Protestant area. But while he felt under no threat, his sister lived in the Shankill Road in Belfast, and she was under threat: 'Because someone might finger her as a Mick.' The situation made him angry—angry at people 'at home' who didn't realize the danger she was facing.

And so every anecdote in Northern Ireland has to come accompanied by its refutation. One person will tell a story pointing up the ubiety of the sectarian divide, and how both groups can instantly identify one another—and then someone else will chime up and say: but what about so-and-so. I had no idea he was a Catholic. Glenn Patterson told this anecdote: 'If you walk around certain areas of Belfast you're bound to be stopped and asked what you are. So one night Robert and I were coming back from somewhere and this drunk asked us. And we looked at each other, trying to guess what the right response was, but then we just shrugged and told him the truth. Then the drunk said: "Are youse two actors?"'

Neither Patterson nor Wilson was comfortable with an ascription of nationality at all. I asked Glenn if he thought of himself as Irish. 'I don't really have any understanding of that . . . people are always trying to get you to define yourself in their terms.'

Then Wilson chimed in, lighting what seemed like his eighty-seventh Silk Cut of the evening: 'Last year I went to a conference in Dublin with the exciting title "Imagining Ireland". I got there and I looked around at all these bloody writers and I thought, you fools, you aren't the people who are imagining Ireland, it's guys wearing balaclavas with names like "Stompy" and "Squinty".'

It was an emphatic comment, well up to standard, and yet earlier that same evening Robert had contradicted himself: 'For years,' he had said, 'I couldn't see this whole business of violence the right way round. I couldn't understand that the basic fact is murder, all the persiflage that comes with it, is entirely logical. Look, you have to understand, you remember those three soldiers who were lured up on to the mountain by those girls, right when the Troubles began? Well, they were all shot with the same gun, they were shot by somebody who had seen what a bullet does to the head. You see, the act of political murder isn't a moral act—it's an act that's possible because of a fatal lack of imagination.'

There was the paradox: Ireland was being imagined by people with no imagination. Both Wilson and Patterson were attempting to deny the absolute relevance of the political violence that surrounds them to their work: 'It's the increasing urbanization of Ireland that dominates my thoughts as a writer at the moment,' said Wilson, 'not the questions of nationality.' Yet his own first novel, *Ripley Bogle,* is steeped in 'questions of nationality', just as Glenn Patterson's *Burning Your Own* is.

Carlo Gébler had persuaded me long and hard about the marginal character of the men of violence; their lack of constituency; their status as political dinosaurs, intransigently reacting to the nexus of pressures defined twenty-five years ago and now cast in concrete. Yet his own writerly preoccupations in recent years seem to have been more and more with the narrative of political violence where he lives. When I arrived in Belfast he was just finishing the last of a trilogy of films about Belfast, two of which were concerned directly with the impact of the Troubles. His new novel (as yet unpublished), while ostensibly concerned with the last recorded witch burning in Southern Ireland, is nonetheless couched within a story about what it means to be a writer, what it means to be Irish, and how violence queers the pitch.

'Go up the Falls Road,' Robert Wilson instructed me, 'tell them exactly what you see . . . tell them it looks OK . . . that it's full of ordinary middle-class houses.' So I went up the Falls Road and I saw some middle-class houses, but I also saw plenty of RIR Scorpions driving around (the Royal Irish Regiment can be distinguished from mainland British Regiments, both by cap badges and by the 'Confidential Hotline' numbers stencilled in yellow on the sides of their vehicles), and outside Sinn Fein's 'Advice Centre' some Stompies and Squinties were being searched at gunpoint by a patrol.

The problem for the novelists was that they just couldn't get enough product out to do the 'imagining' that was within their remit. 'We've over three hundred works of fiction concerned with the Troubles here,' Yvonne Murphy, assistant librarian at the Linen Hall Library told me, 'of course the vast majority of them are exploitative thrillers, using the Troubles as a violent backdrop.' Yvonne Murphy was helping to preside over an effluvium of fatal lack of imagination, a comprehensive archive of the Troubles' ephemera. At the Linen Hall Library they had it all, from plastic bullets to bibs inscribed with the Red Hand of Ulster and the slogan 'Baby Prod'. There were bumper stickers reading: 'Keep Ulster Tidy—Throw Your Litter in the Republic'; paperweights inscribed 'You Are Now Entering Free Derry'; a message of support for Bobby Sands from the Ayatollah Khomeini.

'It's a problem for us to keep all of this stuff,' said Yvonne, 'I mean what do you do with a "Kick the Pope" lollipop when it starts to melt?' It would have been flip to point out that that was probably what the 'Baby Prod' bib was for, but on the other hand there is a niceness of fit between signified and signifier in Northern Ireland that recurs over and over again.

At about ten past one, when the IRA active service unit (ASU) hit the security forces checkpoint on the Cullyhanna road out of Crossmaglen, I'd been eating fat, white ketchuppy chips. Eating them from a cone of paper poised between my thighs, and toddling along the lanes from Newry. I had no particular plan of action. I was acting like the worst ironic voyeur, listening to pop music on the hire car radio, goggling up at the stark army listening posts that sat atop every hill bristling with aerials; and every so often stopping to take a photograph of another piece of IRA iconography.

A LITTLE COTTAGE INDUSTRY

As well as the by now familiar triangular 'men at work'-style road signs that proclaim 'Sniper at Work' and show a hooded silhouette brandishing an Armalite in one hand and a clenched fist, there were other usurpations of the Highways Department that seemed to me even more telling.

Outside Camlough, on the A25, there was a crudely lettered sign with letters and numerals done in green, white and orange. It proclaimed: '30 mph', and underneath: 'IRA'. 'We control everything here,' the sign seemed to be saying, 'even the speed limit.'

And then on a minor road heading into Crossmaglen there was the sign I'd been waiting for. High up on a telegraph pole a piece of blackboard had been tacked. The lettering was white on black, and around the slogan a few quavers and semiquavers had been inscribed to underscore the reference. 'Mull of Kintyre,' it read, 'Bodies Rolling into the Sea . . .'

This was on Friday 10 June, eight days after the RAF Chinook carrying twenty-nine people, most of them members of the Northern Irish security establishment, had crashed on a Scottish hillside. Say what you will about the IRA—they aren't slow when it comes to translating events into postures, attitudes and ultimately narratives.

Around the time I was taking this in, the ASU had already detonated its mortar and was presumably making its way across fields, back into the Republic, or somewhere else where it could go to ground. The mortar was of the local manufacture that has become known as the 'Mark 10'. A group of three or four oxyacetylene cylinders sawn off, packed with the explosive charges and then levelled at an angle of forty-five degrees. This assemblage was then attached to the back of a truck and driven to within range of its target.

The charges travelled about 150 yards, hit a house and the side of the checkpoint. One civilian, two RUC personnel and a soldier were injured and flown out by helicopter to hospital in Newry.

I reached Crossmaglen at about 2.20 p.m. I'd been there the day before and had my car searched by a young squaddie from the Scottish Regiment. But today the queue of cars stretched back for a couple of hundred yards from the checkpoint. The area surrounding the two camouflage- and khaki-netting-draped bafflers was buzzing with RUC men and soldiers, all with firearms levelled rather than ported. I didn't think much of this, for all I knew the extra activity could have been part of a routine sweep of some sort. It wasn't until I pulled up in the main square and the Radio 1 news came on that I realized something had gone down: '. . . Two mortar bombs have hit and partly damaged a checkpoint near Crossmaglen in South Armagh, a civilian and three army personnel were slightly injured . . . A new crime of racial harassment is to go on the Statute Book . . .'

But where had the bombs hit? I'm no hard newsman, and the idea of asking a passer-by didn't exactly appeal, so I drove out of the village on the road that leads most directly to the Republic. Through a hamlet with a sign at its crossroads proclaiming: 'Second Battalion IRA', and then down a tree-lined lane. By a bridge two blue-uniformed Gardai leant against the bonnet of their van: 'Where've you come from, son?'

'Crossmaglen.'

'Is it true there's been an incident up there?'

'I just heard it on the news . . . a mortar attack on a checkpoint. I'm press. I was sort of looking for it.'

'I think you'll find it's back up in the village there.'

'Oh really, well then you'll see me coming back again in a few minutes.'

And as I recrossed the invisible border and drove back into the whirring noise-zone of army helicopters, and the fear-zone of hyped-up young soldiers staring at me through the sights of their rifles, I reflected on this nice irony: that it should take foreign policemen and a news report from London to inform me of an event that had occurred some 300 yards from where I'd been sitting.

Truly this had to be a metaphor for the Troubles themselves: a real incident is rendered progressively more unreal by overlay upon overlay of narrative obfuscation. What is physically close becomes instantly distant; and what is temporally remote is yanked into the present moment. By the time I was driving back to Newry, three hours later, the mortar attack at Crossmaglen had fallen down the Radio 1 hit parade of human tragedy; and by the time I reached Belfast that evening, it had been dropped altogether.

I went to see the people who were imagining Ireland, the people who proclaim 'Tiocfaidh Ar Lá' (pronounced 'Chucky Ar La') or 'Our Time Will Come'. I found myself waiting on a vinyl bench behind the barred door of the Sinn Fein Advice Centre. Party activists were coming in and getting assignments—it was the day of the European elections. On the wall there was the 'Roll of Honour', volunteers who had died in action against the British forces were listed. It was the tangible expression of one of the most successful of contemporary Irish fictions—that there is a real disjunction between the political wing of the IRA and those who wage the armed struggle.

Eventually Richard McAuley, the press officer, arrived, and we went upstairs. We settled ourselves in a room with flaking plaster, a scratched kneehole desk and worn carpet tiling on the floor. There followed one of the most soporific interviews I have ever conducted in my life. If McAuley felt the same way, he wasn't showing it.

He talked on and on, his response to every one of my questions unvarying in its espousal of the party line. 'We have no objection to Albert Reynolds talking to Loyalist groups, both the Irish and the British governments have to become persuaders for change. If you don't have a dialogue the alternative is aiming for military victories. And I think it's generally accepted—although possibly not by the Unionists—that that is not going to provide a solution . . .' Other writers have remarked on this sense of the implacable that surrounds Sinn Fein rhetoric. Whatever tactics I tried to draw McAuley out, to get him to admit some of the known facts that seemed to contradict his line, he side-stepped and came up with another reply remarkable only for its vapidity, its failure to add anything substantive.

It was ridiculous. I was sitting in the hub of the Republican movement, a building that had been attacked three times by rocket grenades in as many months, and I felt myself falling asleep. McAuley was imagining an Ireland in which, as he put it, 'It is possible to square the circle. People said it couldn't be done in South Africa and it has been. They said the same thing about Palestine . . .' This was an imagination run rampant. The facts were that he gave absolutely no hint that Sinn Fein would be climbing down on its position regarding the Unionist veto over future constitutional change in Northern Ireland. I don't believe that the party's response to the clarifications of the Downing Street Declaration will contain any movement on this issue. The unstoppable force will continue to butt its head against the immovable object.

After an hour or so I resorted to tactics. I shamelessly employed my own shame, spoke of my own Republican sympathies, implied that I was still more than sympathetic. Nothing doing. Only in the dying minutes did he start to show a little true colour: 'If we can advance the peace process it may no longer be necessary for British Intelligence to control Loyalist death squads, for them to supply information on how to kill me, or my family, or my colleagues . . .' And then, with the tape recorder off, on our way back down the stairs, we stopped to survey the wreckage caused by the last rocket attack.

I probably can't do justice to the change in his manner when McAuley described these events, but my hunch was that as he traced the path the projectile had taken, through plasterboard, brick and paper, he sensed that I knew—and I knew that he knew—imagination had, in a quite ghastly way, given in to intuition.

It isn't the novelists' fault; their inconsistencies and self-contradictions are the only reasonable response of good men to a bad situation. All three of them, Wilson, Patterson and Gébler, are so implacably opposed to the men of violence that they cannot help but try to deny some of these realities. They were no more willing to countenance the idea of a 'split' in the IRA than Richard McAuley. They have to retain a view of the paramilitaries as monolithic, an incarnation of this evil, because to do otherwise is to start negotiating with that fatal lack of imagination.

Wilson had spoken of his concern, as a writer, with the growing urbanization of Ireland. That urbanization has of course a subtext: the urbanization of the conflict, the links between the paramilitaries and the more blatant face of organized crime is ineluctable in any context where there are firearms and social deprivation. But in South Armagh, where the sniper is at work with his Barrett Light Fifty rifle, five feet of gun weighing thirty pounds that can deliver an armour-piercing round over a mile, it is a different story.

It may only be small wedges of territory, but these zones—the so-called 'Bandit Country' of South Armagh and South Fermanagh—are occupied by the British army. The road signs tell you that more than anything else. And I would have liked to have got one of the leaflets that had been distributed in Crossmaglen a week or so before the mortar attack on the checkpoint. Leaflets that cordially suggested that residents of the houses near military installations might like to spend as much time out of the house as possible. In Crossmaglen the IRA parades petty offenders, and even, it is said, adulterers, around the main square after mass on a Sunday, placards around their necks proclaiming their transgressions. I wonder if the

British army patrols that saturate the village draw a bead on these tormented people, just as they draw a bead on everyone else.

We're all bound up in imagining Ireland, but I wonder if for the English this activity has become increasingly lackadaisical. I grew up with the armed struggle in my ears, just as my contemporaries in Ireland did. When I was twelve, the London ASU of the IRA bombed the Angus Steak House in Hampstead village, 100 yards from my prep school. I cannot remember a time when the dull rumble of the Troubles hasn't been going on in the background, erupting time after time into purposeless squeals of public agony and collective rending of hair and garments.

Last year I was on holiday in the Republic, staying in the house that belonged to those great imaginers of Ireland, Somerville and Ross. The house is in Castletownsend, an enclave of the Protestant Ascendancy in West Cork, which was the most implacable area of IRA support, both in the Tan war and the civil war that followed.

At dinner one night the conversation drifted on to the subject of the relationship between the Ascendancy landowners and the native Irish. An Irish woman—the kind who might be described as a 'Castle Catholic'—chimed up saying: 'But you don't understand. The relationship people had with their servants was very different to that in England. Here the servants were—and are—far more familiar. They felt it was their perfect right to involve themselves in every aspect of their employers' lives. There was a refreshing lack of any formality. But, of course, at the same time they would never dream of thinking themselves like "the quality".'

I was gobsmacked. I sat there staring into the mahogany pool of the table. Immediately before dinner I had been reading the memoirs of Earnán O'Maillie, *On Another Man's Wound*. O'Maillie had at one time during the Tan war been the IRA commander in Cork. In it he had written almost exactly the same thing: '[The English officer] had been used to Ireland as a good hunting country in the same way as he had looked upon northern Scotland as a fine place for grouse, deer, fish, and the wearing of kilts. As long as the country provided a Somerville and Martin Ross atmosphere of hounds giving cry, strong brogues, roguish wit, discreet familiarity of servants, and a sure eye for picking out "the quality" and letting them know it; then Ireland could be understood.' Here was another niceness of fit, revealing a terrible gulf of incomprehension.

'Anniversaries are important here,' McAuley had said, ever the man for stating the obvious. He didn't see anything meretricious or objectionable about the BBC's forthcoming twenty-fifth anniversary bonanza on the Troubles. And why should he? It's another contribution to the little cottage industry, another stab at imagining Ireland.

I'll leave the last anecdote to Robert McLiam Wilson, for it unites all concerns: the media, the conflict, the imagination. 'Last July 12th I went down to watch the bands come by at the end of the road. I got down there and this RUC man turned to me and said: "Have you seen the *Newsletter*?" I told him no, and he said: "Well, you better get inside, son." You see, they'd carried a story that morning reporting the publication of my second novel. There was a photograph of me and under it the caption: "Robert McLiam Wilson, prominent West Belfast novelist".'

Observer, July 1994

Street Legal

It's five-thirty in the morning and I'm walking up the Gelderse Kade canal towards Amsterdam's Central Station, skirting the red-light district, which at this hour is quiescent: the ebb of last night's trade washing against the flow of this morning's. Hobbling on the leaf-plastered cobbles is a Surinamese woman, obviously a drug addict. She's wearing a bilious velour tracksuit and begging in a desultory fashion, proffering her upturned claw of a hand to each indifferent face as she passes. For once, the expressions of the Chinese gamblers, wending their way home, live up to their racial stereotype: they are inscrutable.

For me this woman is a point of strange orientation. The previous evening I had seen her further up the same canal, again panhandling, this time outside a traditional Amsterdam bar. The kind that sells mostly shots of jenever, the Dutch gin, and wittebeer, the light lemony beer favoured by Dutch drinkers. She had chosen the wrong place to beg. A couple of the drinkers, Dutch indigenes sporting long fair beards and the tattered colours of the Amsterdam chapter of the Hell's Angels, had grabbed her and were administering punches and kicks to her arms and legs.

This wasn't the kind of work-out her tracksuit had been intended for. It was a beautiful evening, and the canal looked unbelievably picturesque, with its tip-tilted houses, their high gables like fretwork against the sunset. And in the middle of it all, the Hell's Angels were laughing, their girlfriends were laughing, while the Surinamese woman yowled, and the tourists and Amsterdammers went about their business, scrupulously turning a blind eye.

Amsterdam. I remembered the city from my first visit some ten years before. Coming out of the Central Station and heading towards the Zeedjik, the snaking lane which leads to the heart of the red-light district, I had been mobbed by a crowd of some twenty South Moluccan heroin dealers. As they pushed their wares into my face I caught sight of a large sign that had been put up on a bridge: 'Absolute power,' it declared in English, 'corrupts absolutely.' Quite.

But then this was where it was at. This was the city where elected officials smoked dope in the council chamber; the city where the junkies had their own union; this was where the permissive society had come home to roost.

Amsterdam, a city synonymous with the 'Dutch Experiment', a combination of enlightened policing and harm-minimization health care that has, its proponents claim, effectively divided off the nasty hard-drug market from its benign cannabis cousin.

The Dutch Experiment has become a kind of shibboleth for people concerned with drug policy in Britain. For pro-legalization liberals it is an example of an enlightened approach that has paid dividends. They visit Amsterdam to sop up the atmosphere of its cannabis cafés, to revel in the naughty liberty of being able to puff a joint in the street unmolested. But for prohibitionists it is the exact reverse: a sexual Sodom and a narcotic Gomorrah rolled into one horrific sin bin.

What is the reality? This time round the junkies weren't just clustered along the Zeedjik, they were all over the town centre. They were crouched on the benches thoughtfully provided by the municipality, manipulating bits of tin foil. Chasing the dragon, while children kicked footballs around them. Down in Neumarkt station, the platform was lined with junkies. They were dealing, smoking, scratching and altercating.

Ordinary Dutch commuters went about their business, seemingly ignoring what was going on.

An Anglo-Dutch friend who lent me her centrally located flat had told me: 'Before the Olympic bid a few years ago, you knew where the junkies were, so you could avoid them. But when the police cleaned up the Zeedjik it was like lancing a boil: the pus has spread all over the centre of town.' How right she was. The morning after I arrived, there crouching on the basement steps was my own personal addict. He looked up and smiled. He was smoking his morning hit of heroin, as casually as an alcoholic on the streets of London, supping a Special Brew.

Later that day, a Dutch journalist related an anecdote which summed up the native attitude. An Amsterdammer was coming out of his apartment one morning when he saw a shabby figure crouched on the basement steps. Without looking too closely, he assumed that it was a junkie fixing up. 'Make sure you clean up afterwards,' he quipped. The 'junkie' looked up and flashed a warrant card. It was an undercover cop. 'Make sure you clean up afterwards,' the Amsterdammer reiterated, and went about his business, whistling.

The Amsterdammers are a bizarre inversion of the English concept of Nimbys. They don't mind it being in their backyard—as long as it's cleaned up afterwards. Or that's what they would like you to believe. But as I got deeper into the drug world of Amsterdam I began to realize that there were two quite separate versions of the events going on around me.

One version was for the consumption of foreign professionals: policemen, health-care workers, journalists and lawyers, who had come to see the Dutch Experiment in action. The other version was more truthful. A truth that was as unpalatable for the Dutch as it would be for the foreigners; a truth that hides behind the apparent accessibility of Dutch society;

a truth that is politically and morally complex, and therefore not readily packaged for public consumption.

If you contact the Ministry of Health before undertaking an investigative trip to Amsterdam, a helpful secretary will arrange an itinerary for you. There will be visits to Drs Dirk Korf and Peter Cohen, academic specialists in criminology, who have conducted numerous studies on the prevalence of drug-taking in Amsterdam and the Netherlands. There will also be a visit to the Jellinek Clinic, which provides detoxification treatment for addicts and alcoholics.

And, finally, you will be treated to an interview with Dr Theo van Iwaarden, head of the Alcohol, Drugs and Tobacco Policy Department, part of the Ministry of Health. Dr van Iwaarden is a relative newcomer to the job, replacing the more flamboyant Eddy Engelsman, whose writings and publications over the last fifteen years have represented the crystallization of a policy towards drugs that the Dutch themselves invariably describe as 'pragmatism'. You get a selection of Mr Engelsman's articles by mail before you set off, together with statistical bulletins on the drug abuse situation in the Netherlands, and a copy of an instructive book called *Cannabis in Amsterdam: A Geography of Hashish and Marijuana*.

This tome, by A. C. M. Jansen, is a dope smoker's ramble masquerading as a sociological text. Impressionistic and facile, it concludes with a specious micro-economic study of the price elasticity of 'hemp products' in relation to the competition between coffee shops that sell them. And this is what the government puts out! It's as if a journalist investigating alcohol use in Britain were sent a selection of Jeffrey Bernard's columns by the NHS.

Dr Dirk Korf is relentlessly pragmatic. 'I suppose it's true to say that my research has retrospectively alibied [*sic*] government policy.' Dr Korf's research shows that the prevalence of cannabis consumption in Holland has actually fallen in the wake of effective decriminalization. 'Heroin,' he tells me on the other hand, 'is perceived by Dutch adolescents as a "junkie drug". The visibility of heroin use helps to make it appear unattractive, just as much as it helps the authorities to practise harm-minimization policies.'

He agrees that as police statistics are unreliable, it's impossible to prove that the availability of methadone to addicts has actually meant a decline in drug-related theft. But he said that 'the older the addicts, and the more they've been in contact with the methadone programme, the less criminality they exhibit'.

When I charge him with the visibility of heroin use in Amsterdam he retorts: 'Amsterdam is atypical. You wouldn't see anything like it in the rest of Holland. The policy is: make things visible and you can control them. The point is only that the tip of the iceberg you can see is bigger here than it is in countries with a more repressive policy.'

But Ien Jensen, who runs the Jellinek Clinic, is more fatalistic. 'The point is,' she says, 'that all the addicts who are on methadone supplement it with black-market heroin.' And there are a lot of them, an estimated five to six thousand for a city with a population of 1,079,702 (January 1992 figures).

Indeed, the registered addict population of the Netherlands as a whole is quite high: 21,000, exactly the same as that of the UK, a country with over five times the population. Of course, the Dutch would argue that this is simply because their figure represents a true picture of the problem, whereas, as British epidemiologists would admit, the British figure captures only a fraction of the true population. When the Dutch call their policy 'pragmatism', they are voicing a historical truth. During the 1960s, Amsterdam became one of the first European cities to be badly affected by urban blight. Traffic in the centre was appalling, rates were high. Businesses moved out, leaving behind a vacuum into which junkies, prostitutes and criminals moved.

STREET LEGAL

Amsterdam was the northern entrepôt for the 14K Tong, who at that time controlled the trafficking and distribution for Southeast Asian heroin. The drugs scene was large and vicious, attracting addicts and users from all over Europe. The only way to deal with it was 'pragmatism'; it simply couldn't be eliminated. Having accepted that, the Dutch have moved to make the best of a bad thing, retrospectively labelling this 'pragmatism' as an enlightened policy.

'Really the Dutch are very, very conservative people,' my friend told me. 'Try suggesting that Queen Beatrix should abdicate. Even in a hash coffee shop you'd get some very angry replies. The thing is,' she continued, 'that the "liberals" are really just the descendants of the Calvinist conservatives they allegedly oppose.' One such liberal is thirty-three-year-old Inspector Rob van Velsen, head of the Amsterdam Narcotics Bureau. Inspector van Velsen, as well as being one of the most liberal policemen I had ever met, was also the handsomest.

The two of us were chatting in a rather empty squad room, decorated with the pennants and insignia of other drug squads from around the world. The Inspector started off by giving me a lecture about the British involvement in the opium trade, and went on to say: 'There is no drugs problem here in Amsterdam. We regard it either as a health problem, or as a public order problem. We are interested in drugs only in so far as they contribute to the proceeds of organized crime. We are not interested in drug use itself.'

Back in Britain I had spoken to Customs and Excise sources about Holland. 'We regard the Netherlands as a country of origin for drugs. Not so much heroin, but certainly synthetics. We think that Dutch criminal gangs, possibly those ones traditionally involved with cannabis, have seen the Ecstasy market in Britain, and have acted to fill the demand.'

Inspector van Velsen denied that the Dutch authorities regard Ecstasy in the same semi-legitimate light as cannabis, but the way he did so was significant: 'We don't see a problem with using Ecstasy here. There is no public order problem, and we haven't seen any deaths from it. We are aware that some of the criminal groups have been exporting to the UK, and we've started to take an interest in it.'

Inspector van Velsen was also sceptical about the existence of organized crime in Holland. He talked to me about 'groups that know people, that have connections, but no "mob" in the style of the USA'. This is at best a half-truth. While it is undoubtedly the case that there is little high-level corruption in the public service, the Amsterdam police itself has been rocked by corruption cases at middle level. Furthermore, the Dutch not only refer to organized native criminals as 'the mafia', they also point to a particular area of Amsterdam, the Leidseplein, near the Rijksmuseum, as the mafia part of town.

'We are a little bit successful at what we do,' says Inspector van Velsen, 'that's why people from around the world come and see us.' But while he and my other Dutch interviewees struggled to convince me that it was simply a case of 'more of the iceberg' being exposed to view, all my research, and casual encounters, led me to believe that the iceberg was, quite simply, bigger overall.

Monica, an eighteen-year-old prostitute who offers 'suck and fuck' at 100 guilders (about £30) a throw, operates out of one of the infamous shopfront windows in the red-light district. I caught up with her in The Rocket, a hash café near the Neumarkt which is frequented by young 'drug tourists', English and German kids who have come for hash and Ecstasy. A working-class Amsterdammer who's been on the game for a year, she was happy to talk about prostitutes taking drugs.

'Sure, it happens all the time. A girl goes on the pipe or the brown. She gets very skinny, she loses all her clients. She goes away for three months and comes back better.' But what are the people who run the brothels like? 'They're very reasonable. A doctor comes in twice a week to give us a check-up. We get a flat fee, with bonuses.' Do you think these people are involved in any other illegitimate business, like drugs? Monica didn't even answer, she refused to talk to me further.

The police, the criminologists and the Head of Policy at the Ministry of Health may deny it, but there have been a number of newspaper stories recently implicating Amsterdam as the centre of a European network of child prostitution and white slaving. Certainly Amsterdam is a pornography production centre, and some of the most vicious child pornography is known to be produced there. It strains credulity to imagine that it isn't the same 'groups' of criminals who are mixed up in these different trades.

Inspector van Velsen did, inadvertently, give the lie to the political agenda that underpins all this. Apropos of nothing, when discussing the famed 'Balkan route' for heroin coming into Europe, he said, 'Ask yourself why the Americans are so keen to support the Kurds.' I came up with some fatuous explanation, and the handsome narcotics chief smiled enigmatically.

Another Dutch contact filled in the blanks for me. 'Oh, it's easy,' he said, 'they think the Americans are allowing the Kurds to deal in heroin for arms. They sell to the Moroccans, who then bring it into Holland.'

Stuart Wesley, director of the Drugs Division at the National Criminal Intelligence Service, was sceptical. 'I haven't heard anything,' he told me, 'but then there's always a lot of rumours kicking around about the DEA [the American Drug Enforcement Agency].'

We were sitting in the Service's offices off the Albert Embankment in London. 'We don't know about what we don't know,' a detective inspector in charge of a regional drug squad had once said when I was working on another story; and really that's about the most truthful statement I have ever heard about the drugs trade from a police officer. Stuart Wesley and I sat calculating the street value of a kilo of Ecstasy; it was something he hadn't figured out before: 'Err . . . that's three 920 hits per gram, about 960,000 a kilo . . .'

That makes the street value of the British 1991 Ecstasy seizures roughly equivalent to the NCIS's entire budget. And that's just the seizures. Ever since the mid-1980s when the Thatcher government cut the Customs and Excise budget by a third, policemen and customs officers have discovered a new realism about the drugs traffic. 'You calculate that you get about 10 per cent of the drugs that come in, don't you?' I said tactfully to Stuart Wesley.

'We don't know,' he sighed, 'we just don't know. It could be much less.'

'Don't your policemen get cynical?' I had asked Inspector van Velsen back in Amsterdam.

'Oh no,' he replied.

Later that day at the Neumarkt station, the junkies were all gone. Two burly Dutch metro police were patrolling the concourse. 'You've cleared out all the junkies,' I said.

'Oh yeah,' they replied, 'but they'll be back as soon as we've left.'

'Don't you get cynical?'

'How do you say it in England?' he replied. 'It pays for my roast beef. It's a living.'

'We will never accept a harmonization of drugs policy throughout the EU if it involves a step backwards from our current situation,' Theo van Iwaarden had told me. 'Formally we are not proposing a full legalization of cannabis, but informally we are investigating a number of options . . . I personally think it would be very difficult under our current State Secretary for Health, and under our current Minister of Justice. If we take another step there will also be a lot of international political pressure, which wouldn't please the Ministry of Foreign Affairs.'

So the Dutch go on; their 'pragmatism' means that their

STREET LEGAL

tax inspectors submit estimated bills to the hash cafés and the brothels, both of which are technically illegal. 'They've come to believe in their own rhetoric,' an older Dutch friend told me, 'but really the city is ungovernable.'

The Netherlands has an enlightened social policy, and an enlightened drugs policy, and yet nothing seems to help. Like the hero of their best-known folk tale, their fingers are stuck in the dyke, while a tidal wave of drugs pours over the top of it. But really they are taking the buck for the rest of Europe, and their only real crime consists of trying to put a brave face on it. Perhaps if they admitted that, without a supranational dimension, their policy is just as ineffective as everyone else's, then perhaps everyone could sit down and plan a sensible, enforceable drug policy. One that, for a start, fully legalized cannabis. But then, not even a burgomaster likes to admit that his new clothes are really transparent.

Guardian, February 1994

In the Holy Land

It was the Saturday after Christmas and I stood by the side of a cool dusty road in Jordan. I was some thousand metres above the entrance to the narrow gorge that contains the famous ruins of Petra, the Nabataean necropolis so famously used by a famous Jew—Steven Spielberg—as a backdrop for Indiana Jones, his swashbuckling gentile *alter ego*.

On the long coach drive from the Israeli border at Aqaba—and during the still longer wait at that border, occasioned by the mutual antagonism of all officials concerned—I had noticed the pensive, sensitive mien of a bespectacled man of around my own age, who I guessed was an English Jew. We now stood in a loose dyad, watching a young Jordanian lad attempting to persuade some of our fellow tourists to have their names described in coloured sands and encapsulated in glass vials. Improbably large raindrops began plashing from the leaden sky. He turned to me and asked, 'Is this your first visit to an Arab country?' I muttered something negative and returned the query. 'Yes,' he replied, 'and from what I've seen so far it looks . . . interesting . . .'

'Indeed,'—I drew closer to him and, ever the compulsive stirrer, returned the conversational lob with a drop-shot—'and our Jordanian guide's obvious pride in his country is a welcome contrast to the chauvinism of the Israeli guide who brought us from Eilat, wouldn't you say? Even as a Jew I found all that stuff about how the Jordanians would fleece us chang-

ing money, rip us off for horse rides down to Petra and subject us to insanitary toilet facilities a bit much to take.' The
pensive man looked at me with reinforced thoughtfulness
before replying, 'Well, I'm a Jew too and I can't help agreeing with you.'

It had happened, the moment I had been waiting for ever
since arriving at Ben Gurion International Airport three days
earlier—I had finally bonded with one of my coreligionists.
What a delicious and consummate irony that I'd had to quit
Zion to apprehend any of my own Jewishness.

The Austrian Jewish writer Walter Abish once wrote a story
entitled 'In the English Garden', about a German Jew going
back to a small German town that has suffered a convenient,
collective amnesia about its role in the Holocaust. On arrival
the protagonist finds himself transfixed, looking at the map of
the town, experiencing a shocking epiphany. Everything here,
he realises, right down to the very rivets that secure the metal
map-frame, is German. Teutonism is shot through the material
world like words through a stick of rock; it is monadological,
this Germanness, every atom of the German world containing within itself an infinity of German aspects and all of them
implying the greater, encompassing Germany.

Abish's story is about identity and essentialism, about
defining oneself by what one irreducibly is. My problem has
always been to know whether what I am is an essential property, or only something arrived at in contrariety; whether
my Jewishness is an absolute or a relative construct. Of
course, for most of my life I've attempted to avoid the issue,
a task made beautifully facile by the aggressive secularism of
contemporary English society. The only tangible form my
willed ignorance has taken—besides my avoiding any overt
ceremonial—has been a determination not to visit either Germany or Israel. Either destination might, I felt, break down
the partitions within me and expose poorly insulated psychic cavities.

The German trip eventually came about three years ago, when I went to the Frankfurt Book Fair for a couple of days. Even before the Lufthansa jet had lifted off from Heathrow I was getting the Abish sensation; I was surrounded by German people, German metal, German plastic—even German seat covers; and I was Jewish at last, truly, deeply Jewish. So Jewish that like some Woody Allenesque character I could feel skull locks sprouting from above my ears, and the leather bands of phylacteries wrapping themselves around my temples. A few seconds more and I was convinced I would start rocking back and forth like some Hasid at the Wailing Wall.

This sensation of Jewishness stayed with me throughout my brief sojourn in Germany. Everywhere I went I saw lumpen figures stuffing themselves with bloody sausage; every face I looked into that was over sixty-five I scrutinised for traces of culpability—overt or covert. But even at the time I realised that this was a negative Jewishness, a Jewishness arrived at out of fear of exclusion—not desire to be included.

In a way there's no mystery about this. When it comes to being Jewish I am not so much deracinated as never racinated to begin with. My mother, who was a second-generation American Jew, quickly slipped the slack cultural bonds of her upbringing, heading off on an exogamous trajectory that led her first into marriage to a WASP American academic, and then into marriage to an Anglican English academic—my father.

When I was growing up in the Hampstead Garden Suburb in the sixties my mother would oscillate, sometimes quite wildly, between protestations of Jewishness—'We just *are* funnier than other people'—and Jewish superiority—'You have to ask yourself why it is that Marx, Freud and Einstein were all Jews . . .'—and, conversely, really quite craven denials: 'You aren't *really* Jewish; and people here don't know that I'm Jewish. I mean, I don't look Jewish, and anyway of course there's no such thing as a Jewish look—Chinese Jews look Chinese, you know . . .'

This was the identity she retailed me, one made up in equal parts of Semophilia and that most corrosive of anti-Semitisms: Jewish anti-Semitism. In the last analysis I was a Jew not because I had been circumcised or read my portion of the Torah—neither had happened, rather I'd been christened— nor because I identified myself as being Jewish, but because if the Nazis came back *they* would haul me and my mother off before my father. They would know me for a Jew. There was that, and there was also the fact that Jews claimed—and still do claim—me for their own. Thus I have always been in the peculiar position of being freighted with an identity by two, violently opposed groups; groups that have been internalised within my own psyche.

But if this sounds too dramatic, there is always the limiting constraint of Englishness. Time and again English gentiles would reassure me that I really didn't have to 'go on' about being Jewish, that it really wasn't an issue. But on plenty of occasions when I would take this bait, I'd find that it was poisoned, that the invitation to deny my own Jewishness would be a prelude to induction into cosy, clubbable, mild anti-Semitism—that distinctively English anti-Semitism which pivots eternally on the turncoat phrase 'Some of my best friends . . .' etc. etc.

At school in Finchley my demi-Semitism wasn't that remarkable, but with three gangs naturally formed—the Yocks, the Yids and the Pakis—I found myself teetering unpleasantly on the margins. If I went to synagogue with Jewish friends on Yom Kippur I had to wear a paper skull-cap, which felt so insubstantial atop my seventies bouffant that one hand had to constantly hover over it, lest my pate be exposed to the gaze of a deity I wasn't even sure existed.

As a bloodthirsty twelve-year-old I had followed the progress of the October War on my transistor radio, in between hits by Bowie and T-Rex, and secretly exulted in the idea that Jews could be tough guys. Those Arabs—I would chortle—don't know what's hit them. Then came politicisation. Along with the unpleasant realisation that Jews could not only be tough guys, but also be aggressive, chauvinistic thugs, came the acknowledgement that the Palestinians had a point. More and more wedges were being hammered into a log already split. My Jewishness was now so fractured, my loyalties so broadcast, that apart from drunken sallies into atavism and a conviction that my wiseacre absurdism had a distinctively Semitic cast, my Jewishness came to mean little more than an indicator of disjunction from the oppressive, sheltering sky of England.

The last thing I wanted to do was go to Israel. This, I felt, would, whatever my ambivalences and ambiguities, act like a ferret down either leg of my sembled identity. Would I find myself ululating with the best of them as I shoved prayers into the wall? Or would I become transfixed by the kind of anti-Semitism that I often saw afflicting my mother when we went for late-night hot salt-beef sandwich blow-outs in Golders Green? A visceral anti-Semitism, a rejection of the host body by an organ that felt itself to have been crudely transplanted.

Love conspired to get me to Israel on Christmas night. I didn't object to the two-hour grilling the El Al security staff gave me at Heathrow—they were only doing a job. And anyway, nobody apart from for-hire literary critics has shown that much interest in my work for years: 'Tell me, Mr Self, what kind of satire is it that you write exactly?' Nor could I reasonably object when they confiscated my miniature camera and the face-off for my car stereo—it was stupid of me to bring them in the first place.

The same kind of understanding of the excruciating position in which the Israelis find themselves stayed with me throughout my short trip, and cushioned me through repeated interrogations by officials of one sort or another, who suspected the extempore nature of my decision to visit a land notionally holy to me on two counts. The Israelis feel themselves surrounded by enemies and percolated by them as well. The borders of the Jewish homeland are more like the holes in a colander than any straightforward zoning. As I arrived, the whole dog of state was about to get a serious wagging from the tail-end, four hundred and fifty Jewish 'settlers' who have elected to sabotage a possible Israeli-Palestinian deal over the disputed township of Hebron: a state within a state within a state; a peculiarly vertiginous sovereignty.

There was that understanding, but there was no epiphany for me, no antidote to the Frankfurt experience, no acknowledgement of belonging to a people, a faith, or even some nebulous 'look'. I stood in front of the Wailing Wall and stared at it with emphatically secular eyes, impressed but not awed. The Dome of the Rock affected me more—for here was an achieved building of indisputable aesthetic quality, rather than a buttress of a building demolished two millennia ago that cannot be rebuilt for reasons of Messianism. Indeed, overall, the impression the inhabitants of Jerusalem give, in all their polyglot diversity—Muslims, Jews, Christians, of all nations and peoples—is of understudies to an overwhelming history, constantly attempting to make the right gesture, the proper entrance, as they revolve around a tiny enclave where nothing is *not* sacred.

In Jerusalem we stayed in the Christian Quarter, but once we headed south to Eilat I began to experience the peculiar quality of Israeli boorishness. These may sound like tiny, insignificant gripes, but somehow they did add up to more than the sum of their parts. On buses people constantly pushed and shoved with no demurral; adolescent boys shouted and bayed as if to deliberately annoy everyone around them; the women friends I travelled with were crudely propositioned both sexually and fiscally. (One friend who refused to pay an exorbitant sum for a cab to a tourist site was told she was 'a lazy girl' and should work harder so as to be able to spend more money in Israel.) In Eilat itself, Christmas had been marked with a defiant embrace of racial stereotyping: all the charges in the hotel had been put up by 10 per cent!

The sense of arrogant offhandedness that so many Israelis—and in particular the younger ones—seemed hell-bent on projecting inevitably made me wonder about what had put the Swiftian 'yahu' into Benjamin Netanyahu's name. Why, I asked myself, did Israeli parents not teach their kids to at least be polite to those European and American tourists who might reasonably be expected to have some sympathy for their situation? Surely this pervasive rudeness wasn't simply a reflection of kibbutz egalitarianism? Spartan, no-frills social living? For it grated so terribly within the context of obvious affluence. (The Israeli teenagers with whom I shared a row of seats on the return flight, and who were going to London on a group trip, had armed themselves with one thousand cigarettes a head for their London sojourn.)

No, the more I was chivvied and bullied—in Tel Aviv the cabbie didn't want to take me to the Yemenite Quarter: 'I know somewhere better! You will go there!'—the more I saw the Israeli mentality as being that of the laager. It's no wonder ties have been traditionally strong with white South Africa, because like the Boers, certain sections of the Israeli population have decided to define themselves in racial contrast to their—Arab—neighbours. This—as my mother could have told them—is a spurious homogeneity. Israel is teeming with Jews of all shapes and sizes, from the dark, Ethiopian Falashas to blond kiddies who wouldn't look out of place in the choir of King's College, Cambridge. By attempting to make Jews more than a loose amalgamation of peoples, some Israelis have been party to a most bogus and insidious nationalism.

The ironies that danced attendance on me for five days reached a giddy climax as, exhausted, I waited in the departure lounge for my flight out. Looking around me at all the people rushing, clamouring, pushing and yammering, I was visited with my belated epiphany—but not the one I wanted.

They all look the same, I thought to myself. They all have the same peculiarly repugnant, definably *Jewish* faces. It had happened—I'd experienced a pure hit of true anti-Semitism. Of course, it wasn't really anti-Semitism—it was anti-Israelism. The trouble is for a lot of the time neither they—nor we—can tell the difference.

Observer, January 1997

Not a Great Decade to Be Jewish

Like a Member of Parliament about to enter a debate, I feel that at the outset I should declare an interest—the influence of Woody Allen's comic style on my own. Two out of the three collections of humorous pieces included in Allen's *Complete Prose* were my primers, my textbooks, the canonical forms to which I have returned time and again when considering what it is to be funny in print.

I must have been given the American edition of *Getting Even* in about 1974, when I was thirteen. A year or so later, I actually staged a version of the short play *Death Knocks,* in which Nat Ackerman, a balding Jewish schmutter manufacturer, plays gin rummy with Death. At that age I was, of course, unaware that the playlet is an exquisite parody of Bergman's *Seventh Seal.* I may have been a pretentious and culturally omnivorous adolescent, but it was exclusively the strength of Allen's one-liners, and the precision of his comic timing, that fuelled my admiration. There can have been nothing more absurd to the audience of North London middle-class parents and schoolboys than my production.

My mother was a Jewish New Yorker, and one was as likely to come across Mort Sahl, S. J. Perelman and James Thurber dotted around the family home as H. B. Morton or Wodehouse. Despite this, Allen's Yiddish vocabulary (his kvetching and kaddish, his schlep, kasha and noodge) was as alien to me as to any other English boy; and so was his fictional topography, which effectively mirrors that classic cartoon 'A New Yorker's View of the World'. And yet I read, and reread and even memorized, whole passages of *Getting Even* and *Without Feathers*. Almost twenty years later I still find myself cribbing and restructuring some of Allen's gags in conversation. It wasn't until I came to reread these pieces that I recognized the origin of the joke: 'K. would not think to pass from room to room in a conventional dwelling without first stripping completely and then buttering himself'—which I had freely adapted over the years to become: 'he/she has to strip naked and grease themselves to get through a door'. Ditto for exploded metaphors such as: 'She had a set of parabolas that could have caused cardiac arrest in a yak.' Or: 'the zenith of mongoloid reasoning'.

Any canonical work is more than a point of origin, an inchoate text from which others derive: it also acts as a refracting lens. As I grew older I began to appreciate the way Allen's humour both anticipates the evolution of late twentieth-century comedy—the crystallization of the absurdity of urban alienation—and simultaneously reaches back to incorporate the styles and modes of Dorothy Parker, James Thurber, Perelman and Groucho Marx.

For my young self, the crucial juncture occurred when, thanks to *Annie Hall,* Allen became famous in England. Up until 1976 he was an oddity, a little-known Jewish funny man, a minority-interest comedian. With *Annie Hall* all this changed, and, at least for the art-house-inclined, his film became a primary point of cultural reference. I was appalled in the way that only someone can be who feels he has discovered something in advance of the masses. Allen was *my* comic inspiration, and what's more, although I was profoundly deracinated, he had also become the touchstone of whatever Semitism I accorded myself. The idea that the goyim should even be allowed to laugh at this self-lacerating, mordantly Jewish comedy was more than I could stand.

In retrospect I find it difficult to believe that Allen's humour became widely appreciated in England at that time simply because of the Oscar award. Rather, the English were becoming more self-consciously urbanized and decadent in the mid-seventies. Traditional Little England anti-intellectualism was on a partial wane. In a word, the English were becoming more Jewish. So it was that they began to find Allen funny.

Interestingly this acceptance of Allen in England coincided with what critics have identified as the 'epistemological break' in his work. John Lahr, in his 1984 essay on Allen, wasn't the first to take the view that the comic's early films, thin narrative skeletons on to which Allen could graft his anarchic one-liners, were somehow more honest. After the break, according to Lahr and many others, Allen committed the comic's worst crime—wanting to be taken seriously. He made the stilted, boring Bergmanesque *Interiors,* and his execrably self-obsessed version of Fellini's *8½, Stardust Memories,* in which he tried to deflect such criticisms, by placing them in the mouth of a grotesque, importuning fan: 'I prefer the early funny films.' But Lahr's essay, in which he accuses Allen of 'teasing and flattering a middle-class audience with its hard-won sophistication', and defines his humour as deriving from 'emotional paralysis', was written before *Hannah and Her Sisters* and *Crimes and Misdemeanours,* films which arguably united Allen's 'cosmic kvetching' and his nice appreciation of the tragic ironies of ordinary lives.

There has now been an even more profound 'epistemological break', the kind that only an unusual artistry could survive: Allen's life has begun to overshadow his work. Hardly anyone on the planet has been able to watch *Husbands and Wives* without picking apart the seeming artifice to peer at the emotional realities which we now know lie beneath it. At some screenings—although not the one I attended—sophisticated audiences have tittered knowingly as the Allen character, a creative-writing professor called Gabe Roth (shadows of

Portnoy?), discourses to the camera on his attraction to younger women, his belief in fidelity (tee-hee) and so forth.

Husbands and Wives was a depressing experience for me. No one likes to see his idols brought so low. When the news first broke about Allen's alleged child abuse I was appalled. Surely, I mused, this cannot in any way be true? The whole point about Allen's metaphysical schmuck persona was that it represented a fundamental honesty; a willingness to admit to sexual inadequacy, lust, emotional missed connections. How could such a man turn out to be a comprehensive suborner of trust? To compound the unease there was the film's cinematography. Allen's increasing artistic pretension has been mirrored by his use of sophisticated camerawork. But in *Husbands and Wives,* it looks as if Allen forced Carlo Di Palma to undergo a two-week speed-and-brandy binge before shooting the picture on the comedown. Obviously the hand-held judder and frenzied jump-cut were intended as visual counterpoints to the narrative's muddled emotional compromise and painful honesty. But what came across was a kind of dodginess, an evasiveness which of course one knew was there, as Allen denied the reality of his off-screen misdemeanours face-on to the wavering lens.

On returning to the fifty short pieces contained in the *Complete Prose,* a different order of criticism occurred to me. Naturally, post-Soon-Yi, every reference to nubility leaps off the page. In 'The Lunatic's Tale', Allen's enduring obsession with Jehovah's failure to put the mind of a 'charming and witty culture vulture' into the body of an 'erotic archetype' is given full rein, as he enacts a dry run of the fantasy scene in *Stardust Memories,* by performing the Frankensteinian psycho-sexual transplant surgery himself. It is now very difficult to view his plainting on this theme (no less than five of the fifty pieces are concerned specifically with the impossibility of finding a sexy woman who is his intellectual equal) as anything other than retrogressive and callous. If it is true that Allen cannot locate

137

a woman whom he finds both intelligent and sexy, it is surely—
we now feel—a function of his own shortcomings, rather than
the cosmic joke he would have us believe.

It is in his use of pastiche and parody that these pieces represent the seedbed of Allen's humorous vision. And, as such,
all too often I found myself agreeing with Lahr: in Allen's
work—unlike that of, say, Groucho Marx or Thurber—parody
represents 'an imagination submerged more in art than life',
although I would be inclined to say more in culture than in
art. 'Look,' Allen seems to be saying, 'I may have been ex-
pelled from university' (an event which provided him with
the memorable gag: 'I cheated on the metaphysics paper by
looking into the soul of the student seated next to me'), 'but
I'm still just as clever, well-read and philosophically literate as
the people I would like to be.'

The author's note for *Getting Even* was one of the Allen lines
that I found funniest as a child. He stared out from the jacket,
a misshapen little man with glasses, holding a stick or a twig,
with a mien of utter hopelessness. Underneath he declared:
'My only regret in life is that I'm not someone else.' But,
contrary to the impression which his films give, Allen doesn't
want to be Bergman, Renoir, Fellini or Lang. In the *Complete
Prose,* it is clear that he wants to be Sontag, Benjamin, Adorno
or Arendt. His comic one-liners are a painful involution of
the existential aphorism, which traces its lineage back through
the Frankfurt School to Nietzsche: 'Death is an acquired trait.'
His parodic cultural disquisitions—a critique of a Nietzschean
character's laundry lists; an elision of Dostoyevsky and eating
disorders; a pseudo-memoir of a contemporary of Freud's—
are in effect his attempts at the exegetical essay form, which
has come to represent the summit of contemporary intellectual achievement. When Allen quips, 'Epistemology: Is knowing knowable? If not, how do we know this?' he is not simply
flattering his audience, he is flattering himself as well, showing us that he, too, has a vast matching set of Samsonite intel-

lectual baggage. Possibly my discomfort on rereading these pieces was as much a function of recognizing this pretension within myself as of seeing it in Allen.

The influence which Allen exercises on my own comedy, and on that of many others, is based less on the subject-matter of his pieces than on the particular form of the Allen gag. It is important to remember that Allen cut his teeth writing jokes for Johnny Carson, churning out, it is claimed, as many as five hundred a week. The Allen one-liner has three basic forms: the 'bathetic let-down' the 'surreal elision' and the 'silly word'. Here, in the same order, are examples: 'So little time left, he thought, and so much to accomplish. For one thing, he wanted to learn to drive a car.' 'I did not know that Hitler was a Nazi, for years I thought he worked for the phone company.' 'Once, on holiday in Jena, he could not say anything but the word "eggplant" for four straight days.'

Most of the pieces in this collection were first published in the *New Yorker,* and it is to the classic comic vignettes of the 1930s that they so clearly owe their primary inspiration. The *Complete Prose* is an ideal bedside companion, to be dipped into for quick hits of enjoyment. Treated in this way, and severed from the Allen persona and its tendency to topple over into his own work, the pieces remain examples of unalloyed comic genius. In 'If Impressionists Had Been Dentists', Allen produces a hilarious pastiche of the American bio-pics of Van Gogh, Toulouse-Lautrec and Gauguin. Seurat is a hygienist who cleans his patients' teeth one at a time, in order to build up 'a full fresh mouth'. Toulouse-Lautrec is too proud to work on a stool and so, fumbling away, manages to 'cap Mrs Needleman's chin'. Eventually Vincent, unrecognized, reduced to 'working almost exclusively with dental floss', and unhappy in love, confesses to Theo that 'the ear on sale at Fleishman Brothers Novelty Shop is mine'.

In 'The Kuglemass Episode', Allen conceives of a magician, 'the Great Persky', who is able to project his clients into any work of fiction. So it is that Kuglemass, a Jewish academic at Columbia, trapped in a loveless marriage, is able to enjoy an affair with Emma Bovary: "My God, I'm doing it with Madame Bovary!" Kuglemass whispered to himself. "Me, who failed freshman English."' More surreal still is the fact that Kuglemass actually crops up in the text as it is being read: 'At this very moment students in various classrooms across the country were saying to their teachers: "Who is this character on page 100? A bald Jew is kissing Madame Bovary?"' This kind of conceit goes far further than the simple schemas of Allen one-liners, creating a *reductio ad absurdum* of fantasy/reality, reality/fantasy, that is the hallmark of true satire.

In 'The Discovery and Use of the Fake Ink Blot', he seems to be cutting the ground from under himself, with a mock-serious commentary on the very unfunny nature of the pratfall. However, Allen has never been shy of slapstick, either in print or on film, and these pieces abound with casual instances of the cruellest and most pointless violence, visited on those who expect and deserve it least: 'The old man had slipped on a chicken-salad sandwich and fallen off the Chrysler Building.' The Mafia 'are actually groups of rather serious men, whose main joy in life comes from seeing how long certain people can stay under the East River before they start gurgling'. In 'Viva Vargas!' the first-person protagonist cascades off the front patio, 'luckily breaking the fall with my teeth, which skidded around the ground like loose Chiclets'.

Allen's sado-masochism is another slant on his self-hatred. This in turn is inescapably linked to his Jewishness, and the idea of Jewish humour as a pre-emptive strike: we'll run ourselves down so far that the gentiles won't be able to say anything worse. The quintessence of the Jewish joke is not simply its self-deprecatory character—the Jew as mensch gaining strength through oppression—but also the fact that it must be told by a Jew. If a gentile tells a Jewish joke he is an anti-Semite, if Woody Allen tells an anti-Semitic joke he is being funny.

And here is the crux of my anxiety. The revelation of the nebbisch-as-possible-child-molester may be enough to destabilize the careful balance of pressures that have made Allen's comedy such a good vehicle for promoting tolerance and understanding between Jew and gentile. With Allen paraded as the caricature Jewish child molester, defiler of Christian (oh, all right, Korean-American) virtue, the other elements of his comic persona fall into alignment with the traditional slurs on Jewishness, and specifically on Jewish men: androgyny, thanatos, sexual obsession, febrile genius. With neo-Nazis burning down refugee hostels in Germany, the nineties may not be such a great decade to be Jewish in. With Woody Allen committing crimes of pretentiousness and breach of trust, it may not be such a great decade for Jewish humorists either.

London Review of Books, February 1993

Bret Easton Ellis:
The Rules of Repulsion

So, we're sitting in the Saloon Room of the Oyster Bar, underneath Grand Central Station having lunch with Will Self and Bret Ellis. Bret Ellis is wearing a plain, three-button, black, single-breasted suit which could be by Yves St Laurent, or could just be off the peg; a plain white shirt—which could be Thomas Pink or Marks & Spencer; and a tie with an exaggerated, swirly, paisley motif, which might well be Versace, or alternatively one he could have bought five minutes earlier, from one of the barrow boys outside the terminal. As for the black brogues, they might be Church's but they could just as well be Freeman, Hardy and Willis.

Will Self is a little bit more straightforward (after all, I dressed him this morning): Next three-button blazer, gone slightly to seed; black Levis: ditto; Rockport pigskin walking shoes, so stained they have acquired a sort of verdigris; and a Jasper Conran shirt in the slightest of charcoal checks, worn over a Wrangler T-shirt.

Bret Ellis is eating the crab salad entrée and, despite having made inroads into his Coca-Cola, is still glancing thirstily towards an iced tea which the waiter (some Hispanic in an asinine red uniform waistcoat which places him sartorially closer to Yogi Bear than any other biped) is just bringing to the table. Will Self is ignoring this and tucking into the third of his Blue Point oysters on the half-shell, at the same time as he tucks into his third Brooklyn Lager.

The waiter sets down the iced tea by the elbow of the notorious writer. It has a section of the paper covering set on top of the straw like a miniature and ineffectual condom (and Christ knows why I notice this detail . . . surely it's only a function of the atrocity that subsequently occurs . . .), and Bret Ellis looks up from his crab salad entrée, actually looks directly at the waiter and says, very distinctly: 'Thank you.'

How macabre, how black . . . how disgusting! How can Bret Ellis just sit there and for three whole hours not once fail to thank the waiter for bringing something to the table (he later even declines a lobster bib with grace); not once say something arrogant or self-seeking; not once betray any sign of misogynism or contempt? Has he no respect!

And I know, because I taped the whole encounter on my Sanyo M1118 cassette tape recorder, with Voice Activated System and touch-pause capability. Taped it, and then listened back to the whole repulsive 'snuff' interview. An interview in which the received image of Bret Easton Ellis, the author of the reviled *American Psycho,* is put to death.

For a start he's both bigger and better-looking than his photographs. Funny how we're all victims of the media's attempts to slur people. How we actually believe that if someone has been labelled meretricious, adventitious and plain not nice, we imagine his physical attributes will conform.

Bret Easton Ellis is a tall, rangy, well-built man of thirty, who bears a distinct resemblance to the young Orson Welles (something he later tells me I am not the first to remark on). He has strong, fleshy features, warm brown eyes and, dare I say, a perceptible charisma, which emerges in his propensity to dissolve into shoulder-shaking guffaws with charming frequency.

But most of all there is his quality of embodiment. It has to be said that with people who are really creepy, really not nice, you always get those subliminal, yucky messages of physical unease. And with Bret Easton Ellis? None, *nada, rien du tout.*

This is a man who I'd happily let bath my children—should he wish to engage in such an atrocity.

Or, to put it another way: a publicist in New York who both Bret and I know well, a woman in her thirties, the mother of two small children, said of the hated one: 'Oh, Bret? Well . . . he's so sweet!'

With the publication of his fourth book, *The Informers,* Bret Ellis isn't so much ready for rehabilitation, as habilitation. He may have sold many, many thousands of books (*American Psycho* has sold 150,000 copies in the UK alone and still steady-sells at 1,000 copies a month), but *The Informers* is his first work to receive a favourable review (in the *New York Times Book Review*) in any of the keynote American newspapers.

'I guess that's why I've found it easy to dismiss criticism,' he told me. 'If people had begun by saying nice things about me and my work and then got nasty I might have been upset. But they never said anything nice in the first place.'

Ellis wrote his first book, *Less Than Zero,* at the precocious age of nineteen, while still a student at Bennington College: 'I did it as part of my course credits. I was incapable of getting a job, so I did the book instead.' But it really wasn't a great act of precocity, because he'd already written two novels before this, the first when he was fourteen: 'No one's ever going to see them. Every writer has about a quarter of a million words of self-indulgence he has to get out. I was just fortunate to get mine out a little earlier than most.'

As for the filthy-rich, nihilistic Beverly Hills that forms the backdrop for both *Less Than Zero* and now *The Informers,* contrary to received opinion there was nothing particularly autobiographical about it: 'We lived further out in the suburbs when I was a kid, in a much more middle-class area; so, although I was aware of kids like those in the book, they weren't my closest friends or anything like that.'

His father, a real-estate man, did make a lot of money during the eighties, but this was a little too late to impact on the

Bret Ellis lifestyle: 'When he died a couple of years ago, he left a disaster area behind him as far as tax is concerned. It's something we're still untangling, but I don't think the estate will have any value.'

In fact, if there's any flow of money the implication is that it goes the other way: from Ellis to his mother, whom he quite clearly adores: 'I would say she's the chief factor in why I became a writer. She was always tremendously encouraging of any creativity that I displayed.' Her house was hit quite badly in last year's earthquake and Bret has been out in California for three months helping her to get back on her feet.

The tension between paternal and maternal relationships is something that quite clearly underscores Ellis's work, and he admitted to me that he had 'an extremely difficult, possibly even abusive' relationship with his father. Critics have already remarked on the 'X' factor of poignancy which seems to inhabit the story 'In the Islands' from the new collection. A story which concerns the attempt by a distant and unloving father to build a spurious bridge to his nineteen-year-old son, by taking him on holiday to Hawaii. When I remark on this, Bret smiles ruefully: 'Well, I guess it is a far lighter, more Salinger-like story than some of the others, and that's why they find it easier to latch on to.'

As for the controversy that exploded around *American Psycho:* 'I really didn't see it coming . . . I mean, I just had no idea. I had thought there might be problems with the length of the manuscript—that's where my problems usually are, but not with the content.'

And I don't think he is being disingenuous about this—or even flip. Even now, only three years along the line, much of the brouhaha surrounding *Psycho* looks, quite simply, pathetic. Norman Mailer calling, in *Vanity Fair,* for a panel of 'twelve respected novelists' to judge the work before allowing it to be published; Fay Weldon defending the book's right to be published in the *Guardian,* but admonishing readers that they needn't actually go through the hell of the text, because good old Fay has already done it for them. And many, many other writers who really ought to have known better, shooting their mouths off in a most egregious fashion.

Ellis was accused of just about every crime in the production of this text, but the one of being mercenary seems just about the cruellest and least justified: 'I had no idea that the book would earn out its advance—I didn't expect it to earn out its advance. I had been more or less broke in the year before publication. I was doing journalistic assignments—which I'm not good at. And, as I say, I had no idea of the controversy the book would unleash.'

In 1991, Mark Lawson put Bret Easton Ellis in the dock in the *Independent Magazine,* the charge being how he could justify, in particular, the grossest and most sadistic scene of the novel, in which Patrick Bateman, the eponymous anti-hero 'offs' two prostitutes in an extravagantly sadistic fashion. Lawson looked at many possible defences, from art for art's sake, to the moral responsibility of the satirist, before concluding that the jury was still out. Well, the jury is now back in, and, with the publication of *The Informers,* I would say delivers a unanimous verdict of 'not guilty' on all charges. *The Informers* shows the work of a writer at the peak of his powers, deeply concerned with the moral decline of our society. The book takes us from the first to the seventh circles of hell, from Salinger to de Sade, and in doing so shows that *American Psycho* was no gratuitous exercise, but a keynote text in the development of a major writer's *oeuvre.*

Lunch is over. Will Self picks up the tab with his Mastercard, and the two writers head out of the Oyster Bar. Self is going to walk back downtown to where he's staying in TriBeCa, but Ellis, ever the cocaine-honking, money-spunking bratpacker, is going to take . . . the subway. But before that he has to find a post office. Obviously so he can do something

THE RULES OF REPULSION

vile, like send photographs of sexual atrocities to Gloria
Steinem . . . er . . . actually no: 'I found this guy's wallet in
the street yesterday, and I guess I oughta mail it back to him.'
The sick, sick bastard.

Evening Standard, October 1994

High Fidelity by Nick Hornby

If I were Nick Hornby I'd be shitting my whack. Not just shitting myself, mark me, but actually dumping my load, dropping my ballast, in the very demotic eye of north London. Because that's Hornby—as we all know. He's the man standing on the North Bank at Highbury, with a plastic beaker of Bovril in one hand and a Wagon Wheel in the other; he's the anal retentive who can remember—like Borges's Pierre Menard—every nuance of his life, once it is trawled to the surface by his obsessive recall of the 'worlds' of pop music and football; he's the New Man, who's never made the mistake of merely coming, and whose horror of fisticuffs is just about matched by his glee in voyeurism; and last—but by no means least—he's a literary critic who's undertaken to write what on the face of it appears to be a novel-length work of fiction.

No! Not that same Hornby who wrote just a mere three years ago that 'the influence of post-modernism is such that although everyone knows the orthodox novel is dead, nobody is sure what they should be producing in its place'? Not the Hornby who so plangently opined in the same piece, 'It used to be the case that you could not be a proper writer until you had mythologised your adolescence, satirised your friends, deified an ex-girlfriend or excoriated your parents in a novel? Yep, the very same. I have the piece in front of me as I write.

Hornby penned it as a riposte to the Granta list of 'Best Young British Novelists' that had recently been announced.

The piece (for the *Sunday Times*) was subheaded 'Nick Hornby analyses the literary underachievement of the thirtysome-things'; and in column four we have the delicious pull-quote 'Thirtysomething literary fiction is like a doughnut, with a hole in the middle where an overpaid group of coddled literary superstars should be smirking.'

This was a big mistake. Because, even now (three years may be a long time in football, honey, but it ain't in books), he has to confront the fact that he has written *a novel* that: mytholo-gises his adolescence, satirises his friends, deifies an ex-girlfriend and excoriates his parents.

As for the 'overpaid group of coddled [and smirking] liter-ary superstars', I don't believe Hornby thinks they exist any more than I do. But he would have to admit that his footballing memoir *Fever Pitch* sold inordinately well. So well, in fact, that once when I got into a cab, the cabbie, without prompting from me, launched into a disquisition on what a good book it was! The cabbie! I ask you. Yer average Julian Sensitive would tear his own penis off to get a cabbie to so much as glance at a copy of his book, let alone read it.

As I recall, *Fever Pitch* was on the bestseller list for some time; and while I wouldn't go so far as to say that Hornby is smirking on the cover of the proof of *High Fidelity,* he doesn't exactly look consumed by existential angst, or even more quotidian miseries. Like a cash-flow problem, for example.

So, as I say, Nick Hornby must be shitting his whack. Be-cause on top of these lit-crit-type problems—and what are they but mere persiflage—we also know that he has more personal problems with taking criticism. In *Fever Pitch* he mused on the congruences between his profession as a literary critic and his support of Arsenal, a club universally disliked, saving by its fans.

'Like the club,' Hornby wrote, 'I am not equipped with a particularly thick skin; my oversensitivity to criticism means that I am more likely to pull up the drawbridge and bitterly bemoan my lot than I am to offer a quick handshake and get on with the game.' Oh dear, oh dear, oh dear, how is he going to cope with criticism of his first novel then? An experience that may be ranked as the most profoundly, psychically intrusive probing by potentially hostile strangers that you are ever likely to encounter.

Hornby also admitted in *Fever Pitch* that some of his attitudinising as a literary critic derived from the terraces. The tendency to roar in disbelief at the efforts and awards of other writers was so summarised: 'Perhaps it was these desperate, bitter men in the West Stand at Arsenal who taught me how to get angry in this way; and perhaps it is why I earn some of my living as a critic—maybe it's those voices I can hear when I write. "You're a WANKER, X." "The Booker Prize? THE BOOKER PRIZE? They should give that to me for having to read you."'

I resisted reading *Fever Pitch* for a long time. People kept telling me it was a book about much more than football, but I couldn't really believe them. My failure to get to grips with this central shibboleth of male bonding has always made me feel an outsider; and in time my ignorance of all things *sportif* has become something of a badge of pride. As Montaigne so wisely remarked, 'Mistrust a man who takes games too seriously; it means he doesn't take life seriously enough.'

I only read it because I had to for this review. But I'm glad I did. There's something about being charmed by a book you thought you would hate that is truly captivating. I knew within a page or so that it was exceptionally well written. The prose has that implied mutuality of lucidity (you, the reader, understand perfectly what I, the writer, am saying to you) that is the hallmark of good memoir. But on the second page I also laughed aloud, and on the third or fourth my eyes were pricked by tears. In a year that also produced *And When Did You Last See Your Father?* by Blake Morrison, it was remarkable to read another such poignant evocation of a modern boyhood.

I read the book in one sitting, and called up a footie-loving friend to tell him how much I had enjoyed it. Then I turned my attention to its successor, *High Fidelity,* fervently praying that it would be as good.

Unfortunately it isn't. For a start it has a dreadful title. As Rob Fleming, the protagonist of the novel, might say, 'List your top five favourite novels with titles culled from Elvis Costello songs.' To which one would have to reply, '(1) *Less Than Zero;* (2) Err . . .'

But there is a point to it. The title heralds what has to be the novel most replete with ephemeral cultural references you're likely to find outside an airport bookstall dump-bin this year. (Next year it will probably be there itself.) Hornby's characters work in a record shop, so I suppose that does mean that the endless lists of records and musicians lend some veri-similitude, but do we really want to read any text with the following even mentioned in it: Dr Ruth, Danny Baker, Susan Dey from *LA Law,* Gerry and Sylvia Anderson, Paul McCartney, Whoopi Goldberg, John Cleese, Woody from *Cheers*—that isn't the *Radio Times?*

Maybe this is where 'the novel' (rather than the novel) is going to? As the conceit around which *High Fidelity* revolves is the increasingly serial quality of all aspects of life, from entertain-ment to emotional commitment, it must be the ideal candidate for transferral to CD-ROM. With this nice convergence of medium and message, the life of Rob Fleming could be pushed still further into the future at the reader's behest. We'll get myriad new editions of *High Fidelity* in which there will be a place for not just Peter Frampton, but also Mr Blobby; not only Nirvana but also Massive Attack: Hugh Grant in addition to Keanu Reeves. People could sponsor each other to appear in *High Fidelity* . . . No, I'm getting carried away.

And anyway, as the main psychological theme of the novel is that thirtysomethings (there's that coinage again! It doesn't just come up in his journalism, it makes several appearances in the novel as well—three in direct reference to the television show, the rest, as it were, as spin-offs) are all leading dull little lives in which their personalities are defined by a stale pot-pourri bowl of cultural artefacts, it could be argued that they are there to express a deep sense of collective malaise.

On this reading, *High Fidelity* is a sort of *American Psycho* for trainspotters: a friendly, heart-warming sort of attempt to make you appreciate the crass materialism and record-collecting greed that define your life. This defence might work if Rob Fleming were a reasonably hateful character, but he isn't. He's a nice, cuddly sort of bloke aware of the difficulties of making emotional commitments and obsessed by pop music. Not unlike our own dear . . . Nick Hornby!

In most instances, unmasking the autobiographical charac-ter of a fictional work is either crass, or otiose, or both. But remember those quotes from the *Sunday Times* article. Hornby cannot, I must say, have his cake and eat it. There are far too many congruences between Rob Fleming and the authorial persona of *Fever Pitch* for them to be coincidental. All right, Fleming is from Watford and Hornby hails from the Maiden-head locale; Fleming runs a record shop, and every day Hornby writes the book; but beyond this the similarities are legion: physical, psychological, biographical and, dare I say it, tonal. The voices of the two are recognisably one and the same, al-though Fleming's is neither as authoritative nor as funny.

The action of the book—boy loses girl, girl's father dies, boy experiences various epiphanies and regains girl with re-newed commitment—is simple enough. The problem is that the 'girls' and 'boys' in question are in their mid-thirties. Hornby may be speaking for a considerable social trend when he characterises these people, lost in the wildernesses of a grossly elongated adolescence, a stretch limo of the hormones, but he doesn't speak to this reader. It's the same with the record con-ceit, and all the references to TV and radio. It's as if he wanted to write a book that somehow exemplified all his theories on the redundancies of fiction.

HIGH FIDELITY BY NICK HORNBY

In *Fever Pitch,* even though my grasp of football doesn't even extend to knowing the shape of the ball, I was pulled into the game—and actually felt some nascent interest in it—by the way Hornby renders his obsession universal. In *High Fidelity* I found the protagonist's obsession with pop alienating, and his attempt to use it to provide a motif around which to interpret his life—at the beginning of the book he lists his 'Top Five Rejections'—merely irritating.

The art of using an ephemeral cultural reference in fiction—even when it is for a satirical purpose—is understatement. If overstatement is to be employed, there must be no expectation of sympathy with the character who is immersed in such trivia (cf. Bateman). Irony, by the same token, is a form of humour that assumes a small, privileged group of people 'in the know'. But Hornby's attempts at irony, such as the trope 'Bonkus Mirabilis', fall flat because everyone in the country knows what 'bonk' and *'annus mirabilis'* mean. A 'universal' irony is an oxymoron.

And Rob Fleming is just a moron. Hornby wants us to sympathise with Fleming, by laughing at his foibles and feckless forays into the world of romance, but we don't. Or at any rate I didn't, I just rather wanted him to leave.

Eventually he did—taking with him the charismatic supporting cast of Barry and Dick (they work in the record shop and are keen on lists—we never really learn the physical appearance of either), Laura (the girlfriend, who has spiky hair and works as a lawyer), and the exotica, a real, live Texan singer called Marie, who bears a distinct resemblance to Susan Dey in *LA Law.*

Nick Hornby has written a novel that can rank as a reasonable piece of juvenilia. There are passages in it that are affecting and describe emotions that are recognisably those of thinking, breathing adults. Some scenes, notably the post-coital ones, and the girlfriend's father's funeral (deaths small and large), are well-paced and believable.

His turns of phrase can be diverting—although even just an hour after putting the book down I'm buggered if I can remember any of the diverting ones, although I can remember verbatim such honeys as: 'We're like Tom Hanks in *Big*. Little boys and girls trapped in adult bodies and forced to get on with it'; 'People who know dead people, as Barbra Streisand might have sung, but didn't, are the luckiest people in the world'; 'People who are doing OK but have still not found their soul-mate should look, I don't know, well but anxious, like Billy Crystal in *When Harry Met Sally*'; and the absolute corker 'Have you ever looked at a picture of yourself when you were a kid? Or pictures of famous people when they were kids? It seems to me that they can either make you happy or sad.'

It is not by such acute tropes as 'I felt like a new man, but not like a New Man' that Nick Hornby will be making his living. But I'm not worried for him. In the *Sunday Times* piece he characterised his generation as one of late developers (thanks, Nick, speak for yourself). He's now written an autobiographical novel that mythologises his adolescence etc. etc.—obviously because he feels the need to be a 'proper' writer, of novels. With that off his chest at the age of thirty-eight, I suppose we can confidently look forward to his mid-period flowering by the time he reaches sixty. And who knows, perhaps a Mary Wesleyan comeback sometime towards the mid-twenty-first century.

Modern Review, May 1995

Getting Away With It:
Quentin Tarantino

Through the courtesy of the *Guardian* newspaper, and along with a lot of other white liberals, I boogied down to the National Film Theatre the other evening to watch a black film made by a white capitalist man from Los Angeles. How we all laughed at the salty dialogue of those rough ghetto types. Every 'muthafucka', 'niggah' and 'asshole' drew an appreciative burble of merriment from our plump bellies; and each instance of indiscriminate violence, casual sex and gratuitous drug-taking engendered in us a warm sense of being there now.

After the screening of *Jackie Brown,* we were further blessed by the manifestation of the *auteur* himself, Mr Quentin Tarantino. According to Adrian Wootton, the programme director of the NFT, Mr Tarantino's schedule is *very* busy, so it was nothing short of saintly of him to agree to come to London for a few hours to promote his film. We were suitably humbled, with the possible exception of a black man in the audience who had the temerity to suggest to Mr Tarantino that he might have substituted a few more 'muthafucka's and 'asshole's for the profusion of 'niggah's in the film's script.

Mr Tarantino bridled. He had, he told us, grown up 'surrounded by black culture', and had attended an 'all-black school' in Los Angeles. This rather raised the question, did he himself have to black up in order to attend classes? At any rate this black saturation means that Mr Tarantino can address his black friends as 'niggah' with complete impunity, while we uptight British—

whether black or white—are still enmired in asinine political correctness. When the black member of the audience pursued his point, suggesting that Mr Tarantino wouldn't 'get away' with this over here, the director threw his arms wide and proclaimed endearingly, 'But I do.' How we all chortled.

Another black man in the audience queried Mr Tarantino's championing of so-called 'blaxploitation' movies: 'Personally,' he said, 'I always found them rather vulgar and poorly made.' Mr Tarantino launched into long and essentially vapid defence of the genre, in which the word 'vitality' kept popping up, as if it were in and of itself a validator of artistic integrity. Blaxploitation movies represented 'a gigantic wonderful black cinema movement' that had been 'cut down' by the black intelligentsia themselves. Deary me! Those unruly black intellectuals, they definitely need a white black man like Mr Tarantino to come along and resurrect their cinema.

In truth Mr Tarantino's film is a competent, workmanlike adaptation of an Elmore Leonard thriller, *Rum Punch*. The casting of Pam Grier in the title role was inspiring, not because she's a black middle-aged woman (although it is genuinely pleasing to see a lead character of this unusual kind), but because her dignified, controlled performance held the film together. The other stars—Robert De Niro, Michael Keaton, Robert Forster and Samuel L. Jackson—set around this jewel of a performance didn't shine nearly as much.

But to adapt the form of the *Guardian*'s own Pass Notes column, the thing Mr Tarantino is *least* likely to say is anything remotely modest or self-deprecating. According to him, Elmore Leonard on reading the script of *Jackie Brown* pronounced it 'the best adaptation ever' of one of his novels—and went even further, saying that it was 'the best script ever written', and that it was 'my novel'. This Mr Tarantino took to mean that his script had 'the weight of a novel'. One senses that there isn't a great deal of Dostoyevsky being read *chez* Tarantino; and as for Elmore Leonard, the poor man's memory and critical faculties must be seriously awry for him to prefer *Jackie Brown* over and above Barry Sonnenfeld's superb film adaptation of *Get Shorty*.

Mr Tarantino told us that his adaptation took a year to write; and that the process enables him to get in touch with a quality he's lacking in. He didn't tell us what this 'quality' was, but I venture to suggest that it's originality itself. For Mr Tarantino is essentially a *pasticheur* and an artistic fraud. His use of pop music for his soundtracks—'I find the personality of the piece through the music'—is what confirms the status of his films as extended-play pop videos. These are deft promotions of the current generation's desire for unreflective entertainment, uncluttered by either ethics or purpose. His incorporation into his films of knowing little 'in' jokes about film (in *Jackie Brown* we have a character played by Bridget Fonda, watching a Peter Fonda film on television) is what confirms his status as a derivative and second-order filmmaker, rather than the Scorsese he would have us believe he is.

Mind you, this was the one Quentin Tarantino film I've ever managed to sit through. *Reservoir Dogs* got me puking into my popcorn during the torture sequence, and *Pulp Fiction* heading for the door after about an hour of pseudo-hip drug pornography. As for *Natural Born Killers,* I read Mr Tarantino's script and found it to be illiterate. I certainly hope he didn't spend a year writing that one.

There was some evidence the other evening that the Tarantino bubble is deflating. The last time there was one of these interviews at the NFT the crowds were enormous; this time they were merely big. I stuck out the question-and-answer session as long as I could, but when Pam Grier and Robert Forster came on stage to participate, it was time for this 'niggah' to head for home. After all, there's absolutely no point in asking an actor anything—unless they've already got a script.

The Times, January 1998

D'You Know What I Mean?

Two a.m. in Soho, central London. It's been a drizzly late-autumn evening, but the narrow streets are still crowded with a bizarre gallimaufry of characters: gay clones pumped up on butyl nitrate and testosterone patrol the coffee bars of Old Compton Street; stocky African whores stand on the corners looking for business; crusty young beggars sit in doorways smashed on glue and extra-strength lager. Blanketing the whole scene are great processions of the straight by name and the straight by nature: phalanxes of suits heading home after post-theatre dinners, and bedraggled kids in from the sticks for a night of overpriced fun.

Behind the slickly nondescript doors of the Groucho Club, an evening of epic—and typical—egregiousness is grinding to a halt. In the main bar few are left, just the wrack that remains after the high tide of sociability has receded. Dotted around the overstuffed armchairs are the kind of embittered, ulcerated individuals who tend to frequent the joint. The Groucho is a very atelier of arrogance, a palace of preening. I've sat in here on many occasions, and watched A-list Hollywood celebrities struggle to get service from the staff. In the bar of the Groucho, Britishness puts its best and coolest foot forward, refusing to kowtow to any preconceived notions of success or celebrity.

There's this paradoxical, snobbish egalitarianism. There's also the fact that the ratio of 'names' to non-names at any given time is about one to one. But on this occasion, as I totter like a soused foal down the stairs from the upper bar and the games room, I notice a puncture in the atmosphere, a palpable heating up of the cool. Opting for my twentieth unit of alcohol for the evening, I amble to the downstairs bar and prop myself by a tall, dark-haired individual.

He's dressed in preposterously sharp garb. A lilac jacket of anachronistic cut, round-collared and flaring out over the hips. Down below are black drainpipe trousers and winkle-picker boots; up top are a mop of black hair and wraparound shades. I don't so much study the fellow as have his persona forced upon me. Waves of suspicion and hostility emanate from him like white noise from a television. His head jerks backwards and forwards, his fists nervously tense and clench. His entire upper body is like a whiplash aerial on a speeding car. If this guy isn't wired to the gills, then I'm the ghost of Lester Bangs, and Albert Goldman and the King are jamming together in purgatory.

But it isn't just the mutant mop-top's behaviour that's pumping things up in here. Even before the ludicrously pretty blonde in the satin halter top comes and drapes herself against him I notice something absolutely untoward: all the other people in the bar are looking at him! Blatantly regarding him! Have they no self-respect? If Christ himself walked in here he'd be utterly ignored, but this weirdo has everyone's attention.

When the blonde leads him away to the upright piano in the corner and pours herself across it in a pose strongly reminiscent of Michelle Pfeiffer in *The Fabulous Baker Boys,* it begins to dawn on me who they are. He languidly plays half a dozen chords, she essays a few notes. We're all transfixed. Who cares about Princess Di? Forget Tony and Cherie Blair. This is Liam and Patsy. This is the golden couple—the true home-grown and absolutely authentic face of stardom. She sings, he strums, they're islanded by our regard for a while . . . and then it ebbs away.

159

Oasis. I first heard them—over and over and over again—on my friend Mark Radcliffe's prime-time BBC radio show. Mark broadcasts from Manchester; he's known for catching whatever musical vibrations are resounding in this city of many-splendoured musical mutation. 'Maaybay, I don' reely wanna know . . .' Liam Gallagher snarled over and over and over. I dug the rhythm—who couldn't? It was insistent, transmogrifying feet into sticks, carpet into drum—but it wasn't my thing. Too white, too guitar-band, too internally referential to rock music itself.

But when the press items and the rumours and the general babel began to overwhelm, I found myself intrigued. Noel claimed to have robbed a local shop at the age of thirteen. The band had threatened to burn a prominent club if it didn't give them a gig. There'd been a mêlée on board a ferry. Oasis didn't just smash up hotel rooms, they filleted them. They proudly boasted of being bigger than the Beatles—the ultimate in pop hubris. And there were drugs—loads of drugs. And there were women—loads of women.

A month or so later I was back in the Groucho Club, playing snooker in a desultory fashion with some friends, when I noticed a row of holes along one wall. Big holes in the plaster, which looked like the impressions made by a number of large-calibre weapons of ineffectual ordnance. Initially, I thought they must be one of the generally indifferent works of conceptual art the Groucho insists on purchasing. But on looking closer I saw that they were a little ragged, even for a Damien Hirst. They were, I was told, the fruits of Liam and Patsy's first marital tiff—a savage volley of snooker balls unleashed by the Maddened Mancunian. Such is the awe in which Gallagher was at that time held, there was absolutely no question about censuring him. Indeed, I heard some wags say that the holes should be framed.

Later that evening, Liam was busted horning a line of coke in a shop doorway on Oxford Street. When the police released him with a caution, there was the predictable outcry. It was Jagger all over again, but Gallagher is the sort of butterfly who lifts up a wing and uses it to break you.

'D'You Know What I Mean?', the advance single from the Long-Awaited New Oasis Album, *Be Here Now,* hyped up all of my ambivalences. The track opens with a great grind of backward guitar noise, like the evacuation of the steel intestine of some mighty mechanical creature. Then Liam's whining, soaring threnody begins. But while the pay-off line is delivered with plenty of push, it's melodically not really there. And the lyric, instead of appearing as witty as it should ('D'ya know what I mean' is as ubiquitous in contemporary conversational English as 'actually' used to be), comes across as tired, threadbare. It all sounded alarmingly like the jangly, happy-time strumming associated with that late lamented (not) British subgenre: pub rock.

But no matter what I think of the music, there's a transcendent quality about Oasis. Noel Gallagher's songs, with their freightage of solipsistic, adolescent *aperçus,* are somehow the glass bricks of the *Zeitgeist;* the great screaming walls of guitar noise they're embedded in are as timeless as Sumerian ziggurats.

Before I got my hands on *Be Here Now,* I spent two weeks swooping around the crowded streets of London in a large turbocharged saloon equipped with a serious sound system. 'Shakermaker', 'Cigarettes & Alcohol', 'Live Forever' and 'Wonderwall'—all the 'classics', cranked up to the hilt. At times I felt as if the entire car were some vibrating puck being slammed around on a rink of guitar reverb. At times I felt carried away by it all, certain that I was in the refracted presence of genius; but at other times I felt buried beneath the dead, composting weight of pop decadence.

One minute the music is stirring me and all I want to do is wassail with the lads in a local blizzard of cocaine, under a heavy rain of Jack Daniel's and Coca-Cola; the next I'm finding the relentless harping on four chords a pain in the neck, and the posturing a pain in the arse.

Oasis sound best to me when I'm in a bad, self-indulgent mood ('I need to be myself/I can't be no one else'), when I'm rattling down the road intent on the stacked deck life has dealt me, and how no one understands. Then, the proscenium of crashing guitar chords that frame a ditty like 'Don't Look Back in Anger' capture a tale of pure, unalloyed romanticism. At moments like that, the plangent non-sequiturs of Noel Gallagher's lyrics sound almost Confucian: 'I'll start a revolution from my bed/'Cause you said the brains I had went to my head'. And the slight references to some kind of shared nationality, which the argot-heavy lyrics of Oasis are studded with (a 'morning glory' is the bladder-stoppered wake-up call of a hard-on), can wrench a salt of sentimentality from my baggy old eye.

Liam Gallagher, with his birth date comfortably rooted in the seventies, isn't so much post-punk as entirely post-modern. And Oasis are the first global rock band to have their musical sensibilities defined within an atemporal sonic garden, free from the seasons of cultural change and the tempests of social revolution. Though ostensibly Brit-pop, the Gallagher brothers are actually second-generation Irish immigrants. Their musical sensibilities were formed as much by informal family ceilidhs in County Mayo as by the nihilistic antics of the Sex Pistols. Much has been made of the band's affinity with all things Beatle: they've always aimed to outshine their trichological forefathers; they've covered 'I Am the Walrus'; they're not immune to the harmonies; and—most importantly—there's something about the northwestern English accent, whether Mancunian or Liverpudlian, that makes it particularly suitable for shouting the blues. But the truth is that the actual psychodynamic of Oasis owes far more to their poncy, aspirant-bohemian, southern progenitors—the original Satanic Majesties. Indeed: it's Jagger all over again.

D'YOU KNOW WHAT I MEAN?

Like the Rolling Stones, Oasis are a five-piece with an ineffably sexually charismatic frontman. Like the Stones, Oasis thrive on the psychosexual tension between their lead guitarist/songwriter and their froutman/style guru. In the case of Oasis, this is further cranked up by consanguinity. You only have to imagine what it might be like to hear your little brother singing about your sexual and emotional experiences to understand why songs like 'Wonderwall' and 'Don't Look Back in Anger' have such astonishing emotional resonance.

To push the psychoanalysis still further, if there is any parallel between Oasis and the Beatles, it's in the personalities of John Lennon and Liam Gallagher. Both endured difficult childhoods; both suffered the concomitant dislocation of self. Noel Gallagher has described his brother as 'living in his own little world', and averred that the essential effect of stardom has been to intensify the obliqueness of baby bro's relationship with sanity. I don't think you necessarily have to resort to pathologising or crude psychobabble in order to classify Liam Gallagher as a borderline personality; all things considered, it's a poetic judgement.

But unlike Lennon, the Gallagher brothers have never allowed themselves to be straitjacketed by the exigencies of commerce and image. Lennon was driven by cravenness to embrace his (initial) characterisation as lovable, void of class and (for the most part) of sexuality. The Gallagher brothers are inextricably linked to their working-class origins. To understand how important this is, as an American reader, you have to appreciate just how rigid British class distinctions still are.

In Britain, you can make the ascent from working to middle class in one generation, but you can't top out at the summit. If you have any kind of strong regional accent, you can't possibly be pukka. In Britain the industrial proletariat, particularly in the north, has long formed a masculine horde that on Saturday afternoons is dedicated to the fervent worship of soccer.

One of the most moving passages in Paolo Hewitt's procrustean biography of the band comes when Noel describes what these Saturday afternoons were like. The dads would leave their sons by the side of an enormous barrier that ran the length of the stands, while they sloped off to the bar. The Gallagher brothers sat there irradiated by the sound and colour that is a British soccer match in full cry. And then the singing would begin. It's this soccer-crowd bellowing that provides the strongly anthemic feel of so many Oasis tracks: they are purpose-built for mass chanting.

Another important part of the Oasis aesthetic—or anti-aesthetic—that comes direct from soccer culture is their 'casual' fashion stance. The Casuals were the lineal successors of the Mod aesthetic of the late sixties and early seventies who gained their inspiration from chain-store standardisation. Oasis, with their off-the-peg windcheaters and sloppy training shoes or sneakers, exemplify a bizarre hinterland between the amphetamine-fuelled dancers of all-night soul raves and the razor-toting hooligans who blighted British soccer matches in the eighties.

This, in a nutshell (with a healthy dose of whoring, drugging and wholesale bad behaviour), is the post-everything, post-label character of Oasis. This is why, with their hotel-room trashing and sibling pummelling and record-company baiting, they are so deliciously and deliriously iconic.

And the evidence bears this out: in the United Kingdom, *Definitely Maybe,* the band's debut album, sold 100,000 copies in the first four days of its release; by the end of that year it had topped three-quarters of a million. The second album, *What's the Story (Morning Glory)?,* has sold more copies in the UK than any Beatles album—and gone twelve times platinum. Last year's mammoth gigs at Knebworth achieved a ludicrous, overcapacity attendance of 250,000. Pre-sales of the new album (and the new single 'D'You Know What I Mean?') are among the highest for any band ever. Who knows what sort of business *Be Here Now* will drum up. The mind boggles.

D'YOU KNOW WHAT I MEAN?

The assignment finally came to bed late last night during another visit to the Groucho. I'd stopped in for a drink, not in search of Oasis, but it transpired that Liam Gallagher was in the club again. He sauntered past me huddled up in his hood, flanked by discreetly tough and manifestly casual bodyguards. Patsy was nowhere to be seen. Liam was with a close friend who's also an acquaintance of mine. 'What's the story?' I asked. 'Oh, nothing really. I think Liam's leaving—there was a bit of bother at Ronnie Scott's earlier on.' Apparently, there'd been a showcase for another Creation Records band and Liam had been in an ugly mood. 'Do the two of you still go to Browns any more?' 'Nah—he was barred from there months ago. He just can't seem to behave.' My inner-circle friend walked away through the thicket of drinkers with their burning tobacco foliage.

I asked one of the club managers whether Liam was still in the building. 'No,' she snapped. 'And I hope we never see him again—he's a pain in the arse!' How the Mighty was beginning to lose his burnish. And this just a day after Noel had made another of his legendarily contentious remarks in an interview with the *New Musical Express*.

It had been in response to the question 'Do you think that Oasis are more important to the youth of today than God?' 'I would have to say,' he averred, 'without a shadow of doubt that that is true.' There it was—the final act of Beatle-aspirant blasphemy. Noel also spoke to the *NME* about the new album. He said he was increasingly interested in studio-based work, and had been hanging out with Goldie, the flamboyant British jungle star and mix-down supremo. Together they twiddle knobs, sample things and twist rhythms out of the mixing desk.

This may be the future for the band's creative powerhouse. If Oasis are going to develop a career anything like that of their fellow gods (the three other band members no one ever mentions are sort of clandestine demi-gods), Noel will need to sop up some profoundly new and eclectic source material. And at the moment, techno, drum 'n' bass and all that other computer-generated dance music are certainly what Britain does best.

Gallagher seems particularly vulnerable to accusations that his band hasn't evolved. In truth, when *Be Here Now* finally arrived—this afternoon—some of these anxieties proved justified. Suitably enough, I was listlessly hanging out at the elegant, high-bohemian townhouse of Blur's Damon Albarn and Elastica's Justine Frischmann when the courier knocked on the door. Only half of the Other Couple was in residence at the time. Justine unleashed a fairly pithy volley of her own at the Manchester men and their music. 'Utterly derivative' and 'They aren't even trying' were some of her less purple points.

The new tracks I listened to didn't exactly drive me wild, either. But then again, I wasn't in a bad, self-pitying mood. 'Stand By Me' repeats familiar anthemic patterns; on 'My Big Mouth', Noel offers his own, honed, second me-generation apophthegms: 'I'll have my way/I'll have my say', and so on. Elsewhere some McCartneyesque emotional insight is groped for, when Noel—through his mouthpiece—gives the trenchant advice 'Get your shit together, girl' over a background of softly jangling guitars. Predictably this ditty is entitled 'The Girl in the Dirty Shirt'. Presumably, unlike McCartney and Noel, she can't afford a new one. The mix itself is a bit more adventurous: NWA samples, backward noises, and psychedelic guitar accompany the title track, even as we're once again preached a cliché.

I don't know if *Be Here Now* will do everything its creators hope for. I'll have to hear it on a tinny radio while waiting at a sandwich counter before I crack that egg. I do have sympathy for these potentially vulnerable young men and their wives. They are locked into a considerable whirlpool of hype and scrutiny. The British press can be deceitful, vicious and unscrupulous. The Gallaghers' harassment has epitomised this: non-stop paparazzi, total stake-out.

D'YOU KNOW WHAT I MEAN?

But as far as their image and their music are concerned, I can only echo the words of another British bad boy of rock 'n' roll, Pete Townshend; I really do hope—in terms of the intense tradition they represent—they die before they get old.

Details, September 1997

The Lenders

The Lenders live behind the wainscotting of the house. They are small, human figures, perfectly proportioned. Both men and women wear serious business suits and glasses. They are quiet and purposive and have built a network of open-plan offices behind the wainscotting. Here they keep track of all the things they have lent to the people who live in the house.

The children of the house are up early watching Saturday morning television. Cartoons in fact. The smallest child has a toy rabbit she's particularly fond of. She goes to the kitchen to help herself to a glass of apple juice from the fridge. The Lenders appear from behind the fridge. One of them has a clipboard, and reading from it informs the child that they lent her the rabbit. They take it away from her and disappear with it into the wainscotting. Tragic and disturbing image of rabbit being pulled into mouse-hole.

The child, crying, goes to wake her parents, and tells them what has happened. The mother urges the father to get up and deal with it. He does so—with ill grace. He goes with the child back to the kitchen, and there, by the fridge, meets with the Lenders. They consult their clipboard again, then pull a small VDU out from the wainscotting. The father bends down so that he can read this. The Lenders inform him that the money he used to buy the toy rabbit was in fact lent by them. The father disputes this—although he is warned that the consequences of doing so may be disastrous. He puts the youngest child back on the sofa in front of the television, assuring her that he will get the rabbit back.

Cut to bank. The father is being shown in to see the duty manager. The father explains about the Lenders and demands proof from the manager that the money he used to buy the toy rabbit was lent to him by the bank. The manager is smooth and emollient, but confesses that although this was the case, the money the bank lent was actually lent to the bank by . . . the Lenders. Some Lenders appear on the manager's desk at this point, complete with direct computer link to the father's house. Once again the relevant figures are perused by all parties, and the origin of the loan is incontrovertibly proved.

Meanwhile, back at the house, the mother is having difficulty getting up and facing the day. She keeps pulling the duvet back over her head, despite the children who come into her bedroom and importune her to rise and make their breakfast. The Lenders appear, shinning up the side of the bed, and parley with her on the pillow. They explain that the resistance she feels is a result of her having drawn too heavily on her stock of motherhood. She has exceeded her motherhood overdraft.

How, the mother asks, can she repay this, so that she will be able to tend her own children? The Lenders suggest that she mother *them* a bit—this will help. The Lenders strip off so that she may suckle them. This she does, sitting upright in bed, opening her nightdress and placing one adult homunculus on each breast. Her own, neglected children wail and yammer.

Inside the wainscotting, the other Lenders have set the toy rabbit up in a bizarre temple, and are worshipping it as a deity of childhood. The rabbit smiles down on them benignly.

In another chamber in the interstices of the house, more Lenders are 'playing'. They have stripped naked and are swinging on a kind of Newton's cradle, their bodies taking the place of the ball-bearings. As they swing back and forth, banging into each other, they effect penetration in all the obvious combinations.

The father arrives home from the bank disconsolate, and goes to cuddle the frightened children on the sofa, in front of the still-gabbling cartoons. The children tell him about the mother. He races upstairs and finds in the bedroom a grotesque scene. The numbers of Lenders have swollen, and there is a press of them around the mother. Some are naked, others half-dressed, others still are clothed and pushing from the back of the seething, diminutive mob. The mother gives the father a piteous look.

The father rounds on the Lenders and demands to see their management. The management appear from the wainscotting. They are more heavily-built, more serious-looking and more purposive than the other Lenders. The Lenders who have been jostling to be suckled by the mother leave off and gather themselves together, begin dressing.

The father points out to the management the obvious: where did they obtain the money and the motherhood, the credit of which they extended to the family? There is a frozen moment—the Lenders' bluff has been called. Our POV goes back into the wainscotting. The wainscotting, of course, has its own more diminutive wainscotting, and from behind this come the Lenders' Lenders.

Our POV has the micro-bit between its teeth now, and we plunge on into the wainscotting of the Lenders' Lenders, and meet their Lenders. We shrink down each successive stage until we get to the molecular structure of Lenders, the building-blocks of the Lender cosmos. These consist of many many particular men and women, dressed in sober suits, sitting at desks, and joined to one another in the manner of models of molecules by connective rods. Occasionally a free-ranging electron of a Lender will come barrelling out of the void and attack one of these molecular assemblages of Lenders, displacing one from his or her desk and forcing a reconfiguration of the molecular model. It is a harsh and pitiless scene.

We focus in on the desk of one of these molecular Lenders. They are doodling a sketch of the toy rabbit. We fade out on the smile of the sketch of the toy rabbit.

Video treatment for Massive Attack, 1995

Bona Morrissey

It's a well-known fact about Morrissey that his record contracts stipulate various wacky, star-like things. One of them is the presence of certain, very particular kinds of snack food in any interview context. So it is that the first thing that meets my eye when I enter the penthouse boardroom of RCA Records is a table, laid with plates of crisps (plain, or so I've read) and some KitKats; to one side are bottles of pop.

At the outset Morrissey is drinking a cup of coffee, and during our discussion he occasionally elides his way out of anything remotely resembling an impasse by alluding to these eatables, 'This is such great coffee,' he pronounces at one point, and when I ask him what's on his mind he replies, 'This KitKat.'

These are just the sort of tropes that Morrissey comes up with from minute to minute, turning phrases as he does, like rotating signs outside petrol stations. Morrissey is for many people irredeemably associated with the eighties—and even to say this brings that decade into sharper focus. In the eighties a particular kind of male adolescent angst and self-pity infused the *Zeitgeist,* and Morrissey was its avatar. He was the first male pop star to address a whole generation of boys who were growing up with feminism, a heavy underscoring to a period of natural inadequacy and uselessness.

His miserablism came from that archetypally grim, ravaged provincial city Manchester, where, cut off from a supporting popular culture with any remotely intellectual element, or political undercurrent, Morrissey forged the Smiths, the pop band who were to be the spokesmen for the Miserablists, and penned their anthem 'Heaven Knows I'm Miserable Now'.

Morrissey's hipness and artistry were always wedded to an exquisite taste for the most subtle kitsch of the recent English past, and slathered in Yank-worship. But mixed in with all this came his ambiguous campery, and a version of necrophile teen-death obsession that drew more from Cocteau's *Orphée* than from 'Leader of the Pack'. This veritable ragout of source material forged a strong and compulsively watchable performer, a paradoxical inversion of his just as alienated, but far less able, fans and imitators.

Suited darkly, booted sturdily, and wearing one of those jerseyesque shirts that almost define the retro-committed, Morrissey is very attractive in the flesh. The deeply-set blue eyes coruscate from beneath a high, intelligent brow, and given his self-professed celibacy one of the first things any conscientious interviewer does is to try and assess the quality of his physical presence, his essential heft.

Is this a man tortured by his own sexuality and that of others? Is this a man about whom there lingers a faint scent of fleshly revulsion? No, on both counts. His handshake is firm, warm even. His body language is far from craven. Indeed, there is something quite affectingly embodied about him. At one point in our conversation he commented on my face: 'You've actually got the face of a criminal who I've met . . . A very strong face. A very determined face.' Setting aside the content of this remark, it struck me that this was not the sort of thing that someone who is intent on denying corporeality would be likely to say.

And of course, while his well-publicised encouragement of the excessive—and physical—devotion of his fans has a double-edged quality about it—you can touch, but only in this contrived, aberrant way—in person he lampoons his own self-created shibboleths, again and again and again. When I suggest to him that stage invasions puncture the meniscus of stardom, and confront him with fans who are 98 per cent water, he replies, 'Let it be punctured, let it be punctured, that's my motto.'

The following week at Wembley Arena, the star goes so far towards puncturing the meniscus that he almost bodily hauls a would-be stage-invader through the arms of the bouncers, past the rank of monitors, and into his arms. He receives kisses on both cheeks as no more than his due. He also bends down into the thicket of arms waving towards him, and as much takes as gives out the benediction.

There's a submerged incongruity here, but one that works in his favour. Perhaps one of the central ironies about this most ironic of performers is that he clearly seeks adulation from those most indisposed to give it—the Dagenham Daves and Rusholme Ruffians who people his songscapes—and eschews the advances of those who regard his talent as essentially po- etic. When I ask him if he's ever been attracted to the world of the intelligentsia, he is emphatic: 'Absolutely not. In fact, scorn is perhaps all I feel really. I feel quite sad for such people. I think that everything there is to be lived is hanging round the gutter somewhere. I've always believed that and still do.'

Which rather raises the question, exactly how much hang- ing round the gutter is involved in researching his marvellously deadpan little word pictures? He mentions 'certain pubs around north and east London. But I'm not the sort of person you're likely to spot, because I don't go about wanting to be noticed . . . I'm just slipping in and slipping out, and if you were look- ing for me you'd never find me.' A nice echo of the demonic wail contained in 'Speedway', the closing track of last year's *Vauxhall & I:* 'All of the rumours keeping me grounded/I never said that they were completely unfounded'.

Schiller made the distinction between the 'naïve' artist, who works through a cathartic and direct outpouring of creative imagination, and the 'sentimental' artist, who is compelled to intellectualise all he produces. I take it that Morrissey's preoccupation with 'loafing oafs in all-night chemists' is a willed attempt by his sentimental side to indulge his naïve capacities. For he is that most unusual of artists—both naïve and sentimental.

He tells me that performance for him represents 'exuberance', and when I tax him that this goes somewhat against his self-styled anti-fun posture, he grins and admits it. That being said, Morrissey's idea of post-gig kicks is not exactly what we expect from a pop star: 'Just pure silence. A quiet read. Just me. A locked door. Absolute silence.' I found this attitude refreshing, but it did act as a springboard for Morrissey to trot out some of his more *passé* attitudinising about life: 'Life's incredibly boring. I don't say that in an effort to seem vaguely amusing, but the secret of life is that there's no secret, it's just exceedingly boring.'

I got the feeling that these kinds of sallies are a form of bluff for Morrissey, and that he throws them out in much the way that aircraft in World War II dropped strips of metal to fool radar. If his interlocutors rise to such chaff—then they're not really worthy of consideration. But he's also an adept at side-stepping the conventional psychoanalytic thrusts of the interviewer. He manages this by a complex sleight of personality that is fascinating to observe.

When I mention the 'vexed question' of his sexuality, he replies, 'It doesn't vex me. I don't exactly think it vexes other people at all. People have their opinions and I don't mind what they are. I mean there's a limit to what people can actually assume about sexuality, and at least I'm relieved by that. I don't think people assume anything any more about me. I'm sort of classified in a non-sexual, asexual way, which is an air of dismissiveness which I quite like.'

The interesting thing about this speech is, of course, that the exact opposite is the truth: it *does* vex people, he *does* mind, there are *no* limits to what people can assume about sexuality (which is far from being a relief); and it is he himself who has struck the asexual attitude.

Perhaps it would be too trite to suggest that the plaintive refrain of 'The Teachers Are Afraid of the Pupils', the lead track on his latest album, *Southpaw Grammar,* is in some way an echo of this posture: 'To be finished would be a relief,' the singer proclaims, again and again and again.

The sting really comes when I say, 'Do you think you've pulled that one off?' And with another smile he replies, 'Yeah. Quite well. I think the skill has paid off quite well. I've managed to slip through the net—whatever the net is.' Then there's a neat little bit of wordplay, analogous in the Morrissey idiolect to a boxer's centre-ring shuffle. I interject, 'But—' and he overrides me: 'I know you're about to say "but", but so am I. It's not really an issue, there's nothing to say, and there's nothing to ask, more to the point.'

He's right. Unless I choose to be a boor and attempt to crash into his private existence, there really is nothing to ask. This is the 'skill' that Morrissey has perfected, and it's a skill that in anyone else would be described quite simply as maturity.

Yes, that's the only revelation I have to give you about Steven Patrick Morrissey: he is, against all odds, a grown-up. How exactly he has managed this growing up it's hard to tell. The potted biography gives the impression of a direct transferral from air guitar in front of a suburban Manchester mirror, to air guitar in front of hysterical crowds at the Hacienda. followed by thirteen years of—albeit anomalous—stardom. Where exactly did he find those normal interactions, those normal relationships, necessary to effect maturation?

Of course, it's no secret in the business that his 'no touch' persona bears little relation to a man who closely guards his close friendships; and quite clearly something *is* going on here. It was once said of Edward Heath that if he did have sex at all, it was only in a locked vault in the Bank of England. I don't wish to speculate about whether or not Morrissey has sex, but if he does I think it's fairly safe to assume that the 'locked vault' is a function of two things: an unswerving dedication to maintaining a genuine private life; and a capability for generating immense personal loyalty—a loyalty vault, if you will.

When we discuss the notion of camp, which informs so much of his artistic sensibility, right down to the title of one of his solo albums, *Bona Drag* ('bona' meaning attractive or sexy in Polari, the secret gay argot), he veers off into *The Kenneth Williams Diaries:* 'It was quite gruesome, quite gruesome. I've read it a couple of times and each time it's been like a hammer on the head. An astonishingly depressing book. It's incredibly witty and well done, but the hollow ring it has throughout is murderous, absolutely murderous.'

I tax him that some people might view his life as being a bit like that, and he replies, 'It's not. It definitely isn't,' with a deeply-felt emphasis. So deep that I'm moved to put to him the possibility of the most extreme contrast to Williams's life of emotional and sexual barrenness: 'Have you ever considered having children?' 'Yeah,' he says, flatly, in his burring Mancunian voice.

When we tease out this issue, it becomes apparent that what bothers him about having kids is to do with his—quite legitimate—fear of overidentification with them: 'I wonder what they'd do. I mean, what do they do when they're eleven? What would they do when they were seventeen? . . . What happens when your child turns round and says, "Look, I don't like this world. Why did you bring me into it? I don't want to be a part of it. I'm not leaving home, I'm staying here, I refuse to grow up"?'

But if there are shades of his own (allegedly) willed infantility here, also discernible are the lineaments of grown-up Morrissey, Morrissey whose 'skill' has served him well. He seems to understand only too well the impact of the ambiguous images he has created, and the even more ambiguous images they have spawned.

Morrissey, it became apparent to me, is someone who finds his love for other people painful and overpowering. In this he is, of course, like all of us. He has given up on his favourite soap *Coronation Street,* but when discussing its replacement in his affections, *EastEnders,* he lets slip a yearning for a very populated, very unmiserable Arcadia: 'I think people wish that life really was like that, that we couldn't avoid seeing forty people every day who we spoke to, who knew everything about us, and that we couldn't avoid being caught up in these relationships all the time, and that there was somebody standing on the doorstep throughout the day. I think that's how we'd all secretly like to live. Within *EastEnders,* within *Coronation Street,* there are no age barriers. Senior citizens, young children, they all blend, and they all like one another and they all have a great deal to say, which isn't how life is.'

Perhaps here the complex mask of ritual, signs, signals and cultural references Morrissey has devised, to obliterate the very non-contrived human character beneath, slips a little, but I'd be wary of pushing it. To me he says, 'I wish somebody would get it right. I don't mind if they hate me as long as they get it right.' And yet 'getting it right' would be wholly destructive for the imago, if liberating for the man.

Throughout the solo career there has been a strenuous conflation of the notion of 'Englishness' with that of a camp, Ortonesque liking for 'rough lads'. Is Morrissey like William Burroughs, I wonder, possessed of an eternal faith in the 'goodness' of these rough lads? Is this atmosphere, so vividly captured in *Southpaw Grammar,* one he sees as an Arcadia, or merely one of nostalgia?

'It's pure nostalgia, really, and there's very little truth in it. I'm well aware of that. I know that it's all pure fantasy really, and 50 per cent drivel. Everybody has their problems and there is no way of being that is absolutely free and fun-loving and without horrific responsibilities. It just isn't true. And I think I've had the best of it personally. I don't think I'm missing anything because I'm not a roofer from Ilford.'

Did we really expect anything else? Every alleged 'Arcadian' image Morrissey produces is in reality shot through with irony. The eponymous hero of 'Boy Racer' is described thus: 'Stood at the urinal/He thinks he's got the whole world in his hands'. And as for poor Dagenham Dave: 'Head in a blouse/Everyone loves him/I see why'. Yes indeed! But then, by the same token: 'He'd love to touch, he's afraid he might self-combust/I could say more, but you get the general idea'.

The implication being one of what? Chronically repressed homosexuality? Or merely the singer's own *taedium vitae* in the face of the exhausted husk of English working-class culture? The rubric here is one of subversion, subversion and more subversion. This is most graphically shown when Morrissey, thirty-six and rising, comes on stage at Wembley Arena, with his somewhat younger-looking fellow musicians. It's either *Happy Days* with Morrissey as the Fonz and the vaguely bat-eared guitarist as Richie, or else something altogether more sinister.

The backcloth is a giant projection of the cover of *Southpaw Grammar,* the face of an obscure boxer which Morrissey himself plucked from the anonymity of an old issue of *The Ring.* There's a wheeze and a creak from the massive bunches of speakers dangling overhead, and 'Jerusalem' starts up, being sung by some long-gone school choir. The effect, in tandem with the suited, cropped figures striding about the dark stage, is extremely unsettling. Is this the start of some weird Fascist rally?

Then the band crash into the opening chords of 'Reader Meets Author', and Morrissey begins to flail at the air with the cord of his microphone, pirouetting, hip-swivelling, for all the world like some camp version of Roy Rogers. He'd be run out of the British National Party in seconds if they caught him swishing about like this! Once again he has subverted the political in a peculiarly personal way.

Later on in the set, Morrissey and the band perform the dark and extremely depressing song 'The Operation'. Like many of his lyrics, this one is addressed to an unnamed person. Morrissey must be one of the few songwriters who uses the second person more than the first. 'You fight with your right hand,' he yodels, 'and caress with your left'—and as he joins up the couplet he wipes the arse of the air with a limp hand.

This is presumably what he means by 'Southpaw Grammar': and the manifest and ongoing preoccupation with 'the other' in his work is so antithetical to his posture of bedsit isolation that I wonder again just how truly protean a person this is? To me he says, 'I don't feel trapped in your tape recorder and on those CDs. I don't at all. I can do whatever I like and I can become whatever I like, and if next week I want to have thirteen children and live in Barking, then I can and I will, and nobody will stop me.'

This is all very double-edged, very southpaw. On one reading it smacks of an arrested, adolescent will-to-omnipotentiality, but on another it's an indicator of great sanity, and of a refusal to believe wholly in the imago he has created. While in his first incarnation, as the taboo-busting frontman of the Smiths, Morrissey was prone to using his platform for issuing diktats on all manner of issues unrelated to popular music, his fame now appears to have been well worn in, like a favourite old overcoat.

He confirms this when I ask him how he manages to keep such tight control over the empire he has created: 'I only manage it by repeatedly saying "no". And then the obvious reputation gathers around you that you are a problem, because you are awkward, you are difficult, and you don't really want

180

to be famous. But I just don't want to be famous in any way other than that which naturally suits me.'

I wonder what's going to happen to Morrissey. Among the trainspotters of the music press, his break with Johnny Marr, his songwriting partner in the Smiths, has been insistently viewed as a creative death for him. Yet some of the solo material he has recorded is just as strong as anything they ever did together—and by the same token, who outside the music press has heard much about Johnny Marr in the past five years?

My hunch is that he may well find pop iconic status becoming an increasing drag. He is a very funny man to be with, but he keeps his wit well reined in. Just one example of this comes when we dissect the 'vexed question' of my not having a television. 'Is that a political statement?' he asks, and when I say it is, he rejoins, 'Do all your neighbours know that you don't possess a television set?'

I think the wit is reined in because it's so destructive of the ironic edifice he has created. Stardom requires a certain kind of stupidity to sustain it, and Morrissey is far from being a stupid man. He is responsible for—among other things—encapsulating two hundred years of philosophical speculation in a single line: 'Does the mind rule the body, or the body rule the mind, I don't know.'

His ambitions as an artist clearly don't require him to feed the Moloch of celebrity with more creative babies. He once memorably sang, castigating yet another of his shadowy others for their sexual peccadilloes, 'On the day when your mentality/ Catches up with your biology'. But I think the comparable day of reckoning for Morrissey will come when he allows his sense of humour to catch up with his irony.

Even at Wembley Arena it looked as if the band had invited their uncle to come along and do a turn with them. Morrissey has too acute a view of himself—one hopes—to become one of those grandads of pop, perambulating around the stage in support hose, permanently marooned in some hormonal stretch limo. He told me he could 'do anything'; I certainly hope he can. England needs him.

Observer, November 1995

Vagabond: Marianne Faithfull

There's nothing much crasser in life than being told by someone, shortly after you've met them: 'You really remind me of so-and-so . . .' It's bad enough if this aide-mémoire is someone well known to your interlocutor, but far, far worse if it's someone famous. When I was in my early twenties people used to tell me with monotonous regularity that I 'really reminded them' of Pete Townshend; disregarding entirely the fact that inch for inch you could have extruded at least three of the wiry axeman from my lanky frame. It drove me up the wall; reducing—as it did—the unique harmony of my features to his beaky ubiquity. One of the few conceivable beneficial side effects of notoriety that I can imagine would be to discover that Townshend is now afflicted by people who inform him that he really reminds them of me.

But how inconceivably worse it must be for Marianne Faithfull, who, at fifty-two, still resolutely resembles herself. For Faithfull is the very quintessence of notoriety—she's the twentieth-century icon conceived as a supporting role for a composite personality. She's the photofit picture of intimacy itself. The ultimate rock chick, she was a proto–wild child who bedded the most feral of them. Swelegantly squired through the sixties by Keith Richards and Mick Jagger, she ended up shooting smack on the Soho streets in the seventies; and over the last twenty years she's clawed her way back to become the thinking person's femme fatale, a gravel voiced chanteuse whose poignant readings of her own material—as well as the sorrowful standards—have earned her a top billing at the fin de siècle cabaret.

So it hardly seemed suitable to tell her that she really reminded me of my friend Maria. It was in the husky intimacy of her voice, the readiness of her wit and the vulnerability of her crooked elbows when set beside the theatricality of her spread hands. Like Maria, Marianne has a tendency to slide into an arch, Grande Dame-ish tone; but invariably, comments which begin to describe parabolas of pretension are then shot down by rasping laughter, or still more abrasive coughs—for both of them are steady smokers. And like Maria, Marianne is clever, well-read, engaged—everything you could want in a lunch companion.

In truth, I didn't hit upon the Maria resemblance until some time after I'd met Marianne for lunch, because while I was with her she was so much herself that I found myself gulled into the sense that I in fact did know her really well. Marianne was good enough to say that she felt the same way about me—but I wasn't convinced. Indeed, in retrospect I wonder whether her ability to make me experience her as so familiar is not the very essence both of what made her famous and what made her so vulnerable to that ghastly notoriety.

There's that, and there's also the fact that she is a perfect composite character for me to know. If I'd had the opportunity to order up an older, wiser sister for myself from celestial central casting, it would be Marianne. The outsider's upbringing in the suburbs of Reading—her mother a doubly-exiled Austrian aristocrat, her father an errant idealist—has given her a Janus-faced take on Little England. The long sojourn in the Bermuda Triangle of rock stardom has brought a warped insight into the foibles of the egoist; and then, of course, there were the drugs.

If I'd met Marianne twenty years ago I'm sure we'd have been talking highs and lows the way druggies do; but this being

1999 we talk recovery: the virtues of twelve step programmes, vitamins, therapy, acupuncture, friends, isolation and routine. Yet even while discussing these most mature of considerations, there's a mercurial, capricious character about Marianne which won't go away. Intimacy and immediacy—the dramatic synergy so slickly and falsely imparted by narcotics—are qualities that she has written into her character the way 'Brighton' is through rock.

So it was that I found myself utterly seduced by Marianne, reluctant to bother her with tiresome questions, content to talk far too much about myself, and indeed say anything which would provoke more of her fantastic gravelly guffaws. Of course, I had met her before—as a logical pairing we've crossed paths on the publicity circuit—but even so, as she came barrelling across the restaurant I was struck anew by the force of her beauty.

Her face bears the self-inflicted scars of a woman who's been driven to slice away at the looks which have masked her soul. 'An angel with big tits' is how Andrew Loog Oldham, the upper-class thug manager of the Rolling Stones, once crassly described her; and it's easy to imagine how myriad remarks such as this might have forced her to a self-mastectomy as well as the suicide by a thousand cuts of heroin addiction. She has all of that beauty still, but it's now annealed by the hard times. The once ethereal girl has been pressed between the panes of life, and as time has coursed by she's the figurehead that's weathered it.

She was dressed entirely in black: black jacket, black T-shirt, black skirt, black stockings and black shoes. The black clothes suggested restraint—the stockings a lack of. While we spoke her accent moved between haute-bourgeois and mockney as she adjusted its tone with the subtle modulations of a virtuoso trombonist. 'Fucking' was used principally adjectivally; 'darling' mostly in lieu of the second person singular; truly, her presence was the essence of the demi monde.

Initially I'd regretted arranging to meet her at the Ivy restaurant in Covent Garden, for this eatery is like the green room of celebrity itself, so often are famous faces getting filled there. Yet, as Marianne hailed a selection of those she recognised—the artists Sam Taylor-Wood and Peter Blake; the actors William Shawn and Jonathan Kent—I realized that this was more or less the ideal circumstance within which to view her: in amongst the cavalcade.

Yet while Marianne was in it—'I must go and say hello to him, he's a great friend . . .'—with the bluebird tattooed prominently on her left hand, in the approved, criminal fashion, she was clearly not of it. In England for three weeks to promote her new album *Vagabond Ways* and perform two concerts of Kurt Weill songs with the London Symphony Orchestra, she was staying not at some stylish hotel ('I couldn't afford to anyway'), but with Anita Pallenberg, with whom she's still great friends. One of the songs on the album, called 'File it Under Fun' is about long-term friendships and to me Marianne said 'I don't see discard as an option, to give me credit I really try not to discard people.'

Nor do they try and discard her. When it came up that she'd sung a song from the album at the Royal Albert hall memorial concert for Linda McCartney I asked Marianne if she'd known her well: 'I didn't know her well, but she made my friend very happy, that's the main thing . . . Paul and Linda were living their own life, you didn't see them at parties or things . . . but when I was really fucked up they were so kind, not overly understanding . . . but on my side. She was a decent woman really.'

Marianne's rock 'n' roll friends are set to be portrayed in a film of her autobiography (*Faithfull*), which is due to commence shooting this summer. 'This is my big shot,' she told me, 'I can buy my house in Dublin, although I know there's all sorts of things that can go wrong . . .' Nevertheless, in anticipation of being portrayed she'd been to see the putative

'Marianne', Cate Blanchett, who's currently appearing in 'Plenty'. 'She's a big girl,' Marianne purred 'I didn't realise how tall she is.' I demurred, saying I'd met Blanchett and she was, in fact, a wee thing. Marianne pressed on: 'She did look very tall to me—anyway, she's a lovely strong girl, I think she's very beautiful—she's my first choice.'

Beautiful Blanchett may be, however this is no piece of type-casting, the actor is the complete reverse of Loog Oldham's definition of Marianne: she's a small-breasted woman with her feet firmly on the ground. Marianne is finely divided about her own ravaged looks; when, late on in our talk I referred to the forthcoming film again, she thought I was asking whether she still had any acting ambitions, and re-plied 'I don't think I've got a chance in movies because of the way I look . . .' thus simultaneously acknowledging her beauty and its transfiguration.

Her father died a year ago and remembering him drags Marianne back into the purlieus of her eccentric upbringing. Her father had been an intelligence officer during the war and in the fifties he began a commune. 'I went down to the com-mune to see him, he'd had a heart attack which stripped away his defences. He kept saying "Oh my poor love" whenever I came into the room and bursting into tears.' Had they always been close? 'He was the great unrequited love of my life, but when he was dying I was able to ask him these questions—and he answered them. He told me about some of the things he'd seen in the war and it was clear that he'd been terribly traumatised. He came back a committed pan-European, de-termined to help prevent it happening again.'

Major Glynn Faithfull set up something he termed the 'School for Integrative Social Research' but the Baroness Eva von Sacher-Masoch, the high-toned war bride he'd brought back with him, turned out to be non-integrable and she left the commune, taking the young Marianne with her. Had her father, I wondered, died fulfilled? 'No! It was a nightmare! My dear stepmother—who really helped me to get my place back at the family table—became ill with leukemia. She had to go into hospital—and they kicked him out of the commune! I mean, he did run it as if it were an autocracy, but it was a commune and they voted on it. He and my stepmother died within four weeks of each other.'

Marianne had been there to cope with her father's death, alongside her step-siblings, but despite feeling affection for them she told me 'I'm not really able to cope with a family, I mean I'm trying—' '—Trying is lying.' I thoughtlessly quoted a slogan I remembered from my days in drug rehab', but Marianne, rather than laughing, looked extremely hurt. I didn't feel inclined to raise the issue of her son Nick, who she lost custody of during her drug addiction anyway, and this reminder of the thinness of the scar tissue which covers Marianne's emotional wounds disinclined me still more.

She drank two or three hot rum toddies during lunch to try and quell the croak in her voice: 'I shouldn't be having a drink at all,' she said 'but it's a long day.' A long day of interviews and photo shoots, then the concerts with the London Symphony Orchestra, then a brief sojourn back in Ireland before the band arrives from the States to tour the new album for three weeks around Britain. 'I have to be very good on tour now, or I just can't do it.' Good on tour—and continent at home as well: 'The way I have to live is very quiet, very cool, that's part of the reason why I stay in Dublin—it would be much harder in London.'

Marianne admitted to me that following the publication of the autobiography she'd had 'quite a relapse', but she wasn't referring to heroin; that she's eschewed entirely since she cleaned up in the early eighties. Yet there's an assumed bravado about her pronouncement that 'my liver's a little delicate—I have to be careful.' Just as there is when she claims that she can maintain 'a distance' between herself and the grotesque cartoons the world continues to make of her. Clearly the distance needs to be a physical as well as a psychic one: 'I was nine years at Shell Cottage,' (her former home in the Irish countryside) 'and I was very isolated and very lonely—but it works. I learned to be more self-contained, which I really needed to do.'

There's been isolation, there's been routine, and since the release, in 1979, of the album *Broken English* there's been work—work which Marianne takes extremely seriously: 'It's very precious, it's my work so I don't want it to get fucked up by my ignorance or my arrogance.' To me she compared her gift for music to her father's ear for languages: 'he was a brilliant linguist, he could speak any European language.' Clearly she thinks of herself as an interpretive singer rather than an expressive one, yet in performance she conceded that she 'lost herself', and that the emotions were paramount for her: 'How d'you think I keep straight?' she abjured me. 'I do it by work, days and days and days of work.'

She delicately consumed some expensive lettuce leaves, and when I offered her one of my oysters she declined it as follows: 'I won't thanks—they remind me of giving head.' Endlessly assailed by others' sexual projections, she still remains in control enough to tease. Caught in her charm—the very essence of which is to make time an interloper—I wasn't so much sorry as gutted to see her go. However, there was the Albert Hall to look forward to. When I'd asked if I could come to the concert Marianne chuckled and purred: 'Of course you can—you can come and sit in my box with Anita. Stick around and have a drink afterwards.' And that was promise enough to sustain me for the intervening week.

At the Albert Hall, on the night, I found myself peculiarly nervous. I took my wife along, and bizarrely I found myself worrying that she might not enjoy the concert. Bizarrely, because it's my wife who's the fan of Faithfull's music rather than me. She'd bought the albums—I merely listened to them. Together we scrutinised the thronging audience, playing the

189

Zeitgeist game of confronting our own ageing by observing the wear of our contemporaries. This lot were so like ourselves that they all looked like people we might know; we didn't simply spot the odd acquaintance, we kept seeing three or four possible versions, composites from the past.

The allotted seats were in the body of the Hall rather than a box, although I could see Anita Pallenberg a couple of rows in front. I kept saying to my wife 'I do hope she'll get a decent crowd . . .' I realised that I was nervous both of Marianne and for her. Nervous of, because I was still suffering from the delusion that she was my New Best Friend; nervous for, because while I had thought *Vagabond Ways* as good as anything she's done to date, I couldn't quite believe that the vulnerable person I'd met in the Ivy could withstand the dark chill of the great auditorium, nor rise above the massy sound of a full symphony orchestra.

And sitting there it occurred to me that this was the strange essence of Marianne: this ability to generate in me such a fervid comingling of concern and anxiety. It's all there in the voice, which is a beautifully expressive instrument rather than an interpretive device. No wonder Marianne has chosen to sing Kurt Weill, because the half-singing, half-talking expository style his songs require is such a perfect gestalt of her own, divided nature. And in particular the song cycle 'The Seven Deadly Sins', with its 'dual' narrators, presents a twisted take on our ingrained image of the libertine woman as a succubus.

Not that my fear abated yet. The orchestra tuned up magniloquently; Carl Davis strode on and spoke grandiloquently; but would Marianne's voice be all right? Would the cough have ravaged it, or would the hot toddies have mellowed it? When she walked into the spotlight I picked over her appearance the way a forbidding and judgemental mother might: was that thigh-high slit in her formal, black skirt necessary, or even appropriate? Did she have to carry that bottle of Evian onstage with her? And what was she going to do with her glasses? But

VAGABOND: MARIANNE FAITHFULL

when she squared up to the microphone, her round belly pushed proudly forward, and her arms angled as if she were about to embark on Augean washing up duties, there was no mistaking the seriousness of her intent. And when she opened her mouth to sing, the voice emerged intact, at once harsh yet soft, intimate yet remote, beautiful yet damned.

When the gig was over Marianne's friends and acquaintances started to gather in the artists' bar. I wasn't naïve enough to imagine that I was going to be part of some little coterie, but I didn't really want to see her like this: from in amongst all the other stage door Johnnies, hoping to be burnished by association. I wanted to confine my memories of her to intimate ones, whether intimate conversation, or intimate singing. I didn't want to share her with any other Tom, Dick, Keith or Mick. And in this desire I am paradoxically, I suppose, just like all the others; because Marianne really does remind me of herself . . . alone.

Independent on Sunday,
May 2000

Tracey Emin

In life there are many different ways of getting to know someone—which is perhaps why the notional importance of first impressions is just that. There are people who insinuate themselves into your life, skulking away when you approach, tailing you from the front; and there are others who ram-raid their way into your psyche and have a rummage around to see if there's anything they can use. But these aren't the only polarities, as the intense singularity with which Tracey Emin has penetrated my life bears testimony.

Our first encounter was in 1995 at a weekend symposium, organised by a gallery owner in Amsterdam, intended to introduce the new wave of British artists—visual, literary, performing—to their Dutch counterparts. I can't imagine what induced me to attend this event—it's exactly the kind of thing I abhor; if I weren't in the business myself I'd never go near a cultural happening of any sort.

I'd had a crappy journey over, taking the Sally Line to Zeebrugge, then driving my Noddy car Citroen Diane through more low country than anyone should endure. After a hurried and testy lunch with my Dutch publisher, we went to the gallery so I could deliver my contribution: some jawing on London, J. G. Ballard and my rather nerdy enthusiasm for the interface between real and fictional topographies. The gallery was long and thin, as was the audience, all of whom were straight from central casting when the request was made for timeless, existentialist inhabitants of the inner city.

I felt a certain tension in the air as I paced around the end of the avant garde gully. It's always pretty difficult getting English satire across to the Dutch, because they have a tendency to conflate irony and slapstick. But this wasn't just the tension borne of misconception, there was definitely trouble brewing, a few mutterings, then an imprecation—Jesus! I reeled internally, I'm going to be heckled.

But I wasn't—instead I was soundly, nakedly, publically dressed down by a knock-jawed, dark, wrecked beauty of a termagant, who spat invective at me from a mouthful of teeth gone akimbo: 'Who the hell d'jew think you are anyway, Mister Will Self, swanning in here like a fucking prima donna and pushing things all around just so as you can talk this bollocks . . .' I think was the general tenor of her critique, although doubtless Tracey would dispute it. It went on for quite a while, I think we exchanged opinions with some frankness—but in truth this was one of those episodes in my life that I've heartily repressed, ducked in the fluid deep end of the psyche.

Tracey hasn't. She reminded me of it when I went to see her for this piece. And a strange thing happened; not only did I fully recall the incident—which I'd blanked—but I also realised that she had been completely justified in censuring me four years earlier. I had been behaving like a prima donna. I had swanned in to do my bit with every intention of swanning straight off again—even though I knew damn well that anarchic gigs like these demand the most rigid social conduct. It also transpired that Tracey's own performance slot had been jerked about in order to cope with my—now wilfully—late arrival.

She had me bang to rights. I thought I was behaving with icy politeness by not tearing her limb for limb; I now realise that it was Tracey who had the justification for this sort of behaviour—and that she'd been, relatively speaking, very restrained. For the rest of the weekend I made sure that our paths didn't cross, and I vowed that the next time we met it would be me who delivered the devastating character critique.

It wasn't. It was Tracey once more who got the drop on me. I had been commissioned to write and present a new cultural talk show for Channel 4, and against my better judgement agreed to do it. In truth, presenting television, rather than appearing on it as an interviewee, is to my mind wholly destructive of an artist's integrity. It requires of you that you amend your discourse in the most fundamental of ways—that you speak falsely. Now, I hadn't wanted Tracey to be on the show, because of the history we already had, but the producers were keen. Then, a few days before we were due to record, Tracey went on to a set at the Tate Gallery, in the wake of her unsuccessful nomination for the Turner Prize and drunkenly and gloriously upbraided a posse of art luminaries including Roger Scruton, the philosopher, and David Sylvester, the critic. She was smoking, she was swigging and she had an injured hand strapped into a splint. She looked like Edith Sitwell on acid.

Now Tracey was really generating what they call in the industry 'video heat'. Channel 4 were so delighted with the clip of Tracey's bibulous burblings that they aired it several more times, gaining themselves a fine from the ITC. At the time everyone seemed to think it was a marvellously subversive act, squarely within the anti-traditionalism that Tracey and the rest of the Brit art pack were espousing. My producers were now desperate to have her on. I wasn't so sure—when I'd caught glimpses of Tracey in the intervening couple of years since the Amsterdam incident I'd thought her a sad-looking figure. At openings and parties she appeared anorexic as well as pissed. I didn't like the idea of using a broadcast slot to present a pathology; what little I'd seen of her art I was inclined to dismiss as self-indulgent, poorly crafted and conceptually embarrassing.

In the green room at Horseferry Road everything seemed to be going swimmingly. Tracey still had her injured hand strapped up and she was supping away, but she was by no means pissed. 'We were all getting on really well. I was chatting away to Martin Amis and that Suzy Orbach woman, and then we went into the studio and there were all these lights and cameras, and you all began talking in this really false way, just totally unreal . . .' So she saw fit to inform us. Instead of obeying the conventions of the talk show—waiting for the slot to become vacant before inserting a carefully crafted *apercu*—Tracey broke in on us, berated us and trenchantly exposed the very nullity and irrelevance of the cultural context we were in. It was virtuoso stuff—and once again hit home.

In the wake of the recording everyone was extremely sympathetic—to me. The wounded Tracey limped off into the night. She'd done me a favour—exposing exactly what it was I feared about doing this kind of work. She'd activated my conscience—no wonder I loathed the sight of her.

On a chilly February afternoon in the East End of London it looks as if it's Tracey who can't stand the sight of me; or rather, for some minutes after she's swung open the heavy metal door of her new industrial-unit-cum-studio-cum-loft-apartment, it looks as if she can't *understand* the sight of me: 'Um, oh, right—you bin' 'ere long?' The *echt* Essex tones are moistened and damped down from last night's fun; she's in a kimono-style dressing gown, looking thin but not emaciated. Her new building is in-between Brick Lane and Commercial Road, at the very core of the Whitechapel artists' community. Tracey's boyfriend, the artist Matt Collishaw, has an adjacent space. It's an enormous gaff, a commercial unit—iron pillars, concrete floors—of about ninety feet square. Only a small bedroom and a toilet are sectioned off. There's a kitchen alcove at one end and huge, filthy windows range along both sides; implanted in them are rusty, furred extractor fans.

Light irradiates the waste of space, and Tracey's just arrived; boxed and stacked possessions appear suitably anonymous. I recognised her grandmother's chair—one of her *memento mori*, which has been rendered art with a few appliquéd words—set on a square of carpet. Next to it is a wooden truckle which contains an instruction manual for learner drivers, a video of Tony Hancock and a feng shui instructional tape. While the new tenant clomped around, making tea and adjusting to the toxic vision of a day viewed through the bottom of a glass darkly, she threw out bite-sized updates: '. . . Only bin' 'ere sixteen hours . . .', '. . . drinking last night with Matt's brothers . . .' '. . . Very convivial—but I came back 'ere at eleven so as I wouldn't wake up my first day in the new place pissed . . .' '. . . But then they came back as well . . .' '. . . Wouldn't have done an interview today if it wasn't you . . .' '. . . But it was nice drinking . . .'

Nice drinking—if you can get it. I suppose Tracey can get it now—or at least some of it. I know that she's spoken out vehemently about her stuff being secondarily sold to the egregious collector Charles Saatchi, but I also know her dealer, the formidably charming Jay Jopling, is as commercially astute in his clients' interests as he is supportive of their aspirations, perversions and emotional totality. Of Tracey he's said to me: 'She's great—just talk to her; there's so much more to her than you can imagine.'

Is there? I suppose so—and after all there's so much about Tracey that I don't have to imagine, because as well as making a cameo appearance in my own life, she has made it her sole business, since her artistic conversion in 1992, to interfuse her art and her life in order to create a form of intimate, public, confessional discourse. She is the Janeycam of the art world; a *tableau vivante* of drinking, fucking, feuding, emoting, aborting and contriving, all of which is to be carried out in the eye of the lens. Thus we know plenty about her queered Margate upbringing; her Turkish Cypriot, serial begetting father (she has eleven half-siblings); her delinquent twin brother; her underage sex; her relationships (with among others the home-spun nihilist Billy Childish); her abortions (two); and her rape (one).

'I couldn't go on doing art unless it meant something to me emotionally,' she told me 'so I began making things out of bits of me.' The works that have resulted are curiously di-verse. Ordinary things stuck about with slogans, short poems, the names of lovers—the blankets, tents and other life furnish-ings. And less ordinary things—like the fag packet her Uncle Colin was holding when he was decapitated in a car crash. She draws with a crazed yet poised line that wavers somewhere between that of Egon Schiele and Denis Nilsen; and the draw-ings are usually of herself masturbating. She paints as well, most notably at a 1996 installation event in Sweden, where she extemporised in oils for a week, whilst nude and imprisoned within the gallery.

She also gives a lot of interviews and is wholly unashamed of admitting to the pleasure that notoriety gives her. Further than that, the notoriety is, in and of itself, part of the work in hand. It's a closed loop—the Emin universe; and it revolves entirely around Emin. This, in a sense, makes her the perfect interview subject. Indeed, it's possible that if her work is to have any lasting impact it can only be in conjunction with encounters such as these; just as the work of Joseph Beuys (which Tracey's closely resembles) could only be viewed in the context of his own, exaggeratedly didactic, approach to the business of being an artist. With Beuys gone there's just a collection of his tedious possessions, lain out in glass cases, and the ghost of his pedagogy.

Where Beuys used dialectics, Emin employs her sexuality. Indeed, she is arguably as much of a sex worker as any cat-walk model or streetwalker, so vividly is her sexuality and her employment conjoined. In the Emin sex world there is a lot of violence and a lot of tenderness, much abandonment—and little retention. And in the flesh she is very quiet, supremely unaffected, intensely vulnerable and deeply unsexy. Just like a working girl who isn't working. I can imagine crawling into her infamous tent with her, and just lying there holding hands, possibly drinking a can of cider.

Settled down at a table, on upright chairs, Tracey sipped her tea wrapped up in a synthetic blanket, patterned so as to appear like Dalmatian fur. Cruella de Ville—not. Our conversation was calm and circumambulatory, wandering from art to drink to sex to driving and back again. The shadows lengthened across the studio floor. Occasionally her mobile phone played its cretinous serenade and she hastened to it. She was very easy to be with, very relaxing. But did she think she could go on doing this kind of thing indefinitely? 'No, four more years. Four years and I hope I'll 've got it all out of me.' And then what? She wants to write fictions, and began to tell me one oneiric example, but it was too dreamy to make much sense. She was understandably reserved about her current relationship, but says that she's in love 'today—and that's what matters. Now.' She has a terror of anything less than this intensity, of ending up with mere affection 'like a dog'.

She was ambivalent about the idea of having children, and emphatic that she couldn't 'get them out'. 'They're too big,' she proclaimed 'and it's too small.' One of the few, new purchases she'd made for the new home were a couple of tiny chairs which stand marooned in the mid-distance. Set sinisterly beside them are two small pairs of shoes. I remarked that they appeared to be for two, absent children—and, predictably referring to those abortions again, she said that they were.

But the question of children is of course one of permanence; and that is something Tracey Emin seems unwilling to counsel. She spoke lovingly of being drunk because it 'gives you an agenda—all you've gotta do is walk across the room.' In an interview with Waldemar Januszczak last year she'd said she was giving up drinking (even though she was swigging beer at the time), and to me she says the same thing: 'That's why I'm learning to drive—'cos you can't drink and drive.' I wasn't altogether convinced that this was a credible therapy.

Tracey doesn't do drugs—but the oblivion alcohol provides, the relief from her self-confessedly intense *accidie* and anomie, is as much part of her art/life chimaera as the sex. She said to me 'I've never felt happier, more wanted, more supported . . .' and yet there was that hangover, tangibly weighing down her thin shoulders. Although she speaks with equal warmth of relationships with her family, there's still a miasma that clings around her, cloaking her far more than any Dalmatian fur. When I asked her if she was worried that she might lose herself, like a psychic moth frazzled by the combined glare of her own honesty and public scrutiny, she calmly said: 'I woke up two years ago and realised I had murdered myself.'

As it is to love, so it is to the *ouevre*, which is seen by Tracey as essentially decoupled from the rest of the culture; there is no room for any canon here, although when pushed she concedes to reading Warhol when she was young—getting 'the point' of him. Her discussion of her working methods is, perforce, as pedestrian as they are—you really can't say that much interesting about appliqué. The paradox is that in creating these most nakedly 'personal' of art works, Tracey has produced remarkably artefactual work. The now famous 'shop' she ran with her close friend, the sculptor Sarah Lucas, is the concomitant of this.

When I left, Tracey gave me a copy of her book *Exploration of the Soul*. Although one of an unillustrated edition, there are only a few tens of copies of this fearlessly exculpatory account of her own, early sexual experiences. She wrote in the dedication 'I wanted this to be the truth.' And certainly there is a painful honesty in these tense jottings. Is she a good writer? I don't know—there's too little here for me to form a judgement. She told me proudly that it was worth 'a few hundred quid' and then worried—with a laugh—that I might think she was trying to bribe me into saying nice things about her.

As I threaded my way between the fruit stalls and the schmutter shops on Brick Lane I mused on this. No artist needs to have anybody say anything 'nice' about them—least of all by a critic. But Tracey's art—if it is art at all—is all about these kinds of vulnerabilities. In amongst the hard-drinking, hard-living, but essentially playful denizens of the contemporary London avant garde, Emin has found a kind of refuge. It's as if with Damien and Sarah and Angus and Matt and Jay and Sam she has encountered some of the half-siblings she's never met. Yet the very freewheeling character of this environment is also a mark of its transitoriness. Tracey had said she was going to do this art for four more years; might she as well have said four more minutes?

I was grateful to her for pointing out my character defects—she does it with aplomb. I'll be interested to see her whenever she next appears, but to repay her own honesty what can I say about this life that is her work? That it seems peculiarly autistic in its pedestrian solipsism? That it seems astonishing that this particular traumatised individual should be given so much time and liberty to do what so many others do in the art therapy sessions of mental hospitals? Perhaps both of these things. On the other hand Tracey's art-life also seems to be an amazing act of chutzpah—damn it all! She's pulled it off.

And anyway, perhaps this is all the fag end of this century has to offer in the way of creation: autodestructive, autobiographical musings. Only time will tell, Tracey, only time will tell.

Independent on Sunday,
November 2000

Damien Hirst: A Steady Iron-Hard Jet

About twenty minutes before Damien Hirst arrives at the Serpentine Gallery to talk to me, the susurration begins. The leaved minds of those who wait—gallery workers, a photographer, an editor and me—are agitated by his prepresence, the afflatus of what may—or may not—be his genius.

Calls are despatched to try and ascertain where the errant artist has got to. Pimpernel-like he has been sighted here, there and everywhere. I imagine some sort of incident-room map of Central London, with little coloured lights moving about it, showing the relative positions of Hirst, his critics, the buyers of his work. Possibly it could be entitled 'Moving Towards the Inevitable Impossibility of a Meaningful Encounter'. Or somesuch.

'He's definitely coming,' reports a head, poked round—and apparently partially severed by—the door jamb of the staff kitchen where we wait. A new agitation is generated among the waiters. There is discussion of Hirst's antics, the put-ons that have been tried on him by his critics:

'They asked him to draw a banana,' says someone referring to a television appearance by Hirst, 'and then he couldn't do it . . .'

'That's not true!' counters another. Damien is a brilliant draughtsman.'

I'm smoking moodily in a corner, reflecting that this phenomenon is somewhat like J. G. Ballard's concept of the 'Blastosphere', as described in his experimental work of fiction

The Atrocity Exhibition. The Blastosphere is the implicit shape of the way matter is perturbed by an explosion. It is atemporal: it may just as well precede the fact of the explosion as follow from it. We are all waiting in the Hirst Blastosphere, and as such it is inevitable that events, dialogue, thoughts even, should reflect the Hirst anti-aesthetic—a quotidian elision between the surreal and the banal.

A gallery worker shows a suit-wearing man carrying a clip-board into the staff kitchen. She says, 'Over there', pointing at a part of the room, and he replies, 'Mmm, mmm . . .' and notes something on his clipboard. They leave, without saying anything further, or even acknowledging the presence of the waiters. I wonder what the man with the clipboard would look like floating in a solution of formaldehyde.

And then he arrives. There's an almost audible thrumming that precedes the door being opened, an onanistic strumming, the essence of which is summed up by this question: Is it better to masturbate over the image of the Emperor if he has no clothes on, or is it preferable to stimulate yourself discreetly knowing that he is tightly sheathed?

In this sense Hirst's entrance to the kitchen is analogous to the way Ashley Bickerton's *Solomon Island Shark*—one of the exhibits in the current Serpentine Gallery show, 'Some Went Mad, Some Ran Away', which Hirst has guest-curated—impinges on the viewer's sensibility. Hirst is hammerhead down, tightly encased in PVC, rubber and leather, and already garnished with the fatuities of those who observe and comment upon him. Fatuities that are as ordinary and perverse as the coconuts and plastic bags of Scope mouthwash that dangle from Bickerton's shark.

What's immediately apparent is that Hirst has a genuine charisma. Like many spatial artists he is concerned with the interplay between individuals' senses of embodiment and their capacity for extroception. He manifests this as an aspect of his being: his being-in-the-room acts on the flustered gaggle of waiters like an ultrasonic whine on a school of fish; and so they quit it.

We wander out into the gallery to look at the work. Conversation is desultory. We examine details of the various works rather than commenting on their totality. Hirst is annoyed that some of the myriad plastic tags that stipple the surface of Angus Fairhurst's *Ultramine Attaching (Laura Loves Fish)* have been removed. I remark that it reminds me of my days as a shelf-stacker at Sam's Bargain Store in Burnt Oak.

Abigail Lane's *I Spy,* two glass eyes impaled on freestanding hanks of brass wire, calls forth from us both a warm recollection of the girder-impaling-eye sequence in Paul Verhoeven's film *The Fourth Man,* and we go on to bat back and forth anecdotes about other instances of bizarre discorporation, both real and filmic.

Another Lane—this time a full-size waxwork of a naked man crouching on the studio floor—calls forth a dialogue on the sense in which a sculpture can make the viewer aware of the distant provinces, the forgotten Datias and Hibernias of his own body. 'Actually, you know,' says Hirst, 'the genitals of the sculpture are modelled on the real genitals of the subject.' And we stand for a while, thinking about the sensation that the cold stone would make pressed against our own scrotal sacs.

Hirst talks about his interest in depicting 'points of light moving in space'. This, he tells me, was most of the inspiration behind creating the spot paintings, where the aim is to set up a kind of visual humming, a titivation of the air above the surface of the canvas. This calls forth from me a lengthy effusion on 'points of light in space' that runs all the way from the nature of the retinal after-image, through Zeus appearing in a shower of gold, to the experiences of Terence McKenna, the Californian drug guru, on dimethyltryptamine. Hirst grunts non-committally.

And indeed, as we tour the exhibition it becomes increasingly clear to me that not only does Hirst pay very little attention to the way that art critics are describing and categorizing his work, he doesn't even conceive of it in the same terms. For him the ascriptions of certain works as 'gestural', 'expressionistic' or 'conceptualist' are quite void.

What interests him are the details: the way that the butter curdles in Jane Simpson's terminal bird-bath *In Between,* a brackish fusion of brass, butter, halogen bulb and refrigeration unit; the implications of stress set up in Michael Joo's miscegenations of metal construction and Disney or scientific iconography; the way that Andreas Slominski's *Untitled*—a bicycle garlanded with bags of impedimenta—far from being difficult to assemble, in fact arrived at the gallery 'ready to be wheeled out of its crate'; the exact ratio of formaldehyde to water that he uses for his own animal works. He seems most engaged when I remark on the way that little golden bubbles are trapped in the fleece of the lamb he incorporated into *Away from the Flock.*

It's easy to see—talking to Hirst—why so many art critics should have seized upon him as grist to their word mills. They want his apparently gnomic comments on his work to be genuinely gnomic, evidence of a trickster mentality that teases the *cognoscenti.* The art critics who contemplate Hirst's work are like clever children playing with one of those stereoscopic postcards: they flick it this way and that, to show the Emperor alternately naked and adorned. Thus they get their kicks.

In fact Hirst quite clearly thinks about his work in just the straightforward way that he says he does. *Pace* this transcription of our dialogue, which shows Self attempting to schematize, and Hirst quite properly resisting:

w. s.: What I thought was interesting about the way people are writing about you at the moment is that the art critics have to describe your work in their own arcane language—one which prettifies what you are doing. And that does them for at least half an article.

D. H.: They do it all the fucking time . . . they've been doing it for years . . . There's nothing more boring. They say:
You go in, you see a thing . . . blah, blah, blah, just fucking
describe it.

W. S.: But it seems to me that what you're really interested
in is this dark side, this anima, the ingressability and internal-
ity of the body, and the way that culture refracts that experience. Your art is very kinaesthetic, it's about the internal
sensibility of the body.

D. H.: I remember once getting really terrified that I could
only see out of my eyes. Two little fucking holes. I got really
terrified by it. I'm kind of trapped inside with these two little
things . . .

W. S.: Pin-hole camera?

D. H.: Yeah, exactly.

When I attempt to outline some kind of epistemological
development in his work, towards a more 'visceral' approach,
Hirst says: 'I think I'm basically getting more yobbish. Yobbish
is visceral. There's an idea of reality that you get from working with real animals . . . and I like formaldehyde.'

And we go on to discuss the technicalities of suspending
animal carcasses in formaldehyde: what the solution comprises,
how he finds out about its properties, and so on.

Hirst tells me: 'It's ridiculous what I do. I can't believe in
it—but I have to.' And this might reasonably stand as the
motto of any serious contemporary artist. What the critic mis-
understands is that the imaginative condition of an artist like
Hirst is to be continually poised upon the fact of his own
suspension of disbelief. The critic attempts to appropriate
this queasiness as his own. This is because the critic, furthermore, wishes to appropriate the role of the artist for his own
as well.

It's a mistake to be deceived by the ironic hall of mirrors
that Hirst's work seems to present; to be distracted, like the

waiters in the kitchen at the Serpentine Gallery, by the 'phenomenon' of Hirst. While it's true that Hirst—like Warhol—
is an artist who is as much sculpting in social attitudes as he is
in physical materials, his approach to those attitudes is Myshkin-
like in its lack of guile.

D. H.: I'd love to be a painter. I love those stories about
Bacon going into a gallery where one of his paintings was being
sold for £50,000, and buying it and just trashing it. But you
can't really do that with a shark, it would take a whole gang
of men with sledgehammers.

W. S.: That's why I brought up that Mach thing [the man
who immolated himself trying to burn a sculpture by David
Mach]. Because what would you feel like if somebody came
in and destroyed the work? Surely, it is part of a coherent vision and you would feel as if someone had hacked off your
arm?

D. H.: I don't really mind, because I think the idea is more
important that the object. The object can look after itself. It
will probably last long after I'm dead. I'm more frightened of
being stabbed myself. You can always get another shark.

In the course of our conversation Hirst describes many techniques that are explicitly Warholian: working with assistants
who are inadvertently 'preprogrammed'; attempting to generate 'randomicity' in the spot paintings; the idea of a machine
for producing 'great artworks'. But while it may be too much
to assume that he has stumbled upon these concepts wholly
independently—they are, after all, very much part of the air
we breathe—there's no doubt that his formulation of them is
arrived at with a certain freshness. Hirst is a naïve rather than
a sentimental artist in Schiller's formulation.

The comments that Hirst makes that are most interesting
disavow his refusal to articulate a coherent vision. Of fat people
he remarks: 'They just want to fill up more space.' He opines
that what really interests him about space is its purely formal
properties: 'I think it's all like collage . . . d'you know what I

mean . . . that's why doing my own work and the group thing is basically the same. It's collage, shapes in space. As an artist you have these constrictions, when you make a work you have to decide whether it goes on the wall or the floor . . . Well, I hate that. My idea of a perfect art piece would be a perfect sphere in the centre of a room. You would come in and walk around it and it would just be there . . . I love the refractions of light in the liquid pieces. With the shark I just love the reflections in the huge volume of liquid—you don't really need the shark at all.'

We went on to discuss Hirst's new work, entitled *Couple Fucking Dead Twice*. He described it thus: 'Just two tanks, with no formaldehyde in them, and there are four cows—two in one tank, two in the other—and they're just these peeled cows. One's just stood upright, and the other one goes on its back, giving it a really tragic, slow fuck. They're both cows, so it doesn't matter. And they'll just rot. By the end there'll just be a mess of putrid flesh and bones. I just want to find out about rotting.'

There's an eloquence in this description that underscores his comments about the importance of the inspiration for him. He agrees readily enough when I suggest to him that the impetus for the creation of such works is the fact of their having arisen in the imagination in the first place. But this is as far as he can be driven towards intellectualizing his own work or defining an aesthetic.

He is far more interested—both lying on the lawn outside the Serpentine Gallery, and much later drinking at the Groucho—in putting to me teasing choices: 'Which do you hate more, serial killers or flab?'; 'Are you an optimist or a pessimist?'; 'Are you someone who sees the glass half-empty or half-full?' I would hazard a guess that the need to throw up these niggling and trite queries is a dim reflection of the very real battle between appearance and reality that is always going on outside the cave of Hirst's mind, as the Platonic forms of his sharks, cows and lambs are carried by in the flicker-ing firelight.

But I don't want to subside into the kind of waterbed of rhetoric that supports most art-critical speculation, any more than I want my prose to become a fancier description of a very ordinary accumulation of material objects. ('They do it all the fucking time . . . they've been doing it for years . . . There's nothing more boring. They say: You go in, you see a thing . . . blah, blah, blah, just fucking describe it.') William Empson described the introductory copy that prefaces exhibition cata-logues as 'a steady iron-hard jet of absolutely total nonsense'.

The catalogue copy for 'Some Went Mad, Some Ran Away' is a perfect example of this. Richard Shone's essay kicks off with a statement of mind-bogglingly discursive universality: 'An urge to bring order to chaos—the search for meaning in the seemingly random flux of experience—has existed as a fundamental human motivation throughout history.' What are we to gather from this? That this is an art show that somehow manages to bracket and contextualize the fundamental conun-drums of all human experience, for all space and all time?

I think not. Rather, this kind of bombast is an aspect of what I have alluded to above, just as Wittgenstein memorably re-marked on the impossibility of a meaningful musical criticism, on the basis that it was otiose to describe one language in terms of another, completely alien language. So the excesses of contemporary art critics in attempting to define and fix the work of artists such as Hirst reflects a wrong-headed and truly pretentious attempt by manipulators of language to reduce formaldehyde, flesh and bone to some chintzy philosophical abstraction. In literary criticism we have seen the phenome-non of deconstruction—an attempt by critics to hijack the mantle of the metaphysician for their own scrawny shoulders; and this is what we are witnessing here as well.

Shone goes on to characterize Hirst as 'riding freely through the grasslands of art, finding nutrition in the company of his kind'. I hope only one thing, that that 'kind' continues to be artists as interested in the physicality of art as Hirst is himself, and not the pallid poetasters who see his enactments of tangible chutzpah as a springboard for their own aesthetic ambitions.

Empson's phrase is so correct in terms of Hirst's art because Hirst is creating 'steady iron-hard jets', not uttering them.

Modern Painters, Summer 1994

NOTE

*The day after this interview was conducted, a disgruntled artist attempted to destroy Hirst's sculpture *Away From the Flock.*

The Art of Sam Taylor-Wood
Considered in Respect of the A3
Guildford Bypass, Summer 1996

Dylan [Thomas] talked copiously, then stopped.
'Somebody's boring me,' he said, 'I think it's me.'
Rayner Heppenstall, *Four Absentees* (1960)

The vinyl of the steering wheel clammy, buttock-like beneath
his sweating hands. The asphalt of the road scintillating like
frying bread. To the left a Microhard compound of irregular
mirrored rhomboids, reflecting one another. In the stationary
cars to the left of the carriageway they were playing middle-
of-the-road music on their sound systems. In the stationary
cars to the right of the carriageway they were playing middle-
of-the-road music on their sound systems. In the central lane
they were playing middle-of-the-road music on their sound
systems. The grass on the central reservation was painful,
viridian. He looked about at the three lanes of jammed traffic.
He looked at Guildford on its hill. Surprising to see the lineaments of medievalism: castle and cathedral, university and
market, drawn with red bricks and mortared crenellations. He
looked at the Microhard compound and thought of the lives
of the people who worked there. Did they still find the kidney-
shaped lake, with its *faux* Japanese island, diverting? Did they
still find anything diverting?

He knew there might be blue butterflies dancing amongst
the grasses and weeds on the central reservation, and on the

embankments of the road, beyond the endless fenders. He had heard floral friends proclaim that the median strips of the English roadways were paradoxical havens of unusual plants; but squinting at the exhaustive shading that drew the bottom halves of the cars, the road itself and the surrounding territory into a tight crosshatching, he doubted it.

And then gave up doubting it. Neither thesis nor antithesis was worthy of standing into being. Would the traffic ever flow again? Or would they remain thus: capsuled by a two-millimetre-thick layer of steel, artfully bent and shaped so as to resemble a car?

He turned to his companion. 'We're in Hell,' he said.

'Oh come on . . . it's just a traffic jam,' she replied artlessly.

'No, I mean it, we're in Hell. This *is* Hell, this . . . the Guildford bypass. We've died and gone to Hell. I know this with a deep certainty.'

She regarded him sceptically and asked, 'Do you know how we died? Was it in an accident on the way from London, or did we never leave town at all?'

'That I cannot say.'

'Cannot say—or do not wish to. Come on . . . it's you who're coming over all fucking omniscient.' There was appropriate bitterness in her tone.

'No, not omniscient. For example, I don't know if this is just our hell, or if it belongs to all these others as well—' he removed his hands from the steering wheel, each making a tangible 'flotch' of unsuction, in order to gesture; but as soon as he did so the car formation broke up a little. He grabbed the wheel once more and eased the car forwards a few metres, then joined the re-formed unit. 'See! Hell. I bet if you attempt to get out of the car the traffic starts to move, but if you remain in the car it stays jammed.'

'Yeah!' She undid her seatbelt, opened the door on her side of the car, and swung both feet out. They were bare. 'Ow! This is hot.'

'Get back inside!' This he nearly barked. 'We're rolling.'
They rolled another few metres.

'We're in Hell,' he said presently. 'Whatever we do we can't
die—that's what's going to happen to us.'

'What?' Her eyes weren't laughing.

'Soon, when I've managed to convince you that this is the
case, that we really have died and gone to Hell—and it won't
take long: our inability to advance in relation to Guildford,
and the sun's failure to traverse the sky, will pulverise your
scepticism—we will drive hard into the car in front, try and
impale ourselves on the steering column, or shred ourselves
through the windscreen. But if we do so we'll merely find
ourselves back here. Buckled in once more. The car intact.
Our failure to find oblivion will be our particular terror. We
will become poets of suicide. Perhaps for some years. Experiencing more and more ingenious forms of death—using our
limited equipment. Death by anti-freeze. Death by windshield
wiper. Death by eating car mats. Death from rubbing air fresh-
ener into exposed wounds. Perhaps combined with this, or
during some later, later, later era, we will be driven into all
kinds of bizarre experimentation in order to ward off—if only
for a second—the numbing tentacles of oblivion that will
descend upon us. We will, of course, commit unspeakable acts
of brutality against each other; and undoubtedly we shall ex-
plore the uttermost extremities of sexual gratification. My love,
nothing will compare to the titivations and excitations that we
will produce in each other. Nothing, save the same titivations
and excitations when—chillingly—we find ourselves experiencing them once more. We may attempt to enrich the illimitable dullness with the divine spark that remains, despite
everything that has gone before, buried within us. During these
aeons we shall tell each other everything we have ever done,
said, or felt; impart the minutest and most ineffable characteristics of our subjectivities, with all the consummate eloquence
that an eternity can allow you to acquire. Possibly this more

humane approach to Hell will produce some happy results. Ironically—and over millennia the potential for irony is consummately vast—we may find ourselves in a less cerebral state. Then for centuries we could work at adapting the furnishings of the car with as much artistry as we can manage—given the limited materials at our disposal—so as to make it resemble the cockpit of a fighter plane, the bridge of a nuclear submarine, or the control centre of an alien spacecraft, or indeed some vehicle heretofore unimaginable. Then, when we have tired once more of our hands, and our teeth and our tits, no doubt we will recapitulate the vast storehouse of knowledge that our stretched, solitary existence has brought forth in us. They say that those who are marooned on desert islands for years find themselves able to remember all the books they have ever read, verbatim. Well, that will be nothing compared with the lost culture we will recover. Every piece of music that either of us has ever heard will come back, incontinently, eventually. And then manageably, in a controlled fashion, so that we will be able to subject it to scholarly analysis. The same will be true of every film we have ever seen. Every play or exhibition we have ever attended, and every building we have seen, ancient monument we have scaled, city we have strolled around. Right here in the car we shall assemble a treasure house of exegesis, that for sheer duration and ramification will make the Talmud or the Upanishads look like ad flyers. But not even that will save us. For, over the years, we will have come to dislike each other with a stupendous, awesome thoroughness. In milliseconds of communication between us myriad familiarities will be enjoined; and the contempt will match them, point for point. Paradoxically this hatred will be peculiarly painless, and with something like joy we will re-enter the era of attempted suicides. I will put the car in gear'—he put the car in gear—'and once again drive hard into the car in front, try and impale us on the steering column, or shred us through the windscreen . . .' He drove the car a few metres forward, pulled up again, applied the handbrake, put the shift in neutral, turned to her and smiled. He squeezed her thigh.

She sat and looked at him, and at last agreed. She was, quite clearly, in Hell,

Sam Taylor-Wood exhibition catalogue, September 1997

The ICEHotel

Some people have a little difficulty in accepting that they may be a bit eccentric—I'm not one of them. If I see a crowd hurrying in one direction I feel an almost uncontrollable urge to rush off the other way, which is perhaps why I wasn't too fazed to find myself, in December, in a nearly snowbound Stockholm Airport, waiting for a delayed night flight to the Arctic Circle. True, I wasn't feeling exactly rubicund, nor the essence of jolly. In fact, I was moodily sipping beers that required a small mortgage to purchase, and watching the snowploughs—strange robotic things called 'Elephants'—attempt to keep the runways open.

I tried imagining I was a man with a mission—perhaps on my way to interview Santa himself. 'Mr Claus, this is your first interview with a British newspaper—can you explain why you've chosen to speak now?'

'I have bad news—there will be no presents delivered for any of you this year.'

'Any particular reason for this?'

'First there were no elves, then there were no presents. Now the reindeer are off sick—you British should understand these things.'

It was no good. Santa Claus remained a curiously indistinct figure in my mind's eye. Would he live in some kind of igloo, or a more orthodox house? Which ethnic group would he belong to? Would his red suit be made out of Gore-Tex, or some more traditional fabric? Actually, my real mission—to visit the ICEHotel in Jukkas Jarvi—was almost as strange an idea as the Santa exclusive. Despite having seen numerous photographs of this bizarre exercise in tourist accommodation and read the exhaustive blurb produced by its PR people, I was still no nearer to imagining what it could possibly be like.

I think it's because I suffer from the same kind of 'leaves on the line' problem with my imagination as the rest of the British—we just can't quite wrap our heads around the idea of extreme cold. In London, at gathering after gathering in the preceding weeks, when I'd ventured that I would be visiting the ICEHotel, sophisticate after sophisticate would say, 'Oh, I've heard about that; it's that hotel in northern Sweden made completely out of ice. I wonder if it's cold in the rooms?'

Cold in the rooms?! Of course it's *cold*—the thing's made out of ICE! But ever willing to challenge the laws of physics, people would still insist that there must be heating; or failing that they would dredge up from somewhere the idea that Eskimo igloos are really rather toasty on the inside. They are, compared with the ambient temperature, which can be down to −40°C, but they're still made out of ice! And that's where I was headed—me, who even drinks his vodkatinis resolutely straight up; why oh why oh why?

On the flight north I found myself wedged in next to a young woman. I was porting full British Arctic gear, namely fifteen woollies, scarves and mittens. She was in combat trousers and a light mac. It turned out she was going to the far north of Norway; her husband would be picking her up at 1.00 a.m. in Kiruna—where we were bound—and then driving the five hundred kilometres home.

I was incredulous. 'But this is the Arctic—you can't tell me he's doing a round trip of a thousand kilometres over night?'

'Oh yes, it's no problem. Anyway, where we live on the coast it isn't cold like Kiruna. It only gets down to ten below.'

Only? I munched moodily on the coldest slice of pizza I've ever had in my life, and sipped a glass of gelid Rioja. Below, the country was opening out into great swathes of snow and forest; even in the plane the sense of desert emptiness was palpable, and this was only enhanced when the lights of Kiruna came in view and we circled to land. Kiruna is a big mining centre, and it looks it—all vast derricks festooned with lights, clouds of smoke and louring slag heaps. And all of it covered with ice and snow and frost.

We kissed down on to the rink of a runway and coasted to a halt. I needn't have worried about the Swedes having 'leaves on the line'—these are people who really know how to run infrastructure under adverse conditions. Damn it all! Their mobile-phone industry is the best in Europe—perhaps the world. This is a culture that takes side-impact protection seriously. My fellow passengers were out of the plane, through the terminal and on to the taxi rank in seconds.

By the time I got there, the last cab was just about to wheel out. 'To the ICEHotel?' I implored the driver.

'Sorry, I can't—I'll order a cab for you, it will only take fifteen minutes.' And there I was, left staring balefully at a stuffed reindeer in the terminal, standing at an Arctic taxi rank.

The ride was twenty minutes along well-gritted roads. At the Reception to the ICEHotel, tacked to the door there was an envelope addressed to me. Inside was the key to Hut 16. It was nearly 1.30 a.m. and the moon was up. I could see something gleaming beyond the row of chalet-style huts as I crunched towards my quarters—the ICEHotel—and beyond it a vast sweep of frozen river, and beyond that a forested mountain. I crunched on down and stood feeling the spiracles of chill invading my creaking lungs. It was beautiful, with the moonlight infusing the mounded bulk of the hotel. All I needed now was a serious outbreak of the aurora borealis and my long day would be made.

No such luck. I entered Hut 16—a functional, three-roomed, well-insulated structure, the interior of which was predictably sauna-like—supped yet another beer and stared moodily at a poster showing an enormous vodka bottle lighting up the Arctic sky, with the caption 'Absolut Borealis'. Quite so.

In the late morning the sun eventually pushed above the horizon—and it was a clear, beautiful day. I'd heard a lot of activity outside while it was still crepuscular, but when I eventually emerged, the environs of the hotel were buzzing with snow scooters, tractor sleds and even JCBs. Some Japanese women were pulling blocks of ice around on little sleds, and in amongst the huts the maids were doing their rounds, their cleaning gear atop still smaller sleds. It reminded me of nothing so much as a *Dr No*-style installation—the Arctic lair of a sinister character bent on world domination.

Up at Reception I found a shop selling trinkets, tat and clothing made out of every conceivable part of the reindeer, and rendezvoused with my 'ice guide', the charming Asta Vormeier. She looked sceptically at me: 'Is your clothing warm enough for the tour?' And of course, despite being resolutely bundled up, I could only manage about thirty minutes outside—it was fifteen below. On the other hand I was proud—like Robert Falcon Scott—of my ill-preparedness. You can certainly tell national groups by their extreme-weather sartorial tendencies. Inevitably it transpired that the hotel was currently full of French, Belgian and Italian men—in small, outwardly-bound conference-groups—who were all dressed identically in jump suits (the French), Gore-Tex pantaloons (the Italians), or nylon protective suits (the Belgians).

The hotel, which is made of some 30,000 tonnes of ice and 'snice' (compacted half-and-half ice and snow), is rebuilt every year, beginning in the autumn. While I was there they were aiming hard for completion, which is on 30 December, so it was heads-down no-nonsense work. Everywhere Asta and I crunched there were people chiselling and chipping, stacking and smoothing. The hotel comprises a series of interconnect-ing, high-arched, chapel-like halls. These are formed by moul-ding snice around an aluminium arch and then removing it. The vaults are supported with circular columns of pure ice blocks. At the ends there are high 'windows', again of aston-ishing translucent ice, quarried from the frozen river. It is re-ally quite amazingly beautiful.

And yes, everyone, bloody cold! We checked out the bed-rooms. These are caverns of snice, flickeringly lit with candles and each individually decorated with weird, Modernist ice furniture and ice sculpture. The place feels like Superman's polar lair, or Narnia under the reign of the Witch. Asta cheer-fully encouraged me to check out an ice bed. Yup—they're ice: blocks of ice with a wooden board on top of them, then a conventional mattress, then the ubiquitous reindeer hide. 'Really very good for insulation,' as Asta explained.

I exchanged a few hurried words with Arne Berg, one of the architects who started the project, but he, like everyone else, was racing against the deadline—not simply the grand opening, but the all-important launch of the Absolut Ice Bar, which was scheduled for the next weekend. In this cavern of the hotel, an enormous icy S-shaped bar furnishes drinkers with eponymous shots in glasses made from—you guessed it—ice. 'But,' I asked Asta, 'isn't it true that drinking too much in sub-zero temperatures is extremely bad for you?'

'Ah yes,' she replied with Scandinavian rectitude, 'we do try and limit intake a little.'

The ICEHotel is very much conceived of as a gestalt—an involved work of art. While I was there they were putting the finishing touches to an igloo gallery which will mount an exhi-bition of the Arctic photos of Michio Hoshino; the Japanese women were a delegation of ice sculptors from the northern-most island, where apparently they are 'very advanced' at such things. There were Finnish lighting-effects specialists and even an Italian glass blower who had a little hut of his own abutting the hotel. All very impressive—and undeniably aesthetic, although I suppose a cynic might remark that an exaggerated concern with such impermanent architectural forms does smack of a certain decadence.

But then the ICEHotel is really for romantics, as the entirely jolly and rubicund proprietor of the hotel restaurant informed me that evening: 'Its the Japanese, you know. They come here for their honeymoons—lots of couples. And they believe that the Northern Lights give great good—how you say—karma. Yes, they believe a child conceived under the aurora is very lucky. So, I think maybe there's a lot of action down there—!' He collapsed into resolute ho-hoing.

Unfortunately Mrs Self had been indisposed, and the idea of me—a chronic insomniac who can't go to sleep alone unless he is simultaneously reading, smoking, drinking and listening to the radio—spending a long dark night of the soul inside a block of flickeringly-lit ice was right out of the frame. I wimped out and went for Hut 16 again. But in fairness, the hotel isn't in any way conceived of as a permanent residence. The visitors all have a hut as well, to which they can retreat for toenail-cutting, minimal satellite TV and ablutions. The starkness of the frigid rooms is reserved for the wee wee hours, when guests lie entombed in sleeping-bags, presumably musing on how they might copulate without losing their extremities for ever.

Not that the ICEHotel doesn't have other things on offer besides this extreme sleep experience. There's a lot of sled-based action and other such manly pursuits, as well as cultural excursions to grok the Sami people (the Lapland natives) and their ubiquitous reindeer. None the less, I can't help feeling that the main constituency for this sort of venture are very randy couples with a high disposable income, and the kind of hearty fellows who like to snowboard down Everest. Indeed, were there to be a 'Volcano Hotel' I'm sure it would be full of the same types as flock to its chilly counterpart. And they'd be sitting there in the 'Magma Bar' discussing the best kind of flame-retardant clothing.

It's probably just sour grapes, the loneliness of the solo Arctic traveller. As I sat in the restaurant that night, I consoled myself with a few Absoluts (drunk resolutely at room temperature), a chat with the proprietor, and a buffet of gargantuan proportions. This was truly the *ultima Thule* of buffets—the buffet at the end of the world. There were about twenty different kinds of pickled herring alone! There was a cupboard gushing sweets and gingerbread! It made *Babette's Feast* look like a take away. Those Swedes—they may not be the world's most natural hoteliers, but they sure as hell can do a buffet.

Oh, and mobile phones as well. They're dead good at them.

The Times, December 1998

Dealing with the Devil

Last night, I finally penetrated the veils of false memory that have shrouded my mind. It was a chilling and exhilarating moment, the culmination of a personal odyssey which has taken me to some of the darkest regions of my psyche. Over a period of about fifteen minutes—as I became increasingly dizzy and dissociated—I came to understand that for my entire conscious life I have been subjected to a sophisticated form of mind control.

As this impinged upon 'me', I felt my astral body detach itself from my material body and float up towards the ceiling of the room. There it hovered, gazing back down at the figure of the man who lay on the bed. The assumption of my true identity was like a surge of electricity. I was wholly vivified; if you like, enlightened.

This 'Will Self', the lanky form prone on the duvet, was manifestly little more than a puppet, constructed by a cabal of powerful magicians—Satanic cultists. For many years their agents, licentiates, acolytes and creatures have shadowed Will Self, providing him with the sly cues and psychic cover stories that have made it possible for him to believe himself an autonomous, self-aware individual.

Freed finally from this awesome delusion, I realized my true nature, which I will now reveal to you: I am an Illuminatus, a member of a conspiratorial cult that has existed for many thousands of years, in fact as long as human history itself. My thirty-two years spent as Will Self were a kind of initiation rite. All Illuminati must discover their true nature in their own way. Once you have crossed this assault-course abyss you can assume your rightful capabilities and powers.

What was written in 1486 in the *Malleus maleficarum,* or *Hammer of the Witches,* was the truth. I am one of those creatures who 'infect with witchcraft the venereal act and the conception of the womb. First, by inclining the minds of men to inordinate passion; second, by obstructing their generative force; third, by removing the members accommodated to that act; fourth, by changing men into beasts by their magical art; fifth, by destroying the generative force in women; sixth, by procuring abortion; seventh, by offering children to devils . . .'

The two Dominican friars who wrote the *Malleus* were our sworn enemies and their horribly accurate portrait of the Illuminati has pursued us down the ages. Originally intended as a handbook for Inquisitors working in southern Germany and endorsed by Pope Innocent VIII, this Observer Book of the realm of darkness is—as you can see—spot on. It could be offered as corroborative testimony to that of the British children who have given evidence of being involved in the practice of ritual abuse; and that of the 'survivors' of ritual abuse—both here and in the USA—who over the past few years have begun to recover their own buried memories of cult membership.

These are accounts of inter-generational Satanic cults, in which young children are persistently sexually abused and forced, if female, to become 'brood mares' as soon as they are able to conceive. Their function is to provide more sacrificial victims for the cults' hideous rituals: the dismemberment and consumption of foetuses and babies.

But whereas the 'survivors', as they and their therapists style themselves, have woken up to the hideous revelation that they have been victims of a cult to such an extent that they have fashioned multiple sub-personalities, thus blocking out whole swathes of experience, I have found myself to be one of the perpetrators and my authentic being to be one of pure evil.

If the above strikes you as a sick joke of some kind, a piece of malicious fabrication that impugns the very real distress of a great number of people, then you are entirely wrong. My capacity as a writer of fictions means that I must call in such material, allow my imagination free range over the territory of the collective psyche. This has placed me in an interesting position vis-à-vis Satanic abuse.

My novel *My Idea of Fun* is an attempt to examine what is happening to the belief systems of individuals in an age when our relentless practice of applied psychology has kicked the legs out from under our social ethic; in an age when the light of reason, far from burning brightly, is guttering terribly.

It is my contention that the current extraordinary delusion concerning child abuse, Satanic abuse, so-called ritual abuse (this latter is very hard to define), is significant in ways that people are extremely unwilling to accept. My own experience and thought on the matter leads me to believe that there are a number of highly unpalatable truths about our own culture bound up in this phenomenon.

In the process of researching this article I found myself becoming profoundly psychically disturbed. The fantasy sequence with which I began this article is a piece of emotional confabulation that—as I wrote it—had real force for me. The human mind—as I hope I can demonstrate—is indeed a malleable thing. The really secret cult in our culture is the one we all belong to. And it is precisely because membership is so universal that it is proving so hard to get us to break ranks and confess.

'There are,' said Jim Harding, director of children's services at the NSPCC, 'some children who are abused, with some ritual activity or behaviour as an aspect of that abuse, but there is no evidence to suggest the existence of families or extended families where there is an embedded culture of Satanic abuse.

'But look,' he sighed, 'we only speak from experience here—or not at all—and we have only looked into a small number of cases.' Harding spoke with gravitas. When he suggested that the media preoccupation with Satanic abuse had the effect of 'trivializing' the reality of adults' sexual abuse of children, I believed him. When he suggested that the number of children on the NSPCC's 'at risk' registers might be a poor indication of the number actually abused, just as—in the past—the number of women reporting sexual assaults was a poor indication of the number who had actually been assaulted, I believed him as well.

'Look,' he sighed again—a decent man freighted with producing sound bites on the culture's indecent preoccupations—'it could be true to say that there are some unhelpful depressions heading across the Atlantic as far as child protection is concerned. But I think things are different here. We don't have the sheer scale of witnesses coming forward for a start . . .' He tailed off, eyes sliding away to the window. We are trebly compromised—his reticence seemed to say—by our functions, our status, our very preoccupation. What happens to trust in the realm of abuse? 'I think,' he resumed, 'the truth may lie somewhere in the middle.'

Harding told me about studies that were under way to try to fix the extent of the problem. His absence of rhetoric, his determination that the NSPCC was unapologetically committed to children's welfare—and nothing else—had begun to turn the issue around in my mind.

'We have come across a case,' Harding had told me, 'where children were terribly abused and no doubt ritual was involved. But the point is that the significance—in the context of that abuse—of an upside-down cross is from the children's point of view totally unimportant. What's far more significant is understanding a form of coercion such as this—if you're going to help the victims overcome it.'

Heading north towards Birmingham, on the service centre-less M40, I read the fact file from the NSPCC on 'Child Abuse Trends in England and Wales 1988–1990'. Lying open on the passenger seat, black type set against blue vinyl, the quotidian was never more ugly. The summary presented was precise, shading 'abuse' with the solidity of 'neglect'.

The facts amassed about those whose children come to the notice of the social services could have been guessed at in a lounge bar, by anyone with the nous to state the obviousness of suffering at the bottom end of society: 'The findings showed that marital problems, financial difficulties and unemployment were the main factors affecting registered families . . . The sexually abused children were the oldest, followed by the physically injured, emotionally abused and neglected children, with the non-organic failure to thrive cases [where infants are not growing healthily and there's no medical explanation] the youngest . . .'

Sure: they will fuck you, your mum and dad, but only once you're old enough. Before that they beat up on you, scream at you and if you're small enough starve you, or dash your brains out against the wall. But there was one statement in the summary that marked the line between what has been happening in the USA and what has occurred in Britain: 'The number of physically injured children registered increased between '88 and '89, while the number of sexually abused children decreased. Possible reasons for the decline in registrations of sexual abuse could be increased caution on the part of child protection professionals following the events in Cleveland and subsequent inquiries, or the end of a reporting peak.

'The numbers for children in the emotionally abused, neglected and other categories remained constant during the study period, while those for grave concern [cases where they suspect sexual or physical abuse but cannot prove it] almost doubled.'

The NSPCC were talking about 18 per cent of 9,628 children who had been registered between 1988 and 1990. They were talking about fewer than 2,000 instances where actual sexual abuse was proven. In the USA, last year alone, over 30,000 adults came forward with 'recovered memory' evidence of having been subjected to Satanic ritual abuse as children. Even allowing for discrepancies in population base, the NSPCC were clearly not identifying a pool capable of generating such a future upsurge.

The cases in Britain in which evidence of Satanic abuse led to children being taken into care were, most notably, those of Orkney and Rochdale. The 'truth' in both cases—as in that of Cleveland—became engorged by evidence and then ruptured into 'the subsequent inquiries' the NSPCC summary gnomically referred to.

The Butler-Sloss inquiry into the Cleveland case led to new 'guidelines' being issued for the relevant agencies and to a discrediting of the RAD (Reflex-Anal Dilation test) that had set Drs Higgs and Wyatt on the path to placing 123 children in care. But even at the time (1988) of the inquiry's report being published, journalists were asking why it didn't tell the public what the ratio of correct to false diagnoses had actually been.

A highly placed source in the relevant child protection agencies told me while I was researching this piece: 'We think that up to 60 per cent of the children taken into care at Cleveland probably had been abused. But there's nothing we can do about it now.' Likewise, in the Orkney case no one ever disputed that actual abuse had taken place. The father of the 'W' family on South Ronaldsay (who were at the heart of allegations) had actually served time in jail for abusing his children. What the Clyde Report on the Orkney case reiterated was what the Butler-Sloss Report had already implied: that the extent to which social services had believed children's testimony, to that extent were they confabulating, a confabulation being the creation of truth through the admixture of fact and fantasy.

In the USA the accusations of confabulation have been far more widespread and far more damaging. The 'confabulation' school trace the surge of 'recovered memories' of Satanic abuse to the publication in the early eighties of a book entitled *Michelle Remembers,* written by a Canadian called Michelle Smith and her psychiatrist, Richard Padzer. Smith's accounts of Satanic ritual abuse (SRA), as it rapidly became known, were in line with the *Malleus maleficarum* check list: the abuse, torture and mutilation of people and animals; being forced to participate in the sacrifice of human adults and babies; being ceremonially married to Satan.

In 1988 two young psychiatrists, Walter C. Young and Bennett C. Braun, and the psychologist Roberta G. Sachs published a paper which became immensely influential. It was entitled 'A New Clinical Syndrome: Patients Reporting Ritual Abuse in Childhood by Satanic Cults'. Sachs was a specialist in dissociative disorders, states of mind characterized by a confused or diminished sense of identity. The most flamboyant and recognizable of these disorders is termed MPD, or Multiple Personality Disorder. The three authors of the paper interviewed thirty-seven patients diagnosed with MPD and found that over 25 per cent produced congruent accounts of Satanic ritual abuse.

What seems to have happened next is that the cart of effect got put before the causal horse. With only internal and corroborative evidence for the veracity of these accounts of Satanic ritual abuse, the three authors hypothesized that these accounts implied Multiple Personality Disorder. They had unleashed a bush fire of diagnostic supposition. Multiple Personality Disorder, which until then had been a comparatively rare diagnosis for psychiatrists and psychotherapists to make, began to become commonplace.

In the USA three principal responses to this phenomenon have been adopted. First, there are those who, in line with the testimony of *Michelle Remembers* and another self-help guide, *The Courage to Heal,* have taken the evidence of 'recovered memories' of SRA at face value. Second, there have been those who, along with Dr George K. Ganaway (the programme director for the Ridgeview Center for Dissociative Disorders in Smyrna), have accepted the significance of 'recovered memories' of SRA, but seen them as 'screen memories' masking the more prosaic forms of abuse that are inflicted on children—the kind of things the NSPCC 'at risk' register records. Last, there have been influential professionals, such as Professor Richard Ofshe (professor of sociology at Berkeley), who have put forward the thesis that the MPD diagnosis and the SRA memories themselves are a complete confabulation between distressed patients and inept therapists.

Ofshe's publications on the subject question the validity of Freudian psychoanalytic psychiatry in general. Ofshe (along with such critics of Freudianism as Jeffrey Masson) points to the dithering that surrounded Freud's original reclassification of his analysands' accounts of childhood sexual abuse as fantasies or 'projections'. Masson has accused Freud of hypocritically turning his back on what he knew to be the truth: namely that these patients actually had been sexually abused. Ofshe makes the reverse point that Freud was utilizing the same techniques that 'recovered memory' therapists use today, namely hypnosis, interpersonal pressure, leading and suggestion. And that furthermore he never considered the possibility that the 'memories' of abuse were pure confabulations. Rather, he chose to see them as true fantasies, the result of repressed instinctual sexual drives.

None of this would be remotely important or worth running over again were it not for the tremendous impact that Freudian ideas have had on our culture. None of it would be germane were it not that, at the time of writing, fifteen American states have altered their constitutions to admit testimony derived from 'memories' recovered in therapy. There are men and women either already in jail or awaiting trial in the USA on the basis of such evidence.

It is possible to argue that the particular way in which the SRA phenomenon has spread in the USA is unique to that society. The USA is a country where there is still a strong Christian fundamentalist minority. Forty per cent of Americans are regular churchgoers, as against 5 per cent in the UK. The USA is also the culture where Freudian ideas caught on and were institutionalized most rapidly. And lastly there is the relative impact of the various 'strong' schools of feminist psychotherapy. It is ironic indeed that, in seeking to discredit the Freudian attribution of memories of sexual abuse to 'pure fantasy', many feminist psychotherapists may have fallen into the same trap as the Great Paternalist: namely, refusing to accept the role of the therapist herself in leading an unstable or neurotic patient towards a delusory 'answer' to her or his problems.

If I wanted a graphic illustration of the difference between British and American cultural response as regards this issue, I couldn't have chosen a better person to visit than Dr James Phillips. It would be fair to say that with friends like Dr Phillips, the believers in the validity of recovered memories of Satanic ritual abuse don't need any enemies. Entering his surgery in Northfield, Birmingham, was like coming into the fateful snicker-snack atmosphere of a closed psychiatric ward.

Dr Phillips has been carving a media presence for himself as a result of his allegations of Satanism both high and low in British society. He is an enthusiastic propagator of the Multiple Personality Disorder diagnosis. He has been suspended by the General Medical Council (the result, he claims, of a 'Satanist conspiracy'), and is being forced to wind down his practice as a GP.

Dr Phillips and his associate in the 'Jupiter Trust' he has founded, Gordon Lochead, present the 'strong' thesis that up to one in ten Britons are members of a Satanic cult that permeates our entire society. They would both find the first-hand testimony with which I began this article highly credible. Indeed, as I talked to them in a cramped sepia room at the top of the gloomy, deserted surgery, the sunny Sunday outside receded, to be replaced by the fusty coldness of despair and grasping at psychic straws.

I presented myself to Phillips and Lochead as a potential patient, someone who had suffered throughout his life from problems with alcohol and drug addiction (I was misdiagnosed as a chronic alcoholic and drug addict in 1986), someone who felt the presence of an amorphous leviathan of disturbing—but repressed—memory nipping at the heels of his consciousness.

It didn't surprise me at all that they went for this like hounds after a scent: 'If only we could have you with us for a couple of weeks,' said Phillips, 'then we could really do some work together.' The more I showed myself to be compliant, the more flamboyant their revelations of Satanism became. They named government ministers as Satanists, pointed to the suicide of Jocelyn Cadbury as a cult 'hit', and spoke of 'thousands of corpses' buried at the 'ceremonial site' of the Rollright Stones.

It was spooky being with them. They both spoke of their own multiple personalities as if they were in the room with us, floating overhead like dreamers in a Chagall painting: 'Oh, yes,' said Phillips, speaking of his 'John Barleycorn' drinking persona, 'he's a real bugger to get along with, a real drag to have around, isn't he, Gordon?'

Gordon, a pale, intense Scot with a ginger beard, voiced vigorous assent to this. At one point during our conversation, first Gordon and then 'the Doctor' himself had to absent themselves to help a woman alcoholic they were treating in the surgery. 'She has the DTs,' Gordon explained, 'the Doctor is just giving her something to help her out.'

I couldn't wait to get out of the place. But I wasn't being entirely disingenuous. What experience I have of the attribution or diagnosis of childhood sexual abuse as a causal factor lying behind other more obvious psychological disorders comes from my own past on-off membership in twelve-step programmes such as Alcoholics Anonymous and Narcotics Anonymous, and my residence at a Minnesota Method treatment centre for four months in the mid-eighties. It was here that I first ran up against the idea that repressed memories of childhood sexual abuse could be the actual cause of subsequent alcoholism and drug addiction.

Interestingly, of course, the nexus of religion and psychotherapy that you find around the twelve-step programmes resembles the cultural ambience of the USA. Furthermore, the Minnesota Method of treatment for addiction and alcoholism is itself an American import. Among the psychotherapeutic disciplines that have clustered around the twelve-step programmes are such 'eclectic' schools as Psychosynthesis. This is a therapeutic method wherein clients are encouraged both to enact various 'subpersonalities' and to look for some fundamental, buried, repressed trauma, which can explain their subsequent flight from reality into the neurosis of drinking and drugging behaviour.

It had long occurred to me that both the diagnosis of alcoholism and drug addiction as a 'disease' and indeed the very structure of the twelve-step movement itself represented a microcosm of a wider cultural malaise. I myself underwent therapy with a psychosynthesist for some time at the beginning of this year. The therapist—who I would regard as highly responsible within all reasonable bounds—was nonetheless firmly convinced of the significance of memory repression within my malaise. I broke off the treatment when I began to feel that the search for this elusive trauma was beginning to eclipse more immediate concerns.

But now, as I gratefully powered my way out of Birmingham and on to the southbound M5, more of the rows of ratiocination in this strange Rubik's cube of socio-psychological speculation appeared to be clicking into place.

My last port of call was to visit a man called Roger Scotford, who has been attracting a fair share of media interest in the last few months. Scotford has set up an organization called Adult Children Accusing Parents (ACAP). This is the British equivalent of the False Memory Society, the support group for parents in the USA who say they have been wrongly accused of inflicting (usually Satanic) sexual abuse on their children.

Scotford's daughter claims to have 'recovered' memories of his sexual abuse of her during homeopathic treatment. These recovered memories are brutal and graphic although not specifically of SRA. Scotford, an attractive, greying man in his fifties, slightly fey but with an engaging manner, was a positive torrent of information on 'False Memory Syndrome' and all related matters. Everything in his manner said: 'You can't possibly believe that these accusations are real, can you?' His charming house and flower garden were a picture of Kate Greenaway-style homeliness. He was scrupulous in his need to differentiate between the 'robust' hypothesis of 'recovered' or 'false' memories of childhood sexual abuse, and those memories that had elements of continuity, which therefore should be regarded as being probably true.

Since Scotford set up ACAP he told me he had been 'approached by some people who quite possibly were paedophiles. We don't accept people into our organization unreservedly, we ask them to complete a questionnaire which provides a contextualization for the accusations.' Scotford himself is clearly agonized—but by what? the doubters ask. One journalist friend who had already interviewed him voiced reservations about his testimony. His response to the accusations was after all congruent with either guilt or innocence.

His first wife (the mother of the adult daughter who has accused Scotford) has been reported to have said, 'There is no smoke without fire.' Scotford showed me a letter from a former neighbour. The neighbour wrote to a journalist at the *Daily Mail* who had written a piece sympathetic to Scotford: 'I have observed and admired the courage of those two young women [Scotford's daughters] in their attempt to cope and deal with their horrific memories. If Roger Scotford cared about his daughters why would he wish to publicize his views in this way with thinly disguised photographs and his home number?'

But then isn't this the true definition of a modern witch-hunt? A situation in which the accused's very protestations of innocence can be taken as evidence of guilt? I have no wish to come down on one side or the other in any particular case. Which is why, despite Scotford's urgings, I didn't take up the trail that led to his elder daughter (the one who has made the most graphic accusations). Rather, while I was talking to Scotford, I began to arrive at a vivid picture of a culture that has lost its way.

To reiterate: I would agree with Jim Harding at the NSPCC that the widespread existence of sexual abuse of children is an unpalatable truth that has only recently and coaxingly begun to be acknowledged. However, the climate within which it has come to light is not one lit up by 'common sense' or reason. Rather we are a society in which the way we govern our sexuality has become uncoupled from collective ethics. What can we make of a culture in which the rituals associated with menstruation are those of advertising rather than religion? 'Look, no blood!' exclaim the ubiquitous advertisements on the television. In semiotic terms they represent a simultaneous celebration and suppression of a biological reality. In the USA the declivity between feminists and the alleged 'backlash' against feminism has come to encompass the debate about Satanic ritual abuse as well. Feminists here, such as Suzy Orbach, are appalled by the idea that accepting the fictitiousness of 'recovered' memories may lead to some kind of climate in which it becomes difficult, once again, for adults who have been abused as children to come forward and talk about what has happened to them. This is certainly something we should all be worried about.

DEALING WITH THE DEVIL

But when I lay down on my bed after a hard day's driving and talking I found it only too easy to confabulate my way into the hideous scenario I set out at the beginning of this piece. The furniture of the delusion comes from the vestiges of Christianity that lie within my mental prop department. Satanism is after all a construct which owes its existence to its opposite. The mechanics of the delusion I adapted from psychoanalysis with its concentration on the 'false bottom' of self-conscious memory. I can admit to my own suggestibility; what I cannot admit to is being the Devil's disciple.

But however implacable and empirical the testimony of people like Jim Harding, there really is no commonsensical view of these matters. He told me that the NSPCC saw many cases 'where sexual interference with children took place within a context whereby it was judged less damaging to leave the children in their homes than remove them'. Judged by whom? And according to what standard? Which brings us full circle to the proposition I first set out: that we live in a culture elements of which are under threat from forms of cultism. And one thing is for certain: it's not going away.

It is egregious to quote one's own work, but in my novella *Bull* I made an observation which seems to sum up the current introjection of our culture's moral queasiness: 'In this world where all are mad, and none are bad, we all know that the finger that points, also points backwards.'

Harpers & Queen, November 1993

Head-Hunting for Eternity

On a hot day in May I took Highway 99 and drove as fast as I could inland from Los Angeles. Trundling along the broad swathe of concrete, I felt as if I were trying to escape the inundation of this limitless city, which like some urban tidal wave kept on coursing in from the Pacific. But even in the outermost 'burbs, where Mainstreet USA laps against the bleached bones of the Californian hills, there was still an orange tinge of smog in the air. It made everything look underexposed, like a photograph which had been rejected by quality control.

After three hours in Riverside at the headquarters of the Alcor Life Extension Foundation, it was no longer the smog that imparted a sense of unreality, but the fact that I'd been in earnest convocation with a group of people who are deeply committed to sawing each other's heads off after death and then plunging them in liquid nitrogen. Their objective? Nothing short of immortality. They call themselves cryonicists. Lots of other people, including the vast majority of the scientific establishment, call them Dagenham—two stops beyond Barking.

The place where the 'suspensions' take place is far from being some citadel of *Blade Runner*-style hardware. It's just another breeze-block building on another industrial estate, right down to the textured louvres in the diminutive vestibule.

I had seen the smiling likenesses of the already suspended Alcor members. I'd admired the rather dated ambulance the cryonicists had kitted out as a rapid-response vehicle. And I had stood and goggled at the operating table where the 'patients' are prepared for possible immortality.

Now it was show-and-tell time. I was ushered into the aluminium-sided, concrete-floored warehousing unit which contains those members of the Alcor Life Extension Foundation who are already in suspension. The cumbersome lid of the 'neuro-suspension chamber' was being unbolted by Hugh, a huffy cryonicist in his fifties, dressed scoutmasterishly in a tan shirt with epaulettes and pressed chinos.

Coddled inside the chamber were seventeen individual heads. The heads of people who had died of cancer, cardiac arrest and even AIDS. Not that these heads could actually be seen, of course—that would have been macabre. No, no, they were all tidily packed away in individual canisters, in cold store until at least the next millennium. It was like some low-budget version of *Alien* with set design by Texas Homecare instead of H. R. Giger.

The liquid nitrogen gave off a froth of condensation. Hugh and I stared down into the chamber. Among the submerged head-boxes (or 'neurocans', as they are properly called) I could see something else, something that looked decidedly prosaic, something made out of blue linen. 'What's that?' I asked, pointing.

Hugh huffed. 'Oh, it's a pillowcase.'

'I see, and what's it got in it?'

He grunted again. 'Miscellaneous objects.'

'What sort of miscellaneous objects?' My mind reeled. I knew that these people believed in the possibility of whole body cloning; that's why they were prepared to lose their heads after death. Could it be that they also imagined a future science capable of re-creating them from still more slender leftovers? Was the blue pillowcase full of ears? Fingers? Perhaps even toenail clippings? Ralph Whelon, a thin, young cryonicist, spoke up.

237

'They're pets,' he snapped, 'the pets of people who've been suspended.'

Those pets stayed with me throughout my sojourn among the cryonicists, and long afterwards—the pets and the severed head of Saul Kent's mother, Dora, of which more later. Naturally the blue pillowcase was full of pets, for were you to be brought back from death far in the future, with human society incalculably altered, having your very own doggie to hand would do more for your mental adjustment than a spaceship full of psychologists.

That is cryonics in a nutshell: a bizarre marriage between scientism run amok and dewy-eyed sentimentality. As I journeyed around California from one freeze-dried fanatic to the next, a picture of the cryonics community emerged that was at one and the same time reassuring—all too clearly these people were Dagenham—and yet unsettling, because the very form that their delusion takes mirrors the profound spiritual difficulties our culture has in coming to terms with death.

I first became aware of cryonics in the seventies when, as a sci-fi-obsessed teenager, I read an article in the *Observer* magazine, eerily illustrated with pictures of cadavers lain out like presentation salmon on back-lit beds of crinkle-cut ice. It seemed fairly logical to me as a thirteen-year-old materialist. If the mind and the brain are one and the same, I reasoned, and could somehow be preserved at the moment of death, it would be possible for the highly advanced scientists of the future to reboot it, to switch it on again.

But there was another sci-fi story that also gripped me. It portrayed a future in which wealthy people who were terminally ill had their diseased bodies amputated and then went on living as disembodied heads mounted on life-support racks. The first line of the story went something like this: 'For breakfast this morning I had twelve dozen Dover number one oysters and a jeroboam of Dom Perignon—then they removed the bucket.' This seemed an ideal life to me.

Of course, I know now that if I'd joined the Alcor group, or some other gaggle of cryonicists, I'd be spending my summer holidays at life extension conferences at Lake Tahoe. For I had all the psychological factors in place: a genuine willingness to entrust my head to science—whether real or fictional—and an exaggerated fear of death. All the committed cryonicists I met in California had that make-up.

Arguably, the cryogenic dewars (storage canisters) I saw at the Riverside Alcor facility are the lineal descendants of the chamber tombs of the Orkneys, the Sutton Hoo burial ship and the pyramids themselves. But the idea that preserved bodies might be animated by some scientific process dates back to the eighteenth century and Benjamin Franklin, who wanted to be pickled in Madeira: 'I wish it were possible . . . to invent a method of embalming drowned persons, in such a manner that they may be recalled to life at any period, however distant.'

Freezing as a method of preservation came to the fore in this century, predictably from science fiction, which has a lot to answer for in spawning cults. L. Ron Hubbard, the founder of Scientology, was a sci-fi writer, and there's a congruence between Scientology and cryonics. True, cryonicists have no similarly charismatic cult leader. No, the more they spoke, the more I understood what they worshipped. It was their own heads.

The cryonicists' bible is actually a 'factual' book, *The Prospect of Immortality,* published in 1964 by one Robert Ettinger, a junior college physics instructor in Michigan. He argued that cryogenic (or 'tissue freezing') technology and medicine were already well enough advanced for the 'front end', the practical bit, of the cryonics procedure to be worth undertaking. He now runs the Cryonics Institute in Oak Park, Michigan. However, the honour of the first suspension belongs to the

Alcor group and Dr James Bedford, who died in California in August 1967, and who now resides, along with the pillow-case full of pets, at the Alcor facility in Riverside.

It was Steve Bridge, a rather doggily earnest cryonicist, who welcomed me to Alcor and took me through cryonics history. He explained that the Alcor people deny the sovereignty of death—in the literature I had received, the word death wasn't even mentioned; it's referred to as 'deanimation'.

I steeled myself: would Bridge make a play for my head from the off? In the event, he was happy to laugh at some of his odder beliefs. We talked about the early suspensions. 'Oh, they were extremely crude!' he giggled. 'They knew very little about chemistry or biology, and even used mortuary pumps to do the perfusion!'

'Perfusion', a much-used word in Alcor literature, is the pumping out of the blood and its replacement with a cryo-protective fluid, a glycerol and sucrose-based compound which retains its liquidity once the 'patient' is chilled to −196°C. Really, the efficacy or otherwise of perfusion is at the very core of whether or not cryonics has any validity whatsoever.

Contemporary science maintains that cells can be irrepara-bly damaged during freezing: any remaining water in the cells forms ice which expands and ruptures them. But, say cryonic-ists, those clever third-millennium boffins will know what to do. They will send in vast armies of 'nanomachines': tiny, molecular-sized devices, each carrying an on-board computer and capable of physically repairing cellular damage. The nano-machines will communicate with each other, and with vast computers outside the body, in such a way as to reanimate us—not as we were, decrepit and worn out, but restored to the full flower of our youth. And where a 'neuro' (severing the head) rather than a whole body suspension has been done, our missing bodies will be cloned from DNA in surviving cells.

The cryonics literature takes gruesome delight in the makeshift surgery of the suspension procedure. But, as I read case histories of individuals who have fought to be suspended, I found myself becoming emotionally involved. These people spent the last harrowing days of their lives fighting battles with doctors and coroners to ensure that they were pronounced 'dead' as quickly as possible, so that the Alcor team standing by could get perfusing. I felt myself working alongside, champing at the bit, waiting to assist with the insertion of a catheter or a femoral artery cut-down.

Here is the description of the pivotal moment in the cryonic suspension of Eugene Donovan: 'Gene died at 8.19 a.m. on the morning of 21 March 1989. All of us were with him. The hospice nurse pronounced death and from somewhere in the room someone said, "Let's go!" We all quickly wiped our tears and the transport began.

'Jim did manual CPR [cardiopulmonary resuscitation] while Mike and Steve hooked up the HLR [heart-lung resuscitation]. Jerry placed an endotracheal tube. I tried to place an intravenous catheter, and Diane, Gene III and Ray assisted all of us . . .'

Hardly what you'd call a graceful departure from this world. But it drew me—another wannabe surgeon—inexorably towards the question of what it would feel like to start hacking away at the body of someone I'd personally known. Ralph Whelon, the Alcor vice-president, was gung ho on this: 'Even on the first suspension I assisted with, no doubts crossed my mind. It isn't something that's done lightly or nonchalantly. Sure, it takes a strong stomach, but that in itself strengthens commitment.'

But what would Steve Bridge feel, holding my head as it was 'carefully separated surgically at the sixth cervical vertebra'? 'Well, I have to admit,' he said somewhat ruefully, 'once your head has been removed, that becomes the patient. The rest of your body is just a cadaver and we treat it accordingly. But put it this way, I wouldn't have made a good doctor. I can't stand to find myself in a situation where I can't do something for someone.'

Bridge, in fact, used to be a children's librarian, and it transpired that not one of these cryonic pioneers had what amounted to a formal medical training. Had I sought suspension over the past two decades, my front-end manager would have most likely been either a jet-propulsion engineer, a dialysis technician, a surgical assistant, or a vet. But Bridge was unashamed about this apparent lack of formal qualifications. 'In the early days, we thought that once they saw what we were doing, establishment scientists would quickly get involved and improve the technique. But that wasn't the way it worked out. We found we had to do it all ourselves.'

The Alcor Life Extension Foundation is the largest cryonics group, with twenty-seven patients suspended so far, ten of them 'whole body' and seventeen 'neuro': there are three hundred or so cryonicists worldwide, but only forty-eight are suspended. They still offer competitive rates: £80,000 for whole body suspension and £25,000 for neuro. Storage and maintenance costs are only £44 a year for your head and £570 for the whole body. This covers topping you up regularly with liquid nitrogen so that you don't get too clammy and, presumably, changing your pillowcase as well. If money is a problem, insurance policies can be amortized. A modest sum invested will provide the income for storage, maintenance and, who knows, maybe a little nest egg with which to buy your first space station.

Reading these costings was like being droned at by a financial adviser: 'Right, Mr Self. We've sorted out your accident insurance and your PEPs for the kids' education. Now there's just your suspension payments left to arrange.'

Alcor, nonetheless, make no profit, and every board member is fully committed and signed up for suspension. Perhaps mutual aid has ensured their survival. Other cryonics societies have come and gone. When I went to visit Thomas Donaldson, an Alcor member in northern California, he told me of one failed cryonics group where they had all simply 'walked away from the situation, which caused a big stink . . . literally!'

But, notwithstanding Alcor's high ideals, something made me feel slightly uneasy about signing my head over to them. As I talked to Whelon and Bridge, a picture emerged of embattled cryonicists fighting legal battles with the Riverside Coroner and the California Department of Health Services over their right to do suspensions. In 1987, this legal battle had focused on one person—Saul Kent's mother, Dora, and in particular her head.

It was the cryonic suspension of Dora Kent which brought the Riverside Coroner's Department down on Alcor. According to the Riverside Press Enterprise for 3 October 1990: 'The coroner's office determined that Kent died of a lethal dose of barbiturates and sought homicide charges. Alcor officials said the drugs were administered after Kent's death to prepare her body for freezing.'

Alcor won its legal battle with the coroner and the California Department of Health Services, and now has the right to continue doing suspensions and storing bodies. But to this day no one will reveal where Dora Kent's head is. The boys at Alcor will only say that it's not in the neuro-suspension chamber with the other patients.

My head—Dora Kent's head. That night, as I lay tossing and turning on my bed at the Shangri La Hotel in Santa Monica, I dreamed of immortality. I was awakening from a deep sleep, swimming up through the grasping tendrils of Morpheus towards the light. I could feel within my body a strange sensation. It felt as if myriad little pulsing things were moving about in there. Then it came to me. I was being re-animated! The suspension had worked.

243

I'm a little unsteady as the attendants help me out of the re-animation chamber. I look down groggily at my legs. They definitely are my legs, but they look better than they did during my previous animation: smoother, more muscular, more youthful. One of the reanimation technicians comes over. She's shy but a bit puffed up. Like a child about to bestow a gift. She holds up a mirror. 'Would you like to see what a good job we've done for you?' she says. I look at my reflection and then wake up screaming and screaming. They muddled me up! For in the mirror, crudely attached to my own lanky neck, was the wizened bonce of an elderly woman. I was half Self, half Kent.

The following morning, vowing never again to stay in a hotel with any connection to Lost Horizon, I headed off back up Route 99. I was going to confront Son of Head.

Saul Kent was one of the first ten people to become seriously involved with cryonics in the sixties. It was he who persuaded Ettinger that he needed to do something practical in support of his theories. Kent helped to found the Cryonics Society of New York and then came west in search of more converts. Although still a member, he is no longer directly involved with Alcor.

I found him deep in the suburban hinterland of Riverside, holed up in a typical faux adobe Californian house with a large Alsatian called Franklin. 'Franklin is a wonder dog,' he explained, kneading the dog's scruff with a large hand. 'He's been technically dead for over six hours. All the blood was drained out of his brain and he was taken down to around 4°C. No EEG activity at all. Then he was brought back—and look at him!' Franklin wagged his tail reanimatedly. He was in frisky contrast to his master, who looked distinctly liverish.

Kent is the ideologue of cryonics. He has written three books and numerous magazine articles. These are a strange gallimaufry of concepts drawn from the wilder shores of artificial intelligence, futurology and cognitive theory, all of which when added together depict a future in which science will be omnipotent, immortality assured and mankind will be living in self-created worlds gently orbiting the sun.

He fixed me with sag-bag eyes and expounded at length on how as a child of four or five he had decided it would be 'a bad thing' to die. This kindergarten epiphany had led him to a life of cryonics. 'Mind you,' he continued, 'I really view being suspended as the second worst thing that can happen to me after death itself. What I really want is to live healthily for as long as possible.' Now he hardly thought about death at all.

As Saul banged on, I started casting furtive glances around the room. Was there, perhaps, a neurocan tucked behind one of the canework bookcases? After all, Oedipus schmoedipus, what greater love can a son have for a mother than to chop off her head and stash it about the house?

But if Dora Kent's head had gone AWOL, what chance for my own? The boys at Alcor had given me alarming news. They were confident about their ability to keep their patients cool, but at the same time they gaily informed me that Riverside was the Californian city with the highest risk of an earthquake. They were now seeking a new site for the facility, possibly in northern California or Arizona. I began to suspect that, once I had entrusted my head to these people, it might end up doing more travelling when deanimated than it had with me still attached.

So I left LA and took the shuttle north to San Francisco. I was going to meet Thomas Donaldson and encounter the cryonics credo in full flight. For here was a man who had become obsessed by cryonics in the early seventies, and had then discovered in 1985 that he had a brain tumour.

His house was an hour's drive through the rain, down the coast from San Francisco towards Big Sur, and a very modest house it was, too—a little house made of ticky-tacky. The uninformed might imagine that plenty of millionaires would sign up for suspension, just for the hell of it. But, in fact, most cryonicists are fairly typically middle-class. Donaldson was no exception. A former maths teacher and computer software designer, he confirmed my impression of cryonicists as the ultimate computer nerds, with his trollishly sparse hair (for natural and therapeutic reasons) and his vocal delivery, horribly reminiscent of the comedian Emo Phillips.

I found him hunched up in his cardy. 'Aaaaah . . . OK! If they know enough to bring you back, they're going to know enough to grow you a new body . . . aaaah . . . OK?' That's why he was signed up for the head job alone. 'As soon as I knew I had the tumour, I thought: this is it, this is the battle I've been waiting for.' But his fight to have himself suspended immediately, before his legal 'death', proved unsuccessful. Some might think him lucky. His tumour hasn't spread and he is now in his fifth year of remission.

Perhaps it was his distance from the cryonic cockpit in LA that allowed him to talk more casually about his fellow cryonicists. 'When the coroners came for Dora Kent's head,' he confided, 'it wasn't there!' He giggled rather loonily. 'It had been removed.'

But then he went on and on, trotting out exactly the same tedious arguments. Sitting in his dun little room, with the rain coursing down the windows, my head began to deanimate with boredom. I sensed that it was time to leave the cryonicists.

However, back in England, I kept thinking: what if I had a deathbed conversion and decided, after all, that I wanted immortality on the instalment plan? Ralph Whelon had told me there was a front-end facility in England. I called the number he had given me and got one Garret Smyth. Was it true? 'Well, yes,' said a young, educated voice. 'We can perfuse you and lower your body temperature to dry-ice levels, around −79°C. Then we have a cool box to transport you to California. We don't handle storage here.'

'Where's here?' I asked guilelessly.

'Eastbourne,' replied the immortalist.

I could see his point about storage: there are already far too many deanimated people on the south coast of England.

But I didn't feel comfortable about gifting my head to the British cryonicists. There are only sixteen of them and none have actually done a suspension yet. It sounded like entrusting your head to them would be a recipe for guerrilla theatre at the Wintergardens.

That night, Dora Kent's head came to me again, grinning cheesily like a low-rent version of Hamlet Senior's ghost. At 3 a.m. I called Ralph Whelon in California. 'Come on, Ralph,' I said. 'Open up on the question of Saul's mum's head. For Christ's sake, where is it?'

'It's not a question we answer,' he purred. 'I told you that. We won't tell anyone until we're absolutely sure she's safe.'

And when will that be? Orthodox science is still a long way from complying with cryonicists. Saul Kent had told me he had a renegade cryobiologist working at his new laboratory, but that he preferred to remain incognito. The Society for Cryobiology, an official medical organization, states that its board of governors may either suspend or deny membership to anyone who engages in or promotes 'any practice or application of freezing deceased persons in the anticipation of their reanimation'.

Dr David Pegg of the East Anglian Regional Blood Transfusion Service sighed when I cited this. 'What the cryobiological community objects to is the impression these people give that the science has reached a point where some basis for this procedure exists. The suspension process just isn't meaningful when a patient is well and truly dead. They've died of something and there is no known remedy for it. That puts what these people are doing well into the realm of fantasy. What we object to as cryobiologists is the way they use the trappings of science to create a mystical atmosphere. They're just like priests dressing up for some ritual.'

But, in fairness to the cryonicists, isn't their response to the tyranny of death in a godless world at least understandable? They point out that in modern Western societies the vast majority of health expenditure tends to be in the last few months of a person's life. We seem to have created a culture of medical expertise dedicated to squeezing the last pips of consciousness out of near cadavers.

The modern way of death is already tied up in the tubing of an ostensibly life-saving technology: We die in hospitals, laid out on scientific altars. Perhaps the cryonicists are only taking this manifest faith in science to its logical and startling conclusion? The strange truth is that, since cryonicists started perfusing corpses with mortuary pumps in the late sixties, scientific research has been advancing towards the cryonicists' somewhat expanded view of the possible. Parallel computing; nanotechnology (or molecular machines); concepts of cyberspace and, of course, genetic engineering—these are no longer just the dreams of cranks, they are fields of legitimate research eating up many millions of dollars.

And what a delicious irony it would be if cryonics were to work, after all. Saul Kent had told me he had no doubts about his own reanimation: 'If you're being suspended now, you're not going to be one of the first ones back. The people being suspended fifty or a hundred years from now are going to be far easier to work on. If you're being suspended now, you'll have a long time to wait, perhaps thousands of years.'

But there will come a time when even those subject to the guerrilla theatre of the early suspensions will be revived—brave survivalists of time itself. And it will be a shock for the immortals of the future to discover that the pioneers, daring nonconformists all, are just a small posse of rather strident bores. I'll have to sign up for suspension so I can at least have a natter with Dora Kent's head, a frolic with Franklin the wonder dog. We'll all have such a lot of catching up to do.

Esquire, September 1993

On Demolition

To construct, to build, to fabricate, is, in a word, to *make;* or even—if we're being a little bit more high-flown—to *create*. Architects, civil engineers and builders of all stripes have the unalloyed certainty that at least what they do is creative in the purest sense: out of materials will come structures. It's as deterministic a relationship as that between carbonated drinks and burps.

Furthermore, there's the scale in which most of you work. It's big. Even the largest sculptural works of a Henry Moore, or an Anthony Caro, would be dwarfed by the average municipal sports centre. And as for the pictorial and decorative arts, at times you must have difficulty in not seeing these as mere impedimenta, props for your stages, flats for your Bayreuth productions. Thinking about how the architect of a vast building might conceive of such artefacts reminds me of the time I visited my publisher's and found the sales director piling up a teetering ziggurat of hardbacks. 'What're those?' I asked him. 'Don't tell any of the writers,' he hissed, 'but I've got a deal with the manager of—[a world-famous department store]; he buys these remaindered hardbacks off us to put in the bookcases they're flogging.'

Just think of it, labouring for years to produce a decoction of your own experience, or to perfectly realise an imagined (or vanished) world, only to find the result sold by the yard to garnish flatpack pseudo-Hepplewhite. It would have to seem like the most hideous traduction of all that it is to be a creative person.

But at least that's a relatively private matter (or at least it was until now). It must be that much worse in every respect for the originators and fabricators of the built environment who find out that their work is to be destroyed, knocked down, levelled; in a word, subject to *demolition*.

Demolition has intrigued me for many years. Indeed, it's worthwhile reminding you professionals that the blowing up of Ronan Point made just as much—if not more—impression on the general public as the erection of a thousand blocks of flats untroubled by design faults. It was Bakunin, the anarchist revolutionary, who said that 'the urge to destruction is always creative'. I wonder if he moonlighted as a demolition contractor. Indeed, I have been wondering for some time whether or not those who pull down the built environment feel as impassioned about what they do as those who construct it. As children, did these people feel as great a surge of satisfaction when they kicked down a sandcastle as others of us felt when we built one?

Perplexed, I called an old schoolfriend of mine who I'd learned had become a demolition contractor. Actually, Maurice was the boy least likely to raze. A gentle, almost fey character, he always kept his exercise books neatly covered with plastic and labelled with Dymotape. We used to take the piss out of him mercilessly. Now he owns one of the biggest knocking-down shops in the country.

'Maurice,' I asked him, 'you were always so quiet and well behaved—were you always nurturing a secret passion to level every building you clapped eyes on?'

'Not *every* building,' he replied in carefully measured tones, 'but certainly a fair few of them. And yes, I did secretly nurture a desire to demolish from an early age. I would buy plastic models of famous buildings, make them, and then torch

them with lighter fuel, or pound them with a hammer, or simply kick them to bits—'

'What sort of buildings?'

'Well, put it this way, by the time I was fifteen I'd worked
my way through most of the Gothic revival.'

I was prepared to accept that Maurice had a genuine voca-
tion, and certainly when he spoke of the elegance and economy
implied in placing explosive charges within a structure so carefully, so *artfully,* that split seconds after it's subsided it's as if it
was never there, I was impressed. It seemed that Maurice genuinely believed he was benefiting the built environment; that
like some dentist of the carious city he was determined to drill
out decay. But what, I wondered, did he feel like, when having eliminated one monstrosity, another was simply built in
its place? Didn't this entirely vitiate the value of what he was
doing? Wouldn't a truly creative demolition contractor have
to be *proactive,* have to go round to architects' offices and rip
up blueprints, destroy CADCAM files and generally ensure
that the space he'd created remained just that?

Maurice looked pensive for a while, then said, 'I think that's
an absolutely fantastic idea . . .'

Building Design, February 1998

Scab

The scabs on my arms are my sorejeant's stripes. God, what an execrable pun—and yet it's by no means the worst one I have in me, the lowest I could squeeze out. Anyway, within this vector of facile semantic exercise there is, none the less, an important truth: that I, like so many self-mutilators, see my perversion as a long, bitterly-fought campaign, executed in mountainous country, by an overextended conventional ground army, which is being consistently harassed by savage guerrilla bands, who strike at its flanks, slash at its withers, before fading once more into the formlessness of their own, immemorial hinterland.

Seen in this way, the ovoid, vaginal, open weeping sores on my thighs have a more ambiguous message. Unlike the scabs on my arms they are no mere designators of rank—they're more like the squashed semaphore of modern campaign ribbons, wound round my thighs, tightened up into tourniquets.

Anyway, I'm rehearsing these distinctions—while adopting the peculiarly sphinx-like posture required of me, if I'm not to undo the good work the nursing staff do, spreading my stripes and ribbons with antiseptic, and antibiotic, intensively caring cream—when Doc-tor Shamannamundy comes by. I always think that this is a good way to differentiate psychiatrists from the rest of the profession: Doc-tor, that's how their title should be pronounced—and written—so as to rhyme with 'sore'. Shamannamundy is a queer enough thing. Half Tamil,

252

half Irish, he wears three-piece suits cut from three separate weaves of sharkskin, and gunmetal-grey, pointed shoes, with matching, clocked socks. Can you imagine that? A psychiatrist who wears matching socks and shoes—how terrifying can that be?

Shamannamundy bids me, 'Good morning,' very much the sore-side specialist. Shamannamundy also whispers, 'God bless,' when he departs, as if this were the only natural valedictory book-end to his consultations. Why does he whisper? Is his deity omniscient yet marginally deaf? I have vowed to beard him on this matter, as soon as my treatment has sufficiently advanced.

Anyway, he bids me unholster my side-arm, take off my bandoleer, remove my Sam Browne, drop my combat kecks—until I stand, gloriously stippled with sores, maculate with pus, in my true and puckered uniform. Sorejeant de Chirico—ready and waiting. Shamannamundy ignores my badinage; his manner is such as to imprison my rampaging, agonised bull in many many filaments of soft concern, a gauze of seeming-kindness. 'Look,' he says, gesturing at the stripes, the ribbons, 'look what you've done to yourself. Let me see your nails.' And when they've been exhibited, 'See,' he points out the crescent moons of dried blood, 'why d'jew do it? Why?'

Why indeed. Why—indeed. Perversion is a question to which the only answer is a dialectic: pick, open sore, scab. (Where pick is the thesis, open sore the antithesis, and scab the synthesis.) And anyway, precious Shamannamundy, what can you know of the beautiful integrity of my rank? What can you understand of that moment when one's own flesh ceases to be flesh at all and becomes instead an altogether more mortal, more malleable clay?

At night the nursing staff here patrol on the half-hour, for which they receive time and a half. They deploy torches, as if they were Nazi guards, and yet this is an exclusive, private clinic in the very humming heart of London. The wavering beams finger my fucked-up form, where it lies on the grainy mattress; they stroke my face with lucent disregard. In between the patrols I work on the tunnels I am boring through myself— the vermiculation of my very soul. I have arranged pads of antiseptic gauze over the points of ingress in order to fool the medical staff. But once these have been removed, the way is open for my brave fingers to pinch and gouge and distress the flesh. To feel its gritty, bloody, purulent shapeliness. To load it cleverly under my nails. To transport it to the sheet, to the pillowcase, to my stinking T-shirt. Then I replace the bindings, cover up the campaign, and wait for Aurora to ride ahead of me, inaccessible, inviolate in the microwavable bag of her perfect dermis.

Morning finds me in pain, in the basement canteen. Moneyed neurotics toy with sausages that are little more than skin tubes stuffed with greasy breadcrumbs, such is the comprehensive nature of the fiddle the Filipino catering manager is engaged in. I sit, triumphant, over a smallish dish of acerbic grapefruit segments. My arms, my thighs, various junctures of my body—all flare with unbearable pain.

Shamannamundy diffidently approaches across the up-market carpet tiles. 'You did it again last night?'

And will again tonight.

It will be a long campaign, but in the end victory is certain.

Sebastian Horsley exhibition catalogue, February 1999

The Media Estate: Big Brother

In Ray Bradbury's prescient science-fiction novel of 1953, *Fahrenheit 451,* the firemen of the future don't put out fires—they start them in order to burn books. In this painfully delineated utilitarian dystopia, trivial information is good, while knowledge and ideas are bad. The fire Captain, Beatty, explains it this way: 'Give the people contests they win by remembering the words to more popular songs . . . Don't give them any slippery stuff like philosophy or sociology to tie things up with. That way lies melancholy.'

The novel's protagonist, Guy Montag, is a book-burning fireman undergoing a crisis of faith. His wife spends all day with her television 'family', imploring Montag to work harder so that they can afford a fourth wall-sized television monitor. Each morning a script of a kind of real-time soap opera is delivered to the Montags' house, with lines already written in for Mrs Montag. She sits in front of three walls of television images all day, and from time to time one of the actors in the 'family' turns to her and says, 'So, what do you think . . . ?' And she interpolates her own lines.

Even from this brief synopsis, I think you'll have no difficulty in agreeing with me that *Fahrenheit 451* presents a far more accurate view of the society implied by Channel 4's hit game show *Big Brother* than the George Orwell novel *Nineteen Eighty-Four* from which it takes its name. *Big Brother* comes to an end this evening, after a nine-week run. The final three contestants—Craig, the pawky scouser; Anna, the lesbian, skateboarding, former Catholic noviciate; and 'Big Daddy' Darren, the black father-of-three with a nice line in narcissism—will find out who the viewers have voted the 'winner'. One of them will then pick up the £70,000 prize money, while the other two will have to amortise whatever notoriety the show brought them into cash.

Within a couple of weeks of *Big Brother* beginning, the show eased its way into the popular consciousness of the nation. Although only five million or so viewers actually tuned in, the whole implicit concept of death-by-voyeurism seized the imagination not only of couch potatoes, but also of armchair pundits such as myself. While Tracy, my three-year-old's nanny, was happy, downstairs in the playroom, to discuss the character and motivation of the participants—who was to be nominated that week by the contestants from their own number, and who, therefore, would be 'evicted' come Friday—I've been sat upstairs in my office, evoking the name 'Big Brother' as a synecdoche of the British polity, or as an enactment of McLuhanite prophecies, or as a terminal symptom of the death of British television.

Even when the 'Nasty Nick' revelations were transpiring, Channel 4's ratings didn't climb much above seven million, and yet the *Big Brother* phenomenon achieved a huge degree of resonance, like a coaxial cable lashed between high and low culture, and vigorously bowed by contemporaneity. In the *Independent on Sunday* last week, my colleague David Aaronovitch wrote an inspired critique of the current state of British television, to which, as the paper's miserable television critic, I could only nod my head in weary assent. He pointed out that with the Balkanisation of the networks, not only were programmers facing a ratings war, driving them to worse and worse excesses of cheap titillation masquerading as entertainment, but with the very stage upon which high-quality drama

256

might be enacted progressively shrinking, it was questionable whether such productions would even continue to be made.

It's an irony worth noting that the Reithian broadcasting culture, the heyday of which Aaronovitch so eloquently mourned, itself matured in the wartime culture of propaganda that inspired Orwell's *Nineteen Eighty-Four.* For 'the Ministry of Truth' read 'Broadcasting House'. And anyway, the old three-channel television duopoly in Britain had become a state corporatist anomaly in a nation intent on gorging itself on the Big Mac of global capitalism. But during the last few years, it hasn't only been the market that's driven television standards—with some exceptions—into a downward spiral; we've also entered a new era of virtuality, where the interpenetration of a plethora of communications media, from CCTV and mobile phones to webcams and cable channels, has created an environment in which never before have so many watched so many others, doing so very little.

In media-studies faculties at the moment, the debate rages as to whether Marshall McLuhan was right, and these new media are themselves the message—the message being 'buy more media, and everything that they advertise'—or whether, rather, his pabulum should be idealistically reversed to read 'the message is the medium', implying that the global reach and accessibility of the new media will mean a new golden age of participatory democracy. Frankly, I think that the latter view, given streets full of people chatting purposelessly on mobiles, our own Government financing social services through phone franchises, and the stock exchange booming off the anticipation of on-line retailing, is sheer California dreaming.

No, we're living through a period when the face-to-face bonds that personalised even mass societies and made them bearable are being transmogrified into the anonymous encounters of virtual space. *Big Brother* stands as the acme of this culture

of depersonalised anonymity—which explains the painful resonance of its banal triviality. I've watched a fair bit of the show
over the summer, and not only for professional reasons. I've
absolutely no doubt that the way the contestants were selected
for *Big Brother,* together with the editing of the 24/7 footage
from umpteen concealed video cameras, has provided us with
a perfect biopsy of the cancer that as I write is hypostasising
throughout our culture.

It's a culture of equality all right, for the contestants are
equally unquestioning, equally sheep-like, equally directionless,
equally lacking in anything that passes for a social conscience
or a spiritual value. Self-selecting for narcissism, exhibitionism
and a sorrowful dependency on the good opinion of others,
the *Big Brother* contestants are the first cohort among other
equals, in a wholly statistical nation.

It's no accident that the 'tasks' the contestants are asked to
perform are so redolent of other television shows. Whether
doing a turn from *The Krypton Factor, The Generation Game* or
Countdown, these poor saps are only pirouetting in a hall of
video monitors. This is our 'family', and like the twenty-to-
thirtysomething clans depicted in other popular shows such
as *Friends* and *Ally McBeal,* it's made up of 'kidults', those adult
children of juvenescence, the scurf on the collapsing wave of
the baby boom, who are intent on stretching the elastic of their
promiscuous, intoxicated adolescence, until senility snaps it
back in their faces.

Watching *Big Brother* is best done by mixed groups of parents and prepubescent children. All can revel in this enactment of a seventy-day sleep-over, where no one bothers to
get out of their pyjamas except to sunbathe or dress up. Oh
yes, it is heartening to see that in the brave new world of
Blair, a black contestant and a gay contestant have made it
into the last three, but what this suggests to me is that tolerance in our society has only been won at the cost of diversity. The extent to which the viewers haven't been prejudiced

against these minorities is exactly the same as the extent to which they no longer offer any alternative lifestyle choice. With everyone middle-class, childless and a restful shade of beige, we're living not so much in a melting-pot as in a Cup-a-Soup. Or so we wish to believe.

It's no surprise to me that *Big Brother* was originated in the Netherlands, that claustrophobic cockpit of social innovation, where an ancient culture of cheese-making supports an ephemeral one of utter cheesiness. Nor is it any wonder that the format for this show has replicated throughout the globe, like some awful media virus. It offers us the spectacle of pure voyeurism, and its interactivity leads the way to new forms of narration that will no longer require any suspension of disbelief.

In traditional story-telling, whether on page, stage or screen, the audience is invited to emotionally identify themselves with a protagonist whose fate is determined by a *deus ex machina*. But in television shows utilising ordinary people, the action of which is propelled by collective decision-making, there is no need for viewers to exercise that feat of creative empathy, whereby they can 'become' a Prince of Denmark suffering a proto-existential crisis, or a nineteenth-century aristocratic Russian woman tormented by sexual desire—let alone surrender themselves to dictates of chance, or fate. Like mere servomechanisms, extensions of the wilfulness of their contemplators, the pawn-participants in these projects will be required to enact increasingly grotesque playlets to satisfy the jaded palates of their manipulators.

Make no mistake, in terms of what the genre has to offer, *Big Brother* is a mere lukewarm entrée. Novelty, combined with the vestiges of our national rectitude, prevented anything from getting too steamy or nasty in the *Big Brother* house, but in the future, opportunities to interact with sexual and violent experiences will become a *sine qua non* of such shows, as the next tumbrel of entertainment to trundle on to our screens—Channel 5's *Prisoner*—will amply demonstrate.

Yes, we should be worried. The atrophy of the empathetic muscles necessary for the appreciation of traditional narrative is happening in step with the development of entertainment media—the Internet chat room, the interactive television show—that substitute anonymous equivalence for personalised identification. Why bother labouring to translate your being across space, time, gender, ethnicity or religion, when you can watch some bimbo exactly like the one next door plucking her bikini line on live television? Or better still, on a little postcard-sized vignette, in the corner of your PC's screen, while you employ the Intel inside to multitask your way through the next spreadsheet or corporate report.

For me *Big Brother* was over two weeks ago anyway, with Claire, the breast-enhanced flirt interest, sent packing. There was no doubting that poor Mel, the least psychically secure contestant, and the subject of a hate campaign by the herd without, would be the next to go. There was a hideous moment when, as Mel was sprung from behind the razor wire (and how disgusting the setting for this bathos has been, a kind of Ikea Belsen, marooned in Bromley-by-Bow), she heard the lowing of the bovine punters bellowing 'Whore!' and 'Slut!' It took her a split second to adjust to the correct posture of puppetry, and then she leapt up and down like a teenager afflicted with mass hysteria at a pop concert, and began screaming the triumphant affirmation of the eradication of her soul.

Now that it's down to the final triumvirate of trivia, the popular vote will go with the man who best understands and exemplifies populism, Craig, while the dissenting vote will go with Anna. And *Big Brother* being the kind of television show that it is—veritably powered by populism—I hardly think it likely that dissent will carry the day. A few nights ago, chatting to my ten-year-old boy about *Big Brother,* I asked him why it was that the contestants hadn't banded together ages ago and smashed all the cameras in the house save for one. Then they could've taken over the means of the production of the show and broadcast their own demands to the nation. 'They couldn't do that,' he said; 'the people who make it would've switched it off.' 'Ah,' I replied, 'they couldn't afford to do that—it would've lost them hundreds of thousands of pounds in revenue—and anyway, it'd make great television.' He looked at me with the pitying expression of someone who's being parented by an anarchistic dinosaur, while I looked back at him with revulsion at the media dupe I'd spawned.

Marshall McLuhan said that we advance into the future imposing our historic archetypes of communication upon the new media that we invent; thus we steer the car using the rear-view mirror. I think he had a point, but what I can see in the rear-view mirror is Bradbury's *Fahrenheit 451,* and another episode featuring the 'family' is about to be screened.

Independent, September 2000

Wilde

I wonder how many of the hundreds of thousands who gathered along the River Thames to witness the humungous fireworks display that ushered the third millennium into this ancient burg really appreciated why this year was so special? Special, that is, for anyone who fancies himself as a dandy, or a wit, or a bon viveur, or a boulevardier. Special for any of us who is an *homme du monde*—let alone a *fille de joie*. Special for the aesthetic—although certainly not for the ascetic. Special for the classicist, the neo-classicist and the defiantly modern. Special for the straight, the gay *and* the Janus-assed. In Times Square they had a New Year's Eve jollification that would've appealed more than mere fireworks to the man I choose to regard as the presiding spirit of this year. I refer to the traditional dropping of the Waterford crystal globe.

Appealed more because like my hero, Oscar Wilde, the crystal globe originated in Ireland. Appealed more to him because of its scintillating impermanence—and appealed to him more because, like dear Oscar, the globe was beautifully constructed simply to be destroyed.

Oscar Wilde died on 30 November 1900, in Paris, France. He was just forty-six years old—but what amazing years they'd been! The doyen of his Oxford generation, a prodigious classical scholar, Wilde won the Newdigate Prize for poetry and charmed the English academic establishment, despite his habit of dressing excessively showily, compulsive non-attendance,

262

and running up huge debts with local tradesmen. Needless to say he 'went down' (marvellous expression that, signifying— one is tempted to imagine—a headlong descent from the ivory tower of the university to the flesh pots of London) without a degree.

But what need had Oscar of mere paper qualifications? He embarked, more or less immediately, on a hugely successful career as a public lecturer in America. His declaration to cus- toms officials on his arrival at Staten Island of 'nothing but my genius' is probably apocryphal, but little else about his sojourn was. It was all written about fulsomely in newspapers of the day. And written about, and written about, and written about. Wilde tracked back and forth across the country giving lec- tures on the 'House Beautiful' and the Aesthetic movement. He appeared in costumes of his own, highly aesthetical devis- ing. Velvet knee-breeches, a fur-trimmed overcoat, a quilted smoking jacket. Tom Wolfe—eat your heart out, you're so *passé*.

Many flocked to hear this dandy speak without realising that their fascination was provoked by witnessing tomorrow's cultural news today: Wilde—the harbinger of the styles and modes of the twentieth century, an era to be rendered dys- peptic with the gorging of its own decadences. Not only that, he has to be one of the few great writers to have played Peoria and received rave notices. For while Wilde may have been an intellectual and aesthetic élitist, that was the only élitism he espoused. He was no social snob—something Americans understood intuitively.

Wilde initially chanced his arm at high-flown theatrical pieces of almost stultifying impenetrability, and turned to the supreme comedies of timeless manners, for which he is remem- bered, only as a nice little earner. What delicious legerdemain! If only a fraction of today's poetasters could achieve such con- summate insouciance! Still, the reason I'm making Wilde my man of the year isn't simply that it's the centenary of his death (an anniversary that, unlike the millennium itself, is cross-cultural and indisputable), it's that here in benighted Britain, his memory is still under the most pernicious of threats.

A couple of years ago, a statue of dear old Oscar was finally unveiled in the lee of St Martin-in-the Fields, hard by London's Theatreland—the only realm he ever aspired to dominate, and the one he does to this day. The statue, by Maggi Hambling, portrays the artist reclining, smoking one of his trademark opiated cigarettes, and staring towards the West End. The caption on the base of the statue sums him up in his own words: 'We are all in the gutter, but some of us are looking at the stars.' The idea of the piece—which is a kind of granite sarcophagus from which Oscar's head and gesturing arms emerge—was that people could come and sit on his chest and chat to him. Indeed, Hambling's title for the piece is *A Conversation with Oscar Wilde.*

The ribbon was cut by the current British Minister for Culture, Chris Smith, a man who shares with dear old Oscar none of the artist's most important characteristics—to wit, wit, wisdom, immaculate prose style, effortless sartorial style and iconoclastic socialism—and only one of his most salient ones: being openly homosexual. Needless to say, despite being our first uncloseted gay minister, Smith received the attentions of demonstrators during the unveiling—demonstrators who wanted to know what the New Labour Government would be doing about Section 28. This is an infamous piece of legislation introduced by that drag queen of darkness Mrs Thatcher, which makes it illegal for British schools to in any way educate children as to the whys and wherefores of same-sex relationships.

In fairness to Tony Blair and his merry men, the abolition of Section 28 is now under way—but only with tremendous resistance being incurred from every homophobic institution in the land (which is just about all of them with the exception of the Royal National Theatre and the night-club Heaven). But where does this leave dear old Oscar? I'll tell you. Passing by Hambling's statue the other day, on my way to purchase some green lilies in Covent Garden, I was appalled to see that it's been encased in what—for want of a better word—can only be described as a little wooden cottage. If you wanted to have a conversation with Oscar, you'd have to break inside.

The cottage has been put there because the statue kept being vandalised. Yup—it's the solid truth. A hundred years since the man died, his health broken, after a two-year sentence of hard labour for 'gross indecency', the really gross indecency of defacing a memorial to him is being perpetrated.

Well, I for one won't stand for it. One of my projects for this, the year of Wilde, is to finish writing a new movie version of his classic *The Picture of Dorian Gray*. I shall dedicate it to my hero. In the draft I've done so far, I've updated the action from the end of the nineteenth century to the end of the twentieth. *Plus ça change?*—as dear Oscar might say himself. Well, not much. Of course, in the original, the buried metaphor-that-wasn't-really-a-metaphor was syphilis—which Wilde himself suffered from. And in my version it will be Aids. Other than that, the observations of social mores, the melodrama of debauched morals and the superlative epigrams, which apotheosise *everything,* all remain as fresh as the day they were penned.

Indeed, it's the epigrams that have dated best of all. So, it's Oscar's own words that serve best to debunk the freaks who would dare to attack him today—just as they did a hundred years ago: 'A man cannot be too careful in the choice of his enemies.'

Have a Wilde year, everyone.

GQ, February 2000

Andrea Dworkin: The Interview

The Bill Clinton scandals have left Andrea Dworkin, the arche-typal radical feminist, more isolated than ever. Will Self meets a surprisingly vulnerable pariah.

I met her in a coffee bar on Greenwich Avenue in the Village. It was a typical enough joint for downtown Manhattan, called—somewhat grandiloquently—Cafe des Artistes. It had stripped-board floors and distempered walls. There was a base-to-nape counter, overgrown with pot plants and ballasted with a Gaggia, around which hovered a dwarfish collection of waiting staff. The first room was dark enough, but the second—the one she'd told me she'd meet me in—was almost crepuscular.

She'd arrived before me, and arranged herself carefully in a throne-like chair behind a table by the door. She drank sparkling mineral water—although she told me that the food was 'excellent'—while I contented myself with small glasses of tart red wine. The talk strayed—as it will between bookish people—to the reputations of writers we have loved and I asked her about Baudelaire. Her voice was deep and smoothly throaty. She chuckled before replying: 'I still love Baudelaire . . . I just can't . . . y'know . . . intellectually I think he's pathetic, but the poetry still holds me.' She went on to say that she read him in parallel translation.

ANDREA DWORKIN: THE INTERVIEW

A seed was sown and finding myself the following day in the Strand Bookstore, just south of Union Square, with its 'eight miles' of secondhand books, I went looking for a parallel translation of *Les Fleurs du Mal,* thinking that maybe now was the time to renew my quest for the poetic. I found a first edition of Edna St Vincent Millay's translations and, idly flipping the cut and annotated pages, chanced on this verse:

> Hope—if you're hopeful—or despair;
> Nothing's to hinder you; but hark!
> Always the hissing head is there,
> The insupportable remark.

It seemed to me a small piece of uncanniness; St Vincent Millay translates the title as 'The Fang', but L'Avertisseur really means 'the horn', and it's as a foghorn that we perceive this woman, my coffee bar interlocutor: a foghorn blaring out Cassandra-like prophecies of sado-sexual immolation—certainly not as I describe her above, in the guise of a poetry lover, a coffee-bar intellectual, whiling away the early evening in the West Village.

Expectations are made to be defeated, and on this trip one was and one wasn't. I'd expected to turn up at my half-brother Nick Adams's house in upstate New York and have him yawn when I told him why I was in the States; instead, he said 'Andrea who?' 'Dworkin,' I replied, 'the radical feminist—surely you've heard of her?' He hadn't—and I suppose this wouldn't be too remarkable if he were a plumber or a farmer, but he's the professor of architectural history at Vassar and a widely-read liberal intellectual. That evening he returned from the college almost skipping with glee: 'Hardly any of my colleagues have heard of this woman either; a couple of them know of her through her work with a lawyer called Catherine MacKinnon, trying to get anti-pornography legislation enacted—and you say she's well known in Britain—'

267

'Well known?! Her name's almost a synonym for radical feminism.'

'Well, it isn't here. I mean look'—he brandished a copy of that day's *New York Observer*, a tittle-tattle broadsheet printed on salmon-colored paper— 'see here, the headline reads, "New York feminists stand by their bill not by Broaddrick"; and they've gone round interviewing Naomi Wolf, Susan Faludi and Gloria Steinem about their reactions to Juanita Broaddrick's rape accusation against Clinton, but not this Dworkin woman.'

I grabbed the paper off him. It was true: under a garish cartoon which depicted The Great Cocksman and his entourage of Democratically faithful, bikini-porting feminists, tooling along in a red convertible, there were no fewer than three pieces anatomising the unwillingness of prominent New York feminists to countenance the truth of Broaddrick's accusations. Katrina Vanden Heuvel, the editor of *The Nation* (and believe me, well known over there), summed up the prevailing ennui when she remarked, 'Forget Teflon, he's the iridium president. He's like someone from another planet.'

Most of the women questioned were, I realised, not the sort of 'feminists' Andrea Dworkin would have any time for anyway, but Gloria Steinem I knew to be a personal friend. It seemed to me, as the week went on and the strong flows of accusation and counter-accusation continued to course through the American body politic, that I couldn't have chosen a better, nor a potentially more painful time to interview Andrea Dworkin. For she's the woman who has made it her life's work to counter the way she believes existing power structures enshrine the ability of men to exercise violence on women and sexually abuse them. Furthermore, she's someone who has never hesitated to fuse the personal and the political, adding to this most painful of Festschrifts her own accounts of her several sexual assaults, rapes and myriad beatings at the hands of men.

ANDREA DWORKIN: THE INTERVIEW

I first heard of her when I read her book *Intercourse* in the early eighties. It is a searing polemic which advances the proposition that all penetrative sex is freighted with the possibility of being rape. I—as a young man with a more than average obsession with penetrative sex—found the work simultaneously repugnant and beguiling. Repugnant because it forced me to address the basic antinomies of my gender-based sexuality, and beguiling for exactly the same reason. Dworkin's arguments might have been extreme, but they pushed the true agenda to the surface. One thing was clear—this woman was fearless.

A few years later, on its British publication, I read her novel *Ice and Fire* and found it to be not at all what I expected. Beautifully and hauntingly written, this was a description of a woman's *saison d'enfer* in the Hiroshima landscape of the South Bronx. So far from revealing a cold, puritanical sensibility, Dworkin's descriptive prose was lush and sensuous. That was enough for me—I resolved that were I ever in a position to do so, I would meet this writer.

Clanking down the Metro North line and into the throbbing Grand Central heart of Manhattan, I read her latest collection of writings, *Life and Death*. Certainly Dworkin still had all her ice and fire intact. In essays on subjects as diverse as Nicole Brown Simpson, the Serbian death/rape camps and Israeli state-sponsored misogyny, she honed her prose into an incantation of measured outrage. Dworkin always focuses on the language of her opponents, pointing out how the very ascription of Nicole Brown Simpson being a 'battered wife' was disallowed by Judge Lawrence Ito. How, in other words, O.J. Simpson's defence team was able to distort the truth of his persecution and battering, even when his victim was beyond the grave.

My second expectation had been that I would get on well with Andrea, and in this, at least, I wasn't disappointed. I suppose if I'd stopped to think about it for even a few minutes, it might have occurred to me to worry what this much-persecuted woman might make of a large, heterosexual man with an extremely chequered history of relations with women, but I didn't. Perhaps it's the raw quality of Andrea's bulk (she must weigh more than 300 lbs) that effectively muffles such concerns; perhaps somebody being so extravagantly over-weight effectively desexes both them and their interlocutors. The alternative—and I hope true—explanation is that she didn't peg me as a misogynist.

We spoke of Baudelaire, as I say, and of how the degrada-tion of male writers is often perceived as enhancing their aes-thetic value, while the same would never be true for a female writer. It was a point she'd made in her introductory essay to the last collection, *My Life as a Writer,* but she enlarged on it for me, saying she now found Henry Miller's work 'embar-rassingly negligible and repulsively anti-Semitic,' and Ginsberg to mean 'nothing to me, nothing at all'.

I asked what she was currently working on, and she re-plied, 'I'm actually extremely dull because I've been work-ing on footnotes.' The footnotes are for her next book, *Scapegoat,* which deals with a subject as inflammatory as any she has cov-ered before: 'It's about the Jews in Israel and women's liberation. What women-hating and Jew-hating had in com-mon, and then the whole history of how that changed for Jews with the establishment of the state of Israel; how the Jews then subordinated women and created a racial enemy in their image.' Did the Israelis construe the Arabs as effete? I mused. 'Sure,' she went on, 'if you're an Arab you're a castrated individual; so then you go home and take it out on the real woman . . . this chain which never seems to stop.'

But didn't she feel a great sense of achievement having fin-ished this book? A sense of . . . parturition? She paused for a moment, then said, 'When I finished *Intercourse* I remember how I felt . . . Ah! This is done . . . I haven't had that feeling in a long time.' Was it, I wondered, in part because of the recent politico-sexual events? And then it began to come out, the hot effluvia of her pain: 'I'm sure that's part of it, it would be very hard not to be in despair in this country right now. When I sat down each night to write, I had to force myself to believe that I was writing something which somebody, some-where, sometime would read. When I first started publishing I thought there was a community of people I was writing for, but over the years the hostility I've met has changed that vision.'

My brother's analysis of Dworkin's invisibility on the American political scene was succinct, and nothing to do with her nocturnal working habits. 'It's the First Amendment,' he told me—not without a slight smirk. 'This legislation she and Catherine MacKinnon have tried to get passed has been struck down because it infringes a perceived right to free speech. The minute you assault the First Amendment, libertarians of all political stripes are arraigned against you. It's the American way.' So Dworkin was squeezed out of the very middle of the political spectrum; while in Europe her books are in print, in the USA only the last is in circulation. It was an incongruity I'd never heard any British journalist remark on before. What did Andrea think?

'In Britain more people actually read what I write—here my name is a curse word.'

I trotted out Nick's analysis to see if it bore fruit and she said, 'Whatever it is, it's that need people have for absolutes. This is our faith—and it's taken such hold. It's enormously comfortable to have one principle you honour no matter what its consequences are, forget about everything else that has to do with liberty, equality, freedom—just forget it. It's a bril-liant way for people not to have to take the responsibility for what's out there. In this country everything is a legal ques-tion: is it legal or illegal? Then there's nothing more to say about it.'

WILL SELF

'Take Mapplethorpe'—and this was entirely apposite, for
Nick had raised the issue of the 'homoerotic' photographer
to highlight why it was that American liberals had no time for
Dworkin—'It's impossible in America to say anything about
his racism. People only want to know if it's legal.' I concurred,
but went on to hazard that her critics were so vehement because they feared her vision of an egalitarian eroticism as being
a sexless utopia where hermaphroditic beings wandered the
wan earth wearing shapeless dun shifts. She didn't want that,
did she? 'No, I don't. I do think there's a genuine eroticism
of equality, a kind of intimacy that is peculiarly different from
male dominance, regardless of which side is acting out their
role. I have come to believe that it's very hard for people to
even think that their sexual feelings could ever exist in a context of equality.

'What I object to is the taking of pornography for femi-
nine consent—I never used to use those words as synonyms,
it wouldn't've been just. But people don't seem to have noticed the enormous growth of fetishism and voyeurism in this
country—and there are consequences and they are synonymous.' Consequences that Dworkin and MacKinnon sought
to combat, but has their legislative programme ground to a
halt entirely now? 'Pretty much,' she sighed. 'There to be
reawakened at the right time, when people want it. When
people begin to feel that there are consequences to pornography that they find intolerable. The problem is that pornography
changes people—it so desensitises them to any real, authentic
connection with other people. And the more desensitised they
become, the less they can see.'

It was time to broach the barrel of pain and get it out in the
open. How, I asked, would Andrea have responded if she'd
been asked by the *New York Observer* to comment on Broaddrick's rape accusations against the president? Her reply was
presaged by a short, guttural, mirthless laugh: 'I will never be

272

asked that question.' But if she was? 'I believe that Clinton is a rapist. I believe the woman—and if I had doubts about the woman, I trust what I perceive about him—and in my view people have misunderstood what he did to Paula Jones: that was an assault. When you understand that that was an assault, it's a very clear line to rape.'

She didn't raise her voice or speak with odd emphasis, this was the spoken Dworkin, L'Avertisseur, like her prose: a repetitive incantation, designed to honk home the truth. And how did she feel about all of this? 'I am beside myself. If I wasn't numbed by footnotes I don't know what I'd do—it causes me such distress. I'm sure a lot of women will've gone through what I've gone through . . . Suddenly, every time you look at this man you have to think about rape. It's harder to sleep, it's harder to work . . . because this man is the president. That's obscenity—right there.'

And what did she feel about the response of Steinem et al? 'That has been extremely hurtful. I'm about ready to cut up my card and send it back to the office. It's only what the grass-roots women do that keeps me from completely disavowing the mainstream feminism in this country. And, of course, a lot of these women are friends of mine, so it hurts on a personal level.

'I sent Gloria Steinem—with whom I'm very close—a fax a year ago in January. It was just before a piece of mine about Clinton and what he'd done was about to appear. My note said, "People are beginning to circle their wagons. I hope you won't be part of it." Two days later her op-ed piece was in the *New York Times* saying: "Well, he took no for an answer—what is the problem? With Jones he took no for an answer—with Lewinsky it was consensual, so what's the problem?" And I was just appalled and I still am, beside myself.'

I knew that Steinem was one of the feminists who had effectively fed and clothed Dworkin during her dog days. Was this the end of all conversation between them? 'I hope we can find a way to talk, but we can't now. It was so condescending what she said. She said women who had been sexually assaulted did not have the sense of freedom that she had, because she had always been respected and we were ignorant of what consent means. I found that so upsetting. Now that the charge is rape, I think that we're the experts.

'It's this kind of splintering that's so difficult to take— women you consider to have saved your life because of the work they've done, and then they're saying to Ms Broaddrick 'drop dead'; and when they say it to her, they're saying it to me. Essentially, while what's left of the women's movement shows any support for Clinton, they're destroying the movement itself as any kind of refuge for women who've been sexually assaulted.'

That, for me, was a clinching remark and one which made a mockery of the vacuities many mainstream feminists debate, as if theoretical concerns were anywhere near the heart of these issues. Dworkin had said it: support a possible rapist as president and you broach the very hull of the movement, leaving it to flounder and sink; and leaving to sink along with it all of the allegedly pro-women legislation which has been passed during Clinton's administration. 'Of course Clinton is pro-choice,' my wife opined back in London. 'He needs easy access to abortion for all the women he's knocked up.'

But in Manhattan I didn't unleash such incisive irony on L'Avertisseur. Instead I switched off the tape recorder and told Andrea that she no longer needed to sound either sonorous or oracular. And she didn't. We talked about her upbringing in New Jersey, and her 'intensely supportive' father, who's still alive. We spoke also of how her mother, permanently invalided by heart disease, had gone into therapy in her sixties, after 'outliving all her doctors'. Despite her belief in the importance of a personal praxis for those who are political writers, she didn't seem a depressed person: 'I really love being alive—not that I think that every story has a happy ending, but I have an almost biological excitement with the wide world.'

Andrea had pithicisms to make about neuropharmacology: 'I think they're aiming to replace all illegal drugs with legal ones.' And depression: 'In this country it's a blanket term that's pulled over to cover everything: melancholy, sadness, ill-fortune . . .' We also talked—or rather I did—about me. Indeed, the whole interview had commenced with my telling her at length about my other reason for visiting my brother: my need to read the many intimate diaries left by my dead mother, which are in his possession. This is the character of the woman—she is a brilliant and sympathetic listener. I'd read other journalists' accounts of Dworkin and they'd described her as being, surprisingly, 'very nice'. It isn't niceness—it's sympathy. The sympathy of a woman who's had her convictions tempered at the same time as her emotions have been tenderised.

After a couple of hours she asked what I was doing and I said I was going uptown to meet people for dinner. Earlier she'd told me she too had a rendezvous, but now she said she would be meeting them right here in the Cafe des Artistes. I bade her farewell and said I'd look her up when I was next in town. Out in the street I paused at an open-plan phone to make a call. As I was hanging up, I saw a globular figure coming up the street towards me—it was Andrea Dworkin.

What incredible pathos, I thought to myself, for clearly she had finessed my earlier departure, just as she'd arranged to be in situ before I arrived, so that I shouldn't see quite how obese she's become. I hurriedly turned on my heel and walked off. I didn't wish to embarrass her. I'd deliberately avoided discussing either her weight or her sexuality in the interview. In the past journalists have pried, carped and crowed about both. The fact that she lives with a man called John Stoltenberg but, according to both of them, does not have penetrative sex with him, seems to be a source of irresistible, prurient fascination for people. Just as the fact that she has an eating disorder seems to provide her critics with endless ammunition for shooting down her arguments about the war against women: 'Her-her-her . . . the only reason she goes on about pornography/rape/exploitation is that she can't get a man to look at her . . .' and so misogynistically on.

Watching Andrea for those fleeting seconds as she ponderously traversed Greenwich Avenue, I didn't think any of those things. Rather I saw her excess weight merely as a burden, which must, in part, have descended on her as a result of the abuse she's been subjected to; and in my inner ear I raised a toast to her as a brave spirit, for, as long as Andrea Dworkin is with us, '*Always the hissing head is there, / The insupportable remark.*'

The Independent, March 1999

Perfidious Man

When I was a boy I never saw my father run. I don't think I can recall ever witnessing him with both of his feet off the ground, except when he was lying down. When he died, aged eighty, his face was deflated by cancer, and his cheeks were sucked in by his last, ragged gasps as he strained to reach the finish. To me, standing vigil, he looked more athletic—with his big feet akimbo, hurdling his deathbed—than he ever had before.

Not that my father was unsporting. On the contrary, at Oxford he'd been a squash and tennis half-blue. In middle age he'd been a scratch golfer. He had a wicked eye for a ball; he fixed any small globe that orbited within his reach with an almost preternatural fixity, before extending one of his long, simian arms, from his rounded shoulders, and catching it, or swiping it, or batting it away with unnerving accuracy. He seemed to reserve for tennis balls, cricket balls and golf balls a completeness of attention—of recognition even—that he denied to the small, round heads of his offspring.

But I never saw him run. When I happened along he was forty-two, at a time (the early sixties), when for a man of his class and demeanour, 'forty-two' meant elephantine flannel bag trousers, hairy tweed jackets and woollen ties. Throughout my childhood he seemed so monolithic, so leaden-based, that to imagine both his feet off the ground, or picture him with daylight streaming from under his heavy, brogue-shod size twelves, was to conceive of either a fundamental reversal of Newtonian physics, or a peculiarly Anglican instantiation of the Ascension, as a middle-aged professor of political science rose up to heaven from Hampstead Heath.

I never saw him run, and I very seldom saw him manifest any kind of alacrity at all. When he lived with us—which was continuously up until I was nine, and thereafter sporadically until I was seventeen and left myself—he wrote in a Danish Modern chair, at a kneehole desk, in my parents' bedroom. Both chair and desk creaked with the effort of absorbing the stresses imparted by his weighty ruminations on the nature of modern government, or the vagaries of regional planning policy. My mother would put lunch or supper on the table and call up to him: 'Lunch!' or 'Supper!'; and he would bellow down: 'Just coming!', then fail to appear. After five minutes she'd call up again, and receive the same reply; another five minutes would pass and she would get a third groan of imminence. It's small wonder that 'Just coming' became one of her most ambivalent catch-phrases—for she loved to hate everything he said and did.

He never ran—and he rarely hurried. He didn't run for trains or buses, he strolled in the opposite direction from crises. Far from not knowing what to do in an accident—I wonder if he rightly knew what an accident was. When the students rioted at the London School of Economics in 1968, a porter was knocked down, had a heart attack and died, on the staircase outside my father's office. He was entirely unaware of this, until phoned by my mother. Doubtless he was absorbed by the theory, while the practice was going on outside.

My father never ran, and for a man who'd never done any manual labour, he had an uncanny grasp of the fundamental principle involved in expending minimal physical effort for maximal effect. It's no wonder that golf became his game. I say 'became', but he was raised to it, and attempted to initiate my brother and me on the golf course as well. He often told us—for, as with all neurotics, bad behaviour was always justified if it had been inflicted on him already—that our grandfather had disdained even to speak to him 'until I could manage a club'. Anyway, he himself played enough golf, for sufficient years, that it was difficult to ascertain whether golf had tutored him in the exigencies of existence or, rather, he had grown to become entwined with the game, like some ambulatory, bag-toting convolvulus.

I have paradoxically fond memories of him—this round-shouldered, fat-bellied spider of a man, dominating the centre of whichever court or pitch it was he occupied, his sagging arms shooting out to loop in the ball misdirected by us, either through ire, inexperience or indifference. 'You aren't even trying!' he'd bellow, and he was right. There was very little point in trying when he was so much better than we were. It never seemed to cross his mind that a middle-aged Oxford blue with a scratch golfing handicap should by rights defeat all seven-year-old comers; it seldom occurred to him that a mere acquaintance with the rules did not, in and of itself, impart the mind of a seasoned strategist.

He taught us to play chess, backgammon, bridge and five-card stud. Then beat us at all of them. 'You don't concentrate!' he'd shout, as if it might've been possible for us to acquire a mastery of bidding conventions by thought power alone. His tactic of allowing no quarter for youth or inexperience, instead of inculcating us with the virtues of fair play and effort, on the contrary made us surly bad losers, and ultimately non-competitive. After all, what was the point of entering a competition that you couldn't possibly win? For clearly playing was not part of the game at all—it was winning the way that Dad did. In later years I found myself quite unable to explain, either to myself or to others, quite how frustrated almost any competitive situation made me feel, how tiny-dicked, how unmanned.

He had very little sense of modesty—my father. He wore bilious flannel underpants, and capacious grey flannels. This spinnaker of nether garments, together with the tails of his shirts, and even the skirt of a pullover, was cinched around his increasingly bulbous middle parts by a thin leather belt that never knew a loop in its long lifetime. With the inevitability of entropy this bundle would come undone in the course of a few holes on the links, or even a stroll through the city. Unaware and unabashed, feeling things coming adrift down below, Dad would undo his belt, unfasten his trousers, lower them slightly, rearrange the whole assemblage and then retie it. I died a thousand deaths—it drove me to drainpipes and tiny briefs.

He pissed like a horse, flattening bracken along the sides of the many paths we walked together, for ours was a father-son relationship acted out on interminable country walks. His penis was stubby and circumcised, its pink, guttering dome poking out from its ruff of black pubic hair as if it were the tonsure of some tiny monk he kept secluded in his horrible trousers. He drank many many pints of beer—then seemed to void more.

At home there were no locks on the bathroom or toilets; not that this would've made any difference, for he patrolled the house, flat-footed, incautious and often stark naked. In the mornings he stood in my parents' room in his leprous knickers and stringy vests, varicose veins bulging at the backs of his legs like pink grapes growing on tuberous vines, and did his Canadian Airforce exercises. Having learnt these entirely from the manual, in a theoretical fashion, he performed the arm jerks and knee bends with delicious languor, as if they were an act of occidental tai chi. Even as a child I knew this was completely wrong, and I'd laugh at him and urge him to speed things up. But there was no hurrying Dad, no shrillness could affect his all-round orotundity, his decathlon of disengagement.

Of course, I realize now (I and, in truth, probably understood even as a small boy), that this extreme leisureliness was
a defence system, albeit one derived from his essential nature.
Faced on a daily basis with the hair-trigger temper and phobic
anxieties of my mother, what could a man do save retreat into
the vast reserves of his own self-centred imperturbability?

The surprising thing was what a Lothario my father could
be (my mother's nicknames for him were 'Pooter' and
'Polonius'—and I bet she wished that this was all there was to
the man). He didn't learn to drive until he was forty, and he
was a virgin until his early thirties. In the former activity he
never excelled, in the latter he made up for lost time. His was
a compulsively sexualized world; and it was this, mostly, that
my parents recognized in each other.

At disorderly lunches on the crap terrace of our suburban
semi, Dad would swill red wine. The spindly geraniums of
the 1970s sprouted from between oblong, concrete slabs. His
mouth, always wet and pink anyway, grew wetter and pinker.
He'd select a fig from a bowl and bite into it, then display it
to the rest of the table. 'Remember Birkin in *Women in Love*?'
he'd pronounce, scrutinizing the roughly divided fruit, 'and
what he has to say about the resemblance between a fig and a
woman's—' '—Really, Peter!' my mother would break in.
This happened again and again and again, throughout the aeons
of my childhood.

It was not so much an open secret that theirs was an open
marriage, as an open sore. An unutterably grey nimbus of lust
surrounded them, permeated from time to time by the light-
ning strikes of anger expressed by one or the other. I grew up
in this cloud of knowingness, to become that most awful of
things, a jaded innocent, and a promiscuous idealist. Hampered
by age, inconvenienced by the raising of small children, with
which she received little or no assistance, and hobbled by av-
oirdupois, my mother kicked out at the dirty dog she was
married to. She taught us to slow-handclap him, when, after

however many 'Just comings', he finally made his entrance. She ridiculed the way he spoke, walked, acted and thought. Everything about him was—she implied—fit for murder. She taught us to loathe him as she did, and in the way that she did. I grew to biological manhood with the body of a frustrated, depressed, middle-aged woman, not so much trapped—as hiding inside me.

If my father was an inadequate specimen of manhood, then there were no others on offer either. I was given leave to understand early on, that my mother's first husband had been a bastard. 'All men are bastards,' she would say, with the flat certainty of a logician proposing the first premiss of a syllogism. Naturally, given time and testosterone, I would grow to occupy this category, but in the mean time I was her 'Benjamin', her youngest, her baby-talked-to darling. Small wonder that I wanted to stay small and wondered at, like a masturbating prodigy.

So, this was the upbringing I had, from two adulterers mired in their own self-obsession, whilst all around them the sixties— that ape decade—swung through London. I grew up obsessively romantic and compulsively sexual. I grew up with absolutely no idea or conception of what it meant to be a man, or even to be masculine. My parents, with their flabby liberality, made a virtue of devolving on to us their irony and their bitterness in equal part, as if it were a particularly vile cocktail of cynicism. I drank deep. Having no positive model, my role was allocated to me on the basis of how badly I acted. This was to be manhood via the Method.

When, in puberty, I passed through my homosexual stage, I grew my hair long, read poetry, fiddled about guiltlessly. But when I began to be attracted to girls (and this flooded all same-sex attraction; it was as if a dam had burst and swept away the gay village), I became a heterosexual man standing in the wings; waiting to be manly on demand, listening for the cue to put on any act of machismo that might be construed as seductive.

PERFIDIOUS MAN

Without the admiring presence of a female, mine was a penile tree that fell in the forest: who was to say that it had ever existed at all? Yes, when I became a man I hung on to childish things, just as my father had kept hold of his. When we went back to Brighton, to the terraced house where he'd lived as a gentle, interwar boy, my grandmother showed us his toys, his copies of *The Magnet,* and his cricket gear, all neatly stored in his old nursery. It was as if she was waiting for the child she'd known to come back but, of course, neither of them had ever accepted that he'd left home to begin with.

My father was quite astonishingly cack-handed. In the family, the story was that he'd been unable to tie his shoes when he went away to prep school, aged seven, and that his younger brother had to tie them for him. Even as I remember it, his big fingers seemed to elude his mind's governance; and when he tied the shoelaces of golf shoes, or walking boots, it looked as if he were attempting the delicate task of mixing radioactive isotopes, using robotic arms. For my mother, the statement 'Your father can't even open a tin can' was not rhetorical. She seemed to glory in his ineptitude.

They argued—of course. They argued about anything and everything. Both of them being epigones, they always had an air of cosmic bewilderment at the idea that they were required to perform domestic tasks, but my mother attacked cooking and cleaning manfully, while my father absented himself. 'You have to have a division of labour,' he'd say, his evidently consisting in making the Danish Modern chair creak and groan, while everyone else's was all the rest.

Thirty years later, his third wife dead and buried, it was with near pity that I cleaned up the little kitchen of the house he died in. Here, in a suburb on the other side of the world, he had learnt at last to open a tin can; and the evidence of this was set out on the draining board, in the form of several of them, their sharply serrated lids raised in salute to the corpse that lay in the bedroom next door.

No, I don't blame him for anything. In as much as he failed me as a father—I failed him as a son. I was too 'wild'—as he would've put it; too immoderate; too much of a wiseacre. Too much of my mother's son. It's only this that motivates me to write about him at all: this vexed question of masculinity, of what it is to be a man. For when I come to consider it, I find I know all sorts of theories about how a man should behave—and believe me, in recompense for my own behaviours I'm keen on acquiring many more—but I find myself bedevilled when it comes to the consideration of wherein my manhood really inheres. I fondly imagine that other men, when asked this question, can reach inside themselves and feel the shape of their inner man; and that this homunculus, formed from the clay of sensibility, physicality, morality and practicality, feels them in return; that they shake hands on it, seal the masculine deal and high-five fraternity.

I've spent hardly any of my life exclusively in the company of men. I do not support a football team. What the Australians call 'mateship' has not been my estate. If I've been a man at all, it's been largely in the context of finding myself a ham alone. Whether because of my mother's espoused feminism, or her obvious misanthropy, I was helped early on to the conclusion that almost all there was to masculinity was the definition of one's sexuality in terms of aggression. Fucking and fighting, or fucking as fighting, or fighting as fucking. My own father was, according to my mother, so much less than a man; a conscientious objector in the war, who couldn't have put up a set of shelves if his life depended on it. In their relationship he supplied the fucking—she the fighting. They were a schizophrenic hermaphrodite; their marriage a screaming Procrustes, always stretched to breaking point—and beyond.

But I cannot blame them, for even as an adult, when I should by all rights have known better, I've still found myself easily taken in by negative arguments about the condition and the future of manhood. The writer J. G. Ballard once told me:

'The human male sex has become a rust bowl.' And this awesome piece of pessimism has stayed with me, oxidizing in my very masculine brain, oddly like the condition it describes.

So, when it came to the crunch, when someone asked me to write on the subject of 'masculinity', of 'manliness', of what it is to be one—I find myself seized with the most awful sense of inertia. I feel myself to be plunging towards watery extinction, weighted down with the ballast of my own masculinity, yet I cannot assay it, I do not know what it is. I feel like a kitten, spinning around and around in a vain attempt to catch sight of its own tail. Yet whenever I've voiced this sense of indeterminacy which surrounds my masculinity and inheres in my very encoding—the combinations of deoxyribonucleic acids that make me one—men smirk, women laugh, and the consensus is that I could not be any more of a man if I shaved my head, pierced my foreskin, shoved a rag soaked with butyl nitrate in my face and joined a conga line of buggery. I could not be any more of a man if I put on a khaki uniform and went on an imperialist peasant shoot. I could not be any more of a man if I modelled for a statue of Priapus.

In my late twenties I wrote a novella, *Cock,* about a woman who grew a penis and used it to rape her husband, an ineffectual alcoholic. People would ask me—and still do—what it was about. I'd give various answers: that it was about my rage with feminist arguments that all men were rapists by virtue of possessing the requisite weapon; that it was about the breakdown in gender distinctions which implied that all it was to be either one or the other was a mix and match of the requisite parts; that it was about my own nature, for, as Cocteau remarked, all true artists are hermaphrodites.

But I knew then—and know still better now—that it was about none and all of these things; that it was about my own vexed relationship with my gender; that it was about this strange situation we find ourselves in at the moment in Western societies. Marx said of the inevitable caesuras accompanying

285

historical determinism: 'In the interregnum between two different political systems the strangest phenomena will arise.' And it's often seemed to me that we are in the interregnum between two systems of sexuality, and that the strangest phenomena are arising. Is our gender biologically or culturally determined? Are we men or hams alone? Shorn of the requirement for physical aggression or labour is there any *raison d'être* for masculinity any more?

The accepted view of sexual dimorphism is that it is one of the engines of evolutionary change; that in species where there is a radical difference between the genders you find more competition, more exclusion from breeding of the bowerbird with the duff bower, or the peacock with the lousy tail. So why do we need such a radical distinction between human genders? Are the gay clones, the effete young men, the butch lesbians, the assertive career women, all evidence of a tendency towards a third man? Or are these mere little local difficulties, wrack thrown up on the beach by the tides of cultural rather than biological evolution? Who knows—but it does feel . . . odd. It does feel as if gender proposes far more questions than it disposes; that the net result of a century or more of sexology, from Freud and Havelock Ellis to the relentless measuring and categorizing of our own era, has been an utter confusion, with gender roles flung around on the ground of the id like pick-up sticks.

It occurred to me that at least one of the reasons why my own gender status, while undoubtedly compromised, and to me indeterminate, was nonetheless indisputable to those around me, was that although it had never been reinforced by initiation, or celebrated in some corroboree, it had still always been a given. No one had ever endorsed it—but neither had they disputed it. Perhaps what I needed to do, in order to fix the position of the monument of masculinity, as it subsided into the shifting sands of change, was to seek out someone who had fought for their masculinity; who had been compelled to assert it while everyone around them was denying it. If I could talk to a person who, against all odds, had won through to proclaim themselves a man, then perhaps I'd find myself a little closer to knowing what it was to be one?

Stephen Whittle is a lecturer in law at Manchester University, a leading light in Press for Change, the transsexual pressure group, and familiar to me through the other kind of press. Stephen Whittle was the transsexual man who had tried to have his status as the parent of the four children he's brought up, together with his partner Sarah Rutherford, recognized in the European Court of Human Rights. According to British Law, while Sarah—who conceived the children through AI (Artificial Insemination)—is indisputably their mother, Stephen, whom she has been in a steady relationship with for over twenty years, and who has acted in every respect apart from biologically as the children's father, had no rights at all. If one of the children had an accident at school the staff had no legal requirement to inform him.

I knew that Stephen Whittle's case had proved unsuccessful, but beyond this and the bare facts about him published on the Press for Change website, I knew nothing else. My friend ascertained that he was prepared to speak to me; I then called him and arranged to visit him at his house, in a suburb of Stockport, south of Manchester. I told him very little about the project, except that I was conducting a series of interviews with transsexual people for a text that was to accompany a book of photographs of men. I wanted to weight the success or failure of the endeavour entirely on the encounter. I felt it was essential that whatever transpired between me and Stephen was not freighted with expectation; I also think that I realized at an intuitive level that one of the things that transsexual people must find hardest to deal with is the atmosphere of prurience which surrounds any enquiry launched by non-trans people into their lives.

After we had met and talked several times, and Stephen had spoken about his life with candour and insight, he told me that this was indeed the case; or rather, he told me that he had never met a heterosexual man who did not at some level maintain a prurient mien (whether covert or overt) when talking to him. Put bluntly: heterosexual men simply could not get over the issue of what kind of genitals Stephen had and what sexual use he put them to.

I won't make the claim that I'm devoid of such prurience, or that I'm incapable of framing these kind of questions but, for me, when it came to developing a relationship with Stephen, these issues were as circumscribed by good manners and the gradual attainment of intimacy as they would be with any other man. As I've said: I have not spent a great deal of my life with other men; and certainly, the kind of men I have spent my time with have not been in the habit of either asking, or telling each other, what their genitals are like, or what they do with them. I could see no reason not to extend this common courtesy to Stephen.

Beyond this, perhaps unlike other men, I had no preconceptions about whether or not Stephen was what he claimed to be—namely, a man. My whole manner of enquiry into the subject, my own habits of mind—both as a man and as a writer—inclined me to accept whatever he would say at face value. I was not looking for him to convince me of his gender identity at either a dialectical or a physical level; I wanted to enquire into the nature of masculinity with him (he was, after all, an academic specializing in the legal theory surrounding trans-gender issues), and let our conversations illuminate our feelings and thoughts about masculinity, whether they be shared or at variance.

Of course, it would be entirely disingenuous to claim that I was not influenced by everything about Stephen Whittle: his home, his family, his appearance, the way he spoke, the way he held himself. But I was open to all of these impressions as fully and as nonprejudicially as possible. It wasn't that

I was looking for him to prove himself as a man to me—and thereby illuminate what it was that was inherently 'masculine' about being one—but what I did want was for every aspect of who he was to be allowed to speak for itself.

Suffice to say, within the first hour of talking to Stephen I realized that I was in the presence of an exceptional individual, whose life experience and capacity to enquire into it could not help but illuminate the very questions I was seeking answers for. And by the end of the second time we met, I abandoned any thoughts of speaking with anyone else and decided to dedicate this project to Stephen. Stephen told me early on that he had not talked to anyone besides me about his life, in this depth and to this extent (saving, of course, for Sarah and his close friends within the trans community who had accompanied him through it). He also told me that he felt able to open up to me in a deep way. He had always intended to tell the story of his life, but was uncertain about how it should be done. Sensationalism of any kind was to be avoided at all costs. In a sense, my arrival provided him, by chance, with the opportunity he sought.

For my part, as a writer, I understood early on that Stephen and I had between us the kind of rapport that, if tended carefully, might produce a unique kind of testament. As I say, I had no preconceptions about how to deal with the material imparted by Stephen during our conversations, but one point was clear to me from the outset: it was important that he have the right to veto the appearance in print of anything at all. This would be nothing if it was not an exercise in trust.

We met and talked four times over a period of some five months. Three of these occasions were at his home in Stockport, and one was at mine in London. The conversations lasted between one and three hours. Full transcripts were made, and I then edited them so as to eliminate my questions and observations. Stephen then read the edited transcripts and made a few, very minor, alterations, either to elucidate points he felt were unclear, or to protect friends and family. I stress—these were very minor alterations.

It matters, therefore, how you approach this text. If you read it looking for prurient answers to prurient questions—you will not find them. If you skip through it hoping to chance upon the answers to the questions about masculinity that I have proposed—then you will be disappointed. Rather, this text should be viewed as a whole and, like Stephen, allowed to speak for itself. The answers to many of the questions you might wish to propose about masculinity, about the impact of feminism upon it, and about being transsexual, are all here—but they are filtered through the reticulation of an unusual life story. If I was instrumental in prompting this level of enquiry, then I have done a good job, but that is all I have done; the insights themselves are Stephen's alone, just as the life is his alone.

At Stephen's home we talked, sitting on a divan, in his partner Sarah's room. It's a comfortable study-cum-workspace, neatly furnished with a desk, a computer and a dressmaker's form. This headless, genderless torso was an apt totem, given the nature of our discussions. When Stephen and Sarah first met, in the early seventies, Stephen was already passing as a man, and taking hormones, but he was yet to undergo any surgery. One of the things Sarah Rutherford has said about being Stephen's partner is that, perforce, it completely alters people's perceptions of her as a woman: the same prurient searchlight that gets trained on Stephen then wavers across to fix her in its beam. I have no wish to contribute to this, and while I believe that it's important for the reader to have some sense of the family Stephen and Sarah have founded together, I want to make it clear that this is Stephen's story—not Sarah's; and that while Sarah has read and approved this text, her own life and opinions remain to be recorded in another place.

Nevertheless, my impression of Sarah was that she was a woman who was in a long-term relationship with a man. If you want to call this kind of woman 'heterosexual'—then do by all means. If you want to take my word for it that Sarah Rutherford is a very attractive, forthright, intelligent, capable woman, who seemed to be not in one iota strange or peculiar—then please do.

We talked in her room, and very occasionally Sarah would come in to recount some essential aspect of her and the children's day. At the end of each of the Stockport sessions we had supper together: Stephen; Sarah; their long-time friends and housemates Alex and John; the au pair and myself. The younger children were sometimes in bed by then, but their oldest daughter, Eleanor, often came into the conservatory area where we ate and stopped for a while to chat. The conversation between the adults was wide-ranging and by no means fixated upon issues of gender and sexuality, despite the fact that between us six adults there were almost as many different gender statuses and sexual orientations. After all, when six people from different races meet together, they don't necessarily talk about racism or miscegenation. The food was excellent.

Tolstoy said that: 'All happy families are the same, but every unhappy family is unhappy in its own way.' I don't wish to make a facile statement—but the Whittle/Rutherford family is manifestly a happy one. What this means is, that even if I wanted to, I'd find it hard to write about them with any degree of objectivity. Alex and John have lived with Stephen and Sarah for many years and are fully accepted as family members, but the impression I received (and it was one which Stephen to some extent reinforced), was that he and Sarah were, respectively, patriarch and matriarch. All the adults share duties and responsibilities within the home, and all of them are involved to a greater or lesser degree with the childrearing. It's a comfortable, rambling, detached, turn-of-the-last-century house in a leafy suburb. The kind of house that has a tiled hall, herringbone parquet floors and mullioned windows. The furniture and decoration is unostentatious—but good. This is a home full of books and paintings and music. This was a home, I sensed, where disputes are resolved and tensions dissipated. This was a home, I grasped, where there resided a firm consensus on ethics; where the adults agreed on what was to be done. This was a home very unlike the one I grew up in— this was a home where the men and the women knew what their respective roles were, and found them comfortable. This was a home where no one bleated on about the division of labour as an excuse for not doing any.

I don't wish to idealize this—after all, I was only a guest— but you get a nose for these things, especially if your own upbringing consisted in having it repeatedly broken. In their home I felt that peculiar nostalgia for a state which I had myself never really experienced—a dangerous kind of sentimentality. And as for Stephen, how did I regard him? Completely and incontrovertibly as a man—of that I had no doubt. An unusual man certainly—but no more unusual than I am myself. Wherein does his masculinity consist? In all of him: in his appearance, his demeanour, his manner of expressing himself— in his very quiddity; his quality of this-is-Stephenness. But still more importantly—and this is why I've written about the family at all—his manhood resides in his relationships with it, as a partner, as a father, as a patriarch. These aspects of Stephen's masculinity are far more important to me than whether he's big or small, bearded or clean shaven, let alone what kind of genitals he has.

From the Stephen Whittle Interview

STEPHEN WHITTLE: I never saw masculinity—say, in my father's model—as being the slightest bit attractive. So, throughout that period of trying to gauge how not to grow up to be a woman—and an old woman in particular—I couldn't grasp the idea of growing up to be someone like my father. So I spent a lot of time looking for other masculine models. I had a French teacher in primary school, he was kind, he taught you, he listened to you, he had a beard . . . as well as all sorts of other things. I mean, secondary characteristics of masculinity were so desirable, they were overwhelmingly desirable, but I still couldn't think in terms of a penis, it was all about how you physically looked . . . and it was attractive in every shape, it was attractive as something I wanted for myself, it was attractive in other people, and this provided me with all sorts of real issues about sexuality and where my sexual orientation was. I hadn't the faintest idea. I'd read the books and I'd think, Um, well, I'm meant to be a lesbian if I'm like this, 'cos I also knew I found women very attractive, and there was no idea that you could have any other sexuality apart from being straight, as a woman, or a lesbian as a woman. And the idea that you could actually change sex was not feasible at all. I spent so much time reading books and thinking, *Somebody* must have been born a girl and grown up to be a man. It must happen to somebody!

My feeling is that the whole concept of gender dysphoria, the very wide concept, is a really common reason for many adolescents trying to, and actually succeeding, in killing themselves. That, along with bullying . . . the whole notion of being an outsider. To not be an outsider any longer—to just not be any longer. And the more I talk and listen to trans people, and listen to students—y'know, my door's the door they knock on, with their assorted problems, their pregnancies, their arranged marriages—you realize it's this notion of feeling outside of your culture, outside of your society, that you're never, ever, going to fit in. You just think, Let's just stop it, at this point. Y'know—end it, now.

What made it possible for me to survive was firstly—and most profoundly—the school that I went to. I went to an all-girls school near Manchester that was a direct-grant school. I got a scholarship to it. It was a school with no punishment and no praise, that was the whole principle of it, and they did indeed follow that line. Nobody was ever singled out as being better than anybody else, and nobody got punished. It was a group ethos. Eccentricities were totally accepted, they were seen as being strange, but at the same time they were not a reason for a telling-off. There was no reason whatsoever for them to make me conform as long as I stayed within the bounds of the uniform rules and behaved in a reasonably presentable way. I have to say it was the school that made me the man I am today!

I began having relationships with male-to-female transsexuals and found it incredibly comfortable. I mean, this was me, as a man, having a relationship with a woman. Forensically, we would have been perceived as being a straight couple, both of whom were cross-dressers. So, what you had was, all the bits and bobs were the wrong bits and bobs—they'd been given to the wrong people. But you actually felt really comfortable with having that body. I mean, all of us were aspiring to having our bodies sorted out, but we could live with the other person, because the other person said, 'You think your body's a problem? You should see my body!' Before, if I'd been in bed with a woman, prior to my living as Stephen, the trouble was she always wanted somebody who wasn't. And I found it very difficult to say, 'Hold on a minute, that's not me, this is what I am.'

Of course, I kept away from RGs because I was terrified of being in big trouble. They were girls that I knew and fancied but just didn't get involved with 'cos I thought, Oh, what's her mother going to say when she finds out? And that was a mental precursor thing, exactly what did happen.

In '74, when we set up the TV/TS Group, I'd gone to my GP and said, I want to go and see a specialist in this area, I want a sex change. She sent me to see a psychiatrist in Manchester's Withington Hospital, who was an arrogant little toad! I went to see him several times. I told him that I wanted to have hormone treatment, I didn't think I was mad. I said to him, 'I'm not stupid, I did biology 0 Level, I know that I'm physically female, everything works and is perfectly normal, but that's not me and I know that having a sex change is possible, and I want it, and I want hormone treatment . . . and so on and so forth. So, he sent me off to see the psychologist, who was a very strange man, who had a huge big cyst on the top of his bald head, so it was virtually impossible to concentrate on any psychology in the middle of it all. But it was a really bizarre system: I always remember he had photographs of people from the 1950s, and you'd have to say who was more attractive, the male characters or the female characters.

They finally sent me to see another psychologist—a young woman. We sat and chatted for about forty minutes, and then I was meant to go and see her once a week for six months. On the first occasion, I sat there, and after forty minutes she said, 'Well, this is a waste of time.' And I thought she was going to say, 'That's it, I'm not bothering to see you.' But she said, 'It strikes me that you're perfectly sane, you perfectly and absolutely know what you want to do. I can't see any reason for you not to do it, I think you'd be terribly successful, I'll write a letter.' And she wrote the letter in front of me. We didn't hear anything for a while, so I got my GP to chase up the psychiatrist. Eventually I got an appointment and went down to see him again. He just said, 'I won't treat you, you will never, ever, ever make it as a man. Absolutely not, and you'll get nothing out of the National Health Service.'

That must have been May '75, because I had actually been working as Stephen for three months. So I couldn't change my name back. I mean, what the fuck was I meant to do now? I'd changed my name, I'm living as a bloke, I'm working as a bloke, I'm shagging as a bloke and they wanted me to stop it? Jesus Christ, you'd think that changing one way was bad enough, for fuck's sake!

I knew people who were already having treatment. The generation prior to me had not had it easy. They got all of the crap, ended up having a year or two in a locked ward on a psychiatric unit. I think I was really lucky that I was part of the first generation to come through without that, thank God. But when I got knocked back, I went home with the full intention of doing myself in. I was still living with Pat, I knew she'd still be at work, and I went home to kill myself. And my GP was actually sat on the doorstep, and she said, 'I know what he's said, I've had a letter from him, and I'm going to write you out a prescription for hormones.' She was an amazing woman. She got in big trouble for it. I gather she lost her job in the end, she was barred from working for two years in England.

The key thing for my sense of identity was having this life-long experience that came from my relationship with Sarah; it was in the relationship with her that I was able to shift from being just masculine to being a man. Then I became a whole human being, regardless of what state my body was in. You know, as far as she was concerned, I was a man. I could've been a man who was in a wheelchair, I could've been a man who was deaf, I could have been a man who'd lost his willy in an accident, it was simply that I was a transsexual man. From her I was able to come to terms with who I was and I decided it was possible to be just a man, but that included being able to be a transsexual man—and that was it absolutely and completely. I never asked Sarah whether at any point she had thought any differently about me, and I don't want to know. Because I felt it was her total acceptance that allowed me to be who I was. The relationship was a real step from being almost a nothing—an inadequate person—to actually being somebody, and that somebody was distinctly a man.

And that had nothing to do with the sex *per se;* it wasn't to do with money (we didn't have any), but it was a function of being regarded, by somebody else, as a whole human being, a complete and absolute human being, regardless of whatever shape my body was or anything like that. But this is who she saw. I'd always had this sensation of desperately wanting to grow up to be myself—whoever that was. And I couldn't envisage myself growing older and becoming someone everybody else expected to see. Then this person came along who saw who I was—and that was a 'man', a sort of man, whatever that means, because we're all sort of men—and that was distinctly me, and I knew who it was and that I could fit into it, and finally be.

The first time we slept together, we'd gone to a party, and I pointedly looked at her and said, 'Oh, who's coming to bed with me then?' She smiled back and said, 'I am.' And I remember thinking, 'Oh my God, this is terrifying.' And we went upstairs, and I said, 'I just can't take off my clothes.' And she was absolutely fine about it, but she said, 'You know, you're going to have to one day.' And over the next few months I had this realization that she didn't see my body as being any less, or any different—it was me. It was my body. It was entirely labelled by me. And I remember when I had my chest surgery, discussing it, and her saying, 'Well, of course you want your chest surgery and I'm totally behind you, but you do realize that it doesn't matter to me. It absolutely doesn't make an iota of difference to me whether you do or you don't, because you are just you.' But that just 'me' wasn't somebody weird—it wasn't essentially a transsexual person.

Through the system, we got a private clinic in Manchester to accept us. After the first treatment, Sarah conceived, and eventually Eleanor was born, then a couple more treatments led to Gabriel. We did discuss a lot whether or not to try for a third baby, but as it happens we did give it a go—and then we ended up with twins, Lizzie and Pippa—which was terrifying—I mean, was there enough of me to go around that many people? Well, there isn't, sometimes I feel very thinly spread, but somehow it all works, and being a dad has given my life a whole new perspective, which is pretty exciting as well as being totally knackering.

The best way I can answer the inevitable question, Did you feel like a father?, is to say, there was a group of people who we'd practised our birthing techniques with. And there was a reunion at which we all had our babies lined up on the sofa for a photograph, and I can remember looking at them and thinking, 'Well, I don't know how these people can put up with the fact that our child is just so much more beautiful than theirs. Look at them, they're ugly, they're hideous, they're wrinkly and she is absolutely out of this world. And we were talking in the car home and Sarah had thought exactly the same thing. Of course the other parents were also thinking exactly the same thing about their children. And I look at that photograph now, of all these eight babies, and Eleanor's a bit jaundiced, all wrinkly—she looks like a baby. But when she was born I had this overwhelming sensation, and still, when I see my kids in with a group of other kids, they're always the most beautiful.

I've had to cut off from the kids in order to go away and work on occasions. But I found that having the children was a real bonus for me, in terms of work, because it's given me a real incentive to go to work: maintaining a moral and social obligation to my children, to provide for them. And it also gives me a real reason for coming home: I want to come home and see my children. So, I've dealt with work by actually framing it within the concept of my responsibility as their father— and as their father I also want to come back. I do find the social pressures on being what a father's meant to be like quite hard— the fact that you're meant not to touch your children in the same way that women touch them.

I've also been absolutely knackered. I've nearly always been the person that gets up in the middle of the night, simply because I wake up in the middle of the night anyway. Obviously Sarah did the breastfeeding, but once that finished I was

the one who got up, I'm always alert. And I loved those moments in the middle of the night, absolutely loved those moments when there's just them and me, and there's a real sense
now of having the closeness of a relationship that you just never
get without that contact. There've been times when I've been
at work and people have said, 'Oh well, y'know, it's Sarah's
job to do that.' And I've said, 'Pardon! Why would I want
Sarah to do that?' 'Oh well, then you wouldn't be so tired.'
'No thank you, I'll put up with being tired, this is, like, so
special.'

As a father you're also not meant to participate in the
decision-making process in the same way. People always have
been very willing when you do participate, whether it's with
school or the doctor or whatever else, but it's those touchy-
feely bits as well. Gabriel loves to stand and have his back
stroked by me. He'll lift up his shirt and say, 'Scratch my back,
Dad.' My mother will say, 'Leave him alone.' And I'm going,
'Hold on a minute, he's four, he's five, does it matter?' Eleanor
is now at the point—she's seven—where she's saying, 'Oh,
don't give me a kiss as we're going into school.' Well, thank
God I did kiss her on all those other occasions.

I think what having the kids has done for me is to provide
a stage in being a man that most people in my community don't
get a chance to experience. It's provided me with an opportunity to experience another aspect of being a man that I never
expected to have. One of the things I'd always felt before was
that I couldn't quite grow up and I only ever had to look after
me *per se*. And it's quite interesting, because looking after the
kids has made me much more daring than just looking after
me ever did. I mean, I've been much more out—and enjoyed
being out. I took Eleanor and Gabriel to Pride (the Gay Pride
carnival) a couple of years ago and was able to say to them,
'This is our community. This is where we belong.' I wouldn't
ever have taken my mother or my sister or brother or anybody from work, but I took my kids and wanted to introduce

them to where I belonged. And at the same time I wanted my community to welcome them as part of it. Sometimes I find myself thinking, Oh my God, what am I doing to my kids? But then I'm also really pleased that I'm doing it, that I want them to have a much queerer upbringing than I ever had. All this means is that I want them to be able to realize the extent to which there are choices. I realize that when you're responsible for kids you don't have to put your desires on them, you can just desire for them what they want.

Talking about the nature of patriarchy, or what a patriarch is, I try to think about it in terms of what it is one tries to be in life. First of all, I don't know whether it's a masculine thing to do, but the majority of the time I do think I know best. And I think I know best because I think I'm the most reasonable and the most rational. Both within the family, and in its relationship with the outer world, and in my relationship with the outer world as well. I fundamentally believe—and this is absolute categorical madness—that I know best, that I'm the most reasonable and rational and thoughtful person I know. The only person who approaches me as being anything like as rational is Sarah. I have friends who are also sometimes reasonable and rational, but they're not actively involved in my life in that way, and they're not having to make those decisions. Often it's I who provide the voice of the reasonable rationalist within their lives. That, I think, is the reality. I work harder than most of the people I know, I'm the most prepared to listen, and I'm the most prepared to admit when I'm wrong. Well, it that's what being a patriarch is, then that's exactly, precisely, what I think a person in a position of power should be.

It's very difficult to explain, because it's not about having power for the sake of power, or being in charge, or taking things from other people, or having my life at the expense of other people; it's about ensuring that everybody gets a fair whack at everything, about taking your responsibilities seriously. Sarah's always saying to me, 'You know, the problem with you, Stephen, is you always want to make it right for everybody and sometimes you just can't.' Particularly like when her mum died, she said, 'Stephen, you just can't make this any better.' And yes, that's what I want to do. I want to make it better for everybody.

I do think masculinity is facing a massive crisis. What it is to be a man has in itself become so inherently devalued— probably rightly so, through feminist discussion, theory and argument—but, at the same time, the reality is that there's no alternative being provided. We talk about the New Man, the 'nice' New Man, and then women say, 'But I don't want the "nice" New Man.' Or lots of women say they don't. If you push them towards a 'nice' New Man, on the whole they go 'Waargh!' I'm often there being a semi-dating agency for other F-to-Ms. And if there are women who say, 'I can't stand this, I'm straight, but I can't stand the straight men I know,' I say 'OK, I'll introduce you to some really nice straight men.' And it works.

But there's no new model of masculinity. And I think one of the things I've learnt through being a transsexual man, is that transsexual men, we've worked very hard to provide an alternative model of masculinity, because we've inculcated those sort of values, an awful lot of us have come out of the lesbian/feminist community; if nothing else, we sat and we discussed this *ad infinitum:* what were better values.

I was thinking about suddenly becoming a man with Sarah, and the truth is, my masculinity was always there, and it was the bone of contention with everybody else. The masculinity's always, always been there. My mother's argued about it, people at school argued about it, the doctors argued about it, somehow it wasn't meant to be there, but it was always there. What Sarah did was enable me to step over the line into becoming a man.

Excerpted from *Perfidious Man,* Viking (London), 2000

The Book of Revelation

My friend Ben Trainin died thirteen years ago of a heart attack, brought on by an asthma attack, brought on by the complications of a compressed, involuted life: a decoction of existence. He and his girlfriend were living in a shoe box–shaped flat just off the Commercial Road in Whitechapel. The bed—where he died—was crammed under a window, from which you could see the plastic-wrapped schmutter in the windows across the road. Ben was twenty-eight.

He was not a simple soul—he was fucking complex. He came from a convoluted family with connections both bohemian and East End. He'd gone up to Nottingham University to read history, but after doing too much amphetamine he was found giving an extempore, *al fresco* sermon, from the pulpit of the roof of his digs. He served drinks at the Colony Room club in Soho for the next couple of years, courtesy of his—self-styled—'godfather' Ian Board. Then he took the Oxford general entrance paper and scored an unprecedented result. Interviewed by Christopher Hill—then still Master of Balliol—Ben was offered a place to read history. That's how we met.

Ben was fucking complex. Part of his act was to feign simplicity. Gap-toothed, tousle-haired, slack-jawed, he would gawp at me and intone 'Amazing!', 'No!'; 'Really?'; and 'Will!', before gurgling with giggles like an idiot. He walked with knees half bent, as if he were continually going downhill.

Ben was a giver of unexpected presents. I would be sitting in my room reading and Ben would silently tip-toe down on in. He'd deposit a book of Basho's poems, or a manual of Ch'an Zen teaching, then—still without speaking—he'd depart. From Ben I first heard the expression 'random acts of senseless generosity'.

He was brilliant and confused. One time he found me having a bad acid trip, prostrate on my bed, ensnared by a vision of an illimitable cathedral comprised entirely of screaming mouths. 'Bad trip.' He stated on seeing the state I was in. 'You need wine.' He poured two bottles of Burgundy down me, employing a furled magazine as a funnel. An hour later I was dancing to Edwin Starr's *Eye to Eye Contact,* at the Law Society disco. Ben's maxim as far as drugs were concerned was 'little but often'. He constantly smoked tiny nuggets of hashish and snorted less than nugatory lines of amphetamine. With some like-minded souls we formed a rhythm and blues band. Ben loved Robert Johnson and might well have brokered a deal on his own soul in return for guitar picking skill. Together we composed unlikely ditties. I loved him very much.

In the imbroglio of acid, speed, heroin, hashish, cocaine, philosophy, youth, literature, political protest, sex, friendship and dancing, Ben's mind frayed. The dissolution of our peer group seemed congruent with his own mind. When we left the university, Ben began to take day returns from his own sanity. Then awaydays became bargain weekends. We pitched up in Brixton, squatting, in 1982. A very raw, very ragged time—especially for one who was frayed. One night Ben brandished a U-bend bicycle lock in my face and dared me to kill us both, batter us both to death. For someone who practised random acts of senseless generosity, the world had become a screaming, tight fist.

I saw Ben sporadically after that. He moved back to Kennington, a village a few miles outside Oxford. Initially he lived with a bizarre, obese character who was the local 'wise' woman. This was for real—I remember visiting him there and witnessing a sheepish young couple, who had come to consult her on the matter of fecundity. She was so fat she had a reinforced commode with an armchair of a seat. Ben said it was provided by the social services.

Then he moved in with a gay couple who were priests. They seemed caring men when I visited, and genuinely concerned for Ben's health and welfare, but there were nagging undertones—and even overtones—suggesting a less disinterested involvement on their part.

I was living in a borrowed flat in the Gloucester Road area during the hot, early summer of 1985. I had no money and expensive habits. One day Ben called and said he was coming over to see me for the first time in many months. In truth, I had begun to avoid him. The joint suicide attempt had been bad enough, but since then Ben had increasingly taken to interpreting the world through the dark glass of The Book of Revelation.

He carried a pocket bible—leather bound as I recall—with him wherever he went. In the midst of always turbulent, disconnected discourses, he would wrench the tome out and brandishing it cite the applicable prophesy and provide his own piece of exegesis, which constituted impossibly spidery marginalia. Disturbingly his references were always correct— the last piece of mental viability left to him. Montaigne said: 'In my part of the country we call a man who has no memory "stupid".' Ben was never stupid. He spoke of the sharp two-edged sword (ch. 1 v. 13), and the utility of communion with he who has 'the keys of hell and of death' (ch 1 v. 18).

Like many people who are teetering on the edge of psychosis—one foot rammed hard in the door of perception lest it slam shut forever—Ben found in Revelation an awful, immanent level of identification; an apparently fixed point around which his own frail psyche could orbit and then fission. Ben didn't subscribe to any one view of the meaning of Revelations—he subscribed to them all.

I'm not certain that Ben's illness was ever adequately diagnosed. I do know that he was receiving some kind of help or treatment at the time of his death, but I don't think they'd yet managed to hammer this beautifully rounded persona into a square hole of psychopathology. My hunch is that he was hypermanic, or manic-depressive. Perhaps now, with improved drugs, better cognitive approaches, Ben might have been saved—but I doubt it.

For there was an anguished level of insight in this man's disintegration. Even as he ran over—for the nth time—the precise equations that decoded the numerological content of Revelation: four beasts times seven seals, times twelve tribes of twelve thousand—he would still find himself hectored by the furies of his own reason, and pulling himself up short expostulate 'Of course, it's all a load of superstitious bollocks really.'

So Ben paced around the spacious, unpaid-for flat on this hot, early summer day. He wanted us to do *this* together, and to go *there*. He thought we ought to consider becoming *such-and-such,* or dedicating ourselves to this *particular* cause. And all of it was derived from Revelation, all of it was coextensive with—and tantamount to—the determined, ordained, god-directed universe.

He wanted me to go to the Natural History Museum with him, but I wouldn't. He scared me. When someone you love is veering in and out of sanity it's straightforwardly terrifying. They may have their foot rammed in the door, but if they let go the draught could suck you out of rationality along with them; expel you into a screaming void of the id.

Ben said goodbye to me, or rather he said he had come to say goodbye to me. He pocketed the small book of no calm and he left. He died a week later.

He wouldn't have—didn't—want to be in the condition he was. I believe he willed himself to death. On the despairing grapevine that sprang sad roots in the long hours immediately after his death, time and again I heard from other friends and lovers that Ben had been by that preceding week; that he had cropped up for the first time in months; that he had said he was coming to say goodbye—not simply said 'goodbye'.

A few months later I was ordering a takeaway in a fried chicken joint on Haverstock Hill when elements of a familiar litany came floating to me: an anti-prayerful, desperate incantation. It was the hulking man standing next to me in the queue, frayed jeans sagging open at the fly to reveal NHS issue pyjama bottoms underneath. We were—I internally acknowledged—within the crazily paved precincts of the Royal Free Hospital, that ziggurat of social hygiene. The man—who, non-pejoratively was clearly suffering from an array of schizoid symptoms—was speaking of that woman: 'And upon her forehead *was* a name written, MYSTERY, BABYLON THE GREAT, THE MOTHER OF HARLOTS AND ABOMINATIONS OF THE EARTH.'

His speech was Roman, then italicised, then capitalised. It was his own, private revelation.

I became if not exactly fixated, at any rate intrigued by this seam of perverse biblical exegesis, which was being squeezed out from the minds of the insane like variegated toothpaste, ejected from a tube. I would lend an ear to any inapposite mutterer or street ranter I chanced upon, confident that in at least one out of three hits, there would be revelatory pay dirt.

I read the book of Revelation once—I never wanted to read it again. I found it a sick text. Perhaps it's the occlusion of judgmental types, and the congruent occlusion of psyches, but there's something *not quite right* about Revelation. I feel it as an insemination of older, more primal verities into an as yet fresh dough of syncretism—the Neo Platonists still kneading at the stuff of the messiah. The riot of violent, imagistic occurrences; the cabalistic emphasis on numbers; the visceral repulsion expressed towards the bodily, the sensual and the sexual. It deranges in and of itself, and sets the parameters, marshals the props, for all the excessive playlets to come. In its vile obscurantism is its baneful effect; the original language may have welded the metaphoric with the signified, the *logos* with the flesh, but in the King James version the text is a guignol of tedium, a portentous horror film.

I have read the exegetical texts on Revelation and I have read the book itself several more times. I feel no closer to understanding what it is about. Not in the obvious senses—I appreciate the status of Hebraic and early Christian prophecy as pure revelation, decoupled from mere temporal causality, spatial contiguity—but in the sense that I cannot empathise with this piece of writing, I cannot feel what it might be like to feel it.

Last night I plugged into the internet and went looking for Revelation. Funny how the dead get deader. Ben was dead from the moment he died, but five years after his death he was deader, and now he's deader still. I know this because of the anachronistic quality of my vision of him: if he were to be resurrected now, he would look out of place next to my full colour VDU screen, with its weary emphasis that what you see is what you get.

I keyed it into a not especially vigorous search engine, keyed in the bald awfulness of it: the book of Revelation. Hit the return key and waited. The screen departed as a scroll when it is rolled together and I was offered a choice of 2,666,896 websites. And these were by no means all 'Top 10 Revelations in Marcia Clark's New Book'. Oh no, if only. No, they were the real McCoy: the apocalyptic visions visited on the wired generation in the here and now of Christian-defined 1998. They no longer have to mutter in fast food outlets, they no longer have to address themselves to bare precincts, their only witnesses scurrying fast in the opposite direction. Now they can make the screen depart as a scroll when it is rolled together.

Our sense of the apocalypse is steeped in the language of Revelations. In this century the star called Wormwood *has* fallen, and the sea has become as black as sackcloth of hair, and the moon has become as blood. We have heard the silence—about the space of half an hour—that accompanied the opening of the seventh seal, yet still we are here.

I have no truck with personal immortality—it is the dross of the opium of the people. I have no time for the conception of humans as born in sin, screaming for redemption. If Revelations conjures up one single feeling in me, as we stand on the cusp of a new millennium, awaiting television retrospectives that will occupy the space of many hours, it is one of superstitious awe, 'Look on my works, ye Mighty, and despair'. To think this ancient text has survived to be the very stuff of modern, psychotic nightmare.

Not only the good die young—but some do.

In memory of Gregor Benjamin Trainin, 1957–85

Pocket Canons, Canongate Books, Ltd., 1998